THE
CRUCIBLE
OF
STEELE

L M WHITAKER

First edition June 2020

ISBN 978-1-7348496-0-8 (paperback)

ISBN 978-1-7348496-1-5 (e-book)

www.lmwhitaker.com

For Heather

"... man's natural abilities are derived by inheritance, under exactly the same limitations as are the form and physical features of the whole organic world. Consequently, as it is easy, notwithstanding those limitations, to obtain by careful selection a permanent breed of dogs or horses gifted with peculiar powers of running, or of doing anything else, so it would be quite practicable to produce a highly-gifted race of men... I conclude that each generation has enormous power over the natural gifts of those that follow, and maintain that it is a duty we owe to humanity to investigate the range of that power, and to exercise it in a way that, without being unwise towards ourselves, shall be most advantageous to future inhabitants of the earth."

Hereditary Genius,
Sir Francis Galton, 1869

CHAPTER 1

APRIL 1863, LONDON

My dear Berkeley,

I have just come back from Down House, where I was refused entrance and sent away by the great man himself. Charles, or Mr. Darwin as he would have it, would not acknowledge my letter to him, nor accept invitation to discuss my application of his theories.

I trust that some of this is due to the fact that our mutual friend, his half cousin Francis Galton, shared with me his manuscript without knowledge or permission. This does not change the validity of the argument I have put forth.

Natural selection is nature's method—or God's, depending upon which side you take—of changing the face of the world. I prefer the former. Selective breeding is already the method used by the farmer, which Darwin himself cites as proof of his theories. Human selection is simply the next logical step.

Just as we can breed livestock to resist disease, a dog to watch over the livestock, or a fancy pigeon simply to please our eyes, we can also breed man to be stronger and smarter, and woman to be more flattering to the eye. We can create the mankind we want to have. Now that we have this knowledge, we must use it. We owe it to ourselves, or if you prefer, we owe it to God so that we may further his magnificent work. We must be the guardians of humanity.

I did not tell the notable man that I have already started these experiments. Though neither he nor I will live to see the result, as I expect it to take ten or even thirty generations to yield any significant change, and we will be long dead by then. But this does not weaken my resolve, and to this, I am certain that my name will eventually be more famous than the veritable Mr. Darwin.

Yours sincerely,

C. T. Edwards

CHAPTER 2

AUGUST 2019, PERSIAN GULF

"Can you see the World?"

Alex took the cup of coffee offered by the flight attendant but said nothing. Danger was waiting thousands of feet below regardless of the view.

But the woman would not be ignored. She leaned over Alex and pointed out the window. "Have you ever seen anything like that before?"

They were indeed passing over the World. The World Islands, a man-made archipelago in the Persian Gulf comprised of three hundred small atolls, laid out in the shape of the earth. Roughly anyway, Alex thought, struggling to distinguish Iceland from North America.

"I hear Asia's for sale," the attendant said, still leaning over Alex and continuing her one-sided conversation.

"Excuse me?"

"Asia, or at least part of Asia." She tried a smile, which was not returned.

"I'll have to remember that. Do you mind?"

"Oh, sorry." The attendant finally got the message and left, freeing up Alex's personal space.

The private Learjet banked and headed inland. Blue ocean was abruptly replaced by desert of an equal scale. This sea of brown was similarly punctuated with swatches of emerald making the scenery equally impressive. The immense wealth required to create the World Islands was also present here in the transformation of barren land into these lavish estates. Large enough to be seen from the heavens, they appeared as green squares, ovals, and circles with a few shaped in exotic leaf or curl. Each was embellished with glistening blue pools in contrasting shapes.

The plane landed in one of these artificial oases. Armed guards met the aircraft on a runway capable of handling commercial jets and escorted the plane to its final position on the tarmac, where two shiny black armored SUVs waited. Five men, wearing a mix of western and traditional dress, stood next to the cars. Alex managed a few controlled breaths, donned a traditional headdress, then exited the plane.

Alex was immediately overwhelmed by the oppressive heat and blowing sand and struggled to stay composed. One of the suited men approached. Alex recognized him as the son of their client, the sheikh, and eldest brother of the groom. Taking off his sunglasses, the man eyed Alex from head to toe, then grunted. He was a handsome man in his early thirties, with sharp eyes under thick but manicured eyebrows, and a short, equally well-kept beard.

Alex offered a hand and said, "As-salamu alaykum," the traditional greeting.

"Wa alaykumu s-salam," the prince replied, but did not offer his hand in return. He switched to English. "You have everything?"

"Of course."

The man turned around and said something to the others in Arabic. The entourage began to transfer the cargo—heavy-duty marine coolers and boxes—from the plane to the trucks. They would open and inspect each before loading. The coolers held sushi, smoked salmon, and Belgian truffles, while the boxes were laden with cases of water bottles bearing custom-printed labels in three colors, each with a different celebratory message.

"The retrovirus is in the bottles with green labels, the red contains the vaccine against it," Alex said. "The blue is benign. The green is for the bride's side, red for the groom's, obviously. You will have to manage the appropriate distribution."

"My father said we will have to wait many years for this to work. Why?"

"That is deliberate. In the current political environment, you cannot manage your enemies without serious repercussions. True?"

The prince looked over his shoulder back to his men. They were far away, engrossed in the exotic catering. He nodded to Alex to continue.

"I offer you the ability to eradicate the entire tribe using sterilization. And it will never be linked to you or your family." Alex could not suppress a proud smile. "We can silence a specific gene that is required for women to get pregnant. It's a two-step process. The first step, as you know, is administering the retrovirus."

The man looked confused. Normally Alex would not waste time trying to explain this to someone of such average intelligence, but this man was part of an extremely powerful family. This was a tricky, and potentially dangerous, situation.

"Retroviruses are not like other viruses. They do not attack and kill cells; they infiltrate DNA and change the human genome. This virus is very specific. Instead of making the women sterile immediately, it makes them susceptible to future infertility."

"Why should we wait?"

"That's the beauty and power of this retrovirus. The DNA changes are permanent and inherited. It spreads from mother or father to their children."

Now the prince was smiling. He was starting to understand.

Alex continued, "So the longer you wait..."

"The more damage we do, and the less risk we take."

"Yes."

"How do we pull the trigger, so to speak?" He was clearly pleased with himself.

"When you are ready, you will expose them to the activator. It will silence the gene, in effect, shutting it down."

"Is the activation—"

"Activator."

The men had completed the transfer and one of them waved to the prince. He held up his hand to signal for them to wait. "The activator, is it harmful?"

"Only to the gene we are targeting. And only to those with the mutation."

"And you are sure of the effectiveness?" He emphasized the last word, pronouncing each syllable.

Alex hesitated, choosing words carefully. "Yes. But the rate of inheritance depends upon the exposure. If only one parent carries the mutation, then the child may not have it."

The prince frowned.

Alex continued, "So if they marry outside their tribe, their children are less likely to have the genetic mutation."

Sneering, the prince said, "These dogs, they think they are so superior, they only marry within their own tribe." He spat on the ground. "They make my father pay a fortune to them so that my stupid brother can marry that whore."

Alex coughed. It had to be said. "My payment, it's due upon delivery."

"One half will be wired to your account today. The other when we receive the activa…tor."

Alex started to sweat. This was not the deal. There were other interested buyers, of course, but there was no time. They needed all of the money to complete the test. It was do or die.

But fear could not be shown to this man. In a firm and even tone, Alex said, "The activating agent is a simple chemical compound. Once I have confirmed the full payment of thirty million US dollars, I will send instructions for the preparation. You can have someone here make it for you."

The man again gave Alex the once over. But then he nodded and said quietly, as if to himself. "This will change everything. After centuries, we will finally be rid of our enemies."

It was over. Alex smiled and extended a hand.

The prince started to reciprocate, but his face soured. "If this does not work or if you betray us, you will regret it. I swear by Allah."

The smile stayed but was forced this time. "It will work."

"On all of them?"

"Nothing is one hundred percent. Trust me."

"I trust no one."

But he shook Alex's hand, then started after his entourage.

Alex called out, "I forgot to ask, who's the sushi fan?"

The prince grimaced. "The bride. She attended university in New York."

Alex addressed the crowd, "My congratulations to the sheikh."

᠄

The moment the plane's engines roared to life, Alex was on the phone.

"Bruce?"

"Alex, where are you?"

"On my way home."

"I take it you made the drop, against my recommendation?"

"I had to. We made a commitment. These are not people you fuck with, in case you missed the memo," Alex said, fuming. "And you promised me results months ago—June, July at the latest. Do you remember?" It was a rhetorical question. "So? Do you have them?"

Bruce hesitated. "You know, you were taking a huge risk."

"I pay you to get things done, not to advise me," Alex said.

"These are only initial findings. We'll need to do more analysis."

"Tell me."

"The sample size is not large enough for the level of confidence that I am used to reporting. And then there is—"

"Bruce, for God's sake tell me!"

"The inherited transmission rate of the genetic mutation caused by the retrovirus follows standard Mendelian principles for a mono-genetic trait. If both parents were exposed to the virus, we have virtually one hundred percent inheritance, and if one parent was exposed, we have fifty percent inheritance."

Alex suppressed the urge to scream. "Bruce, I know that. I invented the damn thing."

"Of course. Sorry. I just wanted to be clear."

"What about with the second generation?" Alex asked. This was the $64,000 question. Or in this case, thirty million dollars. "What's the sterilization rate?"

"If the mutation exists, my new chemical agent is nearly always effective and permanent," Bruce said, emphasizing the word *my*.

"What does *nearly always effective* mean? Fifty or seventy five percent?"

"Likely higher."

"I knew it." Alex smiled, feeling relieved. "So, what, ninety percent?"

"Higher."

Alex inhaled sharply, tingling with excitement. This was excellent news. "One hundred percent?"

"Nothing is one hundred percent."

CHAPTER 3

ATLANTA, GA

GEORGIA STEELE HATED being the center of attention. This was especially true at the moment, with five pairs of eyes locked on her. The eyes conveyed loathsome sentiments ranging from pity to superiority to pleading. But she had to endure them today at the risk of going to prison, for Georgia had broken the law—not for the first time—but this was the first time she had been caught. She had been stupid. She had not taken the same precautions in her personal life that she normally took in her professional life.

And that was the reason they were here today, seated at an antique walnut table, in a well-appointed conference room with a magnificent view of the Buckhead skyline. Her attorney was one of the best Atlanta had to offer and hence could afford this level of grandeur.

"Georgia?" She felt a hand on her arm, meant to grab her attention.

She had been absently fingering the wooden sticks that kept her long dark hair obediently wrapped in a chignon. The hair sticks were a gift from her parents, embellished with turquoise and silver. She lowered her hand and turned to face her lawyer, an elderly man in an expensive suit. "Do I have to answer that?" she asked.

The question must have startled him. "Well, of course not, but, uh, I recommend that you do."

A broad-shouldered African American man with a crooked nose, bald head, and the pleading eyes said, "George, this is serious. Just tell them everything." Marcus West had insisted on being at this meeting. He had strong ties to the Atlanta political machine, the Atlanta Police Department, and other local law enforcement. His opinion was well respected. Georgia occasionally worked on special projects for his company, West Security, and they had been friends for a long time. And for some of that time, more than friends.

"Everything?" She winked at him.

He closed his eyes and exhaled slowly—an exasperated sigh. Then he buried his head in his large hands, but she saw the slightest grin underneath. She got him.

"I knew that I was adopted from the time I was very young. It's pretty obvious when you look at me. I'm not your normal Caucasian girl next door." Georgia studied the remaining three faces. "But it wasn't that big of a deal. I had my parents and uncle, I mean, my godfather, and we had a small but happy family."

"And your godfather is Frank Anderson? The famous geneticist?" asked Sean Kelly. The local FBI agent had pity in his dark eyes and worry lines beginning to show on his brow. He already knew the answer to the question, of course.

But it registered surprise from the two out-of-town visitors at the table. Georgia's godfather was not only a geneticist, but also a pioneer of in vitro fertilization, and the winner of a Nobel Prize. But it was likely not his medical advancements that made him noteworthy to them. It was what happened later.

Georgia fidgeted in her seat. "Yes, though I suppose at this point infamous is a better description. Anyway, I never thought about looking for a biological family until my parents died in a house fire when I was fifteen."

"It says here that you were a freshman in college," said one of the agents, a young blond woman, as she pointed to a page taken from a stack of notes in front of her.

"I was, but I was home for Christmas. I got in a fight with my parents and went back to school a day early. They died that night."

"Did you feel guilty because you left early? Maybe they'd still be alive if you were there?"

She glared at Blondie, who was emanating the superior attitude. "Or I'd be dead too, which was more likely."

Kelly interjected, "In any case, it must have been very hard on you, as young as you were."

"Well, at that point I still had Frank. It was before he went off the deep end. Plus, I knew that I could look for my biological family once I turned eighteen."

"And did you?" Kelly said. He was leading the conversation in her favor.

"Yes. As soon as I turned eighteen, I requested my original birth certificate. Turns out it's sealed. In some states, New York included, a new birth certificate is issued upon adoption, and the old one can be sealed. It's off limits."

"So then what?"

"While I was in school, I made inquiries to several adoption agencies in New York. None had any record of me, or any record they would release."

"Is that when you started hacking into adoption records?" asked Blondie. Honestly she was annoying. Especially because she looked to be in her mid-twenties, which seemed very young next to Georgia's thirty-two years.

Georgia's attorney whispered a few words in her ear.

"I continued to make requests over the years, in New York and other states, but was unable to find anything," she said, following his advice.

"Did you ever think that maybe your birth parents do not want to be found?"

"Yes," Georgia said. "Of course. But times have changed. Having a mixed-race child is more acceptable than it used to be."

"Is that why, after all this time, you decided to hack into New York State's confidential records?" Blondie asked.

"They updated their system six months ago. They now have a consolidated database of all adoptions, even private adoptions. Many of these were only in hard copy before, lost in old filing cabinets and stored in multiple counties. Now everything is online."

Both agents scribbled on their note pads. This was not a good sign.

"Look, I'm very sorry," she said. "But I wasn't hurting anyone. I just wanted to find my family, a parent, maybe a sister or brother, even a cousin. Can't you understand that?"

Blondie tapped her pen on the table.

The other agent, silent up to this point, spoke. "Why didn't you just send your DNA to those genealogy sites? They have millions of people in them. They can find distant relatives. I found a bunch of cousins in Milwaukee last year."

"I did," Georgia said. "I received no matches. None at all."

"Nothing at all? That's weird, because so many people have…"

Blondie interrupted him with an icy stare. The agent went back to his notes.

"That may be the case, Ms. Steele, but breaking into sealed adoption records is a felony," Blondie said. "If I had my way, you'd be in prison, yet my Southeastern counterparts feel that your services and these extenuating circumstances entitle you to some leniency. But you've admitted to doing this before, and I think you will likely do it again. In addition, there is your relationship to Frank Anderson."

"We have no relationship," Georgia said. "I haven't talked to him in years." She started to say more, but Marcus was staring her down.

Kelly closed his folder, effectively ending this part of the meeting. He said, "I think we covered the reasons behind Dr. Steele's lapse in judgment. Now I'd like to bring in the Atlanta PD and the Georgia Bureau of Investigation to talk about her extraordinary services to our community."

The services to which Kelly referred included testimony Georgia would give in a high-profile case complete with murder and a multi-state drug smuggling operation.

Two years ago, she had been hired for what seemed to be a routine consulting job at Atlantic-Pacific, a mass producer of lumber and other building products. She was to analyze truck routing for the corporation and look for ways to improve efficiency. Georgia was an expert at optimizing complex systems and often performed this type of work.

But instead of suboptimal algorithms, she uncovered a conspiracy to move drugs from Florida across the Southeast using company trucks. Georgia and Atlantic-Pacific helped the FBI set up a sting operation, but before they could act, the Senior Vice President of Logistics was shot to death. Now Georgia's testimony was crucial to the case. They all knew that if she was an accused felon it would not bode well for the prosecution.

While they waited for the detectives from the APD and the GBI, the two out-of-town agents huddled together and talked in hushed tones. Lunch was set out on the credenza near the door and Marcus wasted no time helping himself to a sandwich and a Coke.

Agent Kelly took the seat vacated by Georgia's attorney. Leaning in close, he tapped her arm with his long dark fingers. "You saw we have grand jury selection next week?"

"Yes, starting on 9/11. Whose bright idea was that?"

"You'll be available for the depositions?" Kelly asked. The asking was merely a formality.

৶

"You are one lucky woman, George," Marcus said, after they departed the lawyer's office several hours later. "You know, you didn't make it easy on yourself in there."

"That blond woman, she was so haughty and self-righteous."

"Look who's talking." He grabbed her shoulder and spun her around so that they were standing face to face. Then he loosened his grip and dropped his arm, wrapping it around her and pressing his hand into the small of her back.

She tried to read him, but his eyes were hidden by expensive sunglasses. Marcus always wore sunglasses. She reached up and gently removed them. With heels she was probably 5'9", but he still stood half a foot taller. They were standing very close. The heat between them made the air feel even steamier than it was.

He squinted, though it was a cloudy day. "You need to be more careful."

"Are you saying that because you care about me or because you worry I'll get you and your business into trouble?"

Marcus released her and took a step backward, shaking his head. His phone rang and he turned away to answer it. The moment was gone.

While Georgia waited for Marcus, she absently twirled his sunglasses with one hand and checked her email with the other. One caught her attention. It was from someone named Emiko Mori, and the subject was "Frank Anderson."

Hello Georgia,

My name is Emiko Mori. You don't know me, but I think we might be related.

I was an IVF baby, and Frank Anderson was my parents' doctor. I found out about you through him.

I am playing with the Atlanta Symphony Orchestra tonight. I left two tickets for you at the door. I hope you can come so we can meet.

Yours truly,

Emiko

This was strange. Of course, if Georgia had been the result of in vitro fertilization, with donated sperm or eggs, then she could easily have a half or even full sibling. That thought should have been thrilling. But she had long ago asked her parents about this, given their friendship with Frank, and they had insisted she was adopted. Why would they have lied?

Yet here was a guy, *a guy with an Asian name,* who knew Frank.

Marcus was walking back to her, phone in his hand. "What happened?" he asked. He must have seen the confusion on her face.

She showed him the email.

"That's weird," he said.

"To say the least."

"Do you know this Emiko?"

"Never heard of him."

"Well, let's see." Marcus held up his phone. He swiped and tapped until he read out loud, "Emiko Mori is tonight's guest musician at the Atlanta Symphony Orchestra. At only sixteen, she will be the youngest violinist to ever play with the ASO." He put down the phone.

"She?" Georgia mused.

"Another genius. What do you think? You going to go?"

"I'm not sure."

"What? You've been searching for your biological family for half your life, and here you have a lead like this dropped in your lap and you're not sure?"

"Well, it just seems all too convenient. And weird."

"Why don't you call Frank and find out?" Marcus asked.

"What? No."

"What do you mean, no?"

"He's not part of my life," Georgia said. She handed Marcus his sunglasses. "Besides, he's crazy. And I'm not even sure where he is, or if I can even find a phone number for him."

Marcus looked at her incredulously.

"OK, so maybe I can find a phone number," she said.

"I think you're scared. After all this time…"

"It's not that."

"What, then?" Marcus asked.

"Until now it's all been on my terms. Under my control."

"Ah, yes." He raised an eyebrow. "I know you like to be in control."

Georgia did not respond.

Marcus said, "You really are nervous. Call Frank. Ask him. But regardless, you should go. I'll go with you."

"You? You hate classical music."

"So do you. So I'll pick you up around seven." He looked at his watch. "That's only three hours from now, we better get going."

CHAPTER 4

OLANCHO REGION, HONDURAS

GENE YOUNG LINGERED at the edge of the village square. A handful of adolescent boys occupied its center, laughing and kicking a soccer ball around a loosely formed circle. The sun had dipped below the lush green hills, a beginning to the end of the day. The softening of the light did wonders for the view. It obscured the trash on the roads and transformed the open sewers into simple culverts. The wooden huts surrounding the dirt square were quaint rather than dilapidated. The jungle was coming alive. The daytime fauna overlapped the night, with monkeys, birds, frogs, and cicadas all contributing to the biological cacophony.

"Gene? Dr. Young?"

It was Christine, his nurse.

"Yes, Christine?"

"That's everyone. We can call it a day and wrap up." Short and squat, with dark eyes and hair, Christine resembled the people they served every day, yet she was from Arizona.

Gene searched the horizon. "Everyone?"

"Of course, not everyone. A few days are not enough to see everyone who wants to see a doctor. But we got all the important ones: the broken bones, scabies, parasites, fevers."

Christine disappeared into the narrow wooden shack they used as their makeshift clinic. She returned with a large box of equipment and loaded it into their van. The van served as home base when they traveled for Doctors With Wings, or DWW, which was about two weeks a month. "Boy am I excited to get home and take a hot bath. Don't know how you've managed to do this for what, going on three years?"

"But no pregnant girls."

"What's that?" Christine's head poked around the side of the vehicle. "Did you say something?"

"Never mind." Gene circled the van, giving it a once over. The tires looked fine, but he gave one a kick for good measure. If they left soon, he could still get home before dark. Driving at night in the Honduran countryside was never a good idea.

"What the…? Dr. Young?" Christine sounded alarmed.

Gene hurried to see what had caused her distress. A speeding vehicle came to an abrupt stop in the center of town, a cloud of road dust in tow. It was an old Tiuna truck, the Venezuelan military equivalent of the Humvee, in olive green. Two passengers sat in the front seat, and two more stood in the back cab, rifles in hand. One of these was barking orders at the villagers, telling them to stay away.

The boys scattered and the few adults shrank into open doorways or shadowed alcoves.

A man with a trimmed graying beard in a white dress shirt stepped from the passenger seat and approached them. Gene noticed he wore dark jeans and stylish dress shoes, unusual footwear under the circumstances.

"It's alright, Chris," Gene said. *At least I hope it is, putting my faith in a known criminal, drug dealer, and murderer.*

He walked toward the man and met him halfway. They shook hands.

"Thank you, my friend," the man said.

"It's nothing. It's what we do."

"Not to my sister. She is ever grateful. You saved her only son."

Christine's voice wavered as she called over, "Dr. Young? We should go now."

Gene raised an arm behind him to quiet her. He said, "Thank you for coming."

"What is it you wanted to talk to me about?"

Gene collected himself, then said, "Do you remember Dr. Dumas? The missionary doctor who was here before? He died about ten years ago."

Ramos' eyes narrowed.

"While he was here, there was a time when few women had babies. For three years there were almost no babies."

"I remember," Ramos said, his tone unreadable.

Gene described the lack of pregnant teens he was seeing. "I think it's happening again, but I need to be sure. I have no records from Dumas, and I want to keep this quiet. No need to cause a panic." He caught a drop of sweat before it rolled into his eyes and made his request.

Ramos rubbed his chin in thought. Finally, he nodded. "I will ask around. It will take some time."

"How can I contact you?"

The man shook his head. "You won't. I will find you." He strode back to the truck, waving at the lone boy who had reentered the square. The men drove off, the two in the back still standing and with guns raised.

"Dr. Young, what was that about?" Christine asked, after they were on their way. "That man, is he who I think he is? Juan Carlos Ramos? Nasty man with the army and drug cartel? What were you talking to him about?"

"It was nothing, Chris. He was thanking me for saving his nephew. We saw him a few months ago, the kid who got kicked in the head by a horse, remember?"

"Yes, but…"

"But nothing. Let's drop it. I'm exhausted."

᷍

"Hello, lover," José said, his English thickly accented.

Gene dropped his bags by the kitchen door and submerged his senses in the wonderfulness of his home. A pot steaming on the stove dispersed the comforting aroma of José's chicken and rice. The bank of windows lining the combined living and dining room afforded a spectacular view of the neighboring pasture. The sun had set, but the sky was still aglow with colors that refused to be called orange or yellow but demanded superlative names such as tangerine, saffron, and coral. Inside, they melded together and cast everything in a soft rosy glow.

Ah, to see the world in rose color. Maybe everything was fine, and he was just a paranoid and cynical man.

"I missed you," José said, fitting a lid to the pot. He was standing next to the stove, barefoot in a faded UCLA t-shirt and jeans. His smile radiated. They embraced. Gene plunged his face into José's long curly hair and breathed deeply. He was home.

᷍

Red wine and tortillas accompanied the chicken and rice. As usual, it was delicious.

"You look tired. Was this a busy trip?" José said.

"It was okay. We're not seeing many babies or pregnant women, and that worries me."

"Yes, you told me that before. Anything else?"

"No." Gene squirmed and looked down at his plate. José could always tell when he was lying or even skirting the truth.

"What?"

"Well, I found someone who might be able to help."

"Who?"

"Juan Carlos Ramos."

"Who?"

"You know."

José's brow furrowed, then his eyes widened. "Ramos? Juan Ramos? Why would you talk to *him*?"

"He came to thank me for saving his nephew's life and so...I asked for his help." This was not exactly true, but it was close enough.

"Gene, why are you going to make trouble? Things are finally going well here for us. Your new clinic is open, and more doctors are coming. El Progreso is building a distribution center for medicine and supplies. We are taking Olancho from the stone ages into, *no lo sé*, but something better. And you go talking to the cartel. Who knows what can happen? The mayor, the governor, maybe even the president, they are all watching what we are doing."

Gene started to protest, but José cut him off with a wave of his hand. He stood abruptly, jostling his chair and nearly knocking it over.

"And why? Because young girls are not having sex? Are you *joking* me?" José pressed clenched fists against his chest. "Are you predisposed to a life of misery?" He sighed, dropped his arms, and picked up his wine glass. "I need some air." He left through the back door, disappearing in the dark.

José was probably right. But Gene could not get over the feeling that something very wrong was happening.

CHAPTER 5

ATLANTA, GA

AN ALARM BLARED from the speakers in Georgia's home work-station. She swore, then brought up the interface for her security system. The monitor on her right displayed multiple views of the exterior of the three-story Arts and Crafts home. One camera showed a large black man holding a piece of newspaper over his head and rushing up the stairs to her attic apartment, taking them two and three at a time.

Turning back to her laptop and typing rapidly, Georgia finished the email she had been composing, located the relevant document, and attached it.

A second camera caught Marcus West—newspaper gone—banging on the door. "George, it's starting to rain. Let me in," he said, staring directly into the entrance camera.

She sent the email, hurried to the door, and unlocked it.

Once inside, Marcus brushed the rain from his black bespoke suit and wiped his feet on the mat. He eyed Georgia and made a *tsking* sound. "You're not even ready to go. What have you been doing?"

"Working for you. Tell your client it's done."

"Really?" Marcus raised his eyebrows. "Do tell."

"Not now. I'm late, remember?" she said, already halfway to her bedroom.

Marcus called after her, "Did you talk to Frank?"

"I sent him an email. It bounced back."

"You sent him an email." Georgia heard the disappointment in Marcus' voice. "Did you at least look up Emiko Mori?"

"I didn't have time," she responded through the open door.

"You didn't even do any basic recon on her, like I taught you?" he said, emphasizing the last few words. "You know, I think you're scared. After all this time, all this searching."

"That's not it," she said, defensively. "Marcus, I've been busy. I had to get that case wrapped up, and the security was a bitch. It took me two full days to hack into their payment system." Georgia turned her attention to the closet.

"I do not want to know that. Do not tell me that," Marcus thundered. Then in a softer voice, "Are you serious, you didn't even Google Emiko?"

She found the dress she was searching for, dark red and tiny, and shimmied into it. "She's only fifteen." Georgia pulled the sticks from her long hair and brushed it out. While applying mascara, she continued the conversation. "I don't see how we could be related." She rummaged through a small pouch and found one lipstick, a dark red. It would have to do.

"Oh boy, this is going be quite the surprise," he said under his breath.

That got her attention. She hurriedly put on the shoes she had worn earlier in the day, located a black clutch, and stole a quick look in the mirror. "I'm ready. Now, what about this surprise?"

Marcus' face lit up. "Hot damn, girl, you are gorgeous. Nope, I'm not telling you, and I am going to enjoy this immensely."

Curiosity growing, she stopped at her computer, intending to do a quick search.

"Oh no you don't." With little effort, Marcus picked her up.

He was easily twice her size. He walked out the door with her over his shoulders.

"Marcus!"

❧

In the lobby of the Woodruff Arts Center, Georgia did her best wet-dog shake, which was difficult given the clingy dress and high heels. But her hair more than made up for it, and a few people gave her a "watch it, will you?" look.

"I'm soaked," she whined. The rain had dampened her spirits along with her dress.

Dripping and stamping his feet, Marcus laughed. The rain had not similarly bothered him, it seemed. "Georgia, I told you I'd drop you off at the door, sugar." His southern drawl crept in, and "sugar" sounded more like "shugah."

While Marcus picked up the tickets, Georgia dried off in the restroom. They met afterward at the lobby bar. She was going to need a glass of wine to get through the tiresome ordeal. At least one. Maybe another at intermission.

They found their way down the aisle to their seats in the fifth row, dead center.

"I hope this is worth it. You know how I feel about classical music," Georgia said.

"You'll see. Shh, it's starting."

It turned out that the first half was the normal symphony lineup, and the young violinist never appeared. They both squirmed in their seats and headed to the lobby bar as soon as the intermission began.

"So far, it's pretty much as I expected," Georgia lamented.

"Ye of little faith."

❧

After the intermission it was a different story.

The conductor addressed the audience. "Ladies and Gentleman, we have a very special guest tonight. It is our pleasure to bring to you a rising star and the youngest violinist to play with the Atlanta Symphony. She is a member of the Rochester Philharmonic and a student at Juilliard. May I introduce Miss Emiko Mori."

As the audience applauded, the young virtuoso, clad in the classic white shirt and black pants, walked onto the stage. She nodded to the conductor, turned and bowed to the audience.

"Oh," Georgia said. She found no other words to describe the younger version of herself on the stage.

"Yes," Marcus whispered, handing her a small pair of binoculars.

The conductor continued, "Before we play together, Miss Mori will treat us to a wonderful solo, Bach's Chaconne, the final movement from the Partita No. 2 in D Minor."

The young woman stepped to the front of the stage and began to play.

At first, Georgia was mesmerized by Emiko's appearance, motions, and mannerisms. All eerily similar to her own. But as the young violinist poured herself into the music, Georgia did the same. It carried her on a beautiful journey, full of dancing, joy, and sorrow. She tried not to breathe lest she disrupt the pureness of the air.

A final somber tone ended the movement, and the normally staid crowd jumped to their feet, many with tears in their eyes. It was several minutes before the applause died down to a point where the conductor could continue. Georgia did not stand; she just sat in stunned silence.

The rest of the program was pleasant, but it did not match Emiko's solo performance. At the conclusion, the audience again rose to their feet for the guest violinist, the enthusiastic applause punctuated with shouts of "Bravo!"

"George, she was awesome."

"Marcus, what is going on?" Georgia said, lowering the binoculars. "How could..."

"Let's go find out. We have backstage passes."

They snaked their way through the departing crowd and went to the green room. It was easy to find, but not see, Ms. Mori. A crowd of people surrounded her.

They waited. When most of the throng subsided, Emiko spotted Georgia and Marcus, her eyes and smile widening. She thanked the remaining fans, hurried over to Georgia, and embraced her.

"Finally," she said. She squeezed Georgia again before releasing her. "I am so happy to meet you." The young violinist appeared Asian, but her voice was definitely American.

Georgia stared in shock. She had never seen anyone that even remotely resembled her. She was a mash up of the human race. Looking at Emiko gave her a glimpse of how others must see her: a racial mutt yes, but also an exotic, Latin-Eurasian beauty. They shared a thin but athletic build, shimmering mahogany hair, light olive skin with a gold undertone, prominent cheekbones, and delicate lips. Georgia had hair perhaps a shade lighter and her skin had seen more sun, and of course she was older, though she was often told she did not look her age. Without her heels, Georgia calculated, they were also about the same height. But more than anything it was their eyes. The unusual eyes, almond shaped and amber with flecks of gold, for which Georgia always received compliments. The eyes were exactly the same.

Marcus said, "Miss Mori, I am Marcus West and this is Georgia Steele. You were wonderful and it is truly an honor to meet you."

Emiko did not answer. She mirrored Georgia, staring intently at her older twin.

"You know my godfather, Frank Anderson?" Georgia finally asked.

"Yes, though not well. He moved away when I was very young. But my family kept in touch with him over the years."

More silence. More staring.

Finally, Georgia said, "Did Frank tell you about me?"

"No, not exactly. He does not know I'm here. He would not be pleased."

"Why not?"

She looked around nervously. "How much do you know about Frank?"

"More than enough."

"Then you know he has his secrets. I think we're two of them, and I don't think he wanted us to meet."

"Then why are you here?"

"Isn't it obvious?"

At that moment a petite matronly woman came up to them, and congratulated Emiko on her performance. She said to Georgia, "Are you Emiko's sister? I didn't know she had any family in Atlanta."

Georgia was unable to suppress a smile.

"Mrs. Wilson is my chaperone while I'm in Atlanta," Emiko said.

The woman beamed with pride, as if she was Emiko's mother, and not just a weekend escort. "Isn't she wonderful?"

Emiko said, "Mrs. Wilson, can I talk to my cousin for a few minutes?"

Mrs. Wilson looked slightly embarrassed and excused herself. She wandered away and sat in a chair against the wall but kept her eyes on her ward.

"Can we go somewhere else?" Emiko whispered. "Is there somewhere we can meet in private?"

"Where are you staying?"

"The Georgian Terrace, but I don't want to meet there either."

Marcus handed her a card. "We can go to my club. It's right down the street. I'm the owner. Trust me, it's packed. No one will notice you."

"You can come with us," Georgia said as she touched Emiko's arm. She felt real, but could she be?

"No. You go ahead. I have to pack up and talk to the conductor"—Emiko nodded to the chaperone—"and ditch Mrs. Wilson."

"I can wait for you," Georgia said, trying not to sound desperate.

"Really, it's okay. I'll probably be about thirty minutes."

Marcus said, "Let me call my man, Ty, and he'll come and get you."

Emiko shook her head. "I'll call a ride or catch a taxi. I saw a stand right out back." She glanced over her shoulder. "I gotta bounce."

Scanning the crowd behind Emiko, Georgia saw the conductor beckoning. She just stood there feeling helpless as the young virtuoso turned to leave.

Abruptly, Emiko turned back and hugged Georgia again. As she did, she whispered, "I've been waiting an eternity to meet you."

⌘

This time Georgia opted to stay dry and let Marcus pick her up in front of the Arts Center. The 2016 black Porsche Carrera, spotless and shiny, was a head turner, and she had to work her way around the departing patrons who stopped to gawk.

He had received the car as a present from a local celebrity and multi-millionaire, the R&B singer and songwriter, Raymond. Marcus had literally saved the man's life during an industry party gone wrong. He had tried to refuse the gift, but Raymond would not hear of it, and the two had since become close friends.

"I don't know why we drove. We could've got a ride."

"Today is the first day I've been able to drive my baby in over a week. She missed me." He caressed the leather interior. "Watch that you don't get the seat wet."

She made gagging motions as she wrestled with her seat belt.

Watching her struggle, he said, "You know we're just going one mile."

"Atlanta drivers are crazy. I'm not taking any chances."

They exited the Woodruff Arts Center lot and turned south towards Marcus' club on 11th Street. Cars were lined up bumper to bumper. Midtown was always busy on a Saturday night, but with the symphony and the rain, the traffic was horrid.

Georgia leaned back in her seat and the events of the night hit her. Her head swam and she felt dizzy. "That was unbelievable. Marcus, we have to be related. She looks just like me. She was so amazing." The words tumbled out as she struggled to form cohesive sentences.

"Indeed. Talented and beautiful. Like you, George."

"Why was she worried about where to meet? Seems like more than just losing the chaperone. Maybe she just doesn't want the paparazzi finding out about us before her family does?"

"The paparazzi don't hang out at the symphony. And she doesn't have much family. Her father's dead and so is her older brother. It's just her and her mother."

Georgia stared at Marcus, confused.

He tapped his temple. "Basic recon, remember? You and she have a lot in common, George, a lot more than your looks." Turning his eyes back to the road, he continued, "You're wishing you'd done your homework now, aren't you?"

She groaned.

Finally, they made it the half mile to the West End. A valet ran out with an umbrella and they dashed into the entrance. A young guy, even bigger than Marcus, opened the door for them.

"Hi Mr. West, Ms. Steele. I mean, Dr. Steele." He had an impish grin and towered over Georgia.

"Hi Ty, how are things?"

"Good. Classes are going okay so far." He shrugged. "I do miss football."

"Yeah, but we know who will end up ahead, with the girls and the glam."

"The geeks," they said in unison and both laughed.

Ty had been on the defensive line at Georgia Tech and a star in the making, until he blew out his knee. Marcus was making sure he finished school and did not waste his scholarship or his life. Georgia did not know how many young men Marcus had mentored, but it seemed like he picked up a new one almost every year.

"You look so fine tonight, Mr. West," the buxom brunette working the coat check crooned. "Can I get you anything?"

The music was cranking in the back on the dance floor, but thanks to recent sound baffling one could actually hold a conversation here and at the adjoining bar.

"No, thank you. George, you want anything?"

"Not now, no. I'll just hang out with Ty and wait for Emiko."

Georgia glanced back to where Ty stood at the door. "Look, the rain is already starting to let up."

⌁

Georgia paced outside the entrance of the The West End. The rain had chilled the air, but she did not care. She kept watch on the street.

Marcus was right. She was scared. But not because she wanted to be in control. She was afraid to let herself believe. She had looked so long, in so many places, for so many years. And now, finally, unbelievably, and in the simplest of ways, her dream had come true. There was no way Emiko was not related to her. Closely related. Cousins? Half sisters? *Sisters*?

A car displaying a pink Lyft light stopped catty-corner across the street. Emiko was visible in the back seat, talking to the driver. Anticipation made Georgia excited and nervous at the same time. Emiko finally got out of the car and stepped onto the sidewalk. Georgia lost sight of her in the traffic. She reappeared in the crosswalk in front of the car, violin in hand. The light turned yellow and the teen waited for the second lane to clear. Emiko raised her hand in a wave. Georgia waved back.

As Emiko resumed walking, a dark sedan veered out from the line of vehicles stopped behind the Lyft car. It accelerated rapidly into the inside lane, no doubt to try and beat the light, but Emiko was walking briskly and would be in no danger. Until she stopped, no, rather she jerked back and spun around. Georgia immediately pictured a fish caught on a line at the moment the hook set. Standing behind Emiko on the sidewalk was a man. A tall, older man. A familiar man. *Frank?*

Georgia knew what would happen. She could see the events exactly as they would unfold, but she was too far away in space and too close in time to do anything except scream.

The driver of the dark sedan would not be able to correct course or stop. She watched in horror as it plowed into the young woman and kept going. When it passed, Emiko and the man were both gone.

CHAPTER 6

ATLANTA, GA

EMIKO'S VIOLIN CASE crashed to the ground, landing in front of Georgia. Car tires screeched and someone was screaming. It may have been her.

Ty sprinted past Georgia, yelling "Call 911! Dr. Steele, call 911!" She fumbled in her small clutch until she found her phone. After many rings the call was answered, and she was asking for help when the dispatcher said, "If you are calling from Peachtree and 11th, we've already been called, and help is—" Georgia hung up.

Traffic had stopped and people were getting out of their cars, visibly dazed. No sign of Emiko or the car that hit her. *Probably a drunk driver, the bastard.*

A swarm of activity assembled farther down the road. She forced her body to move in that direction and tripped over the violin case. Her knee hit the ground first and caught most of the impact before her momentum propelled her forward. She braced herself, but runoff from the storm was deep at the edge of the street, and it cushioned her fall.

Georgia rolled to all fours, her dress soaked and torn, her knee scraped and bleeding. She pushed herself up, barely registering her own discomfort. Picking up the violin case, she hurried to where the crowd was forming. She clutched the case to her chest, both protecting it and using it as a shield, and pushed her way through, ducking low to avoid elbows.

A mountain of a man was in her way. It was Ty, bent over with his back to her. Georgia squeezed her way around him. And instantly wished she had not. The halogen street lights above left no doubt as to the horrors below. Emiko was lying on her back and her face was covered in blood. Her eyes were open, but she was not responding to Ty's questions. Her right arm twisted below the elbow and bone ripped through the fabric of her sleeve. The white bone was a striking and perverse contrast to the blood-stained shirt. Georgia felt dizzy and dropped to her knees, using her left hand to steady herself while the right still clutched the case. A siren wailed, sounding far away. The emergency vehicle would be trapped in the tangle of cars and people.

Ty was speaking to Emiko. "Stay with us, girl." He felt the wrist on Emiko's unbroken arm. "She has a pulse, but it's weak." He started mouth-to-mouth resuscitation.

A single EMT pushed through the crowd. "Please folks, give me some room." The young man was out of breath. He must have covered the last few blocks on foot as there was no sign of any ambulance.

Georgia felt an arm nestle under her and start to pull her up. She struggled to stay where she was—with Emiko.

"George, come on, let them do their job." Marcus lifted her off the ground.

"Everyone please move away so we can get to her."

Two more EMTs arrived. They quickly dropped a stretcher to ground level and loaded Emiko onto it with practiced ease. Georgia broke from Marcus' grip and followed them through the crowd and down the street to the waiting ambulance. "Where are you taking her?"

A responder called out, "Either Grady or Atlanta Medical

Center. They have the best trauma units. We'll see who can take her first." Then he closed the door and the ambulance drove away, lights flashing.

✐

Georgia parked her blue Mini Cooper in front of a single-story home in Virginia Highlands. The image of Emiko's maimed figure had haunted her throughout the night, and she was afraid to open the car door, lest she see Emiko lying in the street again, a harsh collage of black, white, and red. She forced herself to focus on today's colors, the brilliant blue of the sky, and a deep green courtesy of a huge poplar obscuring most of the front yard. Everything was going to be all right.

The tree sheltered her as she walked up the sidewalk to the house belonging to her best friend, David Cohen. Here in the deep shade there was still mist in the air, and Georgia felt its cool comfort on her skin.

She knocked while opening the door. "Hello? Anyone home?"

"Hey George, come on in. Want some coffee?" Dave's voice echoed from the back of the house.

Georgia wandered towards the sound of his voice, through the unused living room and into the combination family and dining room. Part of this room was used as Dave's office. Multiple whiteboards hung from the two walls nearest the dining table. As per usual, the table itself was obscured by books, papers, a laptop, and a large monitor. A long, low-slung bookcase under one of the whiteboards was filled with books on artificial intelligence, simulation, statistics, computer science, and the odd historical novel. Dave was a professor at Georgia Tech, in the Industrial and Systems Engineering department. Georgia and Dave had attended graduate school together at Tech.

"Where's Trish?" she asked, looking out a window to the back patio. Her favorite part of Dave's house was the back yard. French doors and a set of wide windows turned out on a brick patio and heavily wooded lot resplendent with every shade of green. But Georgia struggled to see the beauty of it today.

"She's getting ready to go running with you," Dave called.

Patricia Erickson, or Trish for short, was Dave's girlfriend of about six months. Though Trish came off as an airhead, she was no dummy, and Georgia liked her. They had recently started running together.

She found Dave in the kitchen, head in the refrigerator. Trying for some normality after yesterday's insanity she asked, "How's school going?"

"You know, the first few weeks are always fun. You get to scare the bejesus out of the grad students, and the undergrads are still coming to class."

"Yeah, I remember. The old look to your right, look to your left, one of you will not be here at the end of the semester speech. So, you've become one of them?"

"Coffee's ready, splash of milk, right?" He closed the door to the fridge, milk in hand. The perpetual smile Dave normally wore on his face turned upside down. The transformation would have been comical under other circumstances. "George, are you okay? You don't look well."

"I didn't sleep at all last night," Georgia said.

Dave waited, an expectant look on his face.

"I spent the night in the hospital."

"Geez, what happened?" Dave motioned for her to take a seat on a well-worn sofa. "Sit down and talk to me."

She started to tell Dave about the night before but was interrupted when Trish came bounding into the room. "Hi George!" she called out cheerily. Stopping mid-stride, the momentum from her long legs sent Trish's shoulder-length blond hair flying into her face. "What's going on?" she asked, removing a hair band from her wrist and tying back the unruly locks.

Georgia recounted a simplified version of the previous day's events. She did not talk about the meeting with the FBI or her godfather. Though Dave knew about both, she was not ready for his new girlfriend to be privy to such things.

"This girl contacted you just yesterday?" Trish asked.

"Yes. Her name is Emiko Mori."

"And then she got hit by a car, like, right in front of you?"

"Trish," Dave snapped.

"Yes."

"Oh my God! That's awful. Was there blood everywhere?"

Dave glared.

"Sorry," Trish said, looking sheepish. "Is she going to be okay?"

"When I left the hospital a few hours ago, she was out of surgery. She's in the ICU now, in stable condition. They said the next twenty-four hours are the most critical."

Dave put an arm around her shoulder, giving it an awkward squeeze.

"Thanks," she said, extracting herself from his grip. "Hopefully she'll be fine and we'll have plenty of time to get to know each other."

"Do you have a picture?" Trish asked.

"Give it a rest," Dave admonished.

"What? George said she looked like her. I was just curious. Sorry."

"It's alright," Georgia said. "You can look her up online. There's a picture on the ASO website."

That was apparently all the encouragement Trish needed, because she snatched an iPad from the table and began to search.

"Why are you even here? Why aren't you at home sleeping?" Dave asked.

"I tried. It was no use. I figured I could use a run, and it would kill some time before I go back to the hospital and hopefully see her. Visiting hours don't start until eleven."

"Found it," Trish chimed. "Whoa. Wow. Holy crap, George,

she's your twin." Trish read aloud, "Emiko Mori joined the Rochester Philharmonic as a member of the violin section at the beginning of the 2016 season, the same year that she won the String prize in the biennial Young Artists Competition of the National Federation of Music Clubs. Ms. Mori is from Rochester, NY, graduated from Harmony High School, and is currently enrolled at the Juilliard School."

Dave looked at Georgia, eyebrows raised.

"Yes, I went to Harmony."

"You guys went to the same high school?" Trish asked. "You must be related."

Dave said, "Why don't you go get your shoes on."

Trish pouted like a scolded child. "I can take a hint." She shuffled out of the room.

"I'm sorry. Trish is, well, not the most subtle person."

"What she lacks in tact she makes up for in enthusiasm." Georgia grinned. It felt good to smile. "Honestly, I like her. She has no pretense and no hidden agenda."

"That's for sure," Dave said, laughing. "And she likes you too."

Georgia sipped her coffee, letting the rich aroma wash over her.

"After all this time," Dave mused. "Do you really think she could be related to you?"

Before she could say anything, Trish burst back into the room. "I'm ready."

Dave nodded in Trish's direction. "We'll talk later. You go have some fun."

Georgia followed the bouncing Trish to the door. As she left, she glanced back and saw that Dave had picked up the iPad. He was staring at it and shaking his head.

Georgia rapped on the window at the hospital information desk. The elderly woman wearing a volunteer button turned away from her computer and smiled.

"Hi, I'm here to see Emiko Mori. She's my cousin," Georgia said.

The woman peered over her glasses to a clock on the wall, which read 10:50 am. "You're a few minutes early, but I guess I can check you in. Can you spell her name please?"

Georgia complied.

"One minute, young lady." Using only her index fingers, the volunteer poked at the computer keyboard. "Found her. This says she's a minor, and you are her..."

"Cousin. We're first cousins. Her mother lives in New York, and her father passed away. I'm her only family in town." Georgia knew from the previous night that only close family members were allowed in some parts of the hospital.

"I see her mother's been contacted and that you were here last night. If you'll just sign this page, I can let you up to see her. She's in the ICU, on the fourth floor."

Georgia signed the visitors' entry log.

The woman continued hunting and pecking. It was excruciating to watch. "Hmmm, this says she's in ICU but there is no room assigned. Maybe she's being moved. If you can just sit down, I'll try to find someone to help." She handed Georgia a sticker with her name on it and motioned to a waiting area.

"Thank you," Georgia said, affixing the sticker to her shirt. She considered one of the drab, burnt-orange upholstered chairs in the designated seating area and decided to stand. The lobby was bright and airy, but it still smelled of hospital.

The matronly volunteer was on the phone, doing more listening than talking. She frowned. Something was wrong. Georgia approached the desk. The woman raised her index finger in a just-one-minute gesture.

Georgia lifted her hands and mouthed a "sorry." Heart pounding, she backed away slowly. When the woman's eyes dropped down to her screen, Georgia bolted for the elevator.

It was mass confusion at the ICU front desk. Two doctors, a security guard, and a policeman gathered around the front station, and the attending nurse was in tears. They all seemed to be talking over each other, and one of the doctors was pointing down the hallway.

Georgia made for the desk but was met halfway by the security guard. "Not now, young lady, the ICU is closed to visitors. Please go downstairs and we'll call when you can come up."

Georgia hesitated.

"Please. You need to leave."

Georgia turned back towards the elevator. Nearby, a nurse's aide was going through laundry on a cart. "What's going on here?" Georgia asked the young woman. "They won't let me in to see my cousin."

The aide kept her head down, but shifted her eyes to Georgia and then to the station where the conversation was still heated. One of the doctors was repeatedly poking at a clipboard that the other was holding.

The aide returned her gaze to the laundry. When she spoke it was in a whisper with a pronounced Southern accent. "It's been crazy here. A girl died this morning, and they lost the body."

"A girl?"

"The one from the symphony, an Asian girl."

Georgia sucked in her breath, an involuntary reaction. "What?" she exclaimed.

The aide looked up at her, eyes full of sympathy. "Oh no, was she your cousin?"

Georgia fought to remain calm. She grabbed the woman's arm and led her down the hall away from the front desk. "What happened?"

"I'm sorry, but I don't really know much. I know she passed earlier, maybe an hour ago. But instead of going to the morgue, she was taken somewhere else, and no one knows where. And since she was in a car accident the police need the body, I guess. Everyone's freaking out and yelling at everyone else." The girl glanced in the direction of the commotion.

One of the doctors was staring at them.

"I have to go now. I'm really sorry about your cousin." She removed Georgia's hand from her arm, giving it a quick squeeze. "God Bless." Then she hurried back to her cart.

⚬

This can't be happening.

The steering wheel was cool against Georgia's forehead, but it did nothing to soothe the tangle of emotions roiling inside of her. A single tear caught on her cheekbone before spilling down her face. Emiko was dead.

As she fought to gather her composure, her phone rang. Without lifting her head, she felt around on the passenger seat until she found it. "Hello?"

"Georgie?"

That got her attention. "Who is this?" she asked, though she knew who it was. Only one person alive called her Georgie. "Frank, is that you?"

"Georgie, I'm so sorry."

"It was you. You were there. What's going on?"

"I wish I could tell you; I truly do."

"She's gone. Emiko's gone."

"I know."

"Did you have something to do with this?"

"God no!" he exclaimed. Then his voice faltered. "Or maybe I did. I don't know."

"What does that mean? And where are you?" She suddenly got the feeling of being watched. Georgia craned her neck and scanned the area around the car. The parking lot was full, with a steady stream of people passing in and out of the hospital. "Are you here, at the hospital?"

"What did she tell you?"

"Who, Emiko?"

"Yes, what did she tell you?"

"She didn't tell me anything," Georgia said.

"She must have hacked my computer to find you."

At this Georgia could not help but smile.

He went on, "I don't know. I'm not sure how much she found out. I couldn't take the chance." He was rambling now. "If the two of you met, they would have found out. If they think you know..."

"Know what?"

"She didn't tell you anything?"

"She said we were related, and that you were her IVF doctor. You made her. Is it true?"

"Did she say anything else?"

"No. We never got a chance to talk."

He exhaled loudly. "Oh, thank God."

"It's true, isn't it? We are related. Are we sisters?"

"No, uh, look Georgie, I have to go. I have to disappear for a while. I've done too much already." Frank was talking fast, the words tumbling out. "Please let Emiko go. There's nothing to gain and so much to lose. I love you, Georgie. I've always loved you and I will always love you."

"If you love me, why did you leave me?" she said, but he had already hung up. "I needed you," she said to the lifeless phone. The feeling of being watched was also gone.

She dropped the phone into her lap. What the hell? She hadn't spoken to Frank since she turned eighteen. He'd called her then to say he was sorry, that he would be unable to attend her graduation from MIT, and that he was leaving the country. There was a grand conspiracy and *they* were responsible. After that she had refused his calls. Apparently, he was still as paranoid as ever.

She forced the past from her mind and focused on the present. She was certain that she and Emiko *were* closely related, probably through Frank's infertility lab. But her parents had always told her she was adopted. Why would they lie?

And why did it matter if Emiko found her? Sure, Frank would be breaking confidentiality agreements, but it was not unheard of for siblings to try and find each other, even those related only by a sperm or egg donor. Under the circumstances, it certainly didn't warrant him flying all the way from who-knows-where. This pushed the limits, even for Frank crazy.

Then for Emiko to get run over right in front of her. What did Frank mean when he said it was his fault? She thought it was a hit and run. It looked like a hit and run.

And now, Emiko, *her sister*, was gone. It was too much. Tears welled in her eyes and continued along the path of least resistance, streaming down her face and onto her lap.

CHAPTER 7

OLANCHO REGION, HONDURAS

GENE WAS STILL updating the records from his trip with Christine when a dark shadow caught his attention. He removed his reading glasses and rubbed his tired eyes. José, no longer a blur, was standing in the kitchen doorway, holding shopping bags overflowing with produce. Gene said, "You're back from the market already?"

"Did you hear anything I just said?" José over-articulated, dragging each word out.

Gene got the message but could only shrug in response.

José shook his head dramatically and stooped to place the bags on the floor. But when he stood up, he was smiling and his eyes sparkled. "I just found out. We reached an agreement with the mining company. We got everything we wanted. *Everything.* Can you believe it?"

The proposed project for the Olancho Hydroelectric Dam had been in the making for more than a decade. It would bring affordable and clean electricity to the region. The dam was making use of an existing lake but would be extended over an abandoned strip-mining location. The mine had leached arsenic and lead into the land, polluting water and wells. The clean-up had taken years. José had fought bitterly with the mining company and the government to obtain to a fair relocation package for those that would be displaced, primarily indigenous populations.

"That's fantastic," Gene said. "Congratulations."

"I know, it is just unbelievable." José draped his arms around Gene's shoulders and kissed him on the cheek. His smile faded. "Have you been sitting there since I left…" he checked his watch, an expensive present from Gene and a symbol of their commitment to each other, "…over three hours ago?"

"I guess so."

José shook his head again, his black hair flowing in a wave. He sat down next to Gene and rested his elbows on the dining room table. "Tell me."

"Tell you what?"

"Tell me everything. I know you, Gene. Once you get onto something you never let go. You are stubborn. But your heart is in the right place. Tell me."

Gene sighed. "Alright. It's going to take some time. Can you get me a fresh cup of tea?"

Gene consulted one of the many black hardcover notebooks he favored. "To start, we know Honduras has one of the highest population growth rates in the world, thanks largely to the Catholic Church."

José glared at him.

"You know it's true. Women have more children here than almost anywhere in the world."

"But we are making progress," José said. "We have improved access to birth control and education for girls. The birth rate is dropping every year, yes? You said it yourself."

Gene smiled. "People like you make a real difference." As a peasant advocate, José lobbied for the poorest Hondurans.

"We are doing what we can. And the job does have perks. We

get to work with hot doctors from around the world." He winked at Gene.

Gene was unfazed by José's flirtation. "So why am I acting," he said, pausing to recall the exact phrase José had used the night before, "as if I am predisposed to a life of misery?"

José winced and Gene regretted it as soon as the words came out of his mouth. "I'm sorry." He squeezed José's hand. "It's just that something's wrong. We're still seeing some new babies, but hardly any new mothers. I know, that's probably a good thing. But things don't change overnight. I realize we don't see everyone; there are some who never see a doctor. I've seen babies for the first time when they are years old. They were birthed at home. But even so, we should be getting more babies—or at least more pregnant girls."

He turned on his laptop and opened an Excel workbook showing multiple charts and data tables, positioning the screen so that José could see. "Here is the total birthrate in all of Honduras," Gene said, pointing to a bar chart. "It's decreasing slowly but surely, year over year, as you said." He scrolled down the sheet. "And here is the same chart for the past five years broken out by the mothers' ages. Under 15, 15–19, 20–24, 25–34, and so on. The birth rates for each age group are still decreasing over time."

José nodded. "I understand."

Gene continued, "That data is from the World Health Organization." He checked his black notebook, opened a new Excel file, and went to the first tab. "I then recreated it using all the women patients I've seen in the field and at the clinic."

"It looks almost the same," José said.

"Right. But this includes all of the towns I see in the Olancho region, several dozen." He clicked on the second tab. "When you look at just the three in De La Paz…"

The new chart showed that for the last two years, there were no births for any girls under fifteen, and few in the 15–19 age group.

"Are you sure this is right?" José asked.

"Yes."

"But the towns are so small, maybe it is just, how do you say, *anomalía?*"

"An anomaly? No. Not one girl under fifteen has had any children. Between fifteen and seventeen, the birth rate is less than half what I would expect. Girls in all the other villages are having babies, even as young as twelve, unfortunately." Gene rubbed the bridge of his nose, displacing his glasses. "I'm worried it could be happening again."

"It is not the same as before."

"I know. Before there were almost no pregnancies at all for three years. I'm not saying it's related, but we do need to consider that as well."

José stood and clutched the back of his chair. "But the new school…"

"Children from other towns attend the new school. Too many of those girls have gotten pregnant."

José said nothing. His knuckles were turning white, and the chair shook slightly.

"I sent in urine and blood samples for testing," Gene said.

"¿Qué?"

"They found nothing out of the ordinary. But the standard testing is very limited."

José released the chair and faced Gene.

"Does anyone know about this?" José asked.

"Christine, of course. And my boss. I doubt he told anyone else at Doctors With Wings."

"Why? What did he say?"

"DWW is overwhelmed with caring for sick and injured people. He said I should be thrilled that the girls are going to school and not having babies."

"And Ramos? What exactly did you tell *him*?" Now José stood with crossed arms.

Gene couldn't stand up to José's rebuke. He closed his computer and focused his attention on a spot in the middle of the table. "I told him I was worried that whatever caused the problems before was back. I asked him if he knew where I could find the widow of the local doctor who was here when it happened before. I want to see if she has any of his records. I can't find her anywhere."

"I cannot understand why you wanted to talk to him in the first place."

"I told you," Gene said, trying not to sound defensive. "Because he can reach people. He has people all over the place. And, because as weird as this sounds, I think I can trust him. He's not going to tell the government, and he's not going to try to stop the dam project."

José glared at Gene. "What do you mean by that?"

"You know as well as I do, these people, they are going to be scattered to the wind after the dam opens. We have to act now."

"What are you going to do, Gene?"

"I don't know yet."

"You cannot do anything that would hurt this project."

Gene did not respond. José was just doing what he thought was right, but so was he. If someone was hurting these girls, he had to do something. But what?

"Gene?"

CHAPTER 8

ATLANTA, GA

GEORGIA WAS EXHAUSTED and confused. Still sitting in her car in the hospital parking lot, she was not sure if it was lack of sleep or the nightmare of the last day, but she felt unable to think or even move. It was all just too much.

She absently reached for the coffee tumbler Dave lent her that morning. It was not in the center console. That was weird. She could have sworn it was there.

With no coffee to take her mind off things, she closed her eyes and concentrated on breathing, a technique she learned long ago. In for a count of five, out for a count of five. In for a count of five, out for a count of five. Breath by breath, the mental fog began to clear. She came to an obvious conclusion.

It *was* too much.

Emiko finding her, then getting killed—maybe even murdered. Frank, so scared that he came here, after all these years, just to keep them from meeting. And even though she could probably dismiss Frank as crazy, bodies didn't just go missing from hospitals anymore.

Something was going on. Georgia found form from chaos for a living; she could figure this out.

She started her car.

⚬

Fifteen minutes later, Georgia entered the lobby of the Georgian Terrace Hotel, a grand hotel across the street from the equally grand Fox Theater, and momentarily forgot why she was there. Floor-to-ceiling windows, crystal chandeliers, massive marble columns and ornate ceilings stole her attention. Though she had never been there before, she knew the hotel had hosted the opening of *Gone With The Wind*, almost a hundred years earlier. What an affair it must have been. All the Southern belles in their enormous gowns, and the men in top hats and tails. And then she imagined herself at the reception, not as a guest but as a servant, another mulatto.

The glamour disintegrated; she found her way to the front desk and the trim African American man behind the counter. He was talking on the telephone.

"Hi, just one second please," he said, eyes focused below and fingers flying rapidly across a keyboard. "Sorry about that. Now, how can I—are you alright, Miss?"

Georgia was rubbing her temple. She knew she must look fairly awful from crying in her car. She went with it.

"I've been better. I am Emiko Mori's sister... well, half sister. She's staying here. She was in a car accident last night."

"Oh, we heard." He reached across the counter and patted her arm. "I'm so sorry. That is just dreadful. I hope she's going to be okay?"

"I just came from the hospital. She's not doing very well." No exaggeration there. "Would it be possible for me to get some things from her room to take to her?"

He hesitated only a moment. "I just need to see some ID."

She handed over her driver's license.

"You live in Atlanta?"

"Yes, Emiko came here to see me and to play in the symphony."

Georgia felt her voice crack. She made no effort to hold back her emotions.

"Miss Steele, I'll get you a key, one moment." He coded a plastic card, which he passed to Georgia. "Your sister must really be special. I mean, the police were here already. They seem to be giving it their full attention."

In the elevator, on the way to the sixth floor, she pondered the man's words. It was strange that the police would be here for an ordinary hit and run, unless they suspected it was more than that.

The door to Room 621 showed no sign of anything unusual. Inside, the room was empty. Completely empty. No comforter, pillows, or sheets on the bed. No phone or remote control. The room smelled of antiseptic and bleach. She looked in the closet. Empty. Not an iron or even a hanger.

"What the…?"

She turned on the lights in the bathroom. Nothing. No towels, soap, or drinking glasses. Only the shower curtain remained. She pulled it back to inspect the tub. Nothing there. She closed the curtain with some force, venting her frustration, and heard the soft clink of something falling into the bathtub. The next opening of the curtain revealed a clear plastic toothbrush.

Georgia smiled, warmth masking the sadness in her heart. She also brushed her teeth in the shower. She reached into the tub and picked up the toothbrush, taking with her the only remnant of Emiko.

CHAPTER 9

OLANCHO REGION, HONDURAS

ALEJANDRA CASTILLA HAD an unexpected guest. José Rodríguez was leaning on the railing of her deck, head buried in folded arms. She gently touched him, letting her fingers run through his thick hair. As he stood, she brought her hand to his face, cupping his chin. He looked away, and she knew something was wrong.

"My dear José. To what do I owe this pleasure?" Though José's English was very good, she addressed him in his native language.

His dark eyes met hers.

"I hear congratulations are in order. I am very proud of you, José. You got everything you asked for. Those people are very lucky to have you on their side."

José blushed. "It was not just me. Many people worked long and hard for this. I wanted to thank you for your help."

"No need. It's one of the best things El Progreso has supported. So, tell me, what's the timing on everything? Still the same?"

"Yes. The dam should be fully operational by the end of the year. The three villages will be closed two weeks prior to that. Relocation starts next month. It will be traumatic for the people, but we did the best we could."

"Of course you did. And they know that. But I hope you did

not come all the way out here to tell me this? Good news like that travels fast; I heard about it yesterday."

"No, it's something else." José absently twisted a strand of hair.

"What is it?"

"I do not know what to do. I am very worried."

"What is it? You know you can tell me anything."

"It's Gene."

"Dr. Young? Is he sick?"

"No. Nothing like that." José shifted his weight from one foot to the other. "We talked yesterday, and he's concerned that many of the teenage girls he sees are not having babies."

Alex tried to hide her shock by laughing. "Our teen pregnancy initiative is working? How wonderful."

"I know, that's what I thought. But he is certain there's more to it."

"Like what?" Alex asked.

"He does not know. He did some blood tests on some of the girls and nothing unusual showed up. He said it could be environmental."

"Well, he's probably right. There are so many chemicals and heavy metals in the water table. It's just another reason to get the dam online. So we can get clean drinking water to the area."

"I know. It's just that..." José's voice dropped.

"What?"

"He is convinced that it's only happening in the three villages impacted by the dam. He says that he needs to do something now, before all the people leave and the land is flooded. I am scared he could do something to stop the deal. He's obsessed."

Alex said nothing. She could not. She could barely breathe.

"Alejandra?"

She composed herself. "Thank you for coming to see me, José. You're right, we can't let anything stop this. It's just too important."

"What do I tell Gene?"

"What if we help him fast track some testing? Have him collect samples from the girls. El Progreso will submit and pay for any testing that he wants done."

"You would do that?"

"Of course. We're all on the same side here. We all want what is best."

Relief washed over José's face.

"But José, this has to be done carefully and quietly. You know as well as I that this deal could still blow up at the very mention of a new investigation."

"I will make sure he says nothing. Thank you so much."

"Try not to worry. This will all be over very soon."

∽

As soon as José left, Alex found her phone. She did not think Gene Young was too much of a threat, but nothing could be left to chance at this point.

Her colleague answered on the first ring.

"It's Alex. We have a problem." She relayed the meeting with José, speaking in English. "I want to know everything that Gene Young does. I want every call traced; every email read. I want to know where he goes, who he sees, and what they talk about. We can't take a risk with something like this. We're too close."

"Consider it done."

"Better do the same for José Rodríguez, too." It was unfortunate. She liked José and would be sorry if anything had to happen. He had dedicated many years to El Progreso.

"Of course."

"Is the contingency plan we discussed in place?" Alex asked.

"Yes, but it will take several weeks to execute. Do you want to start?"

"Not yet. It's too extreme. For now, let's wait and see what happens."

❧

"It's Gene Young, Dr. Eugene Young. We met last year at the World Medical Conference in London." Gene paced across his living room, running on autopilot. He started on the spiel he'd used a half dozen times already. "I sent you an email a few days ago about a problem I'm seeing here. Did you get my information?"

The response came in the affirmative.

"You did? Fantastic."

The conversation turned less agreeable as Gene answered the man's questions.

"Yes, I am certain the data is correct."

"No, as of now, I cannot corroborate it with a government agency."

"No, not the World Health Organization either." Gene frowned. "No, not Doctors With Wings."

"The source? I collected the data myself. I can get more samples."

"How can you say that? Something is sterilizing these young women."

"And you call yourself a doctor!" Gene yelled, throwing down his phone.

"Who were you talking to?" José asked. He was wearing only a towel, still dripping from a shower.

"It doesn't matter." Gene started for the kitchen. Maybe a cup of tea would help.

"No, I think it does."

Gene kept his back to José. "No one cares anyway."

"What are you talking about?"

"I've called some researchers in the States, a friend at Cambridge, and talked to DWW again. All refused to even look at the data."

Gene heard stomping across the floor, then felt hands seize his shoulders and spin him around. José was livid. "You did not tell me you were doing this. El Progreso is going to do testing for you, is that not enough?"

"It doesn't matter," Gene said, shaking José off. "No one's going to help. They either have no interest or they need verified data. Additional tests run by El Progreso won't help. The universities insist on data gathered by official agencies or themselves. They are not willing to look at my analysis, to come here themselves, or anything. Maybe I'll send it out to the schools in Mexico or Brazil."

"No," said José, his voice firm. "Word could get out that you are asking around."

Gene said nothing. Anything he said would make José even more angry.

"Look, you tried," José said. He grasped his hands together, in a pleading gesture. "Can you just wait until after the dam goes online? Please?"

José looked so pathetic that Gene instantly felt guilty. Who could possibly understand this insane situation? Then Gene had a thought. It was desperate, but desperate times and all.

"Maybe there is one person I could call. He would understand."

"Who?"

"Frank Anderson."

"Who is that?"

"He's a geneticist. We saw a show on him, on *NOVA*."

José made a swirling motion by his head. "The loco baby guy?"

"He won a Nobel Prize. He's also an expert on the impact of pollution on the human reproductive system. And he spent the last decade trying to tell the world exactly this, that there are things out there that can cause large-scale infertility."

"He experimented on babies."

"No. He was accused of stealing eggs and embryos from his clients to use for genetic testing. The research itself was legal. The embryos were just going to be destroyed."

"Do you hear what you are saying? He is a criminal," José said.

"He was never charged with anything. The accusations were overblown, and the government harassed him until he left the country. They wanted to get rid of him."

"Something that could easily happen to us."

"Your work is dangerous too, José."

"I have El Progreso behind me. And I am not breaking the law."

"I probably won't even be able to find him," Gene said.

"I hope you know what you are doing." José retreated into the bathroom, slamming the door behind him.

I hope so too. All of his hopes lay with a drug dealer and a mad scientist.

CHAPTER 10

OLANCHO REGION, HONDURAS

GENE HUNG UP the phone and rushed into the living room. "He says he'll look at it!"

José looked up from the book he was reading. "What?"

"Frank Anderson will look at my data and the new test results."

"I thought you said you wouldn't be able to find him."

"I called the producer of the *NOVA* show and explained that I really needed to get in touch with Dr. Anderson." Gene spoke rapidly, unable to contain his excitement. "Once I told him I was a doctor with DWW, he agreed to forward my contact information. Anderson called me back just now."

José lowered his face and rubbed his forehead.

"I've thought a lot about this," Gene said.

"Gene," José said, pleading.

"I'm only trying to do the right thing." Gene knelt in front of the sofa and pulled José's hands into his.

José turned his head in the opposite direction, refusing to make eye contact.

"I would never do anything to hurt you, and that includes jeopardize what you've worked so hard for. And I'm so thankful to El Progreso for funding the testing. I promise to keep all this quiet until after the dam is open. I promise." Gene rose from his knees and sat next to José. He draped his arms around his lover and began to kiss his neck.

José sighed, "You know I cannot resist you when you do that."

"So don't." José's tight shoulders yielded to his touch.

He groaned. "That feels fantastic."

"Shall I make dinner?"

José's head snapped to face Gene, his eyes squinting. "Okay, what do you want?"

"What?"

"Out with it. You never volunteer to make dinner."

"Am I that transparent?"

"Yes."

Even the guilt at getting caught could not dampen Gene's spirits. He dug a piece of paper from his pants pocket. "He wants me to 'stp' my notes and data to a secure server IP? Do you know what that means?"

"Oh, so it comes out now." One upturned corner of José's mouth betrayed his amusement. "I think you mean SCP, or FTP, and he wants it posted to a server. It's more secure than email, less chance of someone else intercepting it or it getting lost. That seems a little paranoid."

"Based upon what we know about him, is it that surprising?"

José shrugged. "Did he give you the address, a string of numbers?"

"I think so." Gene looked at his notes. "Yes."

"Well, if you get everything you want to send him, I'll zip it up and send it out."

"Thank you," Gene said, then smirked. "I knew I loved you for more than just your dashing good looks."

José flashed his white teeth. "Don't forget my great sense of humor."

"And how about your cooking? What's for dinner?"

With that José picked up a pillow and threw it at Gene.

⚜

Alex and Bruce both jumped at the sound of heavy footsteps coming down the stairs. The basement lab did not see many guests.

Their visitor was a stocky man dressed head to toe in gray camou-flage, with close-cropped graying hair and a semi-automatic handgun strapped to his waist.

"Hello, Anthony," Alex said.

He mumbled a greeting in return.

"This is an unexpected surprise. Bruce and I were just finishing up a project for our friends in the Middle East. What can I do for you?"

"It's Gene Young."

That was not good. Only a few days had passed since she asked him to keep track of the doctor's communications.

"Bruce, would you please excuse us?"

Bruce shifted his eyes from Alex to Anthony. "I have a right to know what's going on."

Alex glared at him.

"Fine," he said, getting up from his seat and running a hand through his unruly white hair. "I needed a break anyway."

When Bruce was well up the stairs, Alex nodded.

"Young contacted researchers and doctors in America and Europe. So far none of them will help him."

"Well, that's fortunate," Alex said. "But he has to stop that behav-ior. I'll give José one more chance to convince him, then we may have to take action."

"There's more," he said. His voice was flat, but Alex knew that meant nothing. "We think he's been in touch with Frank Anderson."

Alex gasped. How was that possible? It had been years since she'd heard the name of her former mentor.

"Young called London. He talked to that producer from *NOVA*," Anthony said. "Then Young got a call from a burner phone," Anthony explained. "It lasted twenty minutes."

"And?"

"We requested a recording of the actual call. That will take time."

"Where did the call come from?"

"Atlanta, Georgia."

Alex relaxed. "That can't be Frank. He's not been in the States for years."

"He is now. He got there Friday. Same-day ticket to Atlanta from Toronto. He used his own name and passport. Some genius." He uttered a guttural sound that might have been a laugh. "The Bureau flagged it. He's still on the watch list. I guess once you're on, you never get off."

"Atlanta?" Alex said, but more to herself. Was Georgia Steele still in Atlanta? He always had a soft spot for her. But why a same-day ticket? "Damn it, Frank." This was not good. Frank had zero credibility, but he could still cause them problems. "We have to find out what he's up to. Do you have anyone at the Bureau in Atlanta?"

"I already called. Anderson's gone."

"Where?"

"They traced the phone. He dumped it at the airport. He flew to JFK, but there is no record of him entering Canada. He's gone underground."

"We lost him?"

"Yes, but there is something."

"What?"

"The last call made from the burner phone was to a local woman, Georgia Steele. We requested a copy of that call, too."

So it was her. Would Frank tell her anything? Alex said, "If we can't find Frank, we have to find her."

"Already on it."

"We have to find out what she knows. Tell your contact to be careful, she's clever."

CHAPTER 11

ATLANTA, GA

IT WAS WEDNESDAY and The West End was hopping, even though it was early. The weekly live jazz show was Georgia's favorite, and judging by the crowds, the rest of Atlanta's as well. She bypassed the long line, trying to look inconspicuous, and found Ty who let her in. She spent many a Wednesday here and usually looked forward to these evenings, but today she was frustrated.

Since the accident on Saturday, Marcus had promised to keep her up to date on the investigation, using his contacts at the police department. As he had to go out of town for work, she gave him a few days. But he had not returned any of her calls, responding only by text. She was at the club to talk to him in person. She had not yet been able to tell him about the call from Frank, or that Emiko's hotel room had been cleaned out, or anything else she had learned. Which was not much.

Georgia passed through the front bar and entered what was normally the dance club, now a lively jazz venue straight out of 1920s Harlem. A half ring of velvet upholstered booths framed the room, and candle-lit café tables filled in the floor. Crimson curtains hung behind the band, obscuring video panels that normally flashed scintillating images. A pair of enormous antique chandeliers and red sconces on the walls completed the transformation. Though Georgia had seen this dozens of times, it still evoked a sense of awe.

The patrons, young professionals and mostly African American, dressed to the hilt. Most of the men wore suits and some sported fedoras while the women adorned themselves in brightly colored African-inspired prints, shapely retro dresses complete with fancy hats, or skimpy cocktail dresses that left little to the imagination.

The band was setting up as Georgia weaved her way through the crowd towards the stage. Marcus was in his normal spot, the U-shaped booth farthest on the left. From there he could keep an eye on most of the club. He was accompanied by his current girlfriend, Kayla, wearing a bright red dress of the skimpy variety. And there was a third person with them, a white guy. A cute white guy, with short dark hair and big brown eyes, wearing a black jacket with a white collared shirt.

"Hey, Marcus, Kayla."

"Hi, George," they said in unison. "Have a seat," Marcus said.

That was not what she wanted to hear. She wanted to talk about Emiko. "Marcus, can we talk?"

"Of course, sugar. In a little while. Come on, sit down." He motioned for her to sit next to the new guy.

Instead, the new guy got out. He was thin, wiry, maybe 5'10". Marcus introduced her to Sam Becker.

"Georgia, as in Atlanta, Georgia?" Sam grinned.

She rolled her eyes. "It's a cruel twist of fate. I grew up in New York with parents who loved Ray Charles. Call me George."

She scooted in next to Kayla and Sam sat next to her. A light, clean scent followed him. It was not unpleasant.

"Do you live in Atlanta?" Georgia asked Sam, mostly out of politeness.

"No. I'm in town to check out a few recording studios for Mythos records. We're planning to move some more work from LA to Atlanta. It's more cost effective. One of our artists told me to look up Marcus when I got here. It turns out we have some mutual friends."

"I'm not surprised. Marcus knows a lot of people."

"George here is a math geek," Marcus interjected.

"Thanks, Marcus." Georgia fake smiled at him. She hated the geek label outside of work, where it often came in handy.

"Oh, really?" Sam asked.

"I do this and that—it's not very interesting." Most people glazed over about thirty seconds into the 'what do you do?' talk with her, which was fine as it kept them from prying. "Anyway, the music is about to start."

"You've got a few minutes. Why don't you show Sam around?" Marcus passed his keys to her with a wink.

Sam was already out of the booth. "I'd love it."

Georgia was not happy. Marcus had tried to set her up a few times before and it had never gone well. But she took Sam on the obligatory tour, starting with the loft which overlooked the dance floor. She showed him the green room and the employees' break room, and the business office where Marcus ran both the club and his security business. Georgia felt around for the lights, turning them all on. The outer office was furnished with blond wooden cabinets and desks, and local art and pictures of Atlanta filled all the available space on the walls.

In the light, she got her first real look at Sam Becker. He had on Levi's jeans with the black jacket and was leaning against a desk, one leg crossed over the other. He looked a little out of place when compared to the impeccably dressed crowd downstairs. But he was cute.

"Impressive," Sam said. He gestured to the door on the back wall. "What's back there?"

"Marcus' office."

"He speaks very highly of you. How long have you known him?"

"Marcus? About four or five years."

"Did you guys ever date?"

"A long time ago, though I can't see how that's any of your business."

"He just seems very protective of you."

"He's protective of all of his friends."

"Hmm…he said you were special." Sam eyed Georgia as if he was trying to get into her head. "He also said that if I did anything to hurt you, he'd fuck me up royally."

"Now that sounds like Marcus," she said, laughing. "Shall we go see the best part of the club?"

Georgia led them back the way they had come, across the loft, and then up an additional flight of stairs to the rooftop patio. Two sides were flanked by much taller buildings, but the others overlooked the corner of Peachtree St. and 11th and were lined with benches and planters. The interior of the patio was set with café tables, chairs, and potted trees. Not many people had gathered there yet, but they would as the night progressed.

"Wow."

"Yeah, I like it up here."

"You want to sit down for a bit?"

She hated being set up on dates, and Marcus knew it. She'd talk to him at the set break and give him a piece of her mind for this and for ignoring her calls. But she acquiesced and led Sam to a spot on a bench with a stellar view of the city.

"So, tell me, what does a math geek do?"

Every few years Georgia was interviewed by the *Atlanta Journal and Constitution* or another news source, so she proffered her canned response. It was sure to drive away unwitting men.

"I guess you could call me a mathematical detective."

"Oh?"

"I have two PhDs from Georgia Tech. My background is in applied mathematics, and I specialize in pattern recognition and complex systems. Basically, I analyze data for large companies. If company executives think there is a problem but they can't find it, I mine their data and tell them where the issues are. Sometimes I can find the root cause; sometimes I just point them in the right direction."

"For example?"

She shrugged. "Well, once I discovered that employees were taking advantage of a client's old point-of-sale system. They worked on commission and found a way to cheat the computer into double commissions by ringing double sales with fake returns. It seems trivial, but it was costing the company hundreds of thousands of dollars. Another time I was able to uncover price fixing in a client's vendor base."

"Fascinating. You must be really great with computers."

Sam held her eyes the entire time he talked to her. This was unusual. Typically, guys were threatened by her intellect and numerous college degrees. They reacted either by trying to one up her or by running away. Sam had done neither.

Sam said, "You said you're from upstate New York? Do your parents still live there?"

"No, they both passed away." She did not recall telling Sam she was from upstate New York. Would Marcus have told him?

"Oh. Was it an accident?" He looked at her with big eyes.

"A fire."

"Do you have any other family up there?"

"No." She hoped the clipped answers would move the conversation onto other topics.

"How about elsewhere? Any aunts, uncles, cousins?"

"No. I don't have any family."

A waitress came by and took their drink order. Sam ordered a beer, a Sweetwater 420, and Georgia got a glass of Syrah. When the waitress left, Georgia used the opportunity to deflect the conversation away from her. "How did you get into the music business?"

Sam explained that his foray into the industry came through

friends in the service. After he got out, he got a job as a gopher and security guard for Mythos Records. He was working his way up through the business and wanted to be an agent. "I'm going back to school for a degree in business and economics, and in another year I'll have it."

They continued to talk for a while until the crowd from downstairs flooded the patio, a sure sign of the set break for the band. Georgia said, "Shall we go downstairs? I should probably get Marcus his keys." Though she was starting to enjoy herself, she needed to talk to Marcus and this would be the best time to do so.

⤬

On Georgia's insistence, she and Marcus went to his office where they could talk privately.

"Why have you been avoiding me?" she asked.

"I have done no such thing," Marcus said.

"Yes, you have."

"I didn't call you because I was busy, and I had nothing to tell you. I told you when I texted you, the APD knows nothing. The case is still open. They have no leads."

"But—"

"They've classified it as a hit and run. There is no reason to believe it was anything other than that. Because of that, they are not investigating Emiko. They are looking for the guy who hit her."

"She was murdered. And they lost her body." *And I lost my sister.*

"I know it's hard, George. I'm sorry."

He reached out to hug her, but she shrugged him off. She wanted to let him, but she was mad. Mad that he did not call, and mad at being alone.

"What did you find out?" he asked.

She wanted to tell him about Frank. And if the police were not looking into Emiko, then who took everything from her hotel room? But what good would telling him do anyway? He'd probably just remind her that Frank was crazy and say that she was being overly dramatic.

"It's nothing. We can talk about it later." Georgia left Marcus in his office. She was nearly out the front door when Sam intercepted her.

"Wait. You can't run out on me like that," he said, pulling her aside. "I'm in town through the weekend. I've never been to Atlanta before. I would love for you to show me the sights on Saturday, if you have the time."

She started to say she was busy, an automatic response, but he pressed a card into her hand. "Please call me." He folded her fingers around the card. "It was really nice to meet you, Georgia Steele. I hope to see you this weekend." And with that, Sam Becker receded into the darkness and commotion of The West End.

CHAPTER 12

OLANCHO REGION, HONDURAS

EVERY DAY SINCE talking to Anderson and sending him data, Gene had checked for a response. Or rather—at his insistence—José had checked, and each day his lover's irritation grew more apparent. Gene hated having to rely on José for this, but he was not tech-savvy and the written instructions, lines of unintelligible code and strings of numbers, made no sense to him.

But the persistence paid off. Three days later, José found the response Gene had been waiting for.

Dr. Young,

I have reviewed the information you sent. Curious, to say the least. I agree that the findings indicate significantly low pregnancy rates for females in your data sample.

If you have dismissed behavioral factors, such as abstinence or birth control, then it is my view that this sudden occurrence cannot have a natural source. This is not uncommon. High male infertility has been documented in many places, such as Argentina and Norway, primarily due to pesticides and other environmental toxins. I'm afraid mankind has made some poor decisions in the name of progress.

However, the conditions that you spoke of: the fact that only three of many villages in the area are impacted, the strict delineation by age of the females, and what seems a near one hundred percent sterility rate may point to more than just an accidental exposure. I think you need to consider that these young women may have been intentionally targeted.

Hopefully, the extended testing results will give us additional information. You can send the results to me in the same manner.

Do you know anything else about the girls? Do they attend the same school? Would they have been seen by the same doctor before you? Can you get their health records?

You also said that this occurred previously, some fifteen years ago, and lasted for several years. Do you have any information you can send in regard to this?

Until we know more, I would encourage you to keep this infor-mation confidential. There is no reason to add to any concerns the girls may have already, and it will do your personal career no good. Trust me on that.

Regards,

Frank

Vindication sent adrenaline rushing through Gene, and he jumped to his feet. "You see? He believes me!" He paraded around the room with his hands held high in celebration.

José had no such reaction. "Of course he does. He is crazy."

"He's not."

"I looked him up. Do you know what he has been doing since that *NOVA* show?"

Gene dropped his arms and folded them across his chest.

"No? I thought not." José switched from English to Spanish, a sure sign he was frustrated. "He has been running all over the world telling his conspiracy theories to anyone who would listen. He thinks that people are being experimented on without their knowledge by governments, corporations, and other "secret organizations"." José used air quotes around the words: secret organizations. He continued, "This includes genetic engineering and, coincidentally, sterilization."

"What's your point?" Gene asked.

"My point is that he has projected his own criminal behavior onto others to try to draw attention away from himself. You have joined his crazy trip."

"He's not a criminal. He's a Nobel Prize-winning scientist."

"He went off the deep end. He has mental problems. You should not talk to him anymore."

Gene raised his hands in frustration. "Why are you saying this? I've finally found someone who believes me."

"I believe you," José said, placing a hand on his chest. "And you have other options. Alejandra is helping you. El Progreso is paying for all those tests you wanted."

"When are the results coming back?"

"You should have them in a few days."

"Good," Gene said, unable to help himself. "I need to send them off to Frank."

José looked furious. "You and the crazy man are on a first-name basis?"

"Why are you yelling at me? We agreed on this." Gene wondered, "Did you tell Alejandra Castilla about Anderson helping me?"

"God no, I was too embarrassed. Once I saw what that man had been up to… I did not want her to think you had totally lost it."

CHAPTER 13

ATLANTA, GA

LENOX SQUARE MALL, an Atlanta mainstay, was busy this afternoon. Searching for a parking place, Georgia chided herself for not taking the MARTA train. It was Friday, what did she expect?

Friday. Just one week since Emiko sent her that email. Only one week ago her life was normal, or relatively normal, and now it had turned upside down and inside out. And she had been left hanging. She'd been unable to get in touch with Frank, and there was still no word on Emiko's missing body.

At least she had the toothbrush. Georgia knew that DNA testing from a toothbrush was far from certain, but it seemed her only option at this point to learn definitively how she and Emiko were related. She couldn't see herself calling Emiko's mother to ask for stray hair.

While they were running, Trish had told Georgia about her standoffish sister-in-law, Diane, a genetics researcher at the Centers for Disease Control and Prevention, or CDC. She was conducting DNA tests on mixed-race people as part of a study on population migration, "or something like that," according to Trish. Once Georgia had learned from Marcus that the police were treating Emiko's death as a routine hit and run, she had asked Trish to introduce her to Diane. And as she'd have only one chance for a DNA test, she wanted Diane's opinion on how to go about it.

She finally found a place to park and hurried through the parking deck into the mall. They were meeting at California Pizza Kitchen, situated in the atrium.

Trish saw her coming and waved her over. She was looking tan and fit in a white shirt and jeans, her blond hair tousled. The woman seated next to her was a few years older, about Georgia's age, with dark hair styled into a pixie cut. Trish introduced Georgia to her sister-in-law, Diane. Her firm, brief handshake aptly accompanied the no-nonsense personality she exuded.

"Have you learned anything more about Emiko?" Trish said, avoiding any small talk. "Did they ever find her body?"

"No, I'm afraid not."

"That is just nuts," Trish said. "I, uh, told Diane about Emiko. I hope that's okay."

"An incredible story," Diane said, her eyes fixed on Georgia, face solemn.

"It's all true," Trish said.

"Patricia said that perhaps I could be of some assistance to you. To be honest, I cannot imagine the circumstances under which that would be likely." The corners of Diane's mouth turned up, but the result was not a smile.

A waiter brought water and took their orders, giving Georgia time to gain her composure. She would need to try a different approach. "I hear you are doing some really interesting research for the CDC. Can you tell me about it?"

Diane's expression softened. "I recently secured a research grant to model the historical movement of people and population mixing. The goals are to understand how populations come together and estimate the rate of socialization and integration."

"That sounds fascinating," Georgia said. "What would you do with that information?"

"Well, how nice of you to ask," Diane responded, emphasizing the *you*.

Trish rolled her eyes.

She continued, "People from different ethnicities are often more welcome before they start marrying into the indigenous population. The first generation of bi-racial children is often shunned by both communities, causing race relations to degenerate. Children in Vietnam born of GI fathers are a prime example. Under certain circumstances this racism dies out pretty quickly, but in others it can persist for many decades, even hundreds of years. One goal of the research project is to recommend policy changes that can support the integration of minorities into our culture."

"I can see why Trish thought we should meet," Georgia said.

This seemed to throw Diane. "Um, yes," she said.

"As I am adopted, I never experienced the clash of cultures exactly as you describe, but being of mixed race, I get plenty of prejudice on a daily basis."

"Just like Emiko," Trish said. "I mean, the mixed-race part. I was curious, so I Googled her. Pretty easy to find out that both her parents were full Japanese. So she had to be adopted, too."

"Not necessarily," Diane said. "There are other scenarios. There are sperm and egg donors, even embryo donation. You said she was sixteen? All those options would have been available to her parents."

"But Diane, you should see, Emiko and Georgia look so much alike. Isn't there a chance they're related?" Trish added.

"Anything is possible. The most likely way would be through a sperm donor. That has been a common practice for over fifty years, and many sperm banks historically did not practice appropriate birth control." Diane uttered a choked sound that might have been laughter. "But Georgia was adopted, and the Moris would probably have had access to Asian sperm or eggs, if they went that route."

Georgia wondered if she should tell them about Frank.

Diane went on, "This would all be a moot point if you had

access to her DNA. DNA tests are not just for paternal or maternal testing, you can look for close family relationships or even more distant ones. The tests have become quite inexpensive, under two hundred dollars."

"Well, that explains the *Maury Povich Show*," Trish said. "But where would you get a DNA sample?"

"I may, in fact, have that covered." Georgia told them about the hotel room. She did not tell them about the cleaning service that got there first.

Diane was frowning, and Georgia wondered which part of the story she found so distasteful.

"A toothbrush may not give you an adequate sample, but you can try," Diane said. "Processing can take up to several weeks. The sooner you can get it mailed, the better. I can give you the names of a few labs that we use, those that are reliable and cost effective."

"Oh, Diane, can't you put in a rush order for George?" Trish asked. "Aren't you doing DNA testing for your new project?"

"Well, yes, but I could get into serious trouble for utilizing my work resources for a personal matter. And the circumstances under which—"

"For God's sake, it's just a standard DNA test and George will pay for it," Trish said. "Just see if you can shepherd it through a little faster. Ask your friends at the DNA lab, the ones you are about to give a lot of money to, if they will do you a very small favor for a friend. Okay?"

Diane ignored the question and checked her phone. "I've got to go pick up my children."

"Is that a yes, then? Come on. I'll trade you a babysitting day."

She looked at Trish, eyes narrowing. "I'll call them. But this is not going through the CDC. And I cannot promise a favorable outcome, or any outcome at all." Addressing Georgia, she said, "And if anything happens, you never told me about how you procured that toothbrush."

Georgia nodded.

Diane got up and gathered several shopping bags. She was shorter than Georgia first thought, but no less feisty. "I have to run by the office in the morning. I can pick up a test kit. If you can meet me around ten, then I can get your DNA and you can mail the kit before the post office closes."

They both thanked Diane, and she walked away purposefully and without looking back.

"She takes some getting used to, but what are you gonna do? She's family." Trish grinned. "Plus, she's totally predictable. She hates leaving her kids with strangers. I can always play the babysitter card."

Georgia's phone rang. It was from an unknown number. She started to put the phone down, but Trish said, "Go ahead and answer it—don't mind me."

"Hello?" Georgia said.

"Georgia Steele? This is Sam Becker."

Georgia felt her cheeks warm. "Sam, how did you get my number?"

"Marcus gave it to me. I pestered it out of him."

Trish's eyes grew wide, and she mouthed, "Sam?"

Georgia ignored her. "I'll have to talk to him about that."

"I was hoping you'd be able to show me around tomorrow. I'll buy you lunch."

"I have to meet someone in the morning, but I guess we could get together after that. I'll text you." Georgia said goodbye and ended the call.

"Who is this Sam?" Trish asked, raising an eyebrow and bouncing in her seat.

"A guy Marcus introduced me to on Wednesday. He's with Mythos Records in LA and is in town to look at some recording space."

Now both eyebrows were up. "And?"

"Alright, I give. He's hot."

Trish grinned, and it was infectious. Georgia felt herself smile.

"He's just damn sexy in a bad boy sort of way. He's got these big brown eyes and mussed up hair, and he's cool and confident. And there's something more, I just can't put my finger on it."

"Ooo, a mystery man," Trish said, dragging out each word.

CHAPTER 14

ATLANTA, GA

SAM WAS WAITING for Georgia when she arrived at the Martin Luther King Visitor Center. He wore sunglasses, Converse sneakers, jeans, and a black Led Zeppelin t-shirt that partially obscured a geometric tattoo on his left arm. She felt an unsolicited flutter in her stomach.

"What have you got there?" Georgia poked the tattoo. Sam's skin was soft, but his bicep underneath was firm.

He lifted his sleeve up to show a lean and muscled arm. Triangles morphed into birds which flew up and over his shoulder.

"Escher?"

"Very good."

"What's it mean?"

He shrugged. "Just liked it, I guess."

"Sure," Georgia said, unconvinced. "Shall we?" She motioned them toward the visitor center.

As they walked, she talked. "Atlanta is a modern city that has changed dramatically over the past few decades. But I think to know it, to really see it, you have to start in the past. The segregation of the South still pulls at the heart of the city. You can see it in the politics and you can feel it in the streets."

"Wow, that's quite an opening, Ms. Steele."

"This is a somber and serious place. Fun and frivolity will come later. And that's Dr. Steele to you."

They started the tour at the visitor center with the permanent exhibition and a short film. Afterwards, walking down the block towards Ebenezer Baptist Church, Georgia spoke first, "It is truly unbelievable that a country could treat its people in such a way. I had always felt, or I guess hoped, that the government does what it does to protect us. But those photos, and the film footage. They show a deliberate attempt to oppress peaceful, law-abiding citizens.

"Anyway, here we are. The church was closed for renovation when I was here last. I'm looking forward to seeing it."

A sermon by Dr. King was playing over an intercom, and they selected a pew in the back where they could listen. Georgia liked the simple brick church with its lack of adornments. A few other tourists were present, and an older woman was on her knees praying.

When the sermon was over they walked back up Auburn Avenue to Georgia's car. "Sam, tell me, did you grow up in LA? How is it that you went into the service?"

"Living the dream." He waved a hand dismissively. "A stupid thing we used to say when I was young. I grew up in a bad part of the city, without a father, and with a mother who worked many jobs to keep me in school. Instead of appreciating and respecting her, I got in with a bad group—a gang of sorts—and dropped out of school. I was eventually arrested for burglary and possession of cocaine. Some dream."

Sam stopped. He shoved his hands into his jean pockets and rocked onto his heels, staring at his toes. "Mom used up all her savings on lawyers. I got off on a technicality. She never even asked for thanks. I got my GED and joined the Marines. I wanted to make her proud and to be able to pay her back one day. Of course, I found that being enlisted in the Marines was not a ticket to paradise. But I'm thankful for it. I'd probably be dead or in jail otherwise."

"Did you know Marcus was also in the Marines?"

"Yes."

Sam did not elaborate, and Georgia did not ask him more. She really didn't care to know too much about this part of his life, or Marcus' for that matter. War was the clear marker of mankind's ultimate failure. She often wondered if life was somehow balanced across some weird fulcrum; as mankind pushed itself to do all sorts of wondrous things—medicine, art, literature, physics—it also dreamed up new ways to kill and torture. Did other worlds have the same dilemma?

"And so, have you found your ticket to paradise?" she asked.

"Not yet. But I'm working on it."

"Transforming yourself," Georgia said, more to herself.

"What's that?"

"Nothing. Want to get some lunch? I'm starved."

∽

Sam and Georgia picked up sandwiches and made the short drive over to Centennial Park, created for the 1996 Olympics. They found a spot on a bench near a fountain crafted in the shape of the Olympic Rings. Young children played, laughing and squealing, among the jets of water that squirted up intermittently from the ground.

"I, uh, read about you online," Sam said. "About how you nearly got killed."

"You mean the Atlantic-Pacific case?"

"Have there been others?"

Though his question was probably meant as a joke, Georgia ignored the comment. There had been another time, but only a few people knew about that.

"The trial is coming up for that guy, right?"

"Yes. I have depositions starting in a few weeks."

"Are you afraid?"

"Of what? Retaliation against me?"

"Your apartment got firebombed. That must have been scary."

"A little unnerving." Georgia paused. That incident had been kept out of the media. Had it been leaked now that the trial was coming up? "Where did you read that?"

Sam frowned. "I don't remember. I looked around a little on the web."

"Since then I've taken steps to protect myself. New apartment, hi-tech security system, self-defense training. Anything could happen, I guess. But you can't live your life worrying."

"I'd love to see your place," Sam said.

Georgia glared at him.

"I mean, to see your security system," he stammered. "I've been thinking about getting one for myself."

Georgia bagged the remnants of her lunch and rose from the bench. "Look, I'm not going to bullshit you. I like you, Sam, and that is why I am going to tell you that I am an exceedingly private person and if you want to get to know me it's going to take a lot more work than a quick Google, and a lot more time than one day. Now, if you just want to screw my brains out, you should just say so, because you'll have a much better chance at that."

Sam flushed.

"I'm going to the restroom, and I'll give you a few minutes to think. When I get back, you can decide if you want to go to Little Five Points with me and see a cool part of town where we can grab a drink and continue to learn about my adopted city. Or you can go back to your hotel and call it a day." With that, she spun around and began walking. "Oh, and Sam," Georgia called out, intentionally not looking back, "about the sex? That does not come in a day, either. Just to set expectations."

⤛

Sam opted for Little Five Points. They walked around for a bit and saw the sights, which in L5P, as it's commonly known, is as much about the people as the shopping or history.

"As you can see, Little Five Points is one of the more colorful parts of Atlanta. Other neighborhoods may be trendier, but I like it here. You've got the best tattoo parlors, vintage, LGBT, and new age stores in the city. This place welcomes everyone and doesn't ask too many questions."

"Georgia? I'm sorry about before," Sam said, after they had settled into a booth in one of her favorite pubs. "I like you and I just want to get to know you."

"I'm sure you've seen from your Googling that, in addition to almost getting killed, I've had some run-ins with the media. It started with me telling a local reporter more than I should have. I am not going to have a repeat."

"I'm not a reporter," Sam said.

"No, I don't think you are. But I did a little research of my own, Sam Becker. And do you know what I found?"

Sam hesitated. "Nothing too bad I hope."

"That's right. Nothing too bad. In fact, nothing at all." She let that sink in. "No listing at Mythos Records, no Facebook account, no Marines coming home list, no public record."

Sam blinked a few times and sat back in his seat. "Well, what do you want me to say?" he said, his voice low. "I'm not important, Georgia. I haven't made a name for myself. I don't have a lot of friends or family or money, it's just me and my mom. I haven't done anything of value, and I dislike social media."

"I'm absolutely sure I could find you if I looked for more than five minutes." She stared at Sam. *Was that anxiety? Maybe he did have a skeleton or two.* "Everyone's life is out there on the web these days. Every American's life, anyway. Your service record, school records, driver's license records. It's all there. You just have to look."

The waitress served them and the conversation turned to lighter subjects as they sipped their beers. They talked about recent news events and his upcoming week of work. Sam showed Georgia the rest of his tattoos: a Marine insignia on his left shoulder and a Celtic band around his right calf.

"What, no Mom tattoo?"

"She hates them and made me promise never to get that."

Georgia finished her beer and Sam looked at his watch. "It's still early, shall we have one more?"

"Sorry, I need to get home. Do you mind if I drop you at your hotel?"

"Tell you what. You can leave me here."

"Are you sure?"

"Of course, I can call a ride or take the train. I'm going to wander around. I may drop by the local tattoo parlor."

"Oh?"

"Just looking, don't worry. I told Mom, no more tattoos. Unless it's something really cool." He winked. "Georgia, can I call you again sometime? I'm going to be in town quite a bit over the next month."

"It's George."

"Sorry?"

"My friends call me George." She bent over and gave him a quick kiss on the cheek. "Bye, Sam."

CHAPTER 15

OLANCHO REGION, HONDURAS

THE PRINTER WAS old. It spewed off page after page of Frank's assessment, each accompanied by a grinding cacophony caused by wear and misalignment.

"Let me see," Gene said impatiently.

José had positioned himself in front of the printer and was catching the pages as they flew from the clunky machine, saving most from spilling onto the floor. He passed a handful to Gene.

"These are copies of the test results we sent to Frank," Gene said. The printed results were covered with hand-written annotations.

Finally, the machine was silent. José stared at the final page before he handed it to Gene. He waited while Gene read.

"I can't believe it. I just can't believe it," Gene's initial excitement had turned to disappointment.

"Why not?"

"He says all the results are normal."

"That is what you found."

"I know, but..." Gene read from the page, "There's no sign of any external factor, and so this must be behavioral. Either the girls are not having sex or are using birth control, even if they say otherwise. I'm sorry, but I just don't see any point in continuing."

Gene slumped to the bed.

José grabbed his shoulders. "Why are you sad? This is great news. Everything is going great. I'm going to call Alejandra to thank her for doing the testing and let her know the results."

José left the compact office. Gene stayed put. How was this possible? He was so certain that there was something amiss. He glanced through the report. Frank had made copious annotations, going every which way on the pages. The man clearly had taken a lot of time on this. Gene decided that no matter what, he owed it to Frank to read his analysis.

He started at the beginning. Frank had marked each test result with an overly detailed explanation that, in the end, simply said the numbers were normal. In some places he described what an abnormal result might mean, though the actual was fine. It was like reading a first-year med student exam. It was all accurate content, but nothing a doctor wouldn't already know. Why would Frank take the time to do this? Maybe he was crazy after all.

Gene continued to scrutinize page after page. He was about halfway through the report when he saw one sentence in the middle of a long annotation that caught his eye. It said, "It would be good to talk about this."

That seemed weird. The mark was in reference to a triglycerides reading, and it was slightly high, but still in the range of normal.

He kept reading. Two pages later, he saw "results are often between 55.547 and 62.294." Though technically accurate, it made no sense to document a reading that would normally be between fifty and seventy to three random decimal places.

Later, he saw another line. "The contact must come from an untraceable source."

Gene kept reading, the hairs on his neck standing on end. A bit later, "These results should be kept confidential." Then finally, "It's your call on this one."

Frank was sending him some sort of message. Gene read the

out-of-place annotations over and again a third time, and then he understood. He would need a new cell phone.

⤸

On Saturday morning, José needed to go to one of the Hydro villages to give the locals information on how to apply for government housing. Gene volunteered to go to the local farmer's market to get supplies for the week. He rarely did the shopping, but it was a useful excuse. He was going to buy a prepaid phone and call Frank Anderson. Since most locals used this type of phone, it was easy to find one, even here in the remote Honduran countryside.

Once at the busy market, he called the number: 555-476-2294. He wasn't sure if he was imagining all of this and would find himself talking to a housewife in Omaha. Half of him wanted Anderson to answer, and half wanted it to be a wrong number.

"Yes?"

"Dr. Anderson?"

"Who is this?"

"This is Gene Young."

"I rather thought so."

"I got your message."

"Where are you calling from?"

"I bought a pre-paid phone. It's brand new."

"Good. Are you alone?"

"Yes."

"Does anyone know you are calling me?"

"No. No one. Not even José."

"Good."

"Why the cloak and dagger?" Gene asked.

"Did you see the report?"

"Of course, how else did I know to call you?"

"That's not what I meant. I ran a small program on the report. The results were doctored. Someone—someone not very savvy at that—thought he could scan in the results, change them, and then re-PDF them. The fonts did not even match."

"I don't understand."

"After the report was created, someone altered the results. You received a digital copy, correct?'

"Yes, I got it via email and José put it on your server."

"If it had been a hard copy, I might have missed it. Stupid, cocky, or, both."

"What was off?"

"That's the thing. The original results were not that unusual. We would expect to see some abnormal results for some of the patients, but all of these appear to have been changed. It's the total lack of anomalies in the modified report that make it suspicious."

"Yes, I see what you're saying."

"But you do understand that's not the primary issue, right?"

Gene did not. "You may have to spell it out for me."

"The problem is that someone cared enough to change the results before sending them to you. Do you know what that spells? Conspiracy."

"Who would do that? And why?"

"Let's focus on the who for the time being. The first results were done in a lab in San José. Who emailed the modified results to you?"

Gene literally felt as if he had been hit by a ton of bricks.

He whispered, "El Progreso."

Gene explained that El Progreso had driven the dam project, that José's role was to negotiate a settlement for the people living in the Hydro towns, and that those were the same towns with the missing teen pregnancies.

"Maybe José changed the results to save his project," Frank said.

"He's not a doctor."

"Exactly. A doctor would have known those results could be caused by anything. It sounds like José has a lot invested in this."

"No," Gene said, in a voice louder than he intended. "He would not do that. He would not lie to me."

"If not José, then who? What does this El Progreso group do?"

"El Progreso has few employees. They give grants and work through other local groups. They mediate and broker deals. They've been around for a long time. It's run by its founder, a woman named Alejandra Castilla."

"Alejandra Castilla?"

"You know her?"

"I hope not. Give me a minute."

Gene heard Frank typing on a keyboard. He was about to say something when he heard a cry on the other end.

Frank wailed, "No, it can't be."

CHAPTER 16

ATLANTA, GA

GEORGIA WAS DRINKING coffee and reading the Saturday *New York Times* on her iPad when she heard the security alarm. Someone was climbing the stairs to her front door. A few clicks on her laptop keyboard and the monitors came alive with camera images surrounding the house. To her surprise, Marcus and Dave were coming up the stairs. Marcus did not hang out with Dave, except on the rare occasions she brought them together. She could not imagine why they both would be here.

She opened the door before they had a chance to knock, and the two men entered her small apartment, muttering hellos. Neither appeared happy.

"Is something wrong?"

Marcus removed his sunglasses. He motioned to the dining table where her coffee and iPad sat. "Can we sit down?"

Once seated, Dave said, "George, it's about the DNA tests that you gave Diane to send off." He glanced at Marcus, who nodded. "She got the results back yesterday."

"Oh." Georgia exhaled in relief. "Well that was fast. We're related, aren't we? Emiko and me? I know we are." Georgia smiled.

She was excited to find out. "You guys didn't have to come down here to tell me that. So, are we cousins? Half sisters?"

Dave stared at her. Marcus played with his glasses.

"Dave, come on, what's up?"

It was Marcus who finally spoke. "George," he said, "Emiko was your daughter."

CHAPTER 17

ATLANTA, GA

"EMIKO WAS YOUR daughter." The words replayed in Georgia's mind.

"Are you sure?"

Dave nodded slowly. "Diane has ordered some additional tests, but yes, she's sure."

Georgia felt, well, nothing. Time stopped. A black nothingness filled her, and she was simply a shell. A three-dimensional outline, taking up space in a four-dimensional world. Detached from her emotions, she contemplated the likely series of events that brought her to this unlikely point. She wanted to stay in this dreamscape birthed by shock, devoid of pleasure and pain.

But this was not a dream, and at some point time thrust its hand into her soul and wrenched it back into its rightful place in the universe. She brought back with her some idea of how it had happened.

"That bastard," Georgia whispered.

Her head and her heart were at odds, and so while she had been able to protect the analytical part of herself with this fantastical cognitive voyage, she could no longer contain her feelings. Anger and sorrow racked her body, and she shook as she sobbed at the loss of the daughter she would never know.

Strong arms surrounded her. Marcus. She sagged into his embrace and stayed there until the horrible pain had run over and through her and left her exhausted. At some point Marcus carried her to the sofa. Georgia slept fitfully, for what could have been an hour or a day. When she opened her eyes, Dave was standing by the window, a coffee mug in his hand.

"You okay, George? Can I get you something?"

"Where's Marcus?"

"He had to go to work. Do you want me to call him?"

"No, thanks." She pushed off a soft blanket and pulled herself up. "It was him, you know."

"Marcus?"

"No." She shook her head. "It was Frank. He did this."

"I figured," Dave said.

"You did?"

"Who else could it be?"

"Of course."

"I'm sorry. It was very wrong of him to do that."

"I'm going to find him. I need to know why. And I need to know if there are others. Others like Emiko, or others like me."

⌇

Georgia holed up in her apartment and spent Sunday trying to locate Frank. She called the phone number he used when she was at the hospital, but there was no answer and the voicemail had never been activated. Searching for Frank on the internet, she found volumes of old entries, but little from the last year. The *NOVA* special a few years ago resulted in a spike of activity, most of it authored by conspiracy nuts. She found multiple chat groups that had referenced him, and a few of the conversations were still active. She threw out some bait but got no bites. One group even accused her of working for the Feds.

She decided to try a little old-fashioned social engineering.

Georgia called all the public utility offices in and around Amsterdam, the last place she knew Frank lived. She pretended to be Frank's niece and said he was in the hospital in the States and she wanted to make sure his utilities were paid. Bingo. A nice lady in a town outside of Amsterdam let her pay Frank's current bill, approximately $68 US, and gave Georgia the account and customer number so she could pay future bills directly online. From the online account, she got his physical address.

Georgia was able to find the name of his landlord from the local tax records. She told the elderly woman who answered the phone that she was Frank's cousin ("first cousin once removed") and needed to get in touch with him. She knew he had been in the States but wondered if he was back home yet.

"Oh my, I hope nothing is wrong?"

"Not at all. I may have an opportunity to come over there for work, and I wanted to make sure I could see him. I must have a wrong number for him, or his voicemail is not working."

"He hates voicemail, he told me," the landlady said conspiratorially. "Try this number."

The number turned out to be a VoIP, or internet-based, number, and thus was not associated with a landline. Georgia called and left multiple messages. There was an email address on the utility account, but a note to that bounced back.

All she had to show for a day of searching was an address of a rented apartment outside of Amsterdam and an internet phone number. Frank knew how to stay under the radar. Appropriate, given the years of paranoia.

But Frank could be found; the technology existed. Georgia knew that the NSA capabilities exposed by Snowden were just the tip of the iceberg. When it came to the NSA, Georgia thought some paranoia was more than reasonable.

As a result of the Patriot Act, the FBI had nearly limitless access to any information gathered in the US. Would it be worth it to involve them? She liked Sean Kelly, the agent in charge of the Atlantic-Pacific case. He had persuaded the New York agents not to press any charges against her for hacking that adoption database. Of course, he needed her testimony.

But could she trust him? Right now, he needed her more than she needed him. Need and trust were far from the same, but could one substitute for the other?

CHAPTER 18

ATLANTA, GA

THE NEW FBI field office in northeast Atlanta was located on the grounds of Mercer University, tucked away at the back of the campus. The juxtaposition was startling. Cordoned off by concrete barricades and a tall wrought iron perimeter fence, the three-story brick and stucco building resembled a prison more than a center for higher education.

Georgia and Marcus signed in with a guard at the front gate and went through security screening once inside the building. They were promptly shuffled into a windowless waiting room ringed with metal-framed chairs. Motivational posters and plastic plants served as decoration. They checked in and were told to have a seat and wait. They passed the time by reading outdated *People* magazines.

"You guys miss me?" The deep voice belonged to Sean Kelly.

They rose to greet the agent. Marcus stood over six feet tall, yet he was a good three inches shorter than the man whose hand he was shaking.

"Sean, good to see you."

He offered his hand to Georgia. "Georgia?" He raised his eyebrows as if waiting for a response, but she gave him none. They had not yet told him the reason for the visit. "Shall we go up to my office then?"

The agent led them up a flight of stairs, down a hallway, and through a maze of cubicles to a spartan office. Two chairs fronted Kelly's desk, which was completely clear of all paper. A college degree and FBI commendations were the only adornments on the otherwise beige walls.

"Georgia, your depositions are next week, right?"

"Yes."

"You ready for them?"

"Of course, or I will be anyway."

"Excellent."

"But that's not why we're here," she said.

"Yes, so I heard," Kelly said, and turned his attention to Marcus. "What's so important that you couldn't tell me on the phone?"

"It's George's story to tell."

They both looked at her. She took a deep breath to calm her nerves. Then she told him everything.

"Wow, that's quite a story." Agent Kelly had been taking notes as Georgia talked, and now he leaned back into his chair and clasped his hands together under his chin.

"So you think Anderson created Emiko Mori using your eggs?"

"I'm sure of it."

"Do you have any idea why he would've done this?"

"I'm not sure. Frank didn't tell me—" she started, then seeing the confusion on both faces, she said to Marcus, "Did I forget to tell you I talked to Frank?"

Georgia then relayed the phone conversation in the hospital parking lot, while Marcus paced around the small office.

"Why didn't you tell me this before?" Marcus said.

"You never returned my calls," Georgia answered defensively. "I told you I thought I saw him. You didn't believe me."

He snapped, "That's BS and you know it."

"You saw Anderson at the scene of the accident and then later talked to him on the phone at the hospital?" Kelly asked.

"She *thinks* she saw him," Marcus said, glowering at her. "But she hasn't seen him in over ten years."

"It was Frank," Georgia insisted. "He was at the accident. But I don't think he had anything to do with it."

"And at the hospital, when he called you?"

"I got the feeling he was close by. I could hear the same kind of sounds through the phone that I heard in the parking lot. But no, I didn't see him."

Marcus exhaled in a sputter and reclaimed his seat. He shook his head, and Georgia knew he was more hurt than angry.

"Well, I'm glad you came to me first. You did come to me first?" She nodded.

"Good. It would not do for this to get out now. That would cause a lot of chaos."

Kelly closed the notebook he'd retrieved during Georgia's recount and placed it and the pen in a desk drawer, leaving the desk spotless. "I'm going to need to consult some of my colleagues."

"Do you have any idea where Frank is?" Georgia asked.

"No, why would I? But he may still be on a travel watch list. You're not looking for us to press charges at this point, right?"

"No. I just want to find Frank so I can ask him why he did this." She left out the fact that Emiko might not be the only one, but Kelly was smart enough to figure that out.

"As tempting as it is for me to open up this can of worms, I tend to agree with you. I'll keep your involvement out of it and simply say we had a tip that Anderson was here in Atlanta."

"Also, we still haven't heard anything about what happened at the hospital, when they lost Emiko's…" Georgia could not bring herself to finish the sentence.

"I'll make some calls. But I doubt I'll find out anything that Marcus can't, given his connections in the APD."

Georgia stole a glance at Marcus. Definitely hurt feelings. He caught her eyes and stood up, then thanked Kelly for his time and help.

"Is there a restroom I can use on the way out?" Georgia asked.

"Sure, I'll show you the way." Kelly took them back the way they had come, then continued past the elevator and led her to a corridor. "Go down to the end of the hall, turn right, the bathroom is on your left. We'll wait for you at the elevator bank."

After using the bathroom, Georgia washed her hands at the basin. The bathroom was a depressing beige rectangle, much like the rest of the building. How horrible to spend so much of one's life in monochrome.

She exited the bathroom deep in thought, strode down the beige hallway, turned, and then came to a dead end. "Damn." She turned around and headed back. Was that a left then a right, or a right then a left?

After a few more hallways and turns, she found an open section full of cubicles with offices on either side. Hoping to ask for directions, she entered the work area.

Two men, both Caucasian with dark hair and white dress shirts, were standing and talking over their connecting cubicle wall. She waved to the one facing her, trying to grab his attention.

"Excuse me, can you point me to the elevators?"

The second man spun around. The first started to speak while the other stood open-mouthed.

Georgia was equally surprised. "Sam? What are you doing here?"

Sam closed his mouth. She turned on her heels and walked briskly back the way she had come, resisting the urge to run. She heard Sam calling behind her, "Georgia, wait!"

This time she found her way to the elevators. Marcus was gesturing wildly in the air and Kelly was laughing. The both saw her and stopped.

"What's wrong?" Marcus asked.

She did not have to answer. At that moment, Sam Becker rounded the corner into the elevator lobby, wide-eyed and out of breath.

CHAPTER 19

ATLANTA, GA

AGENT KELLY USHERED them all to a small conference room. A flat screen panel covered up an entire wall, and multiple cameras supported video conferencing. Standard office chairs crowded around a shiny oblong table.

Kelly said, "I think we need something to drink. Water or coffee? I have to warn you, the coffee's not very good."

They opted for water. With one finger Kelly pointed first at Sam and then the door. Message received; Sam silently departed.

Kelly said, "Please have a seat. I'll be right back."

True to his word, Kelly returned only a minute later, followed by a small, severe-looking woman. She was probably not much older than Georgia, but looked so in her conservative blue suit and tightly-bunned hair. Georgia could not hear the hallway conversation, but the woman was doing most of the talking while Kelly nodded.

"Marcus? Do you have any idea what's going on?" Georgia asked

"No sugar, I don't." Marcus' words were gentle, but his arms were crossed and his stare never left the pair of agents.

Sam rejoined the group, hands full of water bottles. Kelly said something, the other two nodded, and then they all entered the room and took seats around the table.

Kelly made the introductions. "Marcus West and Georgia Steele, meet Katherine Vance and Sam Bennett. Katherine manages surveillance here in Atlanta, and Sam is a new agent transferred here from Los Angeles." Vance nodded. No hands were shaken. "I'm going to cut to the chase. Sam was monitoring Emiko Mori to see if she would be contacted by Frank Anderson, her godfather."

Georgia winced. "Are you kidding me?"

Kelly continued, "I'm sorry, Georgia. The assignment came from New York and I had no knowledge of it. Apparently the Bureau had reason to believe Anderson recently contacted Ms. Mori, and also that he had returned to the US."

"To Atlanta?" Marcus asked.

"He was here, yes. But not anymore," Kelly said.

"Where's Frank now?" Georgia asked.

"We can't tell you that," Vance said.

"Why do you care about finding him? What has he done?"

"What do you know about him, Ms. Steele?" Vance asked.

"If you are going to refer to me by my surname, then it's Dr. Steele, Ms. Vance."

Vance rolled her eyes and tapped her fingers on the table.

Seeing this was going nowhere, Georgia relented. "My godfather, my Nobel Prize-winning godfather, was run out of the country for doing questionably ethical, though legal, experiments on human embryos. It was all over the papers and morning talk shows. Everyone in America knows about that."

"What else can you tell us, Dr. Steele?" Vance asked.

Georgia looked across the table to Sam. He held her gaze for a moment, then looked away.

"First and foremost, Frank is a scientist. To him, the quest for knowledge would outweigh antiquated definitions of acceptable behaviors. He followed the law, but he probably walked the line doing it." She paused. "Ms. Vance? Frank said to me, 'If the two of you met, they would have found out.' Do you know who *they* are?"

This question must have taken Vance off guard. She stammered a bit.

Sam blurted out, "What about Emiko? Was she GM?"

Vance glared at him.

Kelly was the first to respond. "GM?"

"Genetically modified. We were told she was valuable because she may be one of the first GM people on the planet."

"So that's why you want Frank? You think he made genetically modified people?" Georgia asked.

"We didn't know, however, that you were Emiko's, uh...," Vance said.

"What?" Sam asked.

"Emiko was my daughter. I am her biological mother," Georgia said.

Sam's eyes widened and he looked to his boss.

"And you all took her. You stole her body from the hospital to study it," Georgia said.

"No."

"Then who did?"

"No one. It was just a paperwork error. The body was cremated, and the responsible party destroyed the documentation in an effort to save his or her job." Vance's clipped manner seemed a bit rehearsed to Georgia.

"So you found who was responsible?"

Vance frowned. "Ms. Steele, I mean Dr. Steele, do you know anything about why Anderson is back in the US?"

"I told you I don't."

"But you talked to him?"

She hesitated. "Yes, but we're not on the best of terms. As I told Agent Kelly, he wanted to know if Emiko and I had met and if so, what she said to me."

"And what did she say to you at the symphony?" Vance asked.

"All she said was that she wanted to talk. We never got the chance. Obviously I wish we had."

"I have a question," Marcus said. "Why all the subterfuge? Once Emiko was killed, why not simply call Georgia and ask what she knew? Why go through the trouble to create a cover and have Sam infiltrate us like we were the enemy?"

"We couldn't be sure you would tell us—" Vance started, but Kelly cut her off.

"Sometimes people here forget we are on the same team. They watch too much television." He shook his head. "I apologize on behalf of the FBI. Now I am going to ask you to forgive us, and also to help us. Sam, please give Georgia and Marcus your contact information. Georgia, if Anderson calls or contacts you again, please let Sam know immediately."

"Can't I just call you?" Georgia whined.

"Of course you can," Kelly said. "Anytime. But this is not my case. You need to relay any information to Sam or Katherine."

Great. The liar or the witch.

"And please do not mention our meeting. It may be ridiculous, but this is considered a matter of national security, and we do not need it leaking out."

"My friends already know about Emiko," Georgia said. "And I'm not sure I want to talk to Mr. Bennett or Ms. Vance again."

Sam winced.

Vance pointed a finger at Georgia. "Look Ms. Steele, we need to know what you know as soon as you know it. We can do this the easy way or the hard way. Your choice."

"What is that—a threat? I haven't done anything wrong. I came to you."

Marcus wrapped an arm around her shoulder and hugged her into him. He spoke softly into her ear. "Agree to it. They already have enough to tap your phones, scan your emails, monitor everything. Do you want that?"

Georgia pulled back so she could see his face. He stared at her, lips pulled tight. He was serious.

Georgia felt sick to her stomach. This was unbelievable. "Alright," she said, shaking herself free, "just forgive me if it feels like I got the short end of the stick here."

"Also, please do not reveal Sam's actual identity to your friends." Kelly looked at his watch and grunted. "I have to go—I'm late for a meeting. I'm sorry about all of this, Georgia. We'll talk soon."

Sam escorted Georgia and Marcus to the elevator lobby and punched the down button. Looking at his feet, he said, "Georgia, I'm really sorry. Please don't be mad at me. It was my first field assignment."

"And maybe your last," Marcus said. "I don't take kindly to people lying to me, even more so when they do it to get to my friends." The elevator light went on, and the door opened. "We can see our way. George?" He put an arm in and held the door open for her.

She entered the elevator. "It's alright." She faced the front, appraising Sam's plaintive expression. "It's not like anything happened. It's not like there was anything there."

Sam lifted up his hand in a tentative wave as the door closed.

CHAPTER 20

ATLANTA, GA

GEORGIA MANAGED TO keep it together long enough for Marcus to exit the FBI parking lot. Then she pounded the dashboard and stamped her feet on the floor of the Porsche.

"Not my baby, please," Marcus pleaded.

"I'm sorry. I'm just so, so, AAAGGGHH." She slapped the dashboard again.

"I know. It's crazy. Please don't hurt my car."

Georgia crossed her arms and pulled into herself.

They drove in silence for about ten minutes when Georgia said, "This really smells."

Marcus sniffed.

"Not the air, this mess with Emiko. If they wanted to study her, they could have gotten her DNA at any time. They didn't need Frank for that."

"True."

"And I don't buy the hospital story. And what about the hotel?"

"I noticed you didn't tell them about the hotel."

"They didn't ask. Someone went to a lot of trouble to make sure nothing of Emiko remained. They took her body and cleaned out the hotel room. If it wasn't the FBI, who was it? And if it was the

FBI, why have Sam try to squeeze information out of me? Why not just bring me in? Or tap my phone?"

"Speaking of…"

"You think they're tapping my phone? Cretins."

"Your computer too."

"I should be good. You know I'm careful, and I have good security."

Marcus navigated the afternoon traffic on I-85, coming to a full stop as the interstate merged with highway GA 400.

He reached out a hand to Georgia. "You're not going to leave this alone, are you?"

Georgia shrugged. It was a rhetorical question.

"You need to be careful with your online activities. Kelly is not going to be able to protect you from the feds forever. Neither can I."

"I'm not asking you to."

"This is serious. If you go poking around in places you shouldn't, you'll get into trouble."

"I can take care of myself."

Marcus sighed, removed his hand from Georgia's, and put it back on the steering wheel.

᪥

Georgia ran every program and procedure she knew to check her computers and servers for signs she'd been hacked. She found nothing. In the morning, Marcus was going to inspect her house for physical intrusions like cameras or listening devices. She did not expect him to find anything either. Currently the preferred government surveillance approach was to intercept communications and internet exchanges after they left your house.

Fortunately, this technical domain was her territory, and she felt she was well protected. Information passing between her network of computers was fully encrypted, and her IP address was masked whenever she searched the web. When she worked with clients, she set up similar protocols for them. Encrypting data and hiding information was a game to Georgia—one that started a long time ago.

Growing up, Georgia and Frank left each other secret messages, and the method for sending them grew more complex over time. When she was a little girl, he'd leave her coded messages in her shoes or under her pillow. Sometimes she played this game with her mother, but mostly the game was between Georgia and Frank. Her passion for technology came from him, and her skills quickly surpassed his.

Frank. How could she find him? He would eventually show up at his place near Amsterdam. Should she go camp out at his apartment? She wished she could leave him a secret message to find.

The thought nearly bowled her over. "Of course. How could I forget?"

Georgia began a search for an obscure server located at a university in one of the tiniest of European nations. It would be more than ten years old, and the likelihood it was still in service was slim. She could not risk accessing it directly.

She typed in a simple command, *ssh-keygen -t rsa*, which created two tiny files. The first went onto a flash drive. The second file would need to get to the foreign server.

She next ran a program which moved the file to a temporary location—a server she only used to transport data. That server was monitored by a second, which moved the file to the third and last server, and removed it from the first. This third server was their old drop server. She hoped it would still be running after all these years.

A confirmation came back. The file had been received.

"I can't believe it," she said. "It's there."

The communication method was the last one she and Frank used together, one she created. Though dated, she still sometimes used a variant of it when she wanted to hide something. The combination of pushing and pulling encrypted data across small independently run servers—never accessing traditional email or commercial cloud resources—remained secure and hard to trace.

If Frank was still using this server, then a second sequence of pushing and pulling would take place from there to his final access point. Even so, she knew it could take days to get a response back.

Georgia removed the flash drive and set it aside. She wondered if all of these precautions were necessary, or even sufficient.

The file she sent had an innocuous enough sounding name: Readme.txt. 'Read Me' files were associated with software packages, providing basic content description and installation directions. Though less common today, any computer would likely have dozens of 'Read Me' files on it, and they would attract little attention.

The contents of the file that Georgia sent to her godfather had but one string of data that read:

AAAAB3NzaC1yc2EAAAADAQABAAABAQDAwuy3I5BvYp-
Khwph2UbkXNWqLKhmfxgTiNG6fu5ByO6VmkWyt35tHl8rvi-
hbohRGIzp8AXMLJYjZNnk9qo4cvCoV92ucQbaXbUZPDEGFs/
O69GmT+gln+KBrq/U7Qq7sTvKfyckGXfn1SKpGevyhlKf/
hiyy0VfSF+UWnusBWExpMZsKcx9PZkois24tlVpID++Owy68Ks-
G7n6A6x9emklXk8Un0oFzayrKY2gyGSYNKjI7d+s6H6at+-
K4u5mTQY6Du0N4wE5PazOHmGPddRx8qmP8l+LR6GEaa7qg-
DUANtlyvRZTeIjw/69dOSWqeKb0CL/iF4v8Cct3CUd04g+1

This was a public key. Public key cryptography used a pair of keys to encrypt and decrypt information. When one key, called the public key, was used to encrypt a message, only the second, the private key, could be used to unlock it. The private key Georgia created to go with her public key was safely on her flash drive. If her public key made it to Frank, he could respond without hesitation, because any message he sent could only be read by her.

They had used keyed and other types of cryptography to

exchange multitudes of messages over the years. Thinking about those happier times in her life made her feel nostalgic and sad.

She shook her head, trying to dislodge the memories, but the past refused to leave her alone.

CHAPTER 21

OLANCHO REGION, HONDURAS

"Ugh," Gene groaned, stopping at the intersection. Distracted with thoughts of José and Frank Anderson, he had missed the turn-off noted in his handwritten directions. Looking for a house to buy was the last thing he wanted to do under the circumstances, but how could he explain that to José. Especially since this one was on his way to the clinic.

He continued driving until he came across a driveway which would accommodate the bulky DWW van, and Gene turned back. Soon he found the narrow, winding road overlooking a lush valley. Rows of coffee plants, running as far as the eye could see, traced the topography of the land.

Paying closer attention to the directions provided by the realtor, he found the partially built home, under construction and unfinished for years. This was a common sight in Central America, where houses were completed by the owner as money became available. The first floor was made of concrete block, plastered but not yet painted. Rebar extended from the corner beams into the sky at awkward angles, mimicking a strange set of antennas and mapping out walls for a future second story.

Fruit trees shaded the yard, and tall coconut palms formed a perimeter, separating the house from the coffee fields. Gene identified a breadfruit and several mango trees, interspersed with bananas. Someone was keeping the yard mowed and the trees tended, but vines and bush grew up around the house. Some hibiscus and ginger still fought for survival. A heavy bar secured the door and most of the windows were shuttered. The few that were not revealed rough concrete openings. No cars or people were around, so Gene stayed in his van to get his head together.

During their phone conversation, Frank recounted a crazy story about a woman who worked for him, an Alex Castle. It all started almost twenty years ago with a genetic defect that he discovered in one of his patients. The defect was interesting, according to Frank, because it was not in the coding region of the gene—the part usually thought of as supplying the genetic instructions—but in the gene's promoter region, which determined how the gene was expressed. This promoter drove the expression of a protein that was essential for the uterine lining to allow implantation; without it, the embryo could not implant and pregnancy would not be possible.

Gene was able to locate Frank's original publication in an online archive, and it verified his account. Frank did not pursue the genetic research further but used the discovery in his IVF practice. He figured out how to resolve the implantation problem by coating the embryos in the missing proteins. This dramatically increased the success rate for all in vitro transplants, and the field exploded. But it was the original findings about the genetic structure and role of promoters in controlling the regulatory network that the scientific world appreciated. Indeed, this discovery earned him a share of a Nobel Prize given to a group of researchers whose body of work was the catalyst for the Human Genome Project.

Frank also said that Alex Castle had figured out how to mimic this genetic defect, by using a retrovirus along with other drugs. The retrovirus targeted the promoter region, making it vulnerable. After that, certain drugs could bind to the promoter and turn off the gene, leaving the women unable to conceive. Frank had said, "Using retroviruses are common enough now, but this was truly innovative at the time. And it was easy to administer. The virus could remain active for days, even weeks, and be delivered in something as simple as a glass of water."

"Why would anyone want to do that?" Gene had asked.

"Do you think the world is overpopulated?"

"I'm not sure." Frank's question had taken him by surprise.

"How many years?"

"What?"

"How many years until it's over, until there are so many people and so few resources, that something truly horrible happens and mankind either kills the planet or kills itself? That's the question she would ask, continually."

"Well, I guess she has a point." Gene had conceded.

"It's not just Alex. There are many people who feel that way. And some are very powerful."

"But you said it was only temporary sterility."

"The original drug had limited effects. Take away the drug, and over time the gene expression would come back."

"Like what happened here. The first time, the infertility stopped after a few years."

"But Alex was looking for ways to make it permanent."

"And you think she's working on this again?"

"I think she never stopped. Alex Castle is Alejandra Castilla."

⤙

It was crazy. Was he being dragged into the same paranoid delusion that had destroyed the life of this once famous scientist? Or could it be true? And if it was true, did José know? It seemed unlikely. But how could he be certain of José's innocence? His body ached with anxiety and guilt. For the first time, he had lied to José, telling him it was all over—that he was just upset for being wrong about the girls and wasting all of their time. Did José believe him? Gene didn't know.

A dusty blue car pulled into the driveway and parked on the lawn in front of the house. Gene got out of the van, forced himself to smile, and introduced himself to the owner of the property, an olive-complexioned man in his late thirties.

"The land has been in my family for generations." Eduardo led Gene up to the house and unlocked the bar on the door. "This was to be my house, for my family. My father and I worked on it for years. The work stopped when he died. I moved in with my mother, down the road, and my family lives there with her now."

The house was surprisingly clean considering the growth outside. Fresh broom marks on the floor and the smell of Fabuloso greeted them.

Earlier, Gene had almost cancelled the meeting, given his current mental state. Now that he was here, he decided to give the house a proper review, if only to be polite. Clearly someone had put in the effort to clean for him.

As they walked from room to room, Gene asked questions. "How much of the land are you looking to sell with the house?"

"We want to keep most of the land to farm, but we will sell three or four acres."

"The small pasture out in the back, is that part of the property?"

"Yes, we were going to have a few horses and goats."

"Where does the water come from? Is it all cistern?"

"We do have a cistern, but also a very deep well. The cistern was never hooked up to the well. We use the well to water the trees and some of the surrounding acreage. There is plenty of water for the property."

"Can I see the cistern space?"

Eduardo bit his lip. "I have not opened it since…" His voice dropped off. "No telling what has crawled in there."

The cistern cover was a concrete slab of about two feet square, set into the corner of the main room. It had no handle or lever, but Eduardo was able to locate a pry bar. Between the two of them, they wedged the jack between the floor and the cover and pried it open.

Gene squatted to get a better look. Directly under them the concrete container was expansive, maybe fifteen by thirty feet, and eight deep. Dust particles shimmered in the diffused light, and a large shape loomed in one dark corner.

"What's that?"

Eduardo lay on his stomach and poked his head into the cistern opening. "I don't know. One minute." He left the house, returning with a large flashlight. Both men dropped to the floor. Eduardo shined the light into the hole, and they peered inside. The lingering smell of dead millipedes turned Gene's stomach.

Stacked in the corner on a make-shift pallet of two by fours were boxes of supplies. There were probably a dozen cases of bottled water and half that in canned food.

"There is water in the cistern after all," Gene said.

Eduardo shook his head. "I cannot believe this has been here all this time."

"What do you mean?"

"My father must have put these here. After Hurricane Mitch. He worked with the relief organizations. See the water? It is marked with a blue P, for El Progreso. They had their own temporary water treatment and bottling center. It was set up just after the hurricane and saved many lives."

A thought came to Gene. If he was right, this was paramount. "Eduardo, how long ago did you father pass?"

"It has been nearly fourteen years."

CHAPTER 22

ATLANTA, GA

GEORGIA CLOSED HER eyes and let the cool breeze bathe her skin. Fall was finally making its way down south, and this evening the typically muggy air felt crisp and clean. She jumped when something warm enveloped her, but it was just Trish putting an arm around her shoulder. Trish spoke in what was probably supposed to be a comforting tone. "It's nothing to be ashamed of. You were what, maybe sixteen when you had Emiko?"

Momentary confusion, and then Georgia laughed at the obvious conclusion. "Trish, no." Then to Dave, "You haven't told her about me?"

Dave shook his head. "Of course not."

"Told me what?" Trish interrupted.

"Dave?" Georgia asked.

"It's your call. Whatever you decide."

Earlier, while the technician was scanning for bugs in her apartment and fortunately not finding any, Georgia called Dave and requested that Trish and Diane join them at his house to discuss the test results. She could not tell the entire story, courtesy of the FBI, but they needed, and deserved, some level of explanation. Now they were all sitting on Dave's back porch. She looked to the three, from best friend to new acquaintance to something in between.

Dave, she could trust with anything. And he already knew most of her history. A true friend, he never poked his nose in too far but was there when you needed him. Trish was wide-eyed with anticipation. She hardly knew Trish, but she had no pretense, and Georgia liked that. But could Trish keep a secret? And then there was Diane. Georgia was going to need Diane's help in the future, and clearly she was not one to walk close to the edge. She would not do anything without fully knowing what she was getting into. Diane was going to be a problem. Georgia would have to win her over.

Georgia said, "It's a complicated and painful story, and I still don't know everything. It's going to take some time to explain."

The women nodded, and Dave said, "Take your time."

"Diane, you were on the right track when you speculated that Emiko and I may have come from the same sperm donor. Apparently I was the Moris' egg donor, albeit, I had no idea."

Diane said, "How could that be?"

"Emiko knew my uncle, Frank Anderson, and he ran an exclusive fertility clinic for many years in New York."

"Frank Anderson," Diane said, eyebrows raised. "Not *the* Frank Anderson."

"Yes, one and the same. He's actually my godfather. I grew up thinking of him as an uncle, though we're not physically related. Obviously."

"Who is he?" Trish asked.

"Frank was my parents' best friend. They met in graduate school at Harvard. He is, or was, a rather famous geneticist."

Diane threw up her hands, her excitement palpable. "Rather famous? He pretty much invented the entire field of in vitro fertilization and discovered genetic switching and pioneered gene therapy and manipulation. He won a Nobel Prize and the Lasker Award." She stopped to catch her breath and shrugged. "Sorry."

Georgia smiled, amused. "No, go right ahead."

"Years ago he was accused of doing genetic engineering and gene therapy on embryos. These were human embryos left over from in vitro procedures. It was legal at the time; this is a field where technology outpaces legislation. When exposed, he admitted it all. It became a huge scandal. He lost most of his research funding and his clinic.

"It's shockingly hypocritical," Diane continued, displaying uncharacteristic emotion. "Did you know that couples are encouraged to create multiple embryos to increase their chances of getting pregnant, but many are never used and just sit frozen? Dr. Anderson, and others, wanted to use them for research. Pro-life groups hounded him incessantly. But why is it ethical to fertilize eggs and let them sit in perpetuity? Or get thrown away? More than one million embryos have been thrown away over the years." Diane raised her hand and sipped from a glass of Diet Coke. She sighed, "I always felt Anderson got a raw deal. And it probably led to, you know, what happened later."

"No, what happened later?" Trish asked.

"After he lost the clinic, he left the country," Georgia answered. "He got some funding from the Netherlands to research the impact of agricultural toxins on human fertility. He seemed to be fine for a while. Then he lost it and became completely paranoid. He started claiming he had been set up in the States and there was a conspiracy to cover up his research results. He said people were out to get him. Then his funding dried up and he went underground."

"Where is he now?" Diane asked.

"I don't know," Georgia said. That was the truth.

"Wait a minute," Trish said. "You think your godfather used your eggs at his in vitro clinic to make Emiko?"

Georgia nodded.

"First of all, that's disgusting," Trish said, her face scrunched up. "Secondly how would he get them?"

"I had my appendix out when I was thirteen. It could have happened then. But they often ran medical tests on us at school, some of them invasive. He could have arranged it."

"At school? The Harmony thing?" Trish asked.

"Yes," Georgia said, nodding. "Harmony School. It's still one of the top boarding schools in the country, if not the world. My father worked there for many years and I attended every year. They claim to make the very brightest into the absolute best. That's their slogan. It was Fame meets Fermilab."

"Your father?" Trish asked. "Do you think he knows about this?"

Dave glared at Trish, who mouthed 'What?' at him.

"My parents were killed when I was fifteen. Our house burned down and they both died."

"Oh gosh, I'm sorry," Trish said.

They sat for a moment in an uncomfortable silence, sipping Cokes and listening to the cicadas.

"The whole mess with Frank started with Harmony School," Georgia said. "There were rumors the school was performing unethical tests on children, like exposing them to unusually stressful situations just to see how they'd respond. School officials were also accused of giving confidential psychological and medical information to Cornell researchers and Frank's clinic in exchange for recommendations on how to improve their students' performance."

"Creepy," Trish said.

"The school didn't deny it. Most of it anyway. They wanted to develop superior children. But after that, the FBI took a closer look at Frank's clinic, and the genetic engineering came out. The Feds never could prove any illegalities at either Harmony School or Frank's lab and never pressed any charges. But it was too late for

Frank. His reputation was ruined. He closed the clinic and he left the country." *And me.*

"So, we think we know the how," Trish said. "But why? Why would Georgia's godfather take eggs from her?"

And why didn't he want me to meet Emiko? Georgia almost added.

Trish went on, "Stealing eggs from kids in order to make other kids, that's hideous."

"But not just any children," Diane said. She looked at Georgia. "You said it yourself: the most intelligent children in the country, if not the world. What better source for designer babies?"

"There are people out there who would pay a lot for that," Dave added. "That's the why."

"There's another aspect to consider," Diane said.

"What?" Georgia asked.

"Um, well," she stammered.

"Just say it," Trish said.

"Rarely do fertility donors give to only one recipient. If Dr. Anderson went to the trouble to harvest and utilize your eggs, it follows logically that…"

Georgia finished the thought for her. "…there are more Emikos out there."

"Yes. There could be other biological children."

"It makes sense," Dave said. "And there could be others like you, George. If the press got ahold of this, it would be another national scandal. A lot of people would have their lives turned upside down."

"I didn't think about that," Georgia said. She stood up, strode to the edge of the deck and gazed up at the sky. No stars were visible. One rarely saw stars in the city, but sometimes airplanes acted as a reasonable distraction. In her mind she replayed the phone conversation with Frank.

She felt someone standing behind her. "What happened yesterday when you went to see Sean Kelly?" It was Dave, his voice low.

"Who's Sean Kelly?" Trish chimed in from the table.

"Jesus, Trish."

"Sorry," she said, in a sing song voice, not sounding sorry.

Georgia turned back around to face the two women. "He's the FBI agent in charge of the Atlantic-Pacific case. He's a good guy. I told him about Emiko and Frank. He already knew Frank is my godfather." Georgia struggled to think of what she could say to keep them interested and stay clean with the FBI. "In a nutshell, he said there was nothing he could do. It was a matter for the police in New York, and it was likely the statute of limitations had run out in any case."

"Bummer," said Trish. "But we have to do something, right?"

Georgia said, "I'm going to keep looking for Frank. And I still want to look for any family. For my real parents and for any..." she paused, unable to say the word *others*. She folded her arms across her chest, trying to hold in the emotions. "I'm going to keep looking."

Trish slapped her hands on the table. "We'll help."

"You're not going to do anything to get yourself into more trouble, are you?" Dave asked. "George is quite skilled at finding her way into digital databases." The comment was directed at Trish and Diane, but his focus never left Georgia.

"You mean hacking?" Diane asked.

"It was nothing. I was trying to search some adoption records."

"It was illegal, and you are lucky they didn't press charges."

Georgia glared at Dave.

Diane stood up. "I cannot be involved with anything even remotely illegal. I could lose my research project or my job, and I have a family to think of."

"That's right, Diane. You have a family. George doesn't," Trish said.

This was going horribly wrong. "Stop, please," Georgia said, hands raised. "Please. Look, it's true I was able to log into an adoption database. But it was barely secure." This was true, for someone with her skills anyway, so it wasn't a complete lie. "But that is all over, and I would never ask anyone here to do anything illegal." She motioned to Diane, "Please, sit down."

Diane hesitated, then slowly returned to her seat.

Georgia addressed her. "When you said Harmony School would be a good source because it has the best and brightest in the world, it occurred to me that schools, universities in particular, are a good place for me to look for my biological parents."

Diane nodded, "Makes sense."

"I'm confused." Trish's face puckered as if she had eaten a lemon.

Diane continued, "Thirty years ago, the best place to find diversity would be in a university setting."

"Or at a world class boarding school," Dave said.

"True." Georgia nodded. "My mother was a professor at Cornell. My father was the dean at Harmony. Maybe there are no adoption records for me because it was a private adoption. Maybe my adoptive parents knew my biological parents. They could have been students at either school.

"In which case, ancestry testing may give you something to go on," Trish said. "Diane, that is right up your alley. You can order that, right?"

Even in the dim light, Diane appeared flushed and dropped her gaze to her hands.

"It's perfectly legal for George to have her own DNA tested," Trish said, exasperation in her voice.

"Yes of course," Diane stammered. "I am apparently now caught in my own ethical web of deception. I'm sorry, Georgia, but I was quite curious about your heritage. I already ordered the ancestry tests. I was going to tell you, of course, when the results came in. Which should be any day now."

Georgia smiled. This was beneficial on many levels. "Diane, I guess this makes you part of the team."

CHAPTER 23

ATLANTA TO NEW YORK

GEORGIA'S HACKING HIATUS was short-lived. Although, as she reflected on the conversation with her friends, she never promised to stop, just not to involve them in her actions.

Dave had offered use of his souped-up internet search bots to gather information on Frank, Emiko, and the Harmony School. The web crawlers quickly gathered massive amounts of information, and AI programs categorized them. It would take weeks for Trish and Dave to assess it thoroughly, but the initial results showed nothing that could lead her to Frank.

Feeling anxious and impatient, she decided to tackle Harmony's records. She easily found her way into the school's administrative database and accessed a comprehensive student records system: grades, attendance, tuition, and college entrance exam results. She could not locate any medical records or psychological data. She guessed that after the public shaming levied at the school, it now safely secured sensitive documents, perhaps outsourcing to a third party. Or the school could have the records stored on site, either on paper or not connected to any network.

The most interesting thing she found was that Emiko's tuition, room, and board had been fully covered by a scholarship from the Harmony Fund. She looked this up online and found that "especially gifted students are considered for full or partial tuition from the Harmony Fund, which is made possible by alumni, local businesses, and anonymous donors."

She moved on to Frank and wondered whether she should look for him virtually since she could not find him in person. The FBI had confiscated the clinic's records long ago, but it was possible he had hidden a copy somewhere, probably using the very techniques she had taught him.

Georgia finished dressing for a morning run and was considering how she might penetrate the security on a system she herself had designed to be impenetrable, when her computer beeped. The tone told her she had a new message on her primary server.

It was an encrypted 'read me' file. A message from Frank.

"Yes!" she called out, celebrating with some hand waves and dance moves. She retrieved the flash drive holding the private key from its hiding place. It was in a tampon box, the last place a man would look.

The file contained a simple message.

Georgie, I hope you are well, and I miss you so. I know you are not one to let things lie, but it would be best if you forget Emiko and let it go. There are larger forces at play here and it could be very dangerous. I'm going to be leaving the country in a few days after I wrap up some loose ends. I love you. F

She screamed, jerked the USB drive out of her computer, and threw it across the room as hard as she could. Any damage it sustained was irrelevant. By not sending her a key to use in return, Frank did not want her to reply. He was blowing her off again. And he had the nerve to call her Georgie and tell her he loved her. In a blinding rage, she rushed out of her apartment, down the stairs, and through the neighbor's yard to 10th Street. Horns blared as she crossed, but she didn't care. She ran circles around the park until she was exhausted.

In the end, the run did not change her mind about finding Frank, but rather strengthened her resolve. Only he knew if there were other Emikos out there. And Frank was closer to her parents than anyone. He would know about her adoption. But if he left the country he could disappear and abandon her again.

She had to find him and do it quickly. She did not know where he was, but perhaps she knew someone who did. It was a gamble, but what did she have to lose? She took a quick shower, packed up a bag with a few days' worth of clothes, a leather jacket, and her laptop. Then she called for a ride to the airport.

᷈

"Hello, Georgia Steele. I must say this is a pleasant surprise." Sam eyed her through the open passenger window of a red Ford Focus. "When you didn't answer any of my texts or phone calls, I thought I was going to have to…"

Georgia opened the back door of his car and placed an overnight bag and backpack on the seat.

"What are you doing?" Sam asked as Georgia slid into the passenger seat beside him.

"Is this your car? It doesn't look like an FBI car."

"It's a rental, and not all FBI cars are black sedans contrary to popular belief." Instead of putting the car into drive, he removed his hands from the steering wheel and crossed his arms.

"Look, I need a ride to the airport and as my appointed liaison, you need to, well liaise, and so I figured we could kill two birds with one stone." She made a shooing gesture. "Let's go."

Sam engaged the car and pulled away from the curb. "I appreciate your letting me know you are going out of town, but you could have just called."

"I just thought you should know since I'm going to see Frank."

"What?" Sam's head jerked and the car veered right. He slammed on the brakes, barely missing a parked car. "How did you find him?"

"Drive. You're blocking traffic." She nodded to the road.

He headed out slowly, circling the block and turning right on Monroe Drive, taking them south towards the interstate.

"Let's have it. How did you find Frank?" Sam asked.

"The same way you did."

"We lost him when he missed his connection at JFK."

Georgia smiled. Her bluff had worked. Frank was in New York. She might have a chance after all.

Sam asked, "You think he's still in New York? Where?"

"I don't exactly know."

"Then where are you going?"

"I don't exactly know."

"But you said you are seeing Frank. How are you going to do that?"

"Maybe if I throw out a line, he'll grab onto it."

"I should come with you," Sam said.

"You absolutely will not."

"You know I have to report this."

Georgia searched for a plausible explanation. "I have a storage unit in Ithaca, New York. It has my parents' things in it." This was accompanied by a tug in her chest. "I'm going there to see if I can find any answers."

"What?"

"It's true, and that's what you will report."

"I can't do that."

"Sam, I didn't know where Frank was until you told me. How would you like your superiors to know that? Think there will be any more fieldwork in your future?"

His face fell, and she knew she had him.

Sam still looked like a hurt puppy when he dropped her off at

Hartsfield Airport. He was so cute she almost felt sorry for deceiving him. Almost.

✍

Once in the airport, Georgia called Marcus to let him know where she was going.

"I'm not sure about this," Marcus said.

"I have to go. Frank won't talk to me, and he is going to be leaving any day to go God knows where."

"Do you even know where he is?"

"No. I might not even get to meet with him."

"Did you tell Bennett?"

"Oh, him." It might not be a good idea to tell Marcus what she had done. "He'll tell you that I'm going to clean out my parents' storage unit to see if I can find anything."

"You still have that?" Disbelief sounded in his voice. "I thought you got rid of that years ago."

A pang of guilt shot through her. "I, uh, no. I still have it."

"George, you have to be kidding. They've been dead close to twenty years."

"Just forget it," she said. "I'm also thinking of going to see Emiko's mother to see if she could shed any light on this."

"You think that's a good idea?"

"Why not?"

"Oh, gee, I don't know. Your daughter just dies and then a look-a-like shows up at your front door."

"I hadn't thought about that."

"There are a lot of things you don't think about."

"Well, I'm going to New York," she said defiantly. "I'll be fine."

He sighed. "Do you want me to come with you?"

"No. What could happen?"

✍

She didn't have to phone Dave. He called her less than a minute after she hung up with Marcus.

"Dave, I know what you're going to say," she said.

"You do?" He sounded confused. "How? Did you talk to Diane?"

"No." Now it was her turn to be confused. "I saw I had a text from her when I got back from running, but I haven't had time to call. What's up?"

"She got your ancestry results back."

"She did? What did they say?"

"I think we should let her tell you. One sec and I'll conference her in."

While Georgia waited, her flight was called for boarding. She feared she might have to hang up, but then Dave's voice came on the line.

"Hey George, I have Diane."

"Can you make it quick? I'm about to get on a plane to New York."

"You're going to New York?" Dave asked.

"I'll explain later. Tell me the news."

Diane spoke. "Well, you understand how we can examine DNA markers and compare them to different ethnicities to determine your ancestral heritage. Most people living in the US actually have multiple lines."

"The short version please."

"Certainly. Let me think how to communicate this succinctly. Whereas most people have multiple lines, you have significantly more."

"That's pretty obvious."

"No, you are missing the point. You have markers from every major line in the world. There is more research to be done, but I've been studying exactly this in my work, and I can say with confidence that you are quite unique."

"Thanks, I guess," Georgia said.

"No. What I am trying to say is that it is highly improbable you came about naturally."

"What are you getting at?"

"Honestly, I don't know," Diane admitted. "You were born in the mid-80s? Perhaps you were not adopted, but in fact were IVF. Given your relationship with Dr. Anderson, and his large pool of resources, it is a possibility. It may not explain—"

"My parents told me I was adopted."

"When you were born, in vitro fertilization was still new and controversial, and the children were often treated as outcasts. I'm sure it was bad enough for you being mixed race. Can you imagine being IVF and mixed race? They could have kept this from you in order to protect you."

"But you're not sure."

"No. I'm trying to account for your, um, composition, for lack of a better word. You are much more than a designer baby, Georgia. I did not know that anyone like you even existed. To call you one in a million is a massive understatement. More like one in a billion."

The gate attendant announced last call for boarding. Georgia quickly asked Diane to send her details to look at on the plane.

After reviewing only a fraction of the report Diane sent, Georgia had read enough. She stared out the window to the fluffy clouds settled beneath the plane. Her eyes were mollified by the billowing forms stretched across the sky, but her mind raced and bounced. The scientist in her was intrigued, but the rest of her was sickened. What was the point of it all? Was she just the outcome of a science experiment to see how many different kinds of people could be shoved into one body? Did her parents know? There had to be more to this. At least she hoped.

Georgia composed another 'Read Me' note to Frank, this one entirely unencrypted.

It's too late. I know. I know I am her mother. I know you made both of us, and I know the FBI is looking for you. I'm on my way to New York. And I'll be expecting you to pick me up tonight, at the place we last saw each other. G

CHAPTER 24

ROCHESTER, NEW YORK

GEORGIA WONDERED IF little kids still made macaroni necklaces and if mothers still saved them. This one appeared to be a haphazard compilation of elbow and penne. Even now she could recall the teacher's disappointed expression. Of course, the teacher never knew that the necklace spelled "I love you, Mom" in Morse code. She gently placed the pasta jewelry back into the shoe box and hugged it against her chest before returning it to the larger carton labeled Georgie's School Records and Art.

This trip down memory lane was happening in a rented Nissan in the parking lot of a Denny's near the Rochester airport. Georgia had just come from the storage facility where she kept what little remained of her parents' belongings. Their study was about the only thing to escape the fire, and she had long ago moved or given away most of their prized collection of books. What was left should have been household or work-related records. And apparently, some pre-school arts and crafts.

But she did not find any of her parents' research. She uncovered a few scientific books and journals, but that was all. Her parents' computers survived the fire, but both were returned to their employers—the University and the Harmony School. Still it seemed odd no paper documents remained. She did not remember throwing any out. But the days after their death were a haze, and it was entirely possible she had.

There were some medical records. These she went through in detail. Receipts from when her father fell off a ladder and had to be hospitalized. Evidence of her mother's asthma. But nothing about Georgia. There were no adoption papers, no immunization records, no documents from Frank's clinic. Nothing at all. Not even from when she had her appendix removed.

Georgia opened the second box, Vacation Memories, marked in her mother's familiar handwriting. It was not full of photos, as she expected, but of souvenirs of their vacations together: little glass bottles. Her mother had a thing about collecting sand or dirt from all of their vacation sites. They were each labeled. She saw one from "Atlantic City." Another from "St. Croix, USVI," where her parents had honeymooned. She also found a music box, her mother's from when she was a little girl, and some other trinkets. She lifted the lid, and the ballerina began a timeless twirl.

The gentle music was overpowered by an approaching motorcycle. A vintage Indian motorcycle pulled up to where she was parked. The rider dismounted and removed his helmet.

"Hi, Frank," Georgia said, holding her voice flat.

Frank's thinning white hair fluttered in the wind and heavy lines crossed his brow. He looked worn by the years, like creased sandstone bearing witness to a century of tireless wind, yet his eyes were bright and his posture erect. "Georgie, you should not have come."

Georgia got out of the car to face her godfather. "Nice to see you, too, by the way. Is this your old bike?"

"Gather your things. Leave the car here."

"What?"

"It can't come with us."

"But I have boxes from my storage unit."

"Bring what you need. Put the rest in the trunk. I'll have some-one pick up the car." He opened a storage case on the side of the bike and produced a spare helmet and a black pouch. "And please turn off your cell phone and all other electronics and put them in here. Hurry."

Georgia inspected the pouch, turning it over in her hands. "Is this a Faraday bag?" Faraday bags secured electronic devices by blocking cell, RFID, and WiFi transmissions. They were easy to come by, but she had never seen one, never having felt the need to hide her physical location. She rolled her eyes in annoyance but complied with Frank's request.

"Where are we going?"

He handed her the helmet and stowed her things. "You'll see."

"Can I drive?"

Frank answered by getting back on the motorcycle. Georgia sighed, put on her sunglasses and the helmet, and mounted the bike behind him. They raced down I-390, then east to I-590, cut-ting between cars where they could not pass. A world of emotions simmered within her.

Frank checked his rear-view mirror before exiting onto NY 31/Monroe. He repeated the act before turning south onto NY 65/Clover St. This began as a five-lane road, but as they drove it narrowed to two. Their pace slowed as Frank stayed in line with the sporadic traffic. The scenery changed from urban to suburban to rural.

The gray monochrome of the city was gone. Horses fed in green pastures occupied by red barns and deciduous trees glowing in shades of yellow and red. Overhead, wispy pink clouds dotted a bright blue sky as the sun glowed low on the horizon.

They turned and continued east for several miles, until Frank steered the motorcycle into a gravel parking area on the side of the road. He motioned for her to get off the bike. The west side of the lot housed a stand of thick evergreens. On the opposite side scrubby brush punctuated an overgrown field. At the center was a trailhead, which ran due north through a field of high grass along what looked to be an old railway bed.

The sunset was spectacular, with pink and red clouds streaking through the sky. Mist was forming in the warm evening air.

Frank and the bike were gone, a crunching sound emanating from the evergreen stand. A minute later Frank pushed through the dense canopy, a dark shadow against the dazzling sky.

He beckoned to her with one finger, and she followed.

"What are we doing?"

"Waiting. Come with me."

She followed him down the trail, continuing as he cut back through the deep grass and into the evergreen stand. The road was still visible, but they were well hidden.

"OK. That's it. What's going on?" Georgia asked.

"You tell me." His voice was quiet but firm.

"What do you mean by that?"

"Come on, Georgie."

"Don't call me that."

"You fly up here with no warning, and you bring the Feds with you." Muttering under his breath, "At least I hope it was the Feds."

"What?"

"They followed you to Denny's," he said, his tone matter of fact. "And probably have a trace on you, at least on your phone. I find it hard to believe you don't know."

"They said they wouldn't do that." As she said the words, she realized how stupid they sounded. "Wait, why am I apologizing to you?" Anger roiled in her stomach. "You stole my eggs and made Emiko and who knows how many others. And you got her killed."

Frank had been facing the road, but now he wheeled around. "I did not have anything to do with that."

They glared at each other in the fading light.

"What do you want from me, Georgia?" he said, her name sounding forced.

"I want you to tell me everything. Everything. About me, you, my parents, how this whole thing got started, and how far it goes."

"It's too dangerous."

"You keep saying that, but how would I know since you've not told me anything? Please let me be the judge of that, Frank. I'm not a little girl anymore." She crossed her arms in front of her and steeled herself. "And I'm not going anywhere until you tell me."

He sighed and checked his watch.

"I mean it," Georgia said.

Frank glanced over his shoulder, regarding the empty road. "Fine," he said, keeping his voice low. "In 1971, I met your mother at a debate on campus at Harvard. I was pre-med, and she was majoring in Psychiatry. The topic of the debate was intelligence, and whether it was inherited or learned."

"Nature versus nurture."

"Yes. The focus was on the performance of African Americans in our education system. The underlying motive of the visiting professor was to justify segregation. It was quite controversial, but he had his supporters."

A car came along the road and Frank waited for it to pass. "You have to remember, it was a different time. The civil rights bill had been signed only three years before, after Dr. King's assassination.

"Karen and I met at a party after the debate. We were both drawn to the topic. But how much intelligence was inherited versus learned was just part of the interest. It was the controversy it generated. Mankind is simply not able to objectively analyze itself. Whether it's due to religion or the unwillingness of man to put himself in the same spectrum as the rest of life on earth, I still don't know. But it was exciting to talk about these things. We felt like we were walking in the shoes of Da Vinci, Copernicus, or even

Galileo." Frank looked up into the sky, and Georgia followed his gaze. The first stars were coming to light.

He continued, "It was shortly thereafter that we met James, your father. He was an anthropology major. He was the perfect addition to our late-night round tables, and your mother fell head over heels for him. Much to my disappointment," Frank said, his voice echoing his words. "It was James who introduced us to the work of Sir Francis Galton."

"Galton, as in the founder of statistics?" Georgia asked.

"One and the same. He was Charles Darwin's half cousin, and he was inspired by Darwin's discoveries. Galton invented regression and correlation, resulting from studies on inherited characteristics in plants."

"I didn't know that part. Statistics was born from a study of evolution?"

"Biology anyway. He also made founding breakthroughs in meteorology and psychology. But Galton is often most remembered, and misunderstood, for his founding and promotion of eugenics. It's unfortunate, as his initial goal was for us humans to look at ourselves objectively through quantitative analysis. He was likely the first to document how not only physical but also intellectual and behavioral traits can be inherited. Later on, he got swept up in the eugenics hysteria that overtook Britain."

Frank cleared his throat. "Your father agreed with Galton and fiercely believed that we should take as much care with our own future as we do with that of our animals. The human race is so much more important than dogs or chickens, and we should try to make all we can out of it. We did not know it then, but that was their founding principle, too."

"Who are they?" Georgia said.

Frank checked his watch again. "Let's get moving before it's totally dark. These roads are tricky at night."

They motored east for about five miles, passing through a

quaint village before turning south. Pastures turned to farmland and twilight to night. They continued for close to an hour, making multiple turns and encountering several lakes. Georgia knew they were in the Finger Lakes region but had become disoriented in the dark. There was no moon, no street lights, and very few houses.

Finally, Frank slowed and turned onto a nondescript side street which led to a row of older homes and small cabins. He stopped at a gravel drive. What lay beyond was concealed by trees and the blackness of the night.

They had reached their destination.

CHAPTER 25

TEGUCIGALPA, HONDURAS

"ANTHONY, WHAT A surprise. I thought one of your minions was going to pick me up," Alex said. Her colleague, attired in his usual gray fatigues and a frown, had been waiting for her when she exited Customs and Immigration. "Next time send Danny. Such a polite young man."

"We have to talk."

Anthony reached for Alex's wheeled suitcase, an odd display of manners from such a gruff man. She followed him through the airport lobby to the gleaming black SUV parked at the curb. She looked at the white linen suit she wore and smiled. Even in the unending dust and decay that was Tegucigalpa, his car was always spotless.

He stowed her bag and opened the passenger door for her.

"You do realize you are going to have to get some actual clothes at some point?"

He grunted.

"Aren't you even going to ask what happened at the meeting with the Brazilians?"

He put the car into drive, and they pulled away from the terminal.

"Well, since you asked. The Department of Health wants the retrovirus. They learned their lesson with the Zika epidemic. They are developing a vaccine—hell half the world is—but the virus could mutate, or the next Zika could arise. They want our retrovirus as a stopgap. They hope they don't even have to use it. They want us to make a half million doses for now and be able to reserve another half million as contingency. Payment up front." She rubbed her fingers together. "Of course, we'll need a larger operation. What do you think about moving to Cartagena?"

Anthony turned east, taking the longer but nicer route past the Presidential Palace to the apartment she kept in Lomas del Guijarro.

"You'll come with me, of course. I need you, Anthony."

When there was still no response, she asked, "What's the matter?"

"The Steele woman is with Anderson. She found him."

So that was it. "I told you she was clever. Has Frank been in contact with Dr. Young?"

"Not that we know."

"Well, that corroborates what José told me. Young is moping around all depressed now that he doesn't have a health crisis to solve. I recommended a vacation to get his mind off things." Alex adjusted her seatbelt and straightened her rumpled jacket. "Who cares if the girl wants to reunite with Frank? They were very close years ago." She said this with confidence, yet felt a small prickling at the back of her neck. "Where are they now?"

"The Bureau was tailing her. She hooked up with Anderson near Rochester, New York. They lost her."

"So, he went back." Back to where it all started, such a long time ago. Frank Anderson had been a leading researcher, and she'd been so young, a post-doc fresh out of grad school. She'd thought he walked on water. She had been so naive.

They'd found something revolutionary, discovered a key way

genes function, and he told her to drop it. But she wouldn't. And then he got the credit. The Nobel Prize. It should have been hers.

"He has ties to the area," she said. "Maybe some of his old friends are still around. You can give the names to your buddies in the FBI. Buy yourself a favor or two."

"There's more. Before she left, Steele talked to her contact at the Bureau."

Alex listened to the rest, told in short clipped sentences void of emotion. But the conclusion was no less impactful.

"Emiko Mori was her daughter," Anthony said. "But Steele claims she's never had a child, or even been pregnant."

That bastard. He must have made Emiko. What was he trying to do?

"How old is the girl?"

"She was sixteen."

That would have been just after Alex left New York, and too long ago for the FBI to care. She wondered if *they* knew about Emiko. *They* had no statute of limitations.

Anthony said something, but she missed it. "What?"

"The girl died. Hit by a car before Steele could learn anything. That's why she was looking for Anderson."

"What happened to the body?"

Anthony glanced in her direction. "It disappeared from the hospital. Officially an unauthorized cremation, but that is someone's CYA story."

So *they* already knew about Emiko. Did *they* know Frank was in the States? Probably.

The prickling ran from her neck down her back, and she shivered. Could it be more than a coincidence? After Frank read the test results it would have been over. Could there be more? Impossible. No, nothing was impossible.

Nonetheless, she would have to tell Marsten or someone else on the council. Not about what she was doing. They were fully supportive of her "little experiment," being just as concerned as she with the future of humanity and the planet. Indeed, they were actively planning for far more drastic measures to save the Earth, should it become necessary.

No, she would have to tell them about Dr. Young and his quest, and about Frank and young Georgia Steele. They would find out in any case, but it was far better coming from her.

CHAPTER 26

FINGER LAKES REGION, NEW YORK

GEORGIA SMELLED COFFEE. She opened one eye a crack. A bright shaft of light coming in from the window over the bed blinded her. She shut the eye and turned over. Sleepily, she recalled that she was in New York in a cabin with her godfather. She dragged herself out of bed, put on shorts and a long-sleeved shirt, and followed her nose.

An empty mug waited next to the half-full coffee pot. There was no sugar, but at least there was milk in the ancient refrigerator. She poured a cup and searched for Frank. The cabin was empty, the sliding glass doors open.

Frank was sitting at a picnic table on the back deck reading some sort of technical journal. Last night he had refused to talk anymore about her parents or Emiko, claiming he was tired. He forbade her to use her cell phone or iPad. This had ended in an argument, and she had gone to bed early. Though tempted to use her phone, she had respected his wishes.

"I need to call Marcus and let him know I'm alright." This was not really true, but she felt it might add to her cause.

"Good morning to you too," Frank said. He put down the journal and removed his reading glasses.

"You know, I know what I'm doing."

"Like you did last night with the FBI."

She felt herself flush. "That's different; this is technology. I know how to leave no trace."

"Uh huh. We'll figure that out later. Come sit down."

She sighed loudly, demonstrating her disapproval, but took a seat across from him.

"You seem very unfocused."

"I'd rather talk about you and my parents."

"Just humor me."

"Frank."

"Close your eyes and breathe slowly. What do you hear?"

Resigned, she complied. "Birds."

"Come on, you can do better than that."

"Finches, maybe a wren."

"And?"

Georgia let the residual sleepiness relax her body and listened. "Cicadas, still active but not like last night. Wind brushing over the leaves in the trees, making a sound like water in a rocky stream, and the long slow creaking of branches as they scrape across each other." She cocked her head, straining to hear. "A motorboat crossing the lake. Moving slowly, keeping under wake speed. Moving away from us, perhaps into a marina." She sank deeper into the sounds. "Two cars on the road, one speeding up to pass the other. A truck. It's heading for them, no time to correct." She tensed, then exhaled in relief. "Horns blaring, but no accident. That was close."

She picked up her coffee cup, took a sip, and then opened her eyes. Frank was smiling and shaking his head, and she was struck by the juxtaposition.

"You have no idea what you are capable of, do you?" he asked.

"What do you mean?"

"We probably should have told you. You're right. You deserve to know who you are," he said, as if to convince himself. "This way you can reach your full potential." He grunted. "As if any of us even know what that is."

"What are you talking about?"

"Let's go for a walk. We can continue our conversation."

꙰

At the end of the street, they followed a narrow trail into the woods, running parallel to the lake. Frank led the way and the conversation.

"I graduated and went to med school at Johns Hopkins. As you know, your parents stayed in Boston and Karen got her PhD from Harvard, while James went to Boston University. Then Karen got offered a tenure track position at Cornell and your father took a post-doc there to be with her. They were married soon after. I completed my residency, then decided I wanted to go back to research. I was lucky enough to get a job at Cambridge. There I worked with the early founders of IVF.

"During this time, your parents researched the relationship between man's evolution and the changing environment. You know, your father was the first to hypothesize that humans might never have evolved past the hunter-gatherer phase without our best friend, the dog."

"No, I didn't," Georgia said. As mad as she was at Frank, it was wonderful to hear about her parents and their lives together. "But he was fascinated with dogs, even though with Mom's allergies we could never have one."

"There was one aspect that James felt was most important. Selective breeding was not enough," Frank said. "It was the positive interaction with people that reinforced the genetic makeup."

"That makes sense. Dad told me how dogs were bred to communicate with people. Did you know dogs are the only animal to understand pointing? Not even apes do that."

"It can be boiled down to simply, nature *and* nurture, not nature *or* nurture. That was our key belief," Frank said. "I'm not saying our thoughts were unique or original, and there is still plenty of disagreement today about the exact role each plays. But it was clear to us that you need both."

Frank pushed aside a low branch and held it while Georgia passed.

"I say us, because by that time I had started to do some research with them. Among the three of us, we were able to cover our theories from all angles: biological, psychological, and cultural.

"Your parents and I were convinced that people are no different from animals, and one could, in fact, make people with any sort of characteristics. Of course, in the real world, you'd need thousands of people and hundreds of years to make any progress. So it was purely hypothetical."

They emerged from the wooded trail, ending up by the lake. Frank and Georgia sat on a wooden bench bearing the name of a deceased woman. Lily pads and cattails covered the water near the bank.

"It was at about this point that IVF was getting some bad publicity, both here and in the UK," Frank said. "The US was not funding any research, multiple lawsuits were filed in the UK, and my fellowship position was dropped. Back then, most Americans believed techniques like IVF were against 'God's will'." Frank used air quotes to make the last point. "But I digress. In any case, I found myself out of a job and headed back to the States to stay with my best friends.

"We were up late that first night drinking wine and mostly complaining about the fact that groundbreaking science will always be persecuted, with no apologies or praise later when it becomes commonly accepted. Comparing ourselves to Galileo again." Frank grunted. "The young are so haughty."

He gazed out over the water for several minutes, seemingly lost in thought.

"Go on," Georgia said.

"I can't remember which of us came up with the idea for the clinic. At first we laughed it off, but it was exciting to imagine. It took us back to those Harvard conversations, where we were pushing the boundaries of accepted science." One side of Frank's mouth was raised in a half smile. "The world was clearly against the idea of creating a superior race, but on an individual level, we thought people would take a different perspective.

"So we did it. We started an exclusive high-end fertility clinic, with both sperm and egg donation. We recruited our donors very carefully. We played to the egos of the super intelligent and gave them airtight contracts against future parental rights lawsuits. In fact, we never stored their names at all, so there was no way for any individual to be tied to another. Of course, DNA testing had not been developed at that point.

"Our clients came from all over the country. And why not? We had successful doctors, musicians, athletes, and even Nobel Prize-winning scientists. And no, we were not included," Frank said, preempting Georgia's question. "We decided that early on. We were just getting started when the Roe v. Wade decision came down."

"What does that have to do with anything?" Georgia asked.

"In some sense this opened the door for in vitro fertilization," Frank said. "Over the next few years, I performed dozens of successful operations. Many used donor eggs or sperm. We were becoming a hot destination with the upwardly mobile. We even had fertile couples use us to jack up their bloodline. It became quite lucrative, a side benefit we were not expecting.

"We also had a huge amount of data to use in our research. We were able to obtain the sperm and egg donors' complete health and genetic records, and we also got a release from the new parents to access the children's medical charts for use in anonymous research. We had a real-world lab going, and we published articles with the results. It was a fantastic time."

Frank turned to face Georgia. The wistful smile was gone. "Then your father published that damn paper on Galton." Frank shook his head and turned his attention back to the lake. "It was an unabashed soliloquy to his idol. Karen and I were so nervous about the impact it would have on our business and careers. She was still at Cornell. This was a pro-eugenics paper at its core, though we convinced him not to use that word."

Georgia sighed. "I'm such an idiot."

"What did you say?"

"I said, I'm an idiot. When you left the country, we tried to find all we could about you and your research: Marcus, Dave, and myself. I never found that paper. I was only looking at you, not my family. I knew you published papers together. I've read many of them. None of them talk about creating super people."

"I was surprised that you never questioned your birth, that you accepted the story that you were adopted. But there's a good reason why you were never told the truth." He stood up and stretched. He looked grim. "Let's walk." Frank abruptly headed back down the trail, and Georgia scrambled after him. "I swore never to tell anyone about this. Karen, James, and I all made an oath to each other. I must warn you that there could be consequences. I really do not know what could happen."

Georgia caught Frank's arm and stopped him. "What is it with all the conspiracy theory crap? Please get to the point. I get it—you guys decided to make your own designer baby."

"That's just it, Georgie, we didn't make you. They did."

They? Frank tried to move on, but she held him tight. "Who are *they?*"

"After James published that article on Galton, they contacted us."

"Who?"

"The Guardians."

She might have laughed at this, if not for the fact that Frank looked like he was going to cry. He pulled back again and this time she let him go.

"They sent an Englishman. He wasn't much older than us, but he had old-fashioned mannerisms and impeccable speech. He always dressed in a three-piece suit complete with a pocket square.

"He told us he represented a group of people who were working actively to improve the human species. The group had been formed by colleagues of Darwin and Galton, primarily by a man named Christopher Edwards, and had been in existence for 150 years. He said their group worked without regard to race or religion, in a scientifically objective fashion, and privately without any governmental intervention."

"Why do they call themselves the Guardians?" Georgia asked.

"Edwards, Galton, and others were convinced that man should be improved through selective breeding. They believed they owed it to God to further his work. They literally thought of themselves as the Guardians of Mankind. That was the original name.

"Your father went nuts at this revelation. He had found reference to Edwards before but not enough to publish. To think that this was more than speculation, it was enough to send him into academic nirvana.

"On top of that, this Englishman, and thus the Guardians, knew all about us. They knew everything we were doing, even the things we were trying to keep quiet. We had been taking blood from our donors and some of the children and storing it for future use. We knew real DNA testing would happen soon, and we were building a database of sorts. They knew all of that. That alone should have scared us off. But we were enthralled with the idea that this group actually existed.

"And they wanted to use our new technology, my IVF, to expand their program. At first, they just wanted to test it. Would we be willing to perform in vitro fertilization on a number of women if they would supply the eggs and the sperm? Of course we said yes."

"And I was one of their babies?" Georgia's head spun at the implications. Could all this be true?

"Oh, it's not that simple, I'm afraid." Frank waved a hand dismissively. "They sent us sperm from two men. Back then the harvesting of eggs from women was not as accessible and advanced as it is today, so the women had to come to the clinic. There were three women to start. One of them was your biological mother."

Georgia gasped and stopped walking. "You met her?" The implications of this were starting to sink in. "And my parents?" she said, her voice cracking. "Did they meet her too?"

"Yes." Neither Frank's gait nor his tone changed, so Georgia could not tell if he knew how this was affecting her. She ran to catch up. "All three of the women were of mixed race, beautiful, and smart, but she was exceptional. She looked very much like you, Georgie. The other two were younger and kept quiet, but she peppered me with questions on our procedure. I believe she must have been a doctor herself.

"We implanted the two other women with their own eggs, using assigned sperm. We also took eggs from your biological mother, to be implanted in other women at a later time. She herself was not impregnated… and I never saw her again."

"What?" That couldn't be all. Georgia struggled for something to say.

"We were paid half up front and were to be paid half once the two pregnancies were stable, about 6 weeks later. They must have been fine since we were paid in full. But no other women came in to use your mother's eggs, and no further correspondence occurred. We tried to contact the Englishman, but the number had been disconnected. We did not even know what country he was from, or if the name he gave us was real. We were devastated."

Frank stopped. He leaned an arm against a tree branch, keeping his eyes on the trail ahead. "One night we were all having dinner, and I asked James and Karen how long I should keep the extra eggs and sperm from the Guardians. We had started with enough sperm and eggs to make at least two tries at conception. Since we had to assume it all worked, we had leftovers, if you will. I should also mention at this point that your parents had been trying to get pregnant for a while and had actually considered either adopting or going IVF. They looked at each other, and then looked at me, and I knew instantly what they were going to say." He shrugged, "I tried to protest, but it was futile."

Georgia walked around Frank to stand directly in his line of sight. "So you made your own little Frankenstein."

"What?" His face contorted in confusion. "No. Exactly the opposite. We decided to use eggs from the older woman, and the sperm from one of the men. Even though your father had viable sperm, he wanted the best for you. In his own way." Frank reached out to touch a strand of loose hair that had fallen into Georgia's face, but she backed away. "Georgia, you are no Frankenstein, but rather one of the most perfect humans ever to be created. And it did not occur to us at the time, but they knew what we would do. They were setting us up." Frank slid around her and continued walking.

"What do you mean by that?" Georgia scurried after him.

"He showed up at your first birthday party. The English guy. He arrived with a birthday present in one hand and a contract in the other. He said we had to sign and abide by it or he'd take you and we'd never see you again. And he'd make sure that the clinic closed and your parents were fired from their jobs. We'd lose you, and he'd ruin us." Frank stopped. They had reached the end of the trail.

"What did the contract say?" Georgia asked.

Frank did not respond. His cell phone was ringing.

CHAPTER 27

FINGER LAKES REGION, NEW YORK

"I THOUGHT YOU said no phones," Georgia said.

"It's a pre-pay. You can use it to call your friend later when we go out."

He answered the phone. "Hello?... Hi, Martha." Frank's eyes lit up. For a moment he looked a decade younger. Then it was lost, his expression turned grave. "I'll be right over to pick it up. Thanks again."

"Looks like you get that opportunity to call your friend sooner than later. We have to run an errand."

"Where are we going?"

"To the grocery store."

"Good, because one pint of milk and some leftover pizza is not going to cut it." Then she remembered. "I need to call about my rental car before it gets towed."

"That's already been taken care of."

"What does that mean?"

She received no answer.

&

They retraced part of their journey from the night before, navigating north and west. Frank did not have headsets for his motorcycle helmets, so Georgia was left to think about their previous conversation.

The whole thing was unbelievable. Some secret organization had been trying to create a superior race of people, and she was one of them. And her parents were complicit? Maybe Frank was simply lying. No, she believed that Frank was telling her the truth. The truth as he believed it, anyway.

But what did that imply? Could she be the result of more than a century of selective breeding? How would that work anyway? Clearly the decisions did not factor in anything as superficial as race. That much was clear. Intelligence must factor in. She knew that she was smarter than the average person, at least in math and computer science.

So what? That proved nothing. That was just her stupid ego trying to ignore the fact that if this was true, her parents thought of her as no more than a science experiment.

No, that wasn't true either. They had loved her. And all of this would mean that Frank was sane, and the conspiracies were real. Which was more likely? That there existed a centuries old secret eugenics society, and she herself was superhuman, or that Frank was delusional and mentally ill.

She had to get a grip. Literally. Frank was flying around curves and over hills, and if she gave in to her emotions, she'd probably fall off the bike and die.

But what about the FBI? They were still tracking Frank. Were they tracking her too? What could Frank have done to get the FBI so riled up that they were still monitoring him? She doubted it had anything to do with her; they seemed genuinely surprised to hear about Emiko. And the genetic experimentation that ruined Frank a decade ago had been surpassed by the next generation of technology.

Like the tip of the proverbial iceberg, there had to be more to this. A lot more.

 ⁓

Their trip ended by one of the smaller western lakes, in the parking lot of the Lakeshore General Store. The scene was a living picture of the American weekend retreat. Calm blue water filled the background and a two-story log cabin anchored the setting. Fir trees and picnic tables surrounded the store, and a path led out to a dock. A few cars, several campers, and a fishing boat presided over the parking area.

Frank dismounted the motorcycle and strode purposefully into the store. Georgia ran after him, her heart still pounding from the wild ride.

"Is Martha around?" Frank asked the clerk working the single cash register.

"She's upstairs in the office. You can go on up."

"Thanks." He called over his shoulder to Georgia, "You shop, I'll be right back."

Remembering the sparse inventory in the cabin, Georgia found the shopping baskets. She was picking through some local apples when Frank returned, carrying a parcel and accompanied by a gray-haired woman. She was almost as tall as Frank, and close to his age.

"Why, if it isn't Georgia Steele."

"Ms. Meacham?" Georgia reached out a hand to the school librarian, but the woman responded by wrapping strong, spindly arms around her.

"Do call me Martha," she said, releasing her grasp on Georgia. "I saw your name in the papers last year when you took down that drug ring in Atlanta. That was quite something."

"There were many people who worked on that. I guess you're not working at Harmony School?"

"No dear, I retired years ago and bought this store. It keeps me busy."

"I see."

"Well I know you two have things to do. Frank, will I see you soon?" Their eyes met.

"I hope so," he said. He looked like he meant it.

Frank paid cash for the groceries, which he handed to Georgia to carry. As they left the store he rotated the parcel, about twelve inches square, inspecting it from all angles. It was covered in packing tape and multi-colored stickers in several languages.

"What's in the box?" Georgia asked.

"I'm not entirely sure." He headed in the direction of a picnic table set off to one side of the parking lot.

Georgia hurried after him, carrying the bags of groceries.

Frank perched over the box like a vulture guarding a fresh kill. From the pocket of his jeans he fished out an all-in-one tool. Using one of the blades, he carefully cut through the thick layers of tape.

Inside were two brightly colored souvenir shirts, each sealed in a plastic bag. A lime green t-shirt said, "Divers Do it Deeper in Roatan," and a red one had an image of Mayan carvings from Copan. Frank rummaged in the bottom of the box and retrieved a birthday card. He read the card, holding it close to his body.

"It's your birthday?"

"Not even close." Frank replied.

Georgia reached for a shirt.

"Don't touch them."

"The t-shirts?"

He did not reply but instead stood looking out over the lake, eyes unfocused. Frank was so weird. The "mentally unstable" hypothesis was starting to seem more likely.

The groceries they bought were on the other side of the table, along with Frank's keys and cell phone. Georgia gathered them up and went back to the motorcycle. After she stowed the bags, she dialed Marcus.

The call went to voicemail. Not surprising, since it would come up as an unknown caller. She left a quick message telling him she was fine.

Frank was already back, strapping the box to the back of the bike. His hand went out to take the phone. "Let's get going."

৵

Georgia was bored. Frank had left soon after they got back from the store, taking with him the grilled cheese and tomato sandwich she'd cooked for lunch. He'd made her promise not to use her cell phone, and the cabin had no Wi-Fi or cable.

She fetched her laptop from her bedroom, planning to do to some preparation for her upcoming depositions, and was about to head back downstairs when she noticed Frank's bedroom door was ajar. The parcel Frank retrieved from Ms. Meacham's store lay on his bed.

Layers of packing tape and inspection stickers plastered the surface of the cardboard box, written in Spanish and English. It was postmarked Juticalpa, Olancho, Honduras. The sender of the package was Eugene Young. The box was empty except for the card.

Happy Birthday. We wish you could come here to see all Honduras has to offer. In the meantime, here is a little souvenir. Gene.

This was going to be way more interesting than work.

Georgia knew that many Wi-Fi networks were easy to break into, especially those with WEP security, but neighbor's network was not even password protected. Keeping Frank's warnings in mind—though she thought it totally unnecessary—she masked her IP information by logging into a secure VPN server. That should be enough to keep their location a secret.

She typed in *Eugene Young, Olancho, Honduras*. Several references to Doctors With Wings came up, including a picture of Dr. Young at a ceremony for the opening of a new clinic. A slight man with a narrow face and short gray hair, he was smiling and holding the ribbon for a scissor-bearing, rotund Hispanic man. Eugene Young looked like a normal person. What could he be doing with Frank?

She then broadened her search to all Dr. Eugene Youngs but found thousands of results across the country. It would take time to find and track the right one. She needed help.

Dave was online and accepted her video call. He must have had the computer on his lap, for his smiling face and balding head appeared strangely distorted. It was funny and comforting, and instantly made Georgia happy.

"George, how's it going? How are things up north?"

"Interesting," she said.

"Where are you?"

"I'm staying in a cabin on one of the Finger Lakes."

"The Finger Lakes, near Ithaca? Did you find Frank?" Dave asked.

"I did." Georgia waved her hands in the air in a celebratory wave.

"I figured as much. You said you were going to New York." Dave nodded and got even closer to the camera, probably going for conspiratorial but achieving only creepy. "Have you learned anything?"

"He's been pretty cagey. I haven't gotten very far yet."

"Well it has only been a day. How long are you going to stay?"

"Not sure, probably a few more days," Georgia said.

"Anything I can do to help?"

"Maybe."

"Shoot." Dave sat back and picked up a pen, and Georgia was thankful she did not have to look at his nose hairs anymore.

"Can you configure your search bots to look for a Dr. Eugene Young? He's a doctor in Honduras, with Doctors With Wings."

"Of course. Can I ask why? It's kind of random."

"He's been in contact with Frank, and I agree it is random. That's what I want to know. Who is this guy and how would Frank know him?"

"Easy enough to do. Anything else?"

Georgia almost said no. But with Frank around keeping her on a short leash, she wouldn't be able to figure out how much of what he had told her was true and how much was Frank being crazy.

"There is one thing. There was this English guy, named Christopher Edwards, who lived around the mid-1800s. He may be associated with Charles Darwin and Francis Galton. And he may have been part of a group called the Guardians."

Dave was laughing. "Seriously? What in the world are you up to Georgia Steele?"

"I'd rather not tell you, to keep you unbiased."

"Alrighty then. You've piqued my interest. I'll send my crawlers out and see what they find."

"Thanks a ton. We'll talk soon."

∽

Georgia was hoping a nice steak dinner and bottle of wine would relax Frank and keep him seated in one place long enough to talk to her. If she could believe Frank's story, she finally had a lead on who she was. How much was true, and how much was delusion and paranoia?

The kitchen was sparsely stocked but there was a heavy cast iron pan, perfect for cooking the steaks. These she seasoned with salt and pepper and put back into the refrigerator. She sliced half a loaf of bread, added garlic powder and butter, and placed it in the oven. A simple salad with lettuce and tomatoes completed the meal. She opened a bottle of Zinfandel to let it breathe.

"Well that took all of ten minutes. What to do now?"

Between the kitchen and the back deck was a cozy living area with a fireplace, and the only part of the cabin she had yet to explore. Georgia ran her fingers across the arm of the faded recliner. The leather was cracked in places, but still soft. It had aged better than the floral sofa, which was faded and lumpy.

She knelt in front of a bookcase doing double duty as a stand for a television and a DVD player. Jigsaw puzzles, Scrabble, and Go did not gain her interest, nor did most of the books: historical romance, light summer mysteries, an ancient copy of *Lord of the Flies*. Only one book, *Fever Dream* by Douglas Preston and Lincoln Child, looked interesting

She took it over to the sofa, but when she sat down, something sharp scratched her ankle. The culprit was a loose upholstery tack. Determined to keep the tack from its next victim, Georgia kneeled in front of the sofa to work it from the fabric. From this vantage point, she saw magazines caught between the sofa and end table. No, that was not right. The table had a shelf, but it had been turned to face into the sofa, blocking it from view.

Moving the end table, Georgia was surprised to see these were not old magazines, but recent journals from the Cornell Library: *Virology* and *Human and Experimental Toxicology*. Torn pieces of notebook paper marked several articles: "Environmental Toxins: Impacts of Pesticides on Male Fertility," and "Immunological Requirements for Protection Against Acute versus Persistent Retrovirus Infections." Tucked in the back of the toxicology journal was a printout of an online article: "Efficacy of an Endogenous Retrovirus DNA Vaccine."

"What in the world are you up to Frank?"

The answer came as the roar of a motorcycle turning down the street and then into the driveway.

❧

Frank's shoulders stooped as if he was carrying the weight of the world. He shuffled into the house and through the sliding glass door. Georgia followed.

"Hi Georgia, did you have a nice afternoon?" Georgia said. "Why yes Frank, thanks for asking."

His back was to her as he faced the lake. The helmet slipped from his hand and thudded against the deck.

"Frank, why are you in New York?"

"I came to pay my respects to Emiko's mother and to see some old friends," he said, his voice flat.

"Like Ms. Meacham?"

"Yes. I intended to leave earlier, but something came up."

"Something to do with Gene Young? And retroviruses?"

Frank spun around sharply, his expression one of confusion. "How do you know that?"

"The box, the journal articles."

He lifted his hands and opened his mouth, but no words followed. He exhaled slowly. "You have to go," he said.

"What?" That took her by surprise.

"I have some things I need to do here, and they have nothing to do with you."

"No."

"No, what?"

"You're not allowed to do that. You're going tell me exactly what is going on. I still need to know why you created Emiko. And how my parents were involved."

"But—"

"But nothing. She was my daughter," Georgia said, over articulating each word.

Frank winced.

"That's right, my daughter. You don't get to brush over that. You had no right to do that to me."

"Don't you get it? She's dead. And your parents are dead." He lowered his head and pinched the bridge of his nose. "I've already put you in too much danger as it is." His voice dropped, "Georgie, you're all I have left. I don't want to lose you too."

"Frank, I'm not a little girl anymore. Stop trying to protect me. My life is my responsibility now." A cold breeze blew through. Georgia crossed her arms in front of herself. "Let's go inside. I'm going to make dinner, and you're going to finish telling me everything. Then I will consider leaving."

CHAPTER 28

FINGER LAKES REGION, NEW YORK

THE OLD CABIN had little insulation and no heat. The gas fireplace was likely better suited to ambiance than thermal conductivity, but Georgia lit it anyway. Either would help to counteract the gloom in the room.

She sat Frank at the breakfast bar, poured him a glass of wine, and then went for the steaks. "How did Harmony School start?" she said. Georgia glanced around furtively, and Gene could make out heavy bookshelves along the walls behind her. Was she in a public library?

"Frank?"

"Oh, sorry." His lips curled in a forced smile. "Harmony was previously the New York Founder's Preparatory School. It was an elite school and produced senators, governors, and various other politicians. It closed shortly after its hundredth birthday."

"Why?"

"The school blamed it on the '87 economic crisis, but mostly it was mismanagement and pilfering of the trust fund." He sipped his wine. "*They* bought it soon after it closed."

"They? The Guardians?"

"Yes. They changed the name. They fired most of the faculty

and staff and replaced them with a mix of young, talented teachers and organization insiders. Their mission was to accept only those students with the highest potential and to mold them into the most capable and sought-after graduates, which is pretty much the same as today."

"As when I was there," Georgia said.

"They already had a school in the UK with a stellar reputation, and so they had no problem getting students."

"Another school? I didn't know that."

"Yes, it's old and exclusive. But their schools have another purpose. Creating a superior line of humans requires not just education but a lot of research and testing."

"So they were really serious?" Georgia lit a burner on the old range. She turned around to look at Frank. "But how do you know if one human is superior to another?"

He raised one shoulder in a half-hearted shrug. "None of us knew their reasoning, but the staff collected data on just about anything you can imagine." Frank began counting on his fingers. "IQ, reading, writing, math, languages, physical stamina, strength, and health. Creative skills—problem solving, music, painting, literature, and even poetry. We also collected detailed information on the parents—race, ethnicity, religion, income, education, and professional achievements.

"We never knew which were the Guardians' students, although we had our guesses. All of the students were very smart, the brightest in the country. And Harmony is designed to uncover and nurture each child's special gifts, like yours for languages and mathematics. You knew three languages by the time you were in third grade, I believe?"

"Four, if you count English."

"Of course." Frank smiled, though he did not look happy. "Your father was in charge of the testing and reporting. Your mother and I kept our day jobs, so to speak. But the school let us use the data for our research and publish the results. Your mother made quite a name for herself."

"I knew that."

"I also benefitted from the relationship. I kept doing IVF for the super wealthy. By then the human genome had been mapped, and the Guardians were funding any DNA research I wanted that would help our work progress. I think we knew we were selling our souls to the devil, but we were having the time of our lives and riding the intellectual high."

Georgia finished cooking the steaks and served them with the salad and warm bread. She refilled Frank's wine and then poured a glass for herself. Taking the seat next to him, she asked, "So, what happened?"

Frank already had a piece of steak on the way to his mouth, so Georgia motioned for him to eat. "Everything was fine for a long time," Frank said between bites. "My top researcher, Alex, had been working with me to identify a rare genetic defect that could cause infertility in women. Because of a missing protein, embryos were unable to stick to the wall of the uterus. We even published a paper together."

Frank continued to describe the research that ultimately led to his Nobel Prize.

"It was total luck, you know. Finding the gene and determining the defect was in the promoter region. But the important discovery was when we realized these regions control gene expression."

"But you never continued the research," Georgia mused.

"I know. Don't get me wrong. We thought it was very interesting. I just couldn't see how we'd use it in our work. The real benefit to us was that by coating the embryos in the missing proteins, we dramatically increased the success rate for in vitro transplants. The field took off."

"What does this have to do with your researcher? What did he do?"

Frank stared at her.

"Alex," Georgia said.

"Oh yes, Alex," Frank said, with a wave of his hand. "Alex was apparently researching retroviruses, unbeknownst to me."

"Some of those journal articles are about retroviruses. What are they?"

"A normal virus reproduces inside the cells of living hosts, destroying the cells in the process. But a retrovirus inserts itself into the genome of the host. It's replicated along with all the original DNA without destroying the infected cells. It can then be passed on to new generations of cells and potentially to any offspring."

"A virus can be inherited?"

"I guess you can think of it that way." Frank picked at the remains of his steak. "It turns out that Alex had reverse engineered a retrovirus that could deliver the DNA mutation."

"And that caused the sterilization?"

"Not on its own, though I didn't know that at the time. The woman would still need to be exposed to certain drugs or chemicals that would, in effect, turn off the gene."

Georgia shook her head. It just wasn't adding up, and she said something to that effect.

Frank looked up from his steak and turned to Georgia. His expression was solemn. "Alex was testing the retroviruses. At the clinic. On human embryos."

"That's horrible."

"As soon as I found out, I fired Alex. I also asked your parents what they thought I should do. You see, Alex was part of the organization. Your mother wanted to call the authorities, but your father and I thought we should notify our contact first. Turns out we didn't need to argue. He arrived the next day."

"What did he say?"

"That the world, as we know it, was coming to an end. That human over-population and climate change were threatening our existence, and that they were going to do something about it. Alex, he said, was looking for humane options to save us all. He intimated that there were other options being considered, ones that were not as humane. He said Alex would leave, but we could say nothing. Your mother walked out at that point."

"When was this?"

"Not too long before... I guess you were a senior in high school. Anyway, Mar—, our contact, told your father and me exactly how it would be. We would never say anything or we would lose our jobs, our reputations, and you. We would continue to work for them and continue the progress we were making. And then he made a final demand."

"What?"

Frank responded by dropping his head and covering his face with his hands. He was shutting down.

Georgia cleared the plates and did the dishes. She poured him a third glass of wine and led him to the sofa, while she leaned against the fireplace mantle.

"Frank, I know this is hard," Georgia said, trying to keep the rising frustration out of her voice. "You need to tell me. I have a right to know."

"I'm sorry, Georgie. I'm so sorry." His head drooped; his face hidden.

"Stop acting like a child," she was almost yelling now. She went over and shook him by the shoulders.

Frank's head snapped back. Tears were streaming down his face. Astonished, Georgia stepped back. "We had made you against their wishes and they wanted final payment—your eggs."

"That's ludicrous," Georgia said. Then she lifted up her shirt, revealing a small scar on the right side of her abdomen. "I still have my appendix, don't I?"

Frank nodded. "Your mother never would have agreed. We never told her, James and I. Karen was never scared of them.

She never believed in their power. She never believed such evil could exist.

"But somehow, she found out. It was almost a year later, just after Christmas. Maybe your father told her. I don't know. But she called me and left me a scathing voice message. She said she was not going to ignore this. Two days later..." Frank removed his glasses to wipe his eyes.

Georgia's breath caught in her throat and she thought she would faint. She held to the mantle for support and closed her eyes. And remembered....

◈

"Karen, you can't do this."

"Watch me, James." Georgia's mother stood on one side of the kitchen island, wearing an apron, her father on the other, coffee cup in hand. A mixing bowl sat on the counter between them, along with a carton of eggs, flour, and other pancake ingredients.

"I've already made the appointment. I'm going, and you can't stop me. Someone has to know. They can't get away with this."

Georgia's parents were so engrossed in their argument they had not seen her standing in the hallway.

"Who can't get away with what?" Georgia heard herself say. She could smell the fresh coffee and maple syrup, the latter gently warming on the stovetop. But every time she remembered this scene, it was as if she was an independent observer and not an actual participant. She knew what would happen next and was powerless to stop it.

"Nothing, sweetie," her mother said.

"I'm tired of being treated like a child. I'm in college."

"It's nothing, Georgie," her father said, his voice reassuring.

Then, like every other time, she and her mother got into the worst fight they ever had. It ended with Georgia storming up to her room, packing her bags, and her father begrudgingly taking her to the station where she caught a train back to school. She never saw her parents again.

⮟

"They died," Georgia whispered.

"Yes." Frank crossed his arms, rocking back and forth. "Just before New Years, the FBI showed up at my clinic. Your parents were supposed to meet with them the day after the fire."

"Are you saying my parents were murdered?" *It couldn't be true.* "The fire was ruled an accident."

"I don't know for sure. But it seemed too coincidental. After that, I was afraid they'd kill me and you too."

"Me?"

"You were supposed to be home that night, Georgie. You are only alive because you got into that fight with your parents."

Georgia's head was spinning. "You still haven't told me about Emiko."

"I know. I'm getting to that. I didn't know what to do. I wanted to run fast and far away. Except leaving in the dead of night would look too suspicious. I put the clinic and my house up for sale and sold most of my belongings.

"Then a small miracle happened. The Moris came to me and wanted a child. We might all be killed, but something good could come from this. If something happened to me or you, Emiko would carry on your bloodline. You see, I had saved a few of your eggs."

"You made her as evidence?"

"No." Frank shook his head. "Well, I don't know. I thought you were the most wonderful thing in the world. The perfect human. I just couldn't give that up."

"You had no right."

"I know. After the Mori's IVF procedure, the FBI came back. They said I was using embryos for genetic engineering, and that maybe I killed your parents because they were going to report me. They accused me of the very things Alex had done."

"Why didn't you tell them the truth?"

"Why would they believe me? Someone had planted evidence to make it look like I did it all." Frank looked as if he would cry again. "I couldn't tell the truth without exposing everything, which would place you and Emiko in danger. The Guardians wanted me gone. I had no choice but to run. But before I did, I compiled every piece of documentation I could find and hid it away. I told our contact if anything happened to you I would go public. Then I went far away from you. And Emiko."

"It ruined your life," Georgia said. She sat down beside her godfather and put her arm around him.

"It was already ruined. And now she's gone. And you are here, and I am putting you in danger."

Frank was on edge, but she could not stop now. There was one last topic. "What about Gene Young? Who is he?"

"He's a doctor in Honduras with Doctors With Wings. He contacted me because he couldn't find anyone else who would listen to him."

"Go on."

"He found a drop in the birth rate among teenage girls for a few of the villages where he practices."

The normality of the statement shocked Georgia.

It must have showed on her face, for Frank said, "I know. On the surface it means nothing. But he sent me his data, and it was clear that something was going on. It's the second time this has happened there. I think these girls are actually the second generation to be infected. They show no sign of the retrovirus in their blood. That was where I was today. I borrowed a friend's lab."

"The t-shirts?"

"One shirt was soaked with water containing the virus, the other with blood samples. He must have found the original source of the virus. It was heavily degraded." Frank snatched the wine glass and tilted it high, swallowing the last few drops.

"And?"

"I sequenced the RNA in the water. The retrovirus is constructed in the same way as the one Alex made in the lab. In my lab."

"What does that mean?"

"That the Guardians went from here to Central America and decided to expand their testing."

"It would be just the place to start," said Georgia. "What order of magnitude are we looking at here?"

"What do you mean?"

"What is the scale of what's going on in Central America?"

"I'm not sure, but I think just a few villages, probably a thousand people. Maybe more, maybe less."

Georgia got off the couch and slowly circled the small living area, assessing the situation. A thousand people in a remote section of a poor country. No one would care. And they could keep doing to others what they did to her, her parents, and Emiko. Unless she and Frank could find a way to stop them.

"Frank, if we can prove that this is the same virus that was developed years ago, then maybe we can get the FBI off your back and help those people in Central America at the same time."

"I doubt they can he helped; they were infected a long time ago."

"At least we can expose this so maybe it won't happen again. These villagers need to know what's going on. They need to know what they are carrying. We have to control the spread."

Frank looked up, shaking his head. "You don't understand. These people are ruthless. The FBI is nothing compared to them."

"They murdered my parents. They may have killed Emiko. What else can they do? I have no more family outside of you, and I want you back."

Frank stared into the fire. He nodded almost imperceptibly. "I wonder if it's still there."

"What?"

"Before I left the country, I hid a sample of the original retro-virus at Harmony."

"Why didn't you give it to the FBI before?"

"Because it wouldn't have made a difference. They still would have thought I did all those terrible things. 'A secret organization framed me' is not a plausible defense."

"Then why did you keep it?"

"Insurance. I told them, the Guardians. It was part of what would be leaked if anything happened to me, or to you."

"And it's still there?"

"I'm not sure."

Georgia leaned with her back against the mantle and the warmth spread against the back of her legs. The fire had gotten quite hot. Just like this situation.

"Georgie?"

"Sorry, what?"

"I hid it in the basement of the library, where all the records were stored."

"I imagine we can't just saunter up to the school and collect it."

"No. But we can't wait long. I'm surprised the FBI hasn't shown up already."

"Maybe we should just wait for them. Tell them what's going on."

Frank's expression remained blank.

"No, you're right. What do you know about the school operations?"

Frank told her everything he knew, and before the night was out they had a plan.

CHAPTER 29

FINGER LAKES REGION, NEW YORK

GEORGIA AND FRANK rose early the next morning and went to a coffee shop that had Wi-Fi. Being Saturday, the store was quiet with few customers.

Georgia was on her laptop searching the internet when Frank handed her a large latte. "There is a girls soccer game at two thirty," she said. "It's perfect. We can stop at a grocery store on the way for some supplies."

They arrived at the school before two. Harmony had all the appearance of a typical Northeastern prep school, sitting on 160 acres with a central campus of red brick buildings. Not much had changed since Georgia attended, except for an increase in security.

A new guardhouse stood at the front entrance and all the other entrances were gated. According to a posting on the school website, all buildings had security cameras and electronic keyed entrances, and aside from the dorms, were completely inaccessible at night.

But on this bright Saturday afternoon in October, the gates were open and the campus was active. Frank entered by the athletic fields, between cars ferrying students from the opposing teams. He parked the motorcycle in the crowded lot filled with SUVs.

Georgia walked with him to the campus center, where the

library stood off the main courtyard. It was the first time Georgia had been back since her parents died. The trees were taller, the buildings seemed smaller. Students read in the sunshine, and families strolled around the grounds. The younger children pointed out the sights of their new weekday home.

As Georgia and Frank approached the door to the library, it opened. A gangly youth, more student than security guard, held the door as they entered the vestibule. He looked out of sorts, balancing a security belt full of gadgets and a cast on his right wrist.

"Hi," Georgia said, smiling. "How did you do that?"

The guard smiled sheepishly. "Riding my bicycle to work. Some jerk cut me off. My first week on the job."

"I hope you're left-handed?"

"Nope," he said. "Just my luck."

Georgia wrestled a book out of her bag, "My daughter Kaitlyn left this at home last weekend, and I'm sure it's overdue. Can we just drop it off?"

"Sure." He gestured with his cast in the direction of the grocery bags. "Can I ask what else you have in there?"

She opened her bag to reveal a jumbo box of goldfish crackers, a bag of pretzels, chocolate chip cookies, and other assorted snacks. Frank followed suit.

"Wow, what great parents," he said, eyeing the treats. Frank blushed.

"I think you made my uncle's day."

Checking his watch, Frank said, "Kaitlyn's game starts soon. Let's get going."

The smell of old books brought back a slew of memories. Georgia slipped the book into the drop below the front desk, half expecting to see Ms. Meacham. She asked the woman in her place if they could use the restrooms. The librarian eyed them both, then pointed down a hallway. Once away from the desk, Georgia hurried to keep up with Frank as he zig-zagged his way between the stacks to a corner staircase.

Once in the basement Frank led her down a corridor and around a corner, to a door with a placard that read *Records*. The dark window in the door revealed nothing of the room's contents. The door was locked with a keyed deadbolt.

Frank sighed and began to turn around, but Georgia motioned for him to stay. She fished a key chain from her pocket and inserted one of the keys into the lock. Next she pulled a metal flashlight from the box of goldfish crackers. Using the end like a hammer, she hit the key as she turned it in the lock. The door opened.

Frank stared, wide-eyed.

"Bump key. Blame Marcus," she whispered.

Inside, the door's window cast enough ambient light to reveal rows of tall, double-wide filing cabinets. The scent of Lysol clung to the air.

"So this is why I couldn't find anything on line," she mumbled.

"What?" Frank said.

"Never mind, let's go." She nodded.

Frank struck a similar path as he had on the upper floor, weaving in between the rows of cabinets as he headed to the far corner of the room. He stopped at the far wall. "Damn," he whispered, and pointed to a metal filing cabinet against the wall. "It's behind that."

The cabinet was too heavy for them to move. And it was locked. Georgia found several paper clips in the drawer of a nearby cubicle and bent them into right angles. She slipped the metal prongs into the lock, jiggling both until it opened. "Stop staring and help," she told Frank.

They emptied the top drawer, and together pushed against one side of the cabinet. It moved away from the wall, scraping across the concrete floor. Georgia cringed at the sound.

Frank pushed by her into the narrow recess. "Light?"

Georgia held the flashlight for Frank as he poked and prodded at the unfinished brick wall. One brick shifted under his touch, and he slowly rocked it out of its resting place. A second brick followed. Frank stuck his hand into the wall and extracted a small Styrofoam box, about five inches square and two inches high. He opened the container. Georgia shone the light on his find. A dozen glass microscope slides nestled in the case. She was backing up to give him room to get out from behind the cabinet when the lights came on, momentarily blinding her.

"Freeze. Put up your hands where I can see them." The wavering voice came from the doorway.

The student turned security guard was scissor stepping towards them, his right leg leading while the left followed. A bright yellow gun wavered in the air, held awkwardly in a trembling hand. His eyes were wide with fear.

Georgia raised her hands, palms out. "I'll hold him off," she whispered to Frank, but kept her attention on the guard. "We need to get you and that box out of here." With what she hoped was a calm voice, she said, "Please be careful with that."

The youth brought his cast up to the gun, and the trembling lessened.

"That's better," she said, her heart pounding.

Frank slowly extracted himself from the cabinet.

"Don't move," the guard said, voice pleading.

"It's okay," Georgia said. She glanced back until she made eye contact with Frank, then rolled her eyes in the direction of the door, willing him to move. Addressing the guard, she said, "Is that a Taser? Do all you guys have one?"

"We find Tasers less threatening to the student body, but our head of security carries real weaponry." The cool, composed voice belonged to a short blond woman wearing a navy suit with conservative pumps. Next to her was a pudgy, prematurely balding man pointing a real gun. At Frank.

"Hello, Marcie," Frank said.

"Frank Anderson? What in the hell are you doing here? Haven't you caused this school enough heartache and shame?"

"You know I never did any of that. You know who the real monsters are."

"I know no such thing. You were the one who broke the law. What in God's name are you doing here now?"

Georgia searched for a way out of this predicament. The hole in the wall was hidden by the filing cabinet. But Frank still held the box in his hand.

"And Georgia Steele. You don't remember me, do you Georgia? Marcie Smith, I'm the assistant principal now. I've read all about you. We keep up with our more notable grads. I'm guessing you picked the lock on the door?" She smiled; her lips pinched tight. "These locks are old and easy to pick. But we now have motion detectors and silent alarms. Since most of our break-ins are caused by students, we prefer to handle these things internally."

"You didn't call the police?" Georgia asked.

"No, not yet."

"Marcie, we just came for this," Frank held out the box.

"It could help clear Frank's name," Georgia said.

"If you just let us go, you'll never see me again. You know it's the right thing to do," Frank said.

The woman appeared to be weighing her options.

"Mrs. Smith?" the pudgy man asked.

A door banged against a wall, and they all jumped. "FBI. Put down your weapons," a voice yelled. "Don't move."

"You called the FBI?" Frank asked.

"No," Marcie said.

Footsteps echoed off the tile floor and shadows jumped across the walls. Georgia caught glimpses of a few figures as they fanned out across the room, methodically searching the maze of cabinets.

"Don't move," the same voice called out again. It came from a middle-aged agent in a suit, the first to reach them. He was accompanied by another in an FBI-emblazoned jacket. This man held a gun, steady in two outstretched hands.

More agents converged upon them, weaving trails through the cabinets like ants rushing to attack an intruder threatening the mound. She caught a familiar face standing in the back. "Sam?" Georgia yelled. "What the hell?"

"Put down your weapons," the man in charge repeated. "Both of you."

The young guard was shaking all over now. He was all thumbs as he attempted to extract the Taser from his left hand with the one in the cast. An agent standing behind him reached around, as if to help.

"No!" Georgia screamed. She felt all the attention in the room shift to her. But she was only concerned with the guard, and the series of events that she could see unfolding but could not stop.

The agent grabbed he guard's arm and the Taser went off, rattling and snapping. The probes sailed through the air into the armed FBI-jacketed agent. Piercing shots rang out as he fell down, twitching. Georgia dropped to the floor, face down, hands over her head and ears. A metal chair screeched against the floor. She heard shouts, scuffling, and a thud.

"Get on the ground!"

"Cease fire!"

"Put your hands up!"

Then it was over. Silence. Georgia moved her hands, turned her head to the side, and opened her eyes.

Frank lay on his side, staring at her. His face was clenched in pain, a widening circle of red spread over his white t-shirt.

"Frank," she cried. Georgia pulled herself to him, crawling on her elbows.

"My Georgie," he whispered. "I love you so much. I'm so sorry."

Georgia touched her forehead to Frank's. She brushed his cheek with her fingers. "I love you, too." She sat up and cradled his head in her lap.

"I acted like a coward." Frothy blood dripped from Frank's mouth as he struggled to speak. "You're brave. I'm so proud of you."

He said something else, too soft to hear. She bent over, but he had lost consciousness.

Rough hands pulled at her, and she struggled to keep Frank's head from hitting the ground. An agent removed Frank's leather jacket and examined his chest. He cut a swath of fabric from his shirt.

"Put pressure here." He placed her hand and the cloth over the wound in Frank's chest. "We've got internal bleeding." He felt for a pulse, counting the beats. "Come on, man."

Georgia barely registered the commotion in the room, though she thought Sam might be talking to her. All her focus was on Frank. Her godfather. Her only family left. His breathing was shallow and irregular. He grew paler by the minute.

"Please, please," she whispered. "Please don't leave me."

The agent gently placed Frank's hand by his side. "I'm afraid he's gone."

"George." Sam tugged her arm. "Come on. There's nothing you can do."

She leaned over on her hands and knees and kissed Frank's forehead. She buried her face in his neck, willing him to come back.

Sam lifted her off the ground and embraced her. She leaned against him, steadying herself. The trail of blood was still seeping from Frank's body—the only vestige of life that remained, and it was fleeing. It was nearing his leather jacket, hastily thrown aside.

She broke free of Sam's grip and snatched up the jacket before the blood reached it. She hugged it to her body, then put it on and wrapped it around herself tightly. Keys in the pocket poked against her stomach. She tried to see Frank, pushing between two men.

"Take her outside," one of the senior agents said.

Sam ushered her out of the room, his arm around her shoulder. Marci Smith and an agent stood together in the hallway. Smith's arms were folded in front of her, and she spoke in a low voice. The agent was recording their conversation on his cell phone.

Georgia felt a sudden urge to get out of there. She bolted down the hallway to the staircase, pushing past the assistant principal. She heard Sam call out and knew he would follow. Georgia ran up the steps to the main floor and out an emergency exit door, through the central campus, past the athletic fields, and to the parking lot. She grabbed Frank's helmet from the seat of his bike.

Blind with tears and rage, she started the bike and took off. A police car blocked the nearest exit from the campus. She braked hard, the bike fishtailed, and Georgia struggled to keep it under control. She just managed to steer it around the cruiser and onto the road.

She had no idea where she was going, and it did not matter.

CHAPTER 30

FINGER LAKES REGION, NEW YORK

GEORGIA COULDN'T WAIT to get out of the funeral home. This was nothing short of torture.

"…and we also carry carved marble or wooden urns. Or these modern ones, which hold an eight by ten of your loved one. We have some nice stands and plaques, and we also make movies. Here let me get you the materials for that." The fat man lifted his arm to open a cabinet drawer, exposing a yellowed armpit.

"No, please. I'll just take the ashes now. I'm going to scatter them."

"Well, if you're sure."

"I'm sure."

"Take this with you, in case you change your mind. I'll be just a minute." He handed her a glossy brochure and waddled off into the back.

Georgia put down the brochure and wiped her hand on her jeans. The funeral home was a freakish place with plastic ornaments on the lawn and a life-size statue of the Virgin Mary at the center of a fountain. Inside was no better. Themed rooms presented a myriad of ways to send loved ones off to their "next state of being." The

Mount Olympus theme, the Disney Theme, and the Zen theme—
she could've been buying a timeshare.

The sweaty man finally appeared with Frank's ashes in what
looked to be a cardboard shoe box. She took the box from him and
propelled her way out, repeatedly declining additional memorial
products and services.

She found Sam leaning against his car, a black sedan. He had
on sunglasses and a dark suit, every bit the stereotypical FBI agent.
She cursed her eyes for enjoying the sight. How could they betray
her so?

"Can you take me to my rental car?"

"Georgia, come on. I'm your dedicated bodyguard until we
get to Atlanta. I'm going to do my best not to screw that up." Sam
nodded to the box she held. "Where would you like to go?"

"Taughannock Falls."

❧

The roar of the falls was deafening. Georgia leaned against the railing
of the footbridge for a long time, staring at the hypnotic wall of
water. But instead of quieting her mind, the sounds only amplified
the inner voices in her head. The day's earlier conversation would
not go away.

It had culminated with Sam's boss, that bitch Katherine Vance,
blackmailing her. "Ms. Steele, we have an agreement then? You
are not to discuss the circumstances of Anderson's death, his little
Honduras research project, or any ties the two might have into a fic-
tional, secret organization known as the Guardians." She laughed.
"I can't believe I'm even saying that. It sounds like a Bond movie.
An old Bond movie."

"If it doesn't exist, then why do you care if I talk about it?"

"And in return, we will not press charges against you. You can
return to your life in Atlanta as if nothing happened. You are lucky,
Ms. Steele, that Agent Kelly likes you."

"He needs me."

"I assure you, he could get what he needed, and we could still put you away for a long time. But you know what he doesn't need? Your accomplices."

"What are you talking about?"

"Marcus West, David Cohen, Patricia Erickson, and Diane Erickson."

"They have nothing to do with this." Georgia had been both surprised and horrified at the mention of the names.

"Oh, but they might. Marcus has some questionable accounting practices that could be very injurious to his business, and David, well, you never know what inappropriate things you might find on a university laptop. Pornography, for example."

"He would never—" and then the realization hit. "You bitch."

"I've been called worse." Katherine Vance leaned back in her chair and smiled, a cat-that-ate-the-canary smile. "So, we have an agreement, then?"

◈

Georgia held the box against her chest. Everything had been taken away from her, and she had put her friends into harm's way. She put her hand in the box and rubbed the rough powder between her fingers. A crack of lightning flashed above the falls. The sky had turned dark gray, and the air smelled of rain. The first drops mixed with the ashes spilling into the river below, washing away the last vestige of her family.

Sam was dutifully waiting by the car, standing under a large black umbrella. "I know it doesn't mean much coming from me, but I'm really sorry," he said, opening the door for her.

"Can I go back to the cabin and get my things?" She already knew the answer but wanted to make a point.

"You know you can't. It's a crime scene."

"Sam, the only crime here is that your team got my godfather killed." That wasn't really true. She was the one responsible for Frank's death. The FBI was looking for him, and she knew they were following her. She should have expected something god-awful to happen.

"You'll get your things back, I promise. You got your phone, right?"

He started the car, and they headed out of the state park to the airport.

Georgia looked back over her shoulder. The last time she visited the falls was long ago for a family vacation. "The bottles."

"What?"

"I left some things in the rental car…things from my family, mementos. I need to find my rental car. Frank said it was safe."

"But the flight."

"Fuck the flight. Find out where the car is."

"How should I know?"

She glared at him.

Sam pulled the car to the side of the road and made a phone call. He explained the situation, and after a few minutes of holding, he said, "Thanks," and hung up. "It's been impounded. Not far from where you left it."

❧

The lot was part junkyard, part impound. A middle-aged man, balding and bulging, showed them to the car.

The blue Nissan appeared untouched on the outside. Georgia breathed a sigh of relief, prematurely. Inside, the car was trashed. The contents of the glove compartment littered the front seat and remnants of a fast food lunch lay in tatters on the floor boards.

She popped the trunk latch. The inside looked like a bomb had gone off in an elementary school art class. One of the boxes was missing, the artwork strewn randomly about. Macaroni covered the trunk's floor. The second box, containing the vacation bottles, was ripped and dented. Something like dirt got on her hands as she maneuvered the box closer to her. No, it was sand. Several of the bottles inside had been broken.

"Damn."

"Sorry, Georgia."

She felt Sam's hand on her shoulder and brushed it off. "Stop saying you're sorry and do something useful. See if you can find me a few new boxes will you?"

As Sam walked away in search of packing supplies, the lot owner said, "You know, he told me it was going to get broken into. That's why I brought it here. To keep it safe. Those rental car companies, they'll charge you for everything."

"Sam told you that?"

"Frank."

"You know Frank?"

"Not well, but I've known him a long time. He used to come here to source parts for his bike."

"When did he tell you to come get the car?"

"Frank said to come around six thirty or seven before it got trashed. Wouldn't think a Denny's parking lot would be so unsafe."

"Six thirty? At night?"

"Sure, Thursday night."

"And it looked like this when you got it?" The car had sat less than an hour.

"I didn't look in the trunk. The rest of the car, yeah."

Sam was already on his way back with two boxes and a roll of packing tape.

"There's a storage place right across the street," he said, by way of an explanation.

She reached her hand out to the man. "Thanks for everything."

"Don't mention it. It's my job. I'll charge the rental company, but I'm sure you'll be getting the bill."

"You can send it to him." She pointed to Sam. "Sam, give the man your address."

CHAPTER 31

ATLANTA, GA

SHOULDERING HER MESSENGER bag, Georgia marched up the sidewalk and knocked on the door. No answer. Relief flooded through her, followed by guilt.

"Just a quiet dinner," Dave had said.

But she dreaded the inevitable questioning and did not want to relive the events of the past few days. And couldn't even if she wanted.

Yesterday, as Sam drove them back from the airport, they had called Agent Sean Kelly. Georgia had held out hope that she could tell Kelly everything that had happened in New York, including being blackmailed by Sam's boss, and he could help make it right. But she never got the chance because Kelly had insisted—on speakerphone and in front of Sam—that she keep the details of what happened to herself, at least until after the depositions only a few days away. He was very busy preparing, but they would talk soon. In the meantime, Sam would act as her appointed liaison, and he would make sure she had everything she needed.

Buck up, George. She tried the knob and found the door unlocked. The tantalizing aroma of pepperoni pizza greeted her as she opened the door. "Dave? Trish?"

"We're out back," came the reply.

The front of the house was dimly lit but light streamed through the French doors from the back deck. Trish and Diane had their backs to her, talking to someone seated at the table. Probably Diane's husband.

What was Diane doing here? What was she going to tell them? Her flight response won this time, and she turned to go. And ran right into Dave.

"Umm, hi."

"I'm glad you came over," Dave said. "I'm sorry..." he stammered, "about Frank. The world can be a cruel place."

"I brought over the notes for the deposition," she said, not able to think of anything else to say.

"That can wait. We're having pizza and beer. Just us pals."

There was no way she could leave now, so she followed Dave out back.

"Hey, George," Diane and Trish said in unison.

Georgia was about to say hi to them, when Diane moved and she saw that the other guest was none other than Sam Becker, aka Sam Bennett, looking rather uncomfortable.

The smug smile on Trish's face told her all she needed to know.

After offering their condolences, everyone kept to small talk during dinner. Trish didn't ask Sam any questions or say much of anything, which was unnerving. Georgia could only imagine what they had talked about before she got there. She'd have to make sure they kept their stories straight.

As soon as Dave took the dinner plates into the house, Trish asked George, "So what did you learn?"

"About what?"

"Did you get to ask your uncle about making you before, um..."

"Trish, give it a rest," Dave called from inside the house.

"It's okay." Georgia had been planning what to say since Dave called her with the invite. "Diane, you were right. I am an IVF baby, a bonafide designer baby created by the infamous Frank Anderson. Made in a test tube, a glorified lab experiment."

"Georgia, you don't have to tell us," Sam said.

"It's alright, Sam. I owe you all an explanation. At the time I was conceived, if that's even the right term, Frank was running a high-end fertility clinic. Donors were very carefully selected, and the recipients paid a small fortune for their sperm or eggs." Georgia tried her best to sound matter-of-fact. "My parents were not able to conceive, so yes, they did IVF through the clinic and got their pick of the parental DNA. As per the protocol then, the donors were completely anonymous. The names were not even recorded, so I'll probably never be able find my genetic parents."

"They must have been super smart," said Trish.

"But your ancestry is so diverse," mused Diane.

"What about Emiko?" Trish was nothing if not persistent.

"It's not especially nice. It was simple payment. The clinic was extremely exclusive. It never performed more than a few pregnancies from any given donor. Which was part of the allure. But the costs were exorbitant. My parents had little money, so they agreed that the clinic could have my eggs to use in exchange."

Sam looked visibly relieved, but the others did not seem to notice.

"That's sick," said Trish.

"I guess they didn't think of it that way."

"Does that mean there are others out there?" Trish asked.

"Emiko was the only one. At least that's what Frank told me."

Trish frowned in apparent disappointment.

"How does Francis Galton fit into all of this?" asked Dave. "And the—what did you call them? The Guardians?"

Sam's eyes widened and he glanced at Georgia.

"Anyone want a beer?" Georgia said, rising from her seat. Coming here had been a terrible idea.

"Who is Francis Galton?" Trish asked.

"Really?" asked Dave. "Basically, the father of statistics."

"Nature versus Nurture," said Diane. "Francis Galton coined the term. He was not only a famous mathematician, but also a founder of the eugenics movement. And a cousin of Charles Darwin."

"Half cousin," corrected Dave. "You're right about the eugenics movement. Georgia thinks that Galton may have been part of an early group that called themselves the Guardians of Mankind."

"So how does this relate to our designer baby?" Trish asked.

"It doesn't," Georgia blurted. "I was wrong."

"About what?" Dave asked.

"There's no such thing as the Guardians."

"But—" Dave said.

She rushed into the house, shutting out any more of the conversation.

⤝

Georgia leaned on the kitchen counter, head down, forcing herself to take slow deep breaths.

"George?" It was Dave's familiar voice, but she jumped all the same.

"Shit, you scared me."

Dave was smiling, a goofy kid-like grin. He was excited. "I found something," he said, "about the Guardians."

The words came back to her... *you never know what you might find on a university laptop.* "No," she said, sharper than she intended.

"Are you okay?" Dave was serious now.

"Delete it. It's none of your business."

"George, you can tell me anything."

"There's nothing to tell."

"You can trust me."

"Look, I don't need your help. And I don't want your help."

"You know Trish and I—"

"Trish is a fucking airhead, just like all the others before her.

What is it with you and dumb blondes?" Georgia said. She found her bag on a chair and slung it over her shoulder. "I have to go."

"George," Dave pleaded.

"Delete it, Dave, I mean it. Delete it. Or I will."

CHAPTER 32

OLANCHO REGION, HONDURAS

GENE WOKE UP alone and groped for his glasses on the bedside table. He had been exhausted when he got home last night after working overtime at the clinic, twelve hours on top of a two-hour commute. Donning a robe, he walked through the house looking for José. He found a note by the half-full coffee pot. José had gone out to get supplies for their trip to Roatan this weekend.

Since he had some privacy, he might as well try to contact Frank Anderson. He had expected to hear from him by now, as a week had passed since he sent the samples, soaked into the tourist t-shirts.

On his laptop, he found an unusual email.

Dr. Young,

I am Frank Anderson's goddaughter. I regret to inform you that he was killed in an accident last weekend.

Frank told me about what's happening there. After he died, I told the FBI everything I know. I don't know if they can help you, but maybe they will notify someone who can. Good luck to you.

Regards,

Georgia Steele

Gene's heart was pounding, and he forced himself to take a few deep breaths. Was this a joke?

A quick internet search told him it was no joke. Frank Anderson died in an accident at the Harmony School near Ithaca, New York. Apparently, a security guard had found Frank in a restricted section. An altercation followed and the man Tasered him. Frank died from subsequent injuries. The news had not been picked up by the national press, and no mention was made of either Frank's past scientific achievements or his notoriety.

Gene reached for his coffee, his hand trembling. This would be it then. It was over. Frank had been his last hope.

He read the email again, dissecting every word. This woman, who was she? How much did she actually know? Why would she go to the FBI? Frank was fanatically secretive. A quick search for Georgia Steele found many results, but none could identify her as the woman who claimed to be Frank's goddaughter.

He responded, asking her to call him and giving her the number of the burner phone.

᧞

A reply came a day later. Georgia Steele would be willing to talk to him over a web video service such as Skype. This posed a problem. He'd used Skype before but José had always set it up. José would want to listen in on this conversation, and there were so many things he'd already kept from him—the secret call to Frank, the fact that El Progreso was involved, and the samples he had sent. Probably none of that mattered now.

᧞

That night, as José was setting up the call, he said, "I hope it brings some closure so that so you can forget this whole mess."

José was right. He should walk away. He had nothing to gain.

At the appropriate time, one word appeared in the Skype panel.

"Gene?" The avatar accompanying it was a cartoon of a girl, a Japanese anime.

"Yes," José typed.

"Ready?"

"Yes."

José connected the call, and a woman appeared on the screen. She looked to be in her late twenties, with long dark hair. José punched some buttons on the computer. "Can you hear me?"

"Yes. Who are you?" The words were clipped the voice tense. "You're not Dr. Young."

"One moment." José got up, and Gene took his place in the chair. Now he got a better look. The woman was beautiful, part Asian and maybe Latino. "Hello, Ms. Steele?"

The woman's face relaxed. "It's Georgia. You must be Gene Young."

"José, what do I do when I want to hang up?"

"Hit the big red button. Or just let me know."

"Gracias." Gene peered back into the computer.

Georgia started to say something, but Gene interrupted her. "What happened to Frank?"

"There was an accident."

"I read about it. Were you there?"

"Yes."

"What really happened to Frank? Why were you both at that school?"

Georgia Steele bit her lower lip. "Dr. Young, I'm sorry but I don't think I can help you."

"Please, Ms. Steele. Georgia."

She leaned into the computer, and he noticed her unusual eyes, amber flecked with gold. "May we speak freely?"

"Of course, why? Oh, you mean José?" Gene glanced in his direction. José was attentive, listening to every word. "He's my part-

ner and my soulmate. You can say whatever you want." A pang of
guilt pulled at Gene as he said the words, hoping they were still true.

The woman pulled up her hair, pinning it in place with a jew-
eled stick.

"My parents and Frank were best friends since college." She
then told Gene that she was an early IVF baby from his clinic.
"Frank was always part of my life growing up. I thought of him as
family." She described how Frank found the genetic defect and later
suspected that one of his researchers had found a way to introduce
it into others using a retrovirus. "You already know this, right?"

"Yes," Gene replied. "Please, go on."

"Based upon the situation there, he thought that this guy–his
old researcher–might be responsible."

As per Frank, the "guy" was Alejandra Castilla, head of El Progreso, but it seemed Ms. Steele did not know that. And he couldn't
tell her. Not with José there.

"Before he died, Frank tested the virus sample you sent. It was
very similar in composition to what he had seen before."

"What is she talking about?" José asked, in Spanish.

"Later," Gene said, waving his hand to quiet José.

"In order to prove his theory, Frank needed to get a sample of
the original," Georgia said. "We were trying to retrieve it when he
was killed."

"He was murdered for this?" José asked.

"It was really more of an accident," Georgia said.

She looked over her shoulder, Gene noticed shelves of books.
Was she in a public library?

She leaned into the speaker and continued in a whisper, "Frank
thought the people who created the original version and yours
are one and the same. He believes—believed—what you discovered was just a test of the technology. They probably have much
grander plans."

He heard José ask him to turn up the sound, but Gene sat frozen, his heart pounding.

"Dr. Young, did Frank tell you the blood samples you sent did not show signs of direct infection?" she asked.

"Which would mean these girls are the second generation?" Gene had considered that possibility. Indeed, he and Frank had talked about it. But something nagged at him. "It doesn't make sense. If that is the case, why only these girls? Why not others?"

"Frank said the retrovirus was virtually the same, but the activator had probably been improved. It could be delivered on a very specific basis. He also thought the effects could last much longer, perhaps permanently."

"My God." Gene's stomach knotted up. "Georgia, can you help us?"

"I don't see how I can."

"But you know. You understand."

"I would like to help you, really I would. But I can't."

"Can't you find someone to look at the samples? Compare them? You said yourself they will prove what happened."

"I don't have any of Frank's research, and everything you sent was lost. Dr. Young, the FBI took everything."

"I have more samples at the clinic."

"Gene, stop." José stood, a horrified expression on his bronzed face.

"My godfather is dead because of this," Georgia said, her voice trembling.

"I thought you said it was an accident," José said.

"Even more reason we can't let them get away with this!" Gene yelled at both.

José raised his hands in front of him. "Calm down."

"Frank was my last hope." Gene pleaded to Georgia, "Now you are."

Georgia shook her head. "Without Frank's evidence, we can't tie any of this together."

If he could tell her about Alejandra Castilla, she might change her mind. But he could not do that with José in the room.

"Please, just think about it." He looked hopefully to José. "We are going away for the weekend. Maybe we can talk next week?"

She sighed. "Okay."

Gene gave José his seat so he could end the call.

"One more thing…" The young woman said something, but Gene didn't catch it.

"What was that?"

José answered for her, "She wants to know where you found the virus."

"In the basement of a house I went to look at," Gene said.

After the call ended, Gene steeled himself for a fight, but José surprised him. "Why have you been keeping secrets from me?" José asked gently. "Please Gene, tell me everything."

CHAPTER 33

ATLANTA, GA

RAIN WAS FALLING in sheets so thick that Georgia could barely see the street from her shelter under the columned portico of the Richard B. Russell Federal Building.

The deposition had centered on Georgia's role in uncovering the multi-state drug running operation. The defendant, present in accordance with his constitutional rights, glared at her the entire time. The suit and tie did nothing to hide his loathsome personality, and the sound of his constant teeth sucking grated on her nerves.

But it was the defense attorney that did her in. Over the course of two hours, he grilled her ad nauseam, picking at her like the sand fleas on the Carolina coast at sunset. One tiny prick after another—no single bite enough to draw blood. And quickly he found her weakness: the murder of Atlantic-Pacific's vice president which she had witnessed. This was the raw skin most susceptible to his bites. With each question, she would recall, not the split-second shooting nor Marcus' intervention, but Frank's slow-motion death. The Taser going off and hitting the agent, the shots fired. Frank falling to floor and bleeding out. His last, forced whispers. Sam calling to her. The shots still rang in her ears, jumbling her thoughts and answers.

Eventually she broke down, unable to continue. The prosecutor requested a continuance and got one. She would need to come back in a few weeks.

"Georgia!"

It took her a moment to realize the voice was not imagined. Sam Bennett was jogging up the sidewalk, umbrella held like a shield against the blowing rain. Once under the shelter, he threaded his way through the growing crowd of federal workers waiting for the rain to subside.

"Hello," Sam said, panting and dripping. He was smartly dressed in a gray jacket with a black shirt and pants.

She considered her own gray pants and black blazer before asking, "What are you doing here? Are you stalking me?"

"Dammit, Georgia. You have not returned any of my texts or calls." As if to emphasize, he retrieved an aged smart phone from his jacket and waved it in front of her.

"Nice phone," she said, trying not to smile.

Sam shrugged. "It sucks. All the new ones go to the senior people. I got the bottom of the barrel." He put the phone away. "You're supposed to keep me in the loop." His eyebrows gathered in a pained expression. "I'm your appointed liaison, remember?"

"What's it like to be an appointed liaison?"

"I really don't know. You're my first."

A gust of wind blew across the portico, drenching them in a shower of rainwater and eliciting a groan from the crowd.

"I have to go," she said, eyeing the gray storm clouds.

"Georgia, since we are supposed to be friends here and I need to know what you're up to, how about you let me take you to dinner tonight?"

She shook her head. "You mean the department will take me to dinner. No thanks."

"Well, of course I'll let them pay. Appointed liaisons make shit."

She laughed, in spite of herself. "I've had a long week."

"How about tomorrow?"

"I'm not sure that's a good idea." What was it about him? Why couldn't he leave her alone?

"Just think about it."

A cab pulled up to the curb to let out a passenger. Georgia saw her chance. "I gotta go." She walked briskly towards the cab, glaring at a man with similar intentions. He stopped, holding up his hands, giving her a small victory for the day.

Sam caught up and held the umbrella over them while Georgia entered the taxi.

"Tomorrow, then?" he smiled.

"I'll think about it," she said, planning to do no such thing. Sam closed the door, and she did not look back.

CHAPTER 34

OLANCHO REGION, HONDURAS

GENE WAS ANXIOUS to get home. The sun had set and the last pink clouds were fading from sight when he and his nurse, Christine, finally reached the yellow stucco house.

"Here you are, Doc."

Gene gathered his things and exited the Doctors With Wings van. "Thanks for the ride," he said.

"I'll handle the paperwork today. Seeing as you're on vacation tomorrow."

"Thanks." He saw no lights on in the house. Only his car in the carport.

"See you on Tuesday," Christine called after him. "Have a nice time in Roatan. You'll love it."

Gene entered the house through the carport and turned on a light. There was a note on the kitchen counter.

Hello Lover,

Went to a last-minute meeting in Olanchito for the dam project. Back by 8, I hope. The ferry leaves from La Ceiba tomorrow at 9:30, so we need to leave by 7. Pack your things and get ready for a weekend of sun and fun.

Te amo,

Jose

Gene smiled. After the call to Georgia Steele two days ago, José had surprised him by telling him that he supported him and wanted to help. They were a team and nothing should come between them. Gene was so touched he told José it could all wait until they were back from their weekend vacation.

And today had been another nice day. He and Christine had delivered a healthy baby, the second daughter in a family of five. The parents were terribly poor, but they were so happy to see their new baby girl.

These were the people he and José fought for. And they would fight together. Things were going to be fine.

Lights swept across the kitchen wall. A car turned into the driveway. *Could José be back already?* The clock on the stove read 6:43.

Gene peered through the open mini-blinds. It was not José's pickup, but a dark SUV.

CHAPTER 35

ATLANTA, GA

GEORGIA WAS IN her pajamas curled up on the couch watching *Chinatown*. Perhaps watching was too strong a word. It was more akin to zoning out. She was exhausted. Watching Frank die, picking a fight with Dave so the FBI would leave him alone, and enduring a grueling day of depositions added up to one shitty week.

Microwave popcorn was all she could muster for dinner. She ate it while watching TV, then got bored and picked up her iPad.

"What the...?"

Someone had sent her a message using Frank's email address. This was not funny. Who had access to his account? The FBI? Them? She debated deleting it but clicked it open.

Hello Georgie,

This is an automated email. It has been a week since I've checked into my primary account, so something bad has happened to me. Or I'm in Bali with a beautiful woman and forgot to send a code to reset the timer. I'm betting on the former.

Georgie, you are the sole recipient of all of my possessions. There is no will or estate to settle; the few material things I have will be

*donated to charity. What I do have is information. Loads of it.
Much of it is confidential, some is illegal, and some dangerous to
possess. You are the only person I would entrust it to.*

*If you want it and are willing to accept any consequences, reply
to this email and attach a public key and a server FTP address.
I have a program that will place all my data on your server,
encrypted using your key. Then all of my servers will be decom-
missioned and the data destroyed (just as you taught me).*

What's the catch?

*You also have to send a unique identifier that could belong only
to you. You have three chances to send a correct ID, which should
be plenty for you. The data will self-destruct in 24 hours regardless. (I thought you'd appreciate the Mission Impossible flair.)*

*I want you to know that I love you very much. I have always
loved you. It is only to protect you that I have had to distance
myself from you.*

*I've been following your success, my dear Georgie. I am so proud
of you and I truly wish that we could have seen each other again.
Know that you are forever in my heart.*

Love,

Frank

Georgia leaned her head back and stared at the ceiling. This
whole mess was not going away. First Dave, then Gene Young—
even Sam and the FBI. None of them was willing to let it go. Now
Frank, coming back from the dead. What was she going to do?

She sighed. Who was she kidding? Of course she would try to
get Frank's files. How could she turn that down? She'd figure out
the rest later.

Georgia had programs to create all kinds of public/private keys.

But what did Frank mean by an identifier that was unique to her? It was going to be a long 24 hours.

She would need coffee.

⤳

The blaring of the car horn barely registered with Georgia, but she heard a woman scream, "Watch out!" Georgia froze while a dark sedan veered around her, horn blasting. She looked around for the source of the voice—a woman with a stroller on the sidewalk. She waved to signal she was okay, then continued across Morningside Drive.

Georgia had worked late into the night, trying to figure out the key to Frank's document library. She had tried a previous code they used many years before. It was wrong. Strike one.

She had hoped a run would clear her mind. Deep in thought and short on sleep, she only vaguely remembered running around the park and through the west side of Virginia Highlands. Now she found herself close to Dave's house. He might be able to help her figure out the puzzle. But they had not spoken since Monday, after that terrible fight. She never fought with Dave. Not ever.

She needed to apologize. Had planned to apologize. But what would she say? The FBI blackmailed me? Dave and Marcus were her only friends. She had to protect them. Even if it meant lying to them.

Trish was stretching on the front stoop of Dave's house. Georgia steeled herself and jogged up to the steps.

"Hi, Trish."

"What do you want?" Bubbly Trish was gone, replaced by a stone-cold version that Georgia found unnerving.

"I want to apologize for the other night."

Trish stood with her arms crossed. "I'm not stopping you."

"Is Dave around?"

"He's not here." Her blue eyes cast an icy stare. "You know, I can take a dumb blonde jab with the rest of them."

Georgia winced.

"But Dave, he is one of the kindest people I know, and for some reason, he really cares about you. Do you have any idea how much you hurt him?"

"I'm sorry, Trish, I really am."

"You need to apologize to him, not me."

"When will he be back?"

"He's at a conference at Chapel Hill. He'll be back tomorrow."

"Crap, that's right. I totally forgot," Georgia said.

"Why did you do it? What would possess you to say those things?"

Georgia did not know how to answer.

Shaking her head, Trish unlocked the door and went into the house, leaving Georgia alone on the front steps.

Think, George, think.

Georgia had dozens of windows open on her two computer screens, none of them displaying anything meaningful. The least colorful and most important had center stage. The white cursor waited patiently on the second line of the black terminal window.

Why had Frank given her such a vague clue and no time to figure it out? How could he expect her to know what her unique ID was?

Out of frustration and a need to do something, she tried her Social Security number, knowing it was too obvious. Strike two. She banged her fist against the desk.

A fierce growl emanated from her stomach. Not surprising, she hadn't eaten all day. She had no food in the house and couldn't bear another night of popcorn. At least this was a problem she could solve.

❧

Sam arrived promptly at six thirty, and Georgia led him past the small kitchen and into the living room.

He gave it the once over, nodding approvingly. Stepping to the double window, he asked, "Is that the park?"

"Yes. The view is even better in the winter."

Sam turned his attention to Georgia's desk, laden with dual screens, a laptop, and an iPad. "Quite the setup." The monitor on the right captured four views of the house and staircase. "Ditto on the security system."

"I imagine it's nothing like the toys you boys have," Georgia downplayed the compliment, but felt a twinge of pride.

"When did you put it in?"

"Just recently. I needed an upgrade."

Sam nodded, still inspecting the monitors. "Ah yes, the drug running operation. Impressive work."

"I nearly got killed, so I'm not sure you should be that impressed. My condo was destroyed, and my car got firebombed. I was pretty naive. I've learned a lot since."

"Like what?"

"Home security systems to start. Hand-to-hand combat. How to fire a gun, hotwire a car, pick locks, kill a man with a teacup."

Sam turned to her, eyebrows raised. "You're joking, right?"

"Somewhat."

He grinned.

Georgia's stomach fluttered. She silently berated it, reminding herself that he was a liar. It growled in response. "I have a question for you, Sam."

"What?"

"All the stuff you told me about yourself—was any of it true?"

He crossed his arms, clearly taken aback. "Which stuff?"

"About growing up and getting into trouble, your mom bailing you out, you wanting to make her proud."

"That's all true. I was a messed-up kid."

"She must be happy now."

"That's the kicker. I'm not allowed to tell her what I do. Oh, she knows I work for the FBI, but I can't tell her the specifics." Sam's sad eyes bore such terrible regret that Georgia knew he was telling the truth.

"I'm sure she's proud, just the same. Does she live in California?"

"Yes, she does, and yes, I grew up in LA like I told you. I'm just here in Atlanta on temporary assignment."

"And the Marines?"

"I was in the Marines for four years. That turned my life around."

"And after? The college degree you are supposed to be getting?"

"That's partly true. After the Marines I got a degree in history from UCLA. I'm currently working on a Masters in Economics. I'll be done in a year. Everything was true, except the story about me working for a record label. I wasn't allowed to tell you I worked for the FBI."

"And what about New York? You told them I was going to New York to see Frank."

"I had to tell them you went there. It's my job. But I never lied to you about that."

"I want to trust you, Sam…"

Sam put his hands together as if in prayer. "Give me a chance, Georgia."

After one last glance at her computer, Georgia made her decision. "I'm starving. Let's go."

 ❧

"Wow, a death match. This is excellent," Sam said. His unabashed enthusiasm had Georgia grinning with him.

Soft jazz flowed over the hum of the crowd gathered in the

atrium of the Fernbank Natural History Museum. Most seemed
unfazed by the battle going on over their heads.

Georgia and Sam made their way to the base of the display,
which was comprised of two colossal dinosaurs engaged in combat,
frozen for all time, with only their skeletons remaining. A flock
of flying dinosaurs, also in skeletal form, ringed the ceiling and
interior staircase.

The visitors this evening varied as much as the fossils, exhibit-
ing a variety of races, ages, income, and choice of attire.

"It's a nice concept: Martinis, Jazz, and IMAX," Georgia said.

"And dinosaurs," Sam said, his eyes fixed to the ceiling. "This
is a great place."

"You bought me a nice dinner. I thought I should show you a
good time."

"Technically, the FBI bought you dinner."

"Shh, don't ruin it."

They got in line at the closest bar, between a pair of hipsters
and an older couple decked out in a pin-striped suit and a Chanel
dress. "You may not know this, but I am something of a dino-nut,"
Sam said.

"Really?"

"I'm fascinated that we can learn so much from a few small
bones. It's an entire lost world, and we know what these animals
looked like, what they ate, how they lived, and what killed them."

Georgia pointed to the T-Rex. "How do they do it?"

"Heavy wire and super glue."

"Smart-ass. I mean how can we understand so much from
so little?"

Sam's phone rang. Georgia laughed as he first fumbled in his
pockets and then struggled to type in the code to unlock it. The
ringing stopped. "I guess I'll have to wait for the message."

"You know…"

"I know, I know. If only I had a new phone, then all I would need is a simple tap." He held up his index finger. "The lone finger-print. Simply and securely identifying the phone's rightful owner and stopping bad guys in their tracks."

Georgia gasped as she recalled the missing metal coffee tum-bler, last seen when she was parked at the hospital to visit Emiko. She swatted Sam in the chest.

"What?" Sam asked, clearly confused.

"That's it! What time is it?"

He glanced at his watch. "8:23. Why?"

"Sam, I have to get home. Fast."

⊷

Georgia took the stairs to her apartment two at a time. Sam hurried behind her.

"Will you tell me now why we—"

"Shut up, please. We don't have time."

The key snagged in the lock, but finally it turned. Georgia pushed open the door, keys dangling, and punched in her security code. She rushed into the kitchen and searched drawer after drawer until she found what she wanted.

"Is that a Sharpie?" Sam asked.

Georgia ignored him. Instead, she blackened her right index finger, and then pressed it onto a clean sheet of paper several times, creating a few rough fingerprints. She used scissors to cut out the clearest print, then placed the square of paper face down onto the glass surface of her all-in-one printer. She pressed the scan button. "Now where is that program?"

Sam looked on in silence, shaking his head.

Georgia swiftly typed in multiple sets of commands. "Found it." She drew in a deep breath. "Cross your fingers," she said, and dramatically pressed the enter key. The time on the monitor read 8:58.

Nothing happened.

Georgia tapped her fingers on the desk. Nothing. She paced back and forth across her living room floor, never taking her eyes from the terminal window. Nothing.

"Hey, do you mind telling me what's going on?"

"Probably nothing. It was a long shot, but I thought it was worth it."

"Georgia?"

"It's nothing. Sorry for dragging you over here, I guess that..."

A bleeping sound interrupted her explanation. She dashed to her computer, read the notification and then logged onto her drop server. There was a sizable tarball, a type of archive file, being FTP'ed to her partition on the server.

She let out a victory whoop and wriggled with pleasure. She had done it. "Thanks Sam, I owe you one."

"How about you just start by telling me what's going on?"

"Frank was going to send me all of his research into this virus and everything he had from Gene Young. He had it all packaged up but never had a chance to tell me how it was encrypted. You helped me figure it out." This was a stretch, but technically true.

"A fingerprint?"

"Yes. My fingerprint to be exact. And a simple data conversion program. It takes a black-and-white picture and converts it to a binary string."

"So why the rush?"

"He put a time limit on it. It was on a server waiting for me to enter the key, and it would have erased itself, in... oh, two more minutes, give or take."

She was expecting a smile but got the opposite. Sam pressed both hands against the sides of his head. "Do you think this is Hollywood? This is the real world. You know I'm going to have to report this. You know they'll take it away from you. What do you think you have to gain here?"

She walked over to him and placed her hands around his, gently bringing them down and holding them together. His eyes blazed, and she found the passion irresistible. On impulse, and to stop his ranting, she kissed him. She was quite surprised when he kissed her back.

⤚

Next to her in the bed, Sam's breathing was slow and regular. Groping in the dark, Georgia found a t-shirt and his boxer shorts and put them on as she tiptoed to the living room.

The file from Frank was over thirty gigabytes in size. She logged into a second server which contained a program that would move the file to a more secure location. She would decommission this server once the file had been moved. Though it was only the first of many levels in her security process, she'd not take the chance of it being found.

She typed in the command to initiate the transfer, followed by the IP address of the secure server, and the path to the archive file. After the transmission started, she went back to bed.

CHAPTER 36

ATLANTA, GA

GEORGIA WOKE UP alone. She found Sam in the living room, a raised arm propped on the window frame, squinting against the morning sun. He was wearing his jeans from the night before but was shirtless, and her eyes lingered on his hairless, sinewy chest.

"Going commando?" She was still wearing his boxer shorts.

"Good morning," he said, but without moving. His attention was elsewhere.

Frank's files. Panic rippled through her and a burst of adrenaline carried her halfway across the room. But the computer screens were dark.

"Don't worry. I haven't invaded your private space."

"I didn't—" she stammered.

"Georgia, we need to talk."

"Is this where you tell me to turn over the goods? That you'll throw my friends into jail if I don't? That you'll hack into Dave's computer and put pornography on it?"

"What are you talking about?" Sam turned from the window, his expression one of confusion and frustration.

"You know."

"I do not know." Sam had not been present when Georgia met with his boss.

"Your boss, the bitch. She threatened to go after Dave, Marcus, Trish, and Diane." Georgia recounted the conversation for Sam. "How did she even know about Diane?"

Sam shook his head, his brow furrowed. "I didn't know anything about this."

Georgia moved in close to Sam, her upturned face only inches from his. She searched for any sign of a lie, but she found only steady brown eyes.

"Then what do you know?" she asked.

"It's BS."

"Of course it is." Georgia stepped back but Sam caught her hand, keeping her close.

"That's not what I mean," he said. "It's a lie. The FBI wouldn't plant anything on Dave's computer to get back at you. And I can't believe they'd do anything to Marcus, as well connected as he is. Besides, they don't work like that. She made it up to scare you."

The momentary relief was followed by anger, partly at herself for being so stupid. Could it all have been a lie? A current of uncertainty rippled over her skin.

"At least one thing makes sense now," Sam mused. "You were so mean to your friends the other night. I couldn't figure that out."

Georgia was struggling to get her emotions under control and could only whisper. "I was trying to protect them."

"Yes." His face softened, and he smoothed her tangled hair. "So what are we going to do about it?"

"We? What about the 'Do you think this is Hollywood?' speech from last night?"

"That was before I knew what Katherine had done. She really is a bitch."

"Then you won't tell them about Frank's data?"

"I didn't say that."

Georgia backed away from him. "You just told me…"

"Shh, calm down. I've been up this morning thinking. And this threat from Katherine," Sam paused to take a deep breath. "When it all started, we were following standard procedure. Frank was on the terrorist watch list. Tracking him, following him, that's what we do. We work with Homeland Security to protect our country."

She bit her lip to stop herself from lashing out.

"I'm not saying it was right, but it made sense. Unlike the rest." Sam ran a hand across his face. "Suppose it's all true. A few hundred girls in a faraway poor country can't get pregnant. Much worse than that happens every single day, and the United States doesn't get involved. The FBI would never get involved. And this Guardians thing." He stared at Georgia with an expression she could not quite place. Incredulity? "A secret organization has been breeding super humans for 150 years and you are one of them?"

"I know it sounds crazy."

"Do you believe it? Do you believe Frank's story?"

She nodded, knowing it seemed ridiculous. "I do. Do you?"

"I don't know, George." Sam shook his head back and forth several times. "Obviously, someone at the Bureau has taken an interest. So at least part of Frank's story could be true. What part, I don't know. This is out of my league."

"We have proof—Frank's original virus sample, and the evidence from Dr. Young."

"I don't have access to that."

"And now I have Frank's data."

"That can get buried like the rest."

"So you aren't going to do anything?"

"Stop putting words into my mouth." Sam drifted towards the kitchen. He stopped, then slowly turned back to her. "How long have you known Sean Kelly?"

"Not long. Just since the Atlantic-Pacific case. Marcus has known him for a long time."

"Do you trust him?"

"Kelly? Before all this happened, I would have said yes."

"I'm going to go into the office and see if I can find anything in our records on the Guardians or Dr. Young. Maybe I can find something to explain all the interest."

"It's Sunday."

"Exactly. I'll talk to Kelly tomorrow morning. We'll need to take everything to him including whatever you can find in Frank's documents."

"Tomorrow's not possible. I need more time."

"Time is not a luxury we have. If we do not act quickly and carefully, they could easily get me out of the way. Appointed liaisons are easy to come by."

He had a point there. "What about my friends?" Georgia asked.

"I wouldn't worry about them. Once I document the threat, they should be safe."

"Can I tell them about all this?"

"Legally, I think so. But Georgia, someone thinks it's important enough to have an FBI agent threaten you."

"I need to tell Dave and Marcus."

"It's your call. I trust you."

Trust. That word again. This time accompanied by a pang of guilt. She had not told Sam about her conversation with Gene, or that the file she got from Frank contained much more than research on the virus. Or that she had no intention of turning it all over.

⁓

Georgia hesitated, her knuckles resting on the smooth wood. What would she do if Dave wouldn't see her? Was she here to apologize, or because she needed him? What kind of a friend was she?

She felt the door give way and wondered for a split second if she had pushed it open. But then Dave appeared and stared quizzically at her raised hand. Georgia began to apologize, but he hugged her, awkwardly squashing her raised arm between them and pinning the other against her side. The gesture touched her.

"Come on," he said, and motioned for her to enter. She followed him to the kitchen, where they found Trish, arms crossed and lips tight. At least today she did not exude hatred. Merely extreme unhappiness.

"I can't defend my actions from the other night," Georgia said, addressing both of them. "I said horrible things."

"Are you scared of the Guardians?" Dave asked. He must have seen the shock she felt, for he nodded. "I thought about this a lot, and it's the only thing that explains why you turned on me. To protect us."

"From scientists who lived in the 1800s?" Trish said, now seeming exasperated.

"It started then," Dave said. "But I think they're still out there."

"What did you find?" Georgia asked, unable to help herself.

"No," Trish said. "You first."

"It started with Frank and his paranoid delusions," Georgia said. "But enough things have happened that I think he was telling the truth."

"Go on."

"Can I sit down? It's going to take a while."

They sat down at Dave's dining table turned desk. Georgia began with the history of the Guardians, and then told how her parents and Frank became ensnared in their grasp.

"First, they blackmailed Frank and my parents, using me as collateral. Not that my parents cared all that much. Frank said they were all on an intellectual high. The Guardians funded all their research and Frank's business." She then described how Frank caught one of his researchers experimenting on human embryos, and instead of doing anything about it, they demanded her eggs so they could continue their bloodline.

"My father and Frank kept this last part from my mother,

knowing she would go ballistic. She did find out, almost a year later. She had planned to go to the authorities, but she and my father died before that could happen. Frank thought the Guardians killed them and he left the country to protect himself and me."

"Do you believe that?" Dave asked.

"I don't know. Their deaths were ruled an accident, but the timing is too coincidental."

"This all happened a long time ago," Trish said.

"Right," Georgia agreed, "and I can't prove any of it, anyway." She paused. This was the point of no return. "But there are some bad things happening now."

"Go on," Dave urged.

Georgia then described how Gene Young, a doctor in Honduras, identified high infertility in teenage girls and could find no one to help except Frank. How Frank recognized the retrovirus as being similar to that developed by his old researcher, Alex. Then when Frank died trying to get a sample of the virus, the FBI confiscated everything. She ended by telling them of the threats against her and her friends.

Dave leaned back in his chair, a blank expression on his face.

"Oh George," Trish said. She squeezed Georgia's hand.

"I tried to shut it down, to shut you all down, to ignore everything. But it's not going away." She filled them in on her call with Gene Young, and the data she got from Frank's account.

"Geez," Trish said.

"Yeah. But on the bright side, Sam said the FBI would never actually retaliate against me by hurting you guys. They were lying to scare me off. To be sure, he is going to take all of this to Agent Kelly tomorrow. He also wants any analysis of Frank's data that I can get to him."

Dave and Trish stared at her in confusion.

"I know. It's a long shot. But maybe the data will help us understand something."

More confusion. Sam.

"Oh. That's right. You don't know about Sam Bennett a.k.a. Sam Becker."

She completed the briefing, leaving out the part about Sam staying the night.

"That lying creep," Trish said. "I thought he was so cute."

"Sam?" Georgia asked. "He's not so bad. Once you get to know him."

Trish arched an eyebrow. Georgia shrugged in response. Trish grinned and Georgia smiled, happy to see the old Trish.

Dave missed the entire exchange, staring off into space.

"Dave, what are you thinking?"

"I'm trying to decide if I want to climb out of the rabbit hole or continue to fall into it."

"What did you learn about the Guardians?" Georgia asked.

"Rumblings. I went to the dark net. Nothing to do with anything you told us. More like these guys have infiltrated top positions across governments, big pharma, and high-tech companies across the world. Could be typical conspiracy theories."

"So in a nutshell, we have an FBI agent pretending to be George's boyfriend, some crazy scientist sterilizing girls in remote Central America, a secret organization of super humans that has infiltrated the highest levels of government and industry—of which our pal George is an undocumented member—" Trish paused to breathe, "and a Nobel prize-winning godfather, recently deceased under suspicious circumstances, who tied the whole thing together and sent you information from the grave that could put all of us in jail if we even look at it." Trish deadpanned, "Does that sum it up?"

Georgia and Dave both laughed. "Yes," Georgia said. "That about does it."

"What are you going to do, George?"

"I'm not exactly sure, but I'm going to start by looking at the information Frank sent."

"Okay, I'm in," Trish said.

"You're in what?" Dave asked.

"I'm going to help George. I forgive her for acting like a stupid jerk because she had good intentions. Dave, you'll help too, right?"

Dave shrugged. "Why not? What's the worst that could happen?"

∽

The Georgia Institute of Technology is consistently ranked as one of the top public universities in the United States. The central campus, in Midtown Atlanta, was quiet this Monday morning. Georgia waited in front of the Industrial and Systems Engineering department, housed in an aged three-story brick building across the street from the modern Campus Recreation Center, home to the 1996 Olympic Pool.

A ride share car pulled into the front parking lot and Sam got out, the quintessential FBI agent in a black suit and tie. Awkward greetings followed. Georgia was unsure whether to kiss him or shake his hand.

"Thanks for coming," she said.

"When you called last night, you said it was important."

"I wanted to meet with you before you talked to Agent Kelly."

Georgia led Sam into the building, the interior as nondescript as the facade, up a flight of concrete stairs, and down the hall to Dave's office. She opened the door. "Dave will be here in a minute. He's just getting out of class."

The cramped room was a souped-up version of Dave's home. Two walls were floor-to-ceiling bookshelves, and a third was a whiteboard wall packed with multicolored equations. Papers covered the desk, file folders the floor. Georgia moved a pile of papers from the lone visitor's chair just as Dave arrived. The professor dropped his armload of books onto the desk with a thud.

"I didn't know you were bringing him," Dave said, clearly not excited to see Sam in his office.

The two men eyed each other warily. Georgia snapped her fingers to get their attention. "Come on. We don't have time for this now." Gently but firmly, she pushed Sam into the chair. Addressing Dave, she said, "We talked about this. Sam was doing what he thought was right."

"He lied to us."

"Yes. But now he's taking a big risk by going over his boss' head." Georgia snatched a green marker from a bowl on the desk and held it out to Dave. "Please. I wanted Sam to hear this from you directly. Can you please tell him what we found?"

Dave's shoulders dropped and his face softened. He took the pen. "The data contained a list of young women and teens with birthdates, and their children's birthdates." As he spoke, he cleaned a section of the white-board wall. "It's all anonymous, so people are identified with a numerical ID and towns by a letter. I guess Dr. Young wanted to preserve client-patient confidentiality."

"You can't tell who anyone is?" Sam asked.

Ignoring the comment, Dave drew multiple circles on the board. "We have data for three small communities. If we had the actual locations, we could tell how the virus was spread, whether through wells, community water sources, or even a river. But without location information we can't know."

"Then you can't tell anything," Sam said, looking annoyed.

"Oh, au contraire," Dave said. "We know a lot. Do not underestimate the power of mathematics." Dave was in full professor mode.

Sam rolled his eyes.

Georgia interjected, "Remember that before Frank died, he was able to test the samples Dr. Young sent for the virus. He found genetic fragments of the retrovirus in the water, but none of the expected antibodies in the blood samples of the teen girls. No antibodies means no retrovirus," Georgia explained. "The genetic modifications have to be inherited."

Sam checked his watch. "We knew that, but we have no proof."

"Let's assume that much is true. The data supports his findings, which is remarkable considering the small sample size," Dave
added. "I can't understand how no one saw this earlier."

"It's the two-step process, which is why it's so clever," Georgia added.

"And why it would be a bitch to uncover," Dave said.

Sam raised his hands, clearly exasperated. "OK geniuses, tell
me in simple terms."

"The first step, the retrovirus, makes populations vulnerable,"
Georgia said. "Then at any later time you can make the women or
their descendants sterile, using some sort of activator."

"The first time, the activator may not have been as effective and
did not last long. The data shows a period of time sixteen to eighteen
years ago with significantly fewer births, but nothing like now."
Dave filled in three of the circles on the board. "This time, it's just
three villages. But all of the teen girls in those villages appear to be
sterile. At least everyone in this data sample. And the duration has
already exceeded that of the time before."

"That's an important point," Georgia said. "The sterilization is
highly localized, highly effective, and it could last a long time. The
second point is the future potential." She nodded to Dave.

Using a red marker, Dave drew two stick figures on the board.
"Say we start with one infected pair of parents, and they have two
children, a boy and a girl." He drew two more figures and connected
them to the first, creating the beginning of a family tree. "It's almost
certain that all the children will inherit the genetic defects, assuming that the data is complete for these locations."

He kept drawing, adding stick figures, arrows, and equations.
"If those originally infected never leave their respective villages,
then the rest of the world is fine. However, if they travel to other
populations, which of course they will, they transmit the genetic
modifications to their children, causing the new population to
be susceptible to sterilization." Dave pointed to a Greek letter in

the middle of an equation. "The level of population mixing is the key here."

"So, this is bad?" Sam asked, obviously confused.

"In theory, yes. But in this case, not really," Dave said. "The population sizes are so small and the towns so remote. Even with a high transmission rate, it would be fifty or a hundred years before it spread noticeably."

Sam shook his head. "I don't understand then. I mean, it's wrong, of course, but," he muttered, "why would anyone here care about this?"

Georgia smacked her hand on the white board, causing Sam to jump. "It's a test, a designed experiment," she said. "Whoever introduced the original retrovirus picked small, mostly self-contained tribes in a remote area of the world, and then patiently waited to see what would happen." She grabbed Sam's shoulders, wanting to shake the meaning into him. "Imagine if this was put into an urban water supply. Put this in a few key cities around the world and let it go for a few years or a generation. It's virtually untraceable. Later exposure to the activator could effectively put an end to entire countries or cultures."

Georgia let go of Sam and crossed her arms in front of her. "There is also another point to this, Sam. Why would your boss care enough to threaten us?"

"She knows." Sam slumped in his seat. "Or worse, she's part of it."

"Well, it is a novel way to address the overpopulation problem." Dave fake-smiled. "It beats war."

CHAPTER 37

TEGUCIGALPA, HONDURAS

ALEX WAS ENJOYING a pleasant dinner with the Honduran Commissioner of Health. A light breeze swept over their table, keeping the bugs away and the temperature down. The French white burgundy, while not excellent, was certainly acceptable. And the company, though boring, was well-informed about the political jousting in the administrative arm of the government.

A familiar face approached their table, but he was so out of context in civilian clothes that Alex took a moment to recognize him.

"Danny Mears, what a pleasant surprise," Alex said. What in the world are you doing all the way up here?"

The young, freckle-faced Midwesterner looked out of sorts. "Ma'am."

"Have you ever eaten at La Cumbre? I'm having the bouillabaisse. It's delicious."

"You just missed the sunset. The view of the city is spectacular," the Commissioner said. La Cumbre was situated at the highest point of Tegucigalpa, above the Juana Lainez Park.

Danny remained standing in front of them, hands folded behind his back. "Ma'am, can you come with me for a moment?"

The Commissioner's smile dropped. Alex patted his knee reassuringly. "I'll be right back. Be a dear and order us another bottle of wine, will you?"

Alex followed Danny out to the parking lot where moonlight reflected off a shiny black SUV. Anthony's profile was visible through the open window of the front passenger door, but the heavy tint made it impossible to see into the rest of the car.

Danny opened the rear door for her. "To what do I owe this pleasure, Anthony?" It was only as she entered the car and the overhead light activated that she saw the figure in the back seat. Alex's heart skipped a beat, and she was gripped by an overwhelming urge to run back into the restaurant. "Marsten." It was all she could manage to say.

"Hello, Alex," said the white-haired man seated beside her. He must be in his late seventies by now and was, as usual, sharply dressed in a bespoke three-piece suit. She looked into the wizened face and piercing steel blue eyes—the eyes of one of the most dangerous men on the planet—duplicitously wrapped in a grandfather's body.

"Anthony, will you excuse us please?" The man asked politely but they all knew it was not really a question.

Anthony grunted, left the car and joined Danny standing at the edge of the car park, out of earshot.

"It's good to see you again," Alex said, her voice trembling in the lie.

Marsten handed her a printed page from a report, with one paragraph in yellow highlight. "Read it."

She did.

Friday night, Georgia Steele accessed a massive amount of data from Frank Anderson, which was sent to her automatically after his death. She turned it over to the Bureau this morning, and it has been uploaded to a secure site. All of the information related to sterilization and human infertility. Much is medical and

*highly technical. Some originated with Dr. Eugene Young, the
rest appears to have been collected by Anderson, and may span
decades. Steele used the data to corroborate Young's report on the
intentional sterilization of rural Hondurans in several villages in
the Olancho region.*

Alex handed the note back to Marsten.

"The data was turned in to a local team. They secured it before
our contacts were able to intercept."

"Was there anything in there about me?"

"Not Alejandra Castilla, if that's what you mean."

"About," she hesitated, not wanting to say the name aloud,
"the organization?"

"No."

She exhaled.

"I think it's time for you to present to the council. Now that
your experiments have shown promise, you'll need help expanding
the operation."

"We're doing fine here."

"You are not. We have a very limited window of time to execute
this operation. Many on the council—many in the organization—
think this is a charade. And too little too late. If we are going to
make it work, we have to scale up, and fast."

"I have orders from Brazil and the Arabs."

"It's not enough. This is not your personal entrepreneurship.
We funded you and allowed your little project to proceed until
you could prove the results. Now that you've done that, it's time to
move. Otherwise, others will take more drastic action."

"What does that mean, exactly?"

"You don't need to know. But we don't have time to wait multiple generations for this to make an impact. The world is changing
faster than any of us predicted." Marsten reached over and pried

her clenched hand from the door handle. "And Alex, there's more. You've been quite careless."

She felt the hair on the back of her neck rise.

"Georgia Steele spoke with Dr. Young last week," Marsten said.

"That doesn't seem possible."

"It was Friday."

"That was just before Dr. Young and José were due to leave for vacation." *Jesus, Anthony, how could you have missed that?* "If that's the case, she may try to contact him again."

"It would not be good for her to find out he is gone," Marsten said.

"We're so close. We start relocation in just a few weeks."

"Then we need to take her out."

Georgia? "But she's one of us." Alex shook her head. "And she has a permanent FBI babysitter. How would that look?"

"Then bring her here."

"Why?" Alex asked. "Do you think I could convince her to back off? Maybe to join us? She's family, after all."

"In blood only. She was not raised in the organization."

"Marsten, please."

"Bring her here then. You can try to convince her to drop her investigation."

"What if I fail?"

"Then you have options. Like you said when you first began this little experiment. It's the perfect cover. Bad things happen all the time in Honduras."

CHAPTER 38

ATLANTA, GA

GEORGIA OPENED THE door to her apartment when Sam was half-way up the stairs. "Sam, I'm glad you're here," she said.

"I got your message. What happened?"

"Have you talked to Agent Kelly?"

"Briefly. Yesterday after I sent him the report."

"And?"

Sam raised his hands out in front of him. "George, it's been one day. We're meeting tomorrow morning."

Georgia stepped back and motioned for Sam to enter her apartment.

"In the meantime, I'm hiding from my boss. The shit is about to hit the fan."

Georgia took Sam's arm and led him over to her desk. She had turned off all the monitors except one. It displayed an email from José Rodríguez. Sam read it once, then again.

"Jesus."

"Am I responsible for this?" Georgia felt her hands start to shake and clasped them together.

"We don't even know if it's true, or that the email is from Rodríguez. Did you send a response?"

"Yes, as soon as it came in this morning. I tracked the email to a server in San Salvador." Georgia crossed her arms and pressed them tightly against her chest. "I also contacted Doctors With Wings. Dr. Young was supposed to be on vacation, due back today." She looked away, unable to take Sam's penetrating stare. "But he hasn't reported to his clinic yet, he's not answering his phone, and his voicemail is full."

"Huh," Sam said. He read the email again. "I'll see what I can find out."

"I was hoping you'd say that."

Sam fished his cell phone from his jacket pocket and dialed. "Kelly? This is Sam Bennett. Can you talk for a minute?"

Georgia could only hear Sam's side of the conversation. He eyed her as he spoke. "I am here with Georgia Steele. She received an email this morning from José Rodríguez, he's Gene Young's partner, the doctor in Honduras... yes, sir, the one who contacted Anderson, the one in the report. The email says that Dr. Young is missing, as of Friday night. Rodríguez thinks Young was kidnapped or killed. The house was ransacked, and the doctor's computer is gone."

Sam listened for a bit, then said, "Rodríguez thinks all the original data and patient samples are at the clinic, but these will get turned over to Doctors With Wings. Rodríguez has offered to share or copy them if it will help find out what happened to Dr. Young. After that, he plans to leave the country."

Sam rocked from side to side as he listened to the senior FBI agent. After a few minutes, the call ended. "Kelly will get back to us soon. He has to make a few calls." Sam rubbed his temple. "This is sure turning out to be a fun-filled week. And it's only Tuesday."

A half hour passed with no response. It was past lunchtime and the only things Georgia could find in her kitchen were a few diet Cokes and some microwave popcorn.

"I'm not much of a host," she said.

"I see why you spend so much time at Cohen's house."

They sat at her small dining table, eating popcorn from the bag and sipping Diet Coke from the can.

"I think I should go," Georgia said.

"To Cohen's?"

"No, dummy, to Honduras. If I can get a sample of the virus and Dr. Young's files, then we'll have evidence to prove what was done to those girls. If we can expose what was done, maybe we can prevent it from happening elsewhere. Plus, I can clear Frank's name."

"Are you kidding me? You can't go to Honduras."

"Why not?"

His response was an exasperated moan.

"I'll get Marcus to go with me."

"Doesn't he have more depositions this week?"

"Crap, you're right. Well, I'll just go myself."

Sam's jaw was tight, his anger palpable. Fortunately for Georgia, his phone rang. "Bennett," he said, straining through clenched teeth.

This call had Sam doing most of the listening. He tried to interject a few times. "Sir,... but with the recent events... sir, just one minute please." He placed the phone against his chest. "I need to take this in private."

Sam left the apartment and hastened down the stairs. Georgia watched from the window. He continued the phone conversation while pacing around the parking lot, stopping now and again to kick gravel with the toe of his shoe or rub the back of his neck. Ten minutes later, he came back. The frown on his face and the stoop in his shoulders told her he had lost the argument.

"What happened?"

"My boss, Katherine, is gone. She's been reassigned, transferred to another agency. She's already out. As in out of the country."

"Good riddance."

"No, someone very high up pulled strings to get her out of the way. Kelly is freaking out about it."

"Well, what about Dr. Young?"

"Officially, the FBI doesn't know or care about what's going on in some remote region of Honduras. Anything that happens outside of the US is not our business."

"Then why are you so upset?" Georgia nodded to Sam's tightly clenched hands.

He shook them out and rubbed them on his pants. "Kelly told me he wants to keep you happy. He will have someone look into the email and other communications you've had with Dr. Young. If they decide it's all legit, they will contact the State Department. He doubts the Bureau will want anything to do with the villagers, but the State Department should want to investigate Young's disappearance if turns out he is missing." Sam's lips puckered together tightly, as if he had something horrible in this mouth. "They may be able to provide some local support if you go down."

"That's great news," Georgia said.

"No, it's not. Kelly implied that the upper echelon is really worried about something... something to do with your godfather and Katherine. They're not telling me what, and I don't think Kelly knows either." Sam rubbed his hands together. "If whatever is going on in Honduras is related, then—maybe I'm overreacting—it could be very dangerous. Kelly needs you, sure, but not that badly. What if they're hoping to use you as bait? You could draw out the perpetrators, force their hands..."

Georgia stepped toward him, as if closing the physical space would bring their points of view together. "But this could be what I need to get the evidence to clear Frank's name and expose what is going on down there." *And find out who I am.*

Sam lifted his hand to her face. "Please don't go," he said, softly brushing a strand of hair from her eyes.

Georgia backed away. She lost Emiko and Frank. This could be her last chance. "I'm going."

"Then I'm going with you."

✧

On tiptoe, Georgia reached for a suitcase from the top shelf of her closet. It was shocking how quickly the trip had come together. She had received the email from José only yesterday, and they were leaving in the morning.

With the suitcase on the bed, she started to pack. She moved a box sitting on the closet floor in search of a left shoe and heard a tinkle of glass. The new box held the same title as the old one it had replaced: "Vacation Memories."

Absently, she crouched down and opened the box, revealing the miniature bottles. The unbroken ones had been reunited with the wooden display rack. The FBI never had admitted to tearing up the boxes while searching her car as it sat in the Denny's parking lot.

Georgia gently lifted the rack from the box. A printed scroll across the front read "The Sands of Time," and each individual bottle bore a handwritten label. They were originally in chronological order. Every family trip was captured in a bottle. Not all of them were sand; there was some dirt, rock chips, and even coffee, from a vacation to Costa Rica when Georgia was in high school.

The oldest bottles were from before she was born, such as Beach Sand, Jersey Shore, 1974, and Venice Beach, 1977. She remembered Disneyland, 1991, though she was only four years old. Her mother had gone to a conference while her father took her to the theme park.

Absently, she started to arrange them into the correct order, and then one caught her eye: Camping, Tallulah Falls, 1998. Strange. Her family never took that trip. That was the year her father fell off the ladder and the vacation was cancelled.

She picked up the bottle and looked at it, turning it over in her hands. The fine dirt was the color of dark chocolate. She mindlessly rolled it in her hands, stopping when a flash of white appeared in the brown dirt.

Taking the bottle to her kitchen, she emptied it into a bowl. Inside was a small piece of paper, tightly rolled and secured with a rubber band. She carefully unfurled it and found it to be a black and white xerox of a photo, dirty and damaged. The portrait taken against a white background might have been for a work ID or a passport. The person had light skin, dark hair, and was wearing a suit jacket. The photo was so poor she couldn't tell if it was a woman or a man. She carefully placed it under a heavy book to flatten it.

Georgia fetched the full rack of bottles and read all the labels. Two others were for trips that were never taken. She examined these and several others. The bottles from the authentic trips bore only sand and dirt, and she funneled the contents back into the small containers.

The one marked Georgia, 1988 held an actual photo, carefully rolled and wrapped in plastic film. It was faded but in much better shape. It was the picture of a middle-aged man, seated in a car, the picture showing him through an open window. He had blonde slicked-back hair and wore a suit. He was not looking at the photographer. She began to stretch out the photo, planning to place it under another book. It turned in her hands and she caught sight of writing on the back. It said: Marsten, June 02, 1988. That was the date of her first birthday.

She went back to the first and turned it over. There was something written there, a few words scrawled in pencil. Using a new kitchen sponge, she carefully wiped the dirt from the paper. Alex G-a-s-t.... She wiped harder, and moisture from the sponge smeared the pencil into oblivion.

"Damn," she whispered.

She turned it over and studied the picture again. A light skinned person with dark hair, a longish neck, and a sharp chin. She imagined all the men that could fit into this smudge of a picture. Too many.

The last bottle offered up a small piece of plain paper bearing a list of names, caked with the dirt from the tube. Like the xerox, it appeared to have been hastily stashed. She dared not try to clean it for fear of damage.

The pages might be saved with expert reconstruction. But that would have to wait for her return.

CHAPTER 39

TEGUCIGALPA, HONDURAS

The plane had begun its final descent.

"It's beautiful from here, isn't it? The earth?"

Georgia turned from the window and handed the empty coffee cup to the flight attendant. "Yes, it is, thanks."

They were flying over the Yucatan peninsula, and the contrasting hues of sea, sky, and land were breathtaking. But Georgia's thoughts lay thousands of feet below, to what they would find when they got there.

"Here goes," Sam said.

"What do you mean by that?"

"You don't know about the Tegucigalpa airport?" He chuckled. "This is going to be fun. Tegucigalpa is one of the most dangerous airports in the world."

Georgia tensed.

"It's set in the middle of mountains, so the approach is tough and the descent rapid. The weather is unpredictable, and the pilots can't use autopilot to help." Sam leaned across Georgia to peak out of the window. "The kicker is that it also has the shortest runway of any major international airport. And at the end of the runway there is a sixty-foot drop onto a highway below, so if you overshoot it, there's nowhere to go. It's ranked the second most dangerous airport in the world."

"Did the FBI brief you on that?"

"No, I watched it on the History Channel." Sam grinned.

The plane shuddered during the steep descent, but the landing was smooth. The other passengers must have experienced worse. They gave the pilot a round of applause as the plane touched down and slowed to taxi.

∽

Near the terminal exit, a dark-complexioned man in gray camouflage and sunglasses stood with his arms crossed and a handgun resting on his hip. He did not appear to be Latin in ethnicity. Italian maybe? He looked ready to go into a war zone.

"Bennett?" he said, addressing Sam.

"Sam Bennett, and you must be Messina?" Sam reached out his hand to the man.

Messina looked down at the hand, then up at Sam. He uncrossed his arms and awkwardly shook Sam's hand.

"And this is Georgia Steele," Sam said, gesturing to Georgia.

Georgia put out her hand, but Messina was already headed towards the door.

"Let's go," he said, not looking back.

Outside at the curb, Messina lunged into the front passenger seat of a shiny late-model black SUV. He pulled off his hat to reveal close-cropped salt-and-pepper hair.

"Nice ride," Sam said, as he held the door open for Georgia.

The driver, also in gray camo, was young, tall, and muscular with pale skin and freckles.

"The embassy," Messina barked.

∽

Georgia's first impression of Tegucigalpa was that it appeared as many other Central American cities: bejeweled with ancient Spanish churches but carpeted with low-slung, brightly colored concrete-block buildings. The city was further sullied by spider webs of overhead electrical wires and unappealing high rises protected by razor fencing and guards to keep the poor separated from the not-so-poor. The beauty crafted hundreds of years ago had been eroded by modern civilization.

The American Embassy, an unattractive, yellow brick building four stories high, conformed to the modern visage. Concrete barricades and heavily armed guards greeted them upon arrival.

"Leave your things in the car," Messina said. "Bags, cell phone, any electronics." He exited the car and strode up the sidewalk. The guards saluted him as he walked by.

The driver turned to talk to them, bracing his arm on the passenger seat. "I'll make sure nothing happens to your things, sir."

Sam thanked him and got out, with Georgia following.

"Oh, your watch, sir." The driver pointed to Sam's digital watch.

"Really?"

"I'm afraid so, sir."

"Yeah, it might be a secret spy recording device." Georgia laughed.

Sam glared at her. "Just go," he hissed, and handed over his watch.

Full body scanners and a multitude of signs greeted them in the lobby. Messina had been right. There were longs lists in both English and Spanish of prohibited items, including all electronic devices, bags, briefcases, cigarettes, food, or drinks. Documents required for business at the embassy could only be carried in clear plastic bags.

Once through security, they followed the silent Messina down a hallway and up two flights of stairs to the office of the vice-consul. Inside, a middle-aged Hispanic woman seated at a small desk was typing at a terminal, nails clicking on the keyboard. Her eyes flickered to them, then back to her work. "Mr. Evans is expecting you," she said.

Messina had already opened the door to the inner office. It was grandly furnished with traditional leather chairs, antique mahogany bookcases, and an impressive polished desk. The desk, bare except for a closed laptop and a thin manila folder, was occupied by a slight man with thinning auburn hair and wire-rimmed glasses, wearing a conservative navy suit. "Good afternoon," he said, standing. He reached over and shook their hands, introducing himself as Leland Evans. "Very nice to make your acquaintance. Please, have a seat." His deep voice, steeped in Southern drawl, was a contrast to his small stature.

Georgia and Sam sat in a pair of richly brocade chairs facing the desk. Something behind them caught Evans' attention. Georgia turned to see Messina's thick frame filling the doorway.

"Anthony, thank you again for collecting our guests," Evans said. "I'll let you know if we need anything else. Can you please close the door on your way out?"

Messina grunted and turned on his heels, leaving the door open.

The smile remained on Evans face, albeit missing some of its previous charm. He sauntered to the door and pressed it closed with one hand.

"Now, where were we?" he asked, reseated and replete with Southern charm. "Oh yes, I was about to offer you something to drink. Can I get you a coffee or Coca-Cola?"

Both accepted the offer for the latter. He pushed a button on the ancient intercom on his desk and made the request of his assistant.

"Are you from New Orleans, Mr. Evans?" Georgia asked.

Evans brightened, looking delighted. "Yes... well, Lake Charles to be exact. And please, call me Lee."

He leaned forward, placing his elbows on the table and tenting his fingers. "We are always happy to have guests, especially those from the Federal Bureau of Investigation." Evans dragged the words out. "But this is not a social visit, is it?"

"No," Sam agreed. "We are conducting an investigation into a suspected terrorist who was recently killed in the United States."

Georgia choked on her soda. Her uncle was no terrorist. She glared at Sam, but he ignored her.

"He was in contact with a local doctor, Gene Young. He's with Doctors With Wings."

"Yes. We were notified that you were looking for him." Evans fingered the manila folder. "What is the connection with your terrorist?"

"Dr. Young found evidence that rural villages in the Olancho region were exposed to some serious toxins about fifteen years ago."

"Well, I'm afraid that is not too surprising. This is Honduras."

"We believe Dr. Young contacted our suspect because of his medical expertise in this area, not his ties to terrorism. However, we think the group he belonged to may have been the manufacturer of the toxic agents, unbeknownst to Young."

"In other words, our good doctor stumbled into the lion's den?"

"Exactly. And now he's missing."

"My assistant called Doctors With Wings," Evans said. "Your doctor was on vacation this weekend. But he did not show up for work on Tuesday."

"Do they know anything?"

"No," Evans said. "But it's only been two days. It seems a little early to call in the cavalry."

"We also received an email from a friend of his, a man named José Rodríguez," Sam said.

Evans raised his eyebrows. "Who is he?"

"We think he is the doctor's significant other."

"I see." Evans opened the envelope and scribbled a few notes on the back of one of the pages. "But you know nothing more about him?"

"No."

"I'll see what I can find on Rodríguez." He handed Georgia a sheet from the folder. "DWW has an office here in Tegucigalpa. Here is the address. I can have someone drive you over there if you like."

"Thank you. That would be great," Georgia said, reaching to take the page.

Evans kept his grip and Georgia felt tension travel through the sheet of paper. "Be careful, Dr. Steele. Honduras is a very dangerous place, as I'm sure you know. People go missing every day. And the standard of living here, it makes the worst poverty in the Bayou look downright palatial." He let the paper go, leaning back into the chair and resuming his official demeanor. "We'll be in touch regarding Mr. Rodríguez. If you have any other questions, please don't hesitate to call."

They rose to leave. The vice-consul accompanied them to the door. Evans' assistant was still rapidly typing but stopped when Evans spoke to her. "Can you see if someone is available to drive Dr. Steele and Mr. Bennett for the afternoon?"

"Mr. Messina said he would take care of it," she replied.

"Messina is our head of security," he explained. "Can you all find your way out?"

They assured him they could.

⌇

Retracing their steps to the front entrance, they found the freckle-faced driver and the black SUV waiting at the curb. The young man introduced himself as Danny Mears.

"We'd like to go to the University Hospital. Can you take us there?" Georgia asked, climbing into the front seat.

"Yes, Ma'am." Mears smiled. "Would you like to go to your hotel and drop off your things first? It's the Intercontinental, right?"

Georgia caught Sam's surprised expression in the rearview.

"Sure, that's right," he said, recovering. "Thanks. That sounds like a good idea."

On the ride over, they passed a sprawling new hospital, glass walls reflecting the afternoon sun. "Is this it?" Georgia asked.

"No, Ma'am, that's a private hospital. University Hospital, or Hospital Escuela is the only public hospital in Tegucigalpa," Mears said.

"Only one public hospital? For all these poor people?"

"Yes, Ma'am."

"How long have you worked here, Danny?"

"Two years. I did two tours of Afghanistan, then came here."

"You're in the Army?" Sam asked.

"Used to be. Now I work for Messina."

"And Messina? Is he the RSO?"

"Yes, sir."

"RSO?" Georgia asked.

"Regional Security Officer," Sam explained. "The top security officer at the embassy, but not armed forces. Diplomatic Security Service is part of the State Department."

Georgia peeked over her shoulder. "I'm impressed." She turned her attention back to Mears. "How long has Messina been here?"

"I'm not sure. It's been quite a while."

"Do you know if he was here in 2009? For the coup?"

"Yes, Ma'am, I think he came around then."

"And Evans?"

"Less than a year. Most people don't stay long." Mears turned into the driveway of the Intercontinental. "We're here."

⋘

After checking into the hotel, Mears drove them to University Hospital, a mile up Boulevard Suyapa, where Doctors With Wings had an administrative office. He dropped them at an employee access far from the chaos of the main entrance and emergency room.

The guard barely glanced at Georgia and Sam as they passed, perhaps thinking them foreign aid workers. Though no patients waited here, the perfunctory lobby had the ubiquitous hospital stink of urine bathed in bleach.

Georgia was to go alone while Sam waited. The US government was no more trusted here than the Honduran government, and the DWW employees might not be as willing to talk in front of him. And Georgia was fluent in Spanish. Entering the stairwell, she caught sight of Sam standing uncharacteristically rigid, his arms crossed.

It took Georgia some time to find the DWW office, identified only by a number painted next to the door. After a tentative knock, a voice told her to come in.

The office space was as spartan as the door. The first room held a wall of filing cabinets and a folding table, where two college-age men, one white and one black, read through folders and scribbled notes. A pony-tailed man in his late forties was getting coffee from a carafe perched on top of a bookcase, over which hung a map of Honduras and a poster of Bono. A connecting room housed several more folding tables, and from her viewpoint Georgia saw two women sitting at one of the tables. They were speaking in French, something about a planned protest and the impact that would have on the hospital.

The pony-tailed man approached her.

Georgia wondered what language to use. She decided to stick with English. "Hello, I'm Georgia Steele." She offered her hand to the man.

They shook hands and he introduced himself as Ian Standish, the local manager for DWW. "I'm sorry, but we're not open to the public." His accent was Irish, or maybe Scottish.

"Dr. Standish, I'd like to ask you about Dr. Eugene Young."

The room was instantly quiet. Georgia felt multiple sets of eyes on her.

"Are you from the Embassy? I already spoke to them."

"No, I'm here from the States. Can we talk somewhere in private?"

They left the small office and Standish took her to an employee break room, where they found a table in the back and sat on hard plastic chairs. The doctor stared at her from behind crossed arms.

"I'm going to be straight with you," Georgia said. "Dr. Young asked my godfather to help him with something he found here." She described the situation with the sterilization of the girls but left out a few of the more controversial aspects points: the likely cause, secret organizations, her godfather's notoriety.

As she told the story, the doctor's posture softened. His hands dropped to his lap, worry lines traced his forehead.

"He was very upset that no one would listen to him," Georgia said.

The doctor nodded, his head bobbing slowly like the drinking bird Georgia's father kept on his desk, which had fascinated her as a child.

"I spoke to him less than a week ago," Georgia continued. "I expected him to get back to me by now. I'm worried."

"We are too. He was supposed to work the clinic in La Union this week, but never showed up. We've notified the police, but… well, this isn't America or Europe. Most missing people are never found."

"Can you give me his home address?"

"I'm not supposed to give out that information. I'll have to call to get permission."

"Gene had a friend, José Rodríguez? Do you know where I can find him?"

"I think he might work for an activist group, but I cannot tell you which one. I can give you Christine's cell phone number though. She was Gene's nurse. She traveled with him everywhere."

෨

Georgia could hear the concern in Christine's voice coming from the phone halfway across the hotel room. Sam was frantically scribbling notes.

"Seems we are making progress," Sam said after ending the call.

"What did she say?"

"Dr. Young was going on a weekend vacation with José to Roatan, but he did not show up for work on Tuesday. She thought maybe they missed the ferry back or something, but when he didn't call or show up yesterday, she went by their house. It had been broken into and burglarized. She called the police but couldn't wait for them to arrive. She said he never missed work. She is certain something bad has happened."

"Did she know about the sterilization of the girls?"

"Young did not tell her specifically, but she knew he was concerned about the low number of births they were seeing. So concerned that he asked the area drug lord—her words—to gather information for him."

"A drug dealer?"

"Not just a drug dealer. He runs a small cartel. Drug trafficking is a massive problem here."

"One of many, it seems."

"Also, she knows José Rodríguez. She's met him before. He and the doctor have been together for a few years and are a tight couple, but they've had to play it low key. Homosexuality is not widely accepted here."

Sam referred to his notes. "Rodríguez works as an advocate for the poorest indigenous people. His most recent project regards a hydroelectric dam under construction in the Olancho region. His group, Hondurans for Progress, or Hondureños Para El Progreso, is brokering an agreement between the government, the utility company, and the people to be displaced in the deal. It's been quite contentious."

"Sounds like José could have been the target."

"Yes. Or it could have been a simple robbery or kidnapping gone bad."

"Anything else?"

"She gave me directions to Young's house. She didn't know the exact address. It's about two hours from the new clinic in La Unión."

"Does she have a number for José?"

"No."

"Did you ask about the clinic? Can she meet us there?"

"Afraid not. After she went to Young's house and found it broken into, she called into the DWW office and quit. She is currently sitting in the Dallas airport waiting for a connection home to Phoenix. But she did give me directions to that as well." He showed Georgia his notes.

"I see. Nice work, Bennett."

"Why thank you, ma'am." He grinned.

Georgia's stomach rumbled. "I'm absolutely starving." They had not eaten anything since a late breakfast on the plane.

"Me too. But we should call the embassy before Evans leaves to see if we can reserve a car and driver for tomorrow."

"You think he'll do that?"

"I think he will if he can. I think both he and Messina want to make sure nothing happens to us."

Sam got back on the phone and called the embassy. Georgia browsed Google maps while he talked to Vice-Consul Evans. After a few minutes, Sam gave Georgia a thumbs-up sign. "Well that is very nice of you, thank you very much. We'll see you at ten." He said goodbye and hung up. "Well I am two for two today."

"Do tell."

"Evans is going to see what he can dig up on Hondurans for

Progress and try to find us a contact in Olancho. The embassy definitely has a car we can use, and he will ask Messina about a driver."

"That would be great. It looks to be a long drive to the clinic, mostly on back roads." She closed the cover on her iPad. "Thank you for coming with me, Sam. I know you didn't want to be here."

"No, I didn't want *you* to be here. But now that we are, we need to serious about it. Get what we came for and get out."

"No time for any R&R?"

An impish grin spread across Sam's face. "I could be convinced."

Georgia feigned an exasperated sigh. "I'm starving. Let's get dinner. We can discuss dessert later."

CHAPTER 40

TEGUCIGALPA, HONDURAS

For the second time in two days, Messina escorted Georgia and Sam to Vice-Consul Evans' office. Messina closed the door, but this time stayed inside. Evans started to say something, then stopped.

Georgia asked, "Did you find anything on Dr. Young or José Rodríguez?"

"Not directly. But I do have some information." Evans picked up a piece of paper from his desk. "As you know, Rodríguez works for Hondureños Para El Progreso, also known as El Progreso."

She nodded.

"El Progreso is one of the largest activist groups in Honduras. They spend much of their efforts brokering deals and arbitrating settlements between local communities, private interests, and the government," Evans said, consulting his paper periodically. "They appear to be on the up and up but have been accused of being paid off by foreign companies. However, that's not unusual." He put down the paper. "People here don't understand the ways of the world. Development will happen whether they want it to or not."

Georgia said, "José was working to get funding for some residents of Olancho who will be displaced by a new hydroelectric dam."

"There are many hydroelectric projects in various stages of development in Honduras. And there is always opposition from some of the residents. Your Mr. Rodríguez could have been the target, and Dr. Young could simply have been in the wrong place at the wrong time."

He glanced towards the door and Georgia caught a slight nod from Messina.

"Did you manage to get a phone number or address for Rodríguez when you went to Doctors With Wings?" Evans asked.

"No," Georgia replied, not wanting to give away information. It was the nod. "But we did find out that Dr. Young was supposed to work at the clinic in La Unión. We thought we might go there."

"I'm not familiar with that town."

"It looks to be about three hours north of here," Georgia said. On the way to Young's house.

"Well, perfect then." Evans rifled through some papers and passed one to Sam. "Alejandra Castilla is the head of El Progreso. She lives in La Ceiba. It's on the north coast of Honduras. She can meet with you today and in person if you can get there. It's not close, but if you are planning on going north anyway..." He gestured to Messina. "Anthony is the one who arranged it. He knows many more people here than I do."

Messina folded his arms across his chest, looking impassive.

Georgia looked at Sam. He nodded.

"That sounds great," Georgia said. "The more we can learn, the better."

"Good, so I'll see if I can arrange some lodging and transportation—"

"Mears will take them," Messina said.

Evans looked surprised. "What about the protests? They could start this afternoon."

"Mears will take them."

❧

"We're almost there," Mears said. He pointed to a sign that read Pico Bonito National Park with a right arrow, and La Ceiba, seven kilometers straight ahead. Behind the sign, the Pico Bonito Mountain disappeared into the clouds, while the lesser peaks of the Nombre de Dios Mountain Range were fully visible.

"It's beautiful here," Georgia said.

The drive had taken them most of the day. Throughout the interior they passed communities of free-flowing shanty towns interspersed with massive housing projects laid out in stark grids. There was less garbage in the streets and little sign of the homeless and drug addicted that plagued Tegucigalpa, but it was far from picturesque. According to Mears, the projects were completed after Hurricane Mitch left twenty percent of the population homeless.

The last few hours had taken them along the Northern Coast passing through Tela. This section of the Atlantic coast catered to tourists and wealthy locals. Eco-lodges and resorts were plentiful, and several high-end beachside housing developments were under construction.

At the outskirts of La Ceiba, Mears turned away from the coast and onto a rutted one-lane road. After more than a mile of climbing, alternating between winding switchbacks and sloping straightaways, it stopped at a wrought iron gate supported by two masonry pillars. Mears announced their arrival via an intercom embedded in the left column; a few seconds later the gates swung open. They continued to the top, parking between an old pickup and a dark green Land Rover. Barking dogs heralded their arrival.

A retaining wall lined the back of the gravel parking area, with steps cut into the far side. Two Rottweilers at the top were the source of the commotion. Without hesitation, Mears climbed the stairs and patted both on the head. The dogs followed him out of sight, stubby tails wagging.

"That's quite a greeting, Sam said.

"Either he's a dog whisperer or he's been here before," Georgia replied.

The stone steps led to a Satillo tile deck surrounding a curved pool and a yellow stucco house. The 360-degree view was breathtaking. Beyond the pool, Georgia could see to the coastline far below. Brilliant green met Caribbean blue, interrupted only by the town of La Ceiba and the Rio Cangrejal, the brown river snaking into the blue sea. Behind the house to the south, layers of mountains fanned out in all directions, dark green with clouds hiding the higher peaks.

The expansive house was topped with a metal hipped roof. Two sets of heavy mahogany doors matched multiple casement windows, all open. A tanned man in pressed khakis and a white polo shirt met them upon their arrival. He led them through a spacious living space and out to a deck where Alejandra Castilla waited. She stood next to a railing against a backdrop of green. She was a striking woman, with short dark hair that accentuated a long neck and narrow shoulders. She wore a loose white blouse with dark pants and leather sandals.

"Hello, Danny." Her voice was smooth as velvet.

Mears nodded. "Ma'am."

She opened her hands to Sam and Georgia in a welcoming gesture. Georgia could not tell her age but guessed it to be around fifty. Her olive skin was flawless and tight; it was her dark eyes that revealed the years. She did not look any particular ethnicity. Georgia knew the population of Honduras was predominantly "Mestizo," a mix of original Indian and European, mostly Spanish. Perhaps in that sense, she did look Honduran. Except she was a bit taller than Georgia, who at five foot six had felt tall since arriving.

Castilla reached out and grabbed Georgia's hands first, taking both of them firmly into her own. A silver charm bracelet dangled from one wrist. "It's so nice to meet you, Georgia. I've read about you. Impressive."

Georgia raised her eyebrows in confusion.

"We're not totally behind the times here. We have the internet. We Google." She smiled. She turned her attention to Sam and took his offered hand. "And Sam Bennett, of the FBI." She dragged out each letter, her accent more pronounced as she did.

"Yes, Ma'am."

"Be careful, once they get their hooks into you, it can be hard to escape."

"Ms. Castilla, we're here because we need to get in touch with José Rodríguez, one of your employees," Sam said.

"Yes, that's what Anthony told me."

"Do you know where we can find him?" Georgia asked. "It's important."

"Honestly, no. I don't think he's staying at his house."

"But you must have a phone number for him."

Castilla looked at the slim silver watch on her wrist. "How rude of me. You've had a long trip and it's already after five." She beckoned to the servant who had met them at the door. "Manuel will show you to your rooms. You can freshen up before dinner. We'll have plenty of time to talk then."

"That's very generous, but we have a reservation at a hotel in La Ceiba," Sam said.

"Nonsense, you'll stay here. I have plenty of room and the roads can be dangerous at night."

The three guests followed Manuel into the house and down a windowed hallway. Brightly colored prints on the opposing wall danced in the sunbeams cast by the setting sun. On closer inspection Georgia saw they were actually photographs of insects, taken on a microscopic scale. Eyes, antennae, wings, and other body parts—the images exotic and alien. A framed letter from the Entomology Preservation Initiative thanked Castilla for her generous contribution to the South American Insect Ark. Other letters of appreciation followed. One from a seed vault, another from a nature preserve in Brazil.

Georgia caught up to the group as they descended a staircase leading to a light-filled room with a spectacular view. Sliding glass doors opened onto a cantilevered deck that soared over the green valley below. Philodendrons with leaves the size of umbrellas climbed the walls of the house and treetops canopied the deck.

There was a room on the left, which Mears took, a hallway on the right, and a door behind the staircase. The short hallway held two bedrooms, with a Jack-and-Jill bathroom in between. Georgia's suitcase and messenger bag were already in the first room. A colorful painting reminiscent of Georgia O'Keefe hung on the wall over a four-poster antique bed.

Sam appeared through the open bathroom door. "Nice digs, eh? What do you make of our host, Ms. Castilla?"

"She's poised, confident, and obviously quite wealthy," Georgia said. "She's tight with Mears and Messina, which is interesting. Other than that, I don't know yet."

Georgia showered and dressed for dinner. She was waiting for Sam by the staircase when Manuel came down.

"We'll be up in a few minutes," Georgia said, speaking to the man in Spanish.

"That is fine, Señora. I am just getting wine for dinner." He unlocked the door behind the staircase.

Georgia could make out floor to ceiling wine racks. Some of the bottles refracted an electrical blue glow emanating from inside the room. She was moving in for a closer look when Manuel came out with two bottles of red wine.

"That's some wine cellar," she said, trying to appear nonchalant.

"Yes. It is also a hurricane shelter. You want to keep something safe here, you have to encase it in concrete. That is what the Señora says."

～

Georgia, Sam, and Alejandra Castilla sat together at a formal dining table. Manuel poured wine and served local fish for dinner, though Mears had not yet arrived.

They engaged in various small talk, admiring the beautiful sunset and stunning views. Castilla asked about their education and jobs. She seemed particularly interested in Georgia's work, complimenting her on her achievements.

During a lull in the conversation, Sam asked, "Are you from Honduras, Ms. Castilla?"

"Please, call me Alejandra," Castilla said. "No, but I have been here almost twenty years. I went to boarding school with the wife of President Roberto Pinero. He was a man with great plans and had a wonderful vision for the country." She sipped her wine. "Roberto's wife asked me to oversee an ambitious program to improve education, family planning, and employment. Then Hurricane Mitch struck, and everything changed."

Georgia nodded. She had read about Mitch on the plane ride over.

Castilla continued, "It was the worst natural disaster in the history of this country. Over ten thousand people died, and millions were left homeless. Roberto did all he could to secure funding and humanitarian aid. But it wasn't enough, and he lost the next election."

"What made you stay?" Sam asked.

"By that time I had commitments that could not be broken, and I had grown to love this country. I built this home and took matters into my own hands. I started El Progreso. We get things done without waiting for a system that won't change. Though it's a hard place to live, it is the perfect place to make a difference."

"Those photographs in the hallway," Georgia mused.

"The bugs?" Castilla laughed. "A present from the Insect Ark. They also gave me this." She held out her wrist so Georgia could see the bracelet.

"Are those…"

"Insects and an ark. They had it commissioned for me." She pulled her wrist back and absently fingered the charms. "The Ark is gathering as many species of insects as we can find to try and save them." She turned her attention to Georgia. "Did you know that every single year we are losing two and a half percent of the insect population?"

"No," Georgia admitted.

"I'm sure that you are smart enough to know the earth cannot live without its insects, or for that matter, the rest of its ecosystem. We are in the midst of a mass extinction event." Sam must have made some sort of face for Castilla turned on him, glaring. "You think this is a joke?"

"No," he said, bringing one hand up in a half surrender. "I just think a lot of these things are said to scare people, but we always seem to find solutions. The ozone hole, the population explosion, it's all end-of-world hysteria. We'll find a way to make it work."

Castilla shook her head in disgust or maybe disappointment. "This is not about throwing out your spray deodorant or recycling your pizza boxes. People are going to have to make real sacrifices to save future generations. And I can't see them doing it voluntarily. Are you willing to stop eating meat? Or give up your car?" She waved her hand, causing the charms of her bracelet to jingle. "When do you think the world will fall into chaos? When will the Earth's resources and climate collapse and give way to mass starvation, war, and the fall of civilization as we know it?"

"That's a ridiculous question," Sam said.

Castilla ignored him. "Dr. Steele? Give an educated guess."

Georgia had never really thought about it in such stark terms. She took a moment to pull together some of the facts she remembered. Not a pleasant outcome. "A few hundred years, maybe less."

Sam's eyes widened in surprise.

"You're very generous," Castilla said. "Already more than two billion people lack access to clean drinking water. But we'll go with your prediction. Two hundred years from now, it will all be over. Are you okay with that?"

Georgia did not get a chance to respond. The two Rottweilers who had been lying at their owner's feet erupted in excited barking, running from the room and out into the night.

Castilla tilted her head and closed her eyes. Georgia followed her cue and listened. The open windows carried the sound of a car door slamming and footsteps on gravel. The dogs stopped barking when a man greeted them.

Castilla brought one hand to her face, the fingers covering her mouth. She looked distressed. She rose from the table and got as far as the doorway when she stopped.

"What are you doing here?" She was holding the doorframe with one hand, blocking the entrance. Georgia turned and leaned in her seat to see past Castilla to the newcomer.

José Rodríguez wore a dark t-shirt, jeans, and cowboy boots. His long wavy hair fell flat, draping his drawn, tired face. He was almost unrecognizable as the handsome young Latino she had last seen in a Skype window. Georgia turned back and lowered her head, feeling sad to see such a change.

She heard José reply to Castilla's question. "Gene's nurse, Christine, called me. She thought I should know that an FBI agent from the States is here looking for him. Then I called the American Embassy. They told me he had come here. To see you." José turned his head to Castilla. "Alejandra?"

"I wanted to talk to them first, before I called you. To clarify their intentions. I didn't want to get your hopes up." Georgia heard them walk into the room. Castilla said, "This is Sam Bennett."

Sam reached across the table to shake hands with José.

"And this is—"

"What the hell?" José said. He looked from Georgia to Sam.

"We came as soon as we could," Georgia said.

"I should have known," José said. "You're not here to help find Gene, you're here for the information he had."

Castilla reached up and touched José's face. "You know Gene is not coming back."

José swatted her hand aside. He turned to leave.

"Wait!" Georgia cried, "Please." She stood. "I'm so sorry about Gene. I miss Frank so much, too. Maybe we can do something to honor them. If the data Gene sent us was accurate, this is a pretty nasty thing."

"If we can bring enough exposure to it, people will have to listen," Sam said.

José stopped and looked back over his shoulder. "Are you really from the FBI?"

"Yes."

José turned to face them. "There's nothing I can do."

"Gene sent high level data to Frank," Georgia said. "It was enough for us to validate his theory. But it is not detailed enough to do anything about. We need names, and we need DNA samples."

"I don't have anything," José said, his voice trembling. "The house was trashed. Our computers were stolen. His bag is missing. The safe was ripped out of the wall."

"Do you think any records would be at the clinic?"

José exhaled. "Possibly. They shut it down when Gene…" His voice cracked. "Christine was supposed to close the clinic and take the medicine to Tegucigalpa for safe keeping. Maybe the records are still there."

"We can have Mears take us in the morning," Georgia said.

"Mears?" José said.

"You know him? He brought us here."

José nodded in the direction of the parking area. "That ridiculous car. What is Mears doing here, Alejandra?"

"Calm down. He's just acting as a driver for our guests. He will be taking them back in the morning."

Sam started to say something, but José cut him off. "I will take them over to the clinic. I need to go and get a few things from the house."

Castilla frowned.

"Thank you," Georgia said.

"Do not thank me," José said, shaking his head. "Whatever Gene was doing may have gotten him killed, and I am very angry. But I will give you what I can, because I want this out of my life. I will take you to the clinic and find you a ride back to Tegucigalpa or take you myself."

"José, you don't—" Castilla started, but José raised a hand to silence her.

"After that, we are done. I will be here by eight. If we have to drive all the way to Tegu, we need to get an early start."

⁂

Mears joined them after José left. Georgia thought it no coincidence.

Castilla was visibly upset. "That's what I hoped to avoid. José is in no condition to talk about Gene."

Mears eyed them one by one.

"José's giving these two a ride to the clinic tomorrow, so it seems your chauffeur services are no longer required." Castilla informed him.

"You sure? The clinic is in La Unión, right? We could drive that way. It's on the way back to the embassy."

"We'll go with José," Sam said. Georgia was glad he did. She felt they needed to be alone with him.

"I should call Messina. Let him know." Mears got up from the table and went inside.

Castilla took her seat and slowly sipped her wine.

When Mears came back, he looked grim. "It seems I have to leave early anyway," he said. "I'll say goodnight now." He left them and disappeared into the house.

"I think I shall retire as well," Castilla said, a forced smile on her drawn face. "I hope we get the chance to talk again soon, Georgia. I would very much like to get to know you better."

"What do you make of all that?" Georgia asked Sam, once they were alone.

"I don't know. I guess we'll find out more tomorrow," Sam said.

CHAPTER 41

OLANCHO REGION, HONDURAS

GEORGIA HAD AWAKENED in so many places the past few weeks, but this was definitely the most beautiful and tranquil. Light streamed through an emerald mix of mountains, trees, and philodendron leaves. Birds called across the valley. A light breeze brushed fresh air still moist with dew across her skin.

It was almost eight by the time she dressed, packed her bags, secured her cell phone in a waterproof carry case under her shirt, and went upstairs. She found the house empty, except for Sam drinking coffee on the deck and reading emails on his phone.

He gave her a winning smile. "Good morning. You're up late." They had slept alone, in their respective rooms. Both thought it too awkward to share a bed here.

"I couldn't help myself. It's so peaceful," she said. "Where is everyone?"

"Ms. Castilla left. She said to tell you goodbye, and that she hopes to see you again soon. Manuel went into town to shop. And Mears was gone when I got up about six."

"Any coffee left?"

"Yes, but you'll need to take it to go."

Below, José was climbing the stairs from the parking area.

❦

They had been driving for about an hour, sitting shoulder to shoulder in José's pickup truck with Georgia in the center. José was a statue and Georgia's attempts to engage him in small talk had thus far failed.

"This part of the country is so beautiful," Georgia said. The clouds were gone today, and the entire mountain range was visible against a bright blue sky. "Won't you miss it?"

"What do you mean?" José asked. Finally a response.

"When you leave Honduras?"

José looked upset. "Why would I leave Honduras?"

"Your email said you were leaving in a few days."

"What email?"

"José, I got an email from you three days ago. It said that Gene was missing and that you would help me if I came down. And that you were leaving the country. That's why we're here."

"I did not send you any emails."

"Shit," Sam muttered.

A skinny dog darted into the street. José braked hard and the truck narrowly missed the mutt.

"What exactly did it say?" José asked. At least his anger was not directed at them this time.

Georgia told him.

"It makes no sense," José murmured.

"It could have been someone who knew what was going on but was afraid to identify themselves," Georgia said. "Maybe Gene's nurse, Christine?"

"The email was sent Tuesday morning," Sam said. "She couldn't have already known about Gene."

"Someone else then. Or someone who wanted to lure us here to find out what we know," Georgia said. "To see if we are a threat. I think we need to take a look at that email again."

Beep-beep! All three jumped. A car had pulled up behind them and the driver was honking its horn.

Sam said, "We'll have to figure that out later. For now, we'd better go."

José let the honking car pass, then resumed driving.

"How did you meet Gene?" Georgia asked José.

"El Progreso helped DWW get money to open the clinic." José was still frowning. "We met at a planning meeting." His lips pinched into a thin line, holding back the emotion that must be overwhelming him.

Georgia tried a less emotional topic. "And how long have you worked at El Progreso?"

"A long time, since I came back from University, in California."

Georgia waited, hoping to hear more.

"My parents had a successful business here. They sent me to private schools and then to UCLA. I was supposed to take over the company when my father retired." José swerved to miss a pothole, and Georgia bumped into him.

"Sorry," she said.

"Hurricane Mitch hit while I was at school. When I returned everything was gone. Our house, the business. My parents moved to Mexico and wanted me to come too. I saw the horror that happened here and realized I wanted to stay. I wanted to help the people here. That was more important to me than making money. Someone introduced me to Alejandra, and I went to work for El Progreso," José said. "Now I make a real difference in people's lives."

"And the hydroelectric dam is your latest project?" Georgia asked.

José nodded. "It will create electricity and bring clean water to thousands of people. Some of the land was used for strip mining and was horribly polluted. Much work was done to clean up the water and the land."

"Impressive," Georgia said.

"Three small communities will have to move. Their land and their homes will be flooded. But we were able to secure a good payment for them—the largest ever."

"How did you do it?" Sam asked.

"Do what?"

"Get such a good deal."

"I wish I could take the... the..."

"The credit?" Sam asked.

"Yes, the credit, thank you." José said. "After hurricane Mitch the government approved a dam in this region. But the original contracts had no site clean-up and no water supply for the local people. That was when El Progreso got involved. Alejandra got the mine owners and the government to agree to those things. But until a few weeks ago, we still had no payment for the people losing their homes."

"I imagine that did not go over well," Sam said.

"The leaders of the communities said they would not leave. Of course they would have been ordered to go, but the publicity would have been bad. And then, this other thing came up."

"Go on," Georgia said.

José shrugged. "According to Gene, this happened long ago. Before the dam was even planned. I would not be surprised if all of this was due to the mining that occurred before. We know they used arsenic and other terrible chemicals, but we cannot let what happened long ago risk what we have now."

"I'm sorry. I'm confused," Sam said.

"You know, the communities, the villages."

"No," Sam said. "What do you mean?"

"The villages we are paying to move. They were the ones in Gene's study."

Georgia gasped, and José turned to her. "You did not know?"

"Gene sent us only high-level data," she replied. "We knew

the three villages were near each other, but we did not know their names."

"When is the area going to be flooded?" Sam asked.

"Six weeks," José said. "The new dam is complete, and most of the electric grid. There is an old earthen dam farther upstream that was built by the mining company. It is not stable and must be taken down carefully. It will be drained once the people are gone."

"Can you take us to the villages?" Georgia asked, trying to keep her voice steady. This was it. They could get the proof they needed.

José sighed. "I guess so. After the clinic."

"Tell us about the clinic," Sam said.

"It opened last year. Gene was so proud."

"I saw a picture of the ribbon-cutting ceremony on the internet," Georgia said.

"¿Sí?"

"Yes. Will it be impacted by the dam?"

"The clinic? No. It serves La Unión and nearby communities. It is sixty kilometers from the dam site."

"Did Gene see the people from the three villages at the clinic?" Georgia asked.

"Not many. Sixty kilometers may not sound like a long way to you, but to people who cannot afford a car it is very far. Gene and Christine traveled to them."

They stopped to let a man drive a herd of goats across the road.

"José, do you know anyone who would want to hurt Gene?" Sam asked.

José grimaced.

"We want to help," Georgia said.

"You cannot."

"Let us try."

"Gene is, or was, a stubborn man. When he had his mind decided, there was no talking him away from it."

"Sounds like someone else I know," Sam said.

Georgia gave him a quick elbow, and a "Shh."

"Ow."

"Please, José, go on."

"Gene asked Juan Carlos Ramos, a leader of the largest drug cartel in Olancho, to help him gather information about the people." He slammed his hand on the steering wheel. "But why would Ramos care? Why would he want to help? I told him these people care only about themselves and that he could get killed."

The man with the goats waved thanks as the last of his herd crossed the street.

"Do you know where we can find this Ramos?" Georgia asked.

"Are you joking with me?"

"Why would the cartel want to kill a doctor?"

José shrugged and fell silent.

"José, why don't you like Mears?" Sam asked. "What's his story?"

"It is not personal. But you should not expect us to trust any of you."

"Americans?" Georgia asked.

José looked incredulous.

"Please, José, indulge us."

He looked at Sam. "Mears is like him."

"What?"

"CIA."

"I'm not with the CIA," Sam said.

"CIA, FBI, DIA, NSA, Homeland Security, whatever." José rolled his eyes. "Messina, Mears, and half of those at the embassy are not what they pretend to be."

"Really?" Georgia looked at Sam.

"Probably," Sam replied. "It's no secret." To José he said, "But I'm not CIA."

"He seemed so nice," Georgia mused.

"You cannot trust anyone here. Remember that."

◅

Another hour passed before José stopped in front of a white wood-framed cottage. The small front yard needed mowing. Red bougainvillea framed a connecting carport. Mature birds of paradise, twelve feet tall, grew along the side of the house.

"Is this your home?" Georgia asked.

He eased the truck onto the driveway. "We rent the house. We were looking for a house together, before this."

José opened the door leading from the carport and abruptly halted, frozen in the doorway. "I have not been able to come back since Gene left." He propelled himself forward using the doorframe for support.

Georgia entered a sunny kitchen that reeked of rotting garbage. Most of the cabinets and drawers were opened with the contents strewn about. Broken glass sparkled on the floor.

"I'm not sure what you will find. All of Gene's work is gone," José said, directing them into the main room, a combination family and dining room.

Sam searched the master while Georgia looked in the bathroom and home office. These rooms had been given the same treatment as the kitchen. Drawers stood open, the contents scattered, and closets were ransacked.

"They were in a hurry, that's for sure," Sam said, once Georgia and José joined him in the master bedroom. "I'm inclined to agree that whoever did this was probably after Gene's work and just gave the rest of the house a quick once over to make sure nothing was missed. And to make it look like a robbery." He held up a wristwatch, "Is this Gene's?"

José snatched the watch from his hand. "No, it is mine. Where did you find it?"

"Wedged between the bed and the frame. Probably flew out of a drawer. Looks pretty valuable."

José clutched the watch to his chest. "A gift from Gene."

⤜

The clinic was situated on a corner of the street leading into the town of La Unión. A small grocery occupied the space next door and a nondescript two-story apartment lay directly across the street. Further down were a few simple buildings, painted in bright colors. A sign advertising purified water hung on the corner of the next block.

"It looks smaller than in the picture," Georgia said.

"Gene treated a lot of people here. The clinic was always full," José said.

Today no people were in sight, and the grocery store was dark though it was noon.

"That's not good." Sam pointed to the clinic's facade.

Burglar bars crossed the substantial picture window. Sunlight reflected in irregular patterns, revealing broken glass.

"*Demonios*," José cried. He fished a Browning 9mm from under the seat.

"You don't happen to have another one of those handy?" Sam asked.

"Sorry, Señor," he said grimly.

They approached the clinic with caution. The door opened with a push, the lock destroyed. José entered first, then Georgia, followed by Sam.

The clinic's waiting room was in shambles. Papers were scattered across the room. The reception table, fake wood laminate with metal legs, lay on its side blocking an aluminum swinging door. An overturned stack of plastic patio chairs uncoiled across a hook rug covering the concrete floor.

"Do you smell smoke?" Sam asked.

José bolted across the room, leaping over the desk and skidding into the metal door which swung open under his weight. Georgia followed. Past the door were a dispensary-kitchen combination on the right and two patient rooms on the left. The destruction in the waiting room was minimal compared to what had occurred here. The contents of cabinets and drawers were strewn on the ground in a mash-up of liquid, broken glass, and paper. The smoke smell was stronger, mixed with bleach and something sweet.

Sam entered behind them. "If Christine took all the drugs out of here before she left, then what were they after?"

The three carefully made their way across the floor and began to search the rest of the clinic. The two simply-furnished examination rooms across from the dispensary were relatively untouched.

A hallway led to three doors. The first revealed a small operating room, low tech by modern standards. It had met a similar fate as the dispensary, the few electronics smashed and the room in tatters.

José passed the second door, an exit signed in red: *Salida*.

Inside the last room, a shared office with two desks and chairs, material inside a metal wastepaper basket still smoldered. Scraps of burned paper sat atop a mound of ashes. A metal filing cabinet had been pilfered, the drawers left open. Empty manila folders carpeted the floor. Apparently, the perpetrators had casually thrown them down as they fed the enclosed papers to the fire.

José rested his gun on top of the filing cabinet and looked inside. "Nothing left."

Georgia opened the few desk drawers that were not already on the floor. "Nothing here either."

"They may have taken a computer." Sam held up a laptop charging cable. "Is there a safe in here or back-up storage?"

"I think not," José said. "I am going outside to call DWW."

Georgia and Sam spent a few more minutes looking around the clinic. They found nothing of interest.

"It's pretty clear Gene was onto something that got him killed," Georgia said.

"You don't know that for sure. There is a lot of crime here."

"Come on. Vandals and drug addicts don't burn records." Georgia righted an upturned chair. "I think our little trip to Honduras just got extended. We may not be able to get our hands on Gene's records, but we don't need them."

"Why not?"

"Now that we know the villages in question, we can collect DNA from the people who live there. We may want to see if we can get someone from DWW or the World Health Organization to come with us. I'm going to grab my iPad from the truck and make a few notes." Georgia started back towards the front of the clinic.

"Maybe we can get some lunch," Sam said.

Just then, Georgia heard a voice coming from the front room. "Shh," she snapped.

"It's just José on the phone."

"Quiet," Georgia whispered. "There's someone out there with him. A man." She crept through the dispensary. Glass cracked under Sam's feet as he caught up to her, José's gun in hand.

The aluminum door had swung shut, but its Plexiglas window provided a view to the outer room and front entrance. José stood in the front doorway, hands on his hips, blocking her view of the man he was confronting. She caught a bit of slicked back dark hair.

Georgia moved farther left to gain a viewpoint of the clinic's front window. An olive-green military vehicle was parked behind José's truck. It held two additional men, both clothed in black. One stood in the cab holding a rifle while the other sat behind the wheel.

She heard José speaking. "You have no business in here."

"Let me in. I need to see the woman. The one Dr. Young talked about."

"So you can kill her too? When will it end, Ramos?"

"Stop this and let me in." The man stepped forward and into the doorway. Georgia could see him now, a dark-skinned man with a short beard wearing a blue sport jacket, a light blue shirt, and the designer jeans and expensive shoes. He and José were nearly nose to nose.

José stood his ground and Juan Carlos Ramos shoved him. The

two struggled for a moment. Jumping back, José held in his hand a pistol he must have taken from the cartel leader, perhaps from a hidden shoulder holster. He pointed it squarely at Ramos' chest.

"Get out of here, Ramos. Get out now!"

Ramos slowly raised his hands. "Do not be stupid. Put the gun down. My men have you covered." He pointed one finger behind him.

Georgia could see this was true. José must have also, for his shoulders slumped, and he began to lower the gun. Out of nowhere came a loud crack. Both men jumped. Then José's arm went limp, and the gun slipped from his grasp, hitting the ground with a thud. He dropped to his knees, a hand on his chest. Ramos dove for cover, jumping over José. Rapid gunfire erupted outside the clinic.

Georgia dropped to her knees and crawled past the aluminum door. She dragged José out of the doorway and back into the clinic, leaning him up against the concrete wall below the window. She curled next to him, covering her ears. Glass fragments showered them as bullets shattered what remained of the window and ricocheted off the cement floor.

Ramos retrieved the fallen weapon, nearly getting shot. Sam leaned around the metal door, gun in hand. Ramos motioned for him to stay where he was and cover the front entrance. The gunfire continued outside.

The cartel leader studied her with careful consideration, an absurd juxtaposition to the fighting in the street. He set the gun on the floor and reached into the inside pocket of his jacket and retrieved something small, which he placed into her hand. "A copy of what I gave to Dr. Young," he said. "Take it and go. We will take care of Rodríguez."

Georgia chanced a peak out of the window. Ramos' driver was slumped over the steering wheel. The man with the automatic rifle was now crouched behind the truck, firing at the roof of the apartment complex.

"Go now," Ramos said in English, looking past her to Sam. "I have people coming." He picked up the gun and started shooting out of the broken window. He yelled something in Spanish. Tires from an approaching car squealed.

The front of José's shirt was bright red, and his eyes were closed. Sam's hand clamped down hard on Georgia's arm. Shots pelted the wall of the waiting room. The cartel leader swore and reloaded his weapon. As Sam dragged her though the metal door and back into the dispensary, she opened her hand and found that Ramos had given her a memory card. She shoved it into her jeans pocket.

Sam hustled her through the dispensary and into the back hallway. He opened the emergency exit a few inches. Nothing happened. He inched it open until it stopped perpendicular to the building. Distant shots mixed with the roar of vehicles racing away. Then silence.

The door obstructed their view to the street running along the clinic's side. To their right, a parked delivery truck blocked the narrow alley. There was no way to tell what waited in either direction.

"This way," Sam whispered. Ducking, they dashed to take cover behind the truck. Georgia tried the driver's door, but found it locked.

Sam stood up. "I think we're good," he said, just as bullets pelted the clinic door and fractured the truck's windshield. "Shit," he yelled, dropping down to a crouch. The shots seemed to come from the street, but it was impossible to be sure.

Farther down the alley a door opened, behind it a scared face. Georgia bolted and heard Sam's footsteps behind her. She propelled herself through the back door to the grocery store and came face to face with a terrified young woman, her arm protecting the child at her side.

Sam rushed into the store. "Dammit."

"We can't stay here," Georgia said. She tilted her head in the direction of the mother and child. "Stay inside and hide," she told them.

A slow blink conveyed Sam's agreement. Keeping low to the ground, they darted around the alley door and hid behind it. This door was wood, no match for the high-powered ammunition being used against them. A hole blasted inches above Georgia's head.

They ran down the alley staying close to the store. Bullets bit into the bare block wall and concrete chips flew, striking Georgia's legs.

The alley ended across the street from the water supplier. A truck towing an elephant-sized water tank was parked in the adjoining lot, its engine running. Sam got to the trailer first and leapt onto it as the truck started to move. Shots hit the plastic tank and water streamed out. The driver accelerated, spinning tires and throwing gravel.

"Come on," Sam yelled. The truck gained momentum, and Georgia fell behind. *Don't panic, George. Run.* She sprinted and jumped, willing herself towards the trailer's tailgate. One hand caught its lip, and then both hands were on and she was being dragged behind, moving so fast that the ground was a blur. Sam grasped her under the arms and pulled her to safety.

They lay panting between the water container and the walls of the trailer as the truck roared away. Water poured from the bullet holes, cooling the hot metal bed. Georgia heard a few more isolated shots, then nothing more.

She could only see the top half of Sam's body. The rest was curled around the water tank. His white shirt, wet and dirty, was turning deep red.

Even so, Sam was smiling at her.

CHAPTER 42

OLANCHO REGION, HONDURAS

HOTEL CATACAMAS WAS the nicest hotel in the small town of the same name. They were less than thirty miles from La Unión, but the man in the water truck would drive them no farther.

Sam and Georgia entered the lobby as inconspicuously as one bloody American and one mixed-race Asian could. Sam's white shirt was a patchwork of red. He had been cut more than once by shards of flying glass before he pulled Georgia away from José and Ramos. He had not been shot though, as Georgia had feared. She was sweaty and dirty from the trip in the truck but otherwise in one piece.

The hotel was two stories of faded orange concrete, the inside decorated with colorful streamers and a pair of dusty plastic plants flanking a wooden registration desk. A man in his sixties sat at the desk, writing in a spiral notebook.

"We need a room, please, sir," Georgia said.

The man eyed them up and down. "Does your friend need some help?"

"He'll be alright. Do you have a first aid kit?"

The man gave her extra towels and several tiny bandages. "The store down the street should have more."

Their room, one of eight, was simply furnished with a double bed draped in a worn, but seemingly clean, bedspread. It was also unbearably hot. An ancient air conditioner hanging in the window came to life with a series of clicks and a groan.

They had not talked on the ride to Catacamas, apart from establishing that neither had been shot or seriously injured. Georgia felt surprisingly calm; she was probably in shock. But her mind was clear and there were many questions that needed answering.

"Take off your shirt," Georgia said. Sam was a pitiful sight.

He grinned mischievously. "If you say so." He began to undress.

"Really?" she said, feigning exasperation. "You're thinking about sex at a time like this? Go to the bathroom. We need to look at those cuts."

He pouted but did as he was told.

"These are small, but this one could probably use a few stitches." Her fingers traced a path around the cuts on his side and back. "Get in the shower and scrub everything. I'll go get supplies to bandage you up."

She gave him a light kiss on the cheek. "And thanks for saving my life. I have to admit, I did not see that coming."

Sam took her hand, bringing it to his chest. "You saved yourself. I just helped pull you in. That truck was moving fast. You ran it down. That was really incredible."

"Just a will to live."

Georgia returned a half an hour later with several bags in hand and found a seat in the lobby on a white rattan sofa with bright floral patterns. She laid out the memory card from Ramos, a phone cable, and an adapter she bought at what passed for a hardware and convenience store. With a pair of pliers borrowed from the man at the front desk, she rigged up a connection between her iPhone and the card. Using the hotel's Wi-Fi, she transferred the contents of the memory card to a Dropbox folder she shared with Dave and sent him a text. Not very secure, but it would do for the time being. She disposed of the now mangled adapter, returned the pliers, and made another request of the hotelier. He smiled and returned a few minutes later with a small glass.

She found Sam sitting on the bed in their room, a towel wrapped around his waist. One hand pressed a washcloth against the largest cut and the other held his telephone. He hung up as she entered.

"José is alive."

She caught her breath. "Where is he?"

"In a small hospital north of here. I'm trying to find out more. I have Evans looking into it." He noticed the glass in her hand and sniffed. "Is that tequila?"

"Yes, it's easier to find than hydrogen peroxide." She took his washcloth and dipped it into the tequila.

Sam grimaced as she soaked his cuts with the potent liquor. "I'm going to smell like a drunk," he said.

"Better than infection. Be still and stop complaining." One by one, she covered his cuts with bandages, taping up the largest first. "Should we go to the hospital and see José? We can get a doctor to give you a few stitches while we are there."

"He may not be there. After I talked to Evans, I called DWW and told them what happened. They'll make sure he gets the best medical care, which will mean a transfer to a private hospital if at all possible. I'm to call back in an hour or two for an update. I also called Sean Kelly. He's contacting the local authorities. Hopefully they will be here soon to talk to us."

"Good job, Sam." She disposed of the bandage scraps and his bloody shirt. "What should we do now?"

"I have an idea…" Sam placed a hand behind Georgia's neck and kissed her. She did not resist.

❦

"Let's get something to eat." Georgia tossed Sam the contents of the remaining bag. "I got you something to wear."

He held up a bright yellow t-shirt picturing a Mayan temple and the Copan Archeological Park logo. "Stunning."

"It was the best I could do on short notice. Quit your complaining."

The hotel restaurant was empty this late in the afternoon. Their hotelier, who also acted as waiter and bartender during off hours, took their orders of chicken with tortillas, red beans and rice, and Barena, a local beer. The food was mediocre, but the beers were cold.

"I guess I'll try DWW again," Sam said. "See how José is doing." After a few stalled attempts he got through to someone with information. "He's been stabilized and will be moved to another hospital later today. The best trauma surgeon in the country, a DWW doctor, is going to operate."

"That's fantastic news. Did our friend at the embassy know what the hell went on at that clinic?"

"Evans said the cartel was likely to blame."

"That's bull. They were the ones getting shot in the street by snipers."

"I know. I think one of Ramos' men died," he said. "What's that noise?"

"It's Dave," Georgia explained. The sound of the incoming VOIP call grew louder as she extracted her phone.

"Did you get the stuff I sent?" she asked, using the speaker so Sam could hear.

Sam looked confused and mouthed, "What stuff?"

She shushed him.

"Trish and I downloaded it already. It seems to contain complete population records of the three villages in question and at least six others too." Dave sounded excited. "It's mostly pictures of handwritten notes or texts, but we have several open-source readers. We're working on a program to parse and organize the data now."

"Excellent."

"With Dr. Young's previous analysis, it should give us all the data we need to prove that there's something hinky going on. But of course, we cannot tie that to your godfather's research without hard evidence. Are you guys making any progress on that front?"

"Not much. We did find out that the three villages are close to an old mining pit and are being moved to make way for a hydroelectric dam. A deal with them is being brokered by El Progreso. Dr. Young's partner, José Rodríguez, works for them."

"Any other towns being moved for the dam?" Dave asked.

"Nope."

"Seems a little coincidental," Dave said. "Hey, Marcus wants to talk to you. Can you hang on for a minute while I dial him in?"

"Sure." She absently reached for her beer, her hand stopping halfway. From behind Sam, two figures approach their table.

"What's wrong?" Sam asked, turning around.

"Nice shirt, Bennett," Messina said. He was accompanied by Mears, both armed and in their trademark gray camouflage. Messina took an empty chair, turned it around, and sat on it backwards, leaning his arms on the top rail. "Sit," he said, addressing Mears.

The younger man complied, perching on the edge of an unstable bamboo stool.

"If you don't mind, I'm on a call," Georgia said. She pushed her chair back, preparing to stand and move away from the table. Away from Messina. The man gave her the creeps.

"Call them back." The words were benign enough, but the tone was clearly threatening.

"It seems I have to go." Georgia put down the phone.

"We were expecting the local authorities," Sam said. "Who called you?"

"Your Honduran vacation is over. It's time to leave," Messina said.

"We haven't done anything wrong. You can't tell us what to do," Georgia said.

"You broke into the La Unión clinic, met with the leader of a dangerous drug cartel, and almost got José Rodríguez killed."

"That's not what happened," Sam said.

"You could be arrested at this point. For your own safety, I need you to turn over the information you got from Ramos and go back to the States."

Georgia felt her heart quicken. "No chance," she said, her reaction automatic. "Sam and I are not leaving. Not yet."

Sam reached for his phone.

"Go ahead, Bennett, call your boss. ET phone home."

Sam crossed his arms, and the two glared at each other.

"Do it," Messina commanded.

Sam put in a call to Sean Kelly. He paced the floor of the restaurant, on the short end of a one-sided conversation. When he returned and sat back down, his face was flush. "We have to go," he said. "And you need to turn over the memory card."

"Are you kidding me?" Georgia asked.

"I've been recalled. I have to leave as soon as possible." His tone was one of forced composure.

Rage flashed through Georgia. "We can't leave now."

"What about José?" Sam asked Messina. "He's going to Tegucigalpa for surgery. I want to go to the hospital to see him."

"As long as you make the first flight out in the morning. And we'll see that you do."

Georgia took in a deep breath and let it out slowly. She fixed her eyes on Sam and tried to sound calm. "Please send my regards to José."

"What do you mean? You have to come with me."

"I do not."

"You're making a big mistake, Ms. Steele," Messina said.

"It's Dr. Steele to you."

"As you've seen firsthand, this is a dangerous country. It's not safe for Americans traveling alone, especially a woman. You need to come with us."

"Let me talk to her for a minute, okay?" Sam asked. "I'll get the card and meet you out front."

Messina and Mears stood and walked towards the hotel entrance. As they did, Messina laughed and said something to Mears. Mears looked back over his shoulder, and his eyes met Georgia's.

"Look," Sam said. "I know we wanted to see this through, but sometimes you have to know when to call it quits. We could have been killed this morning. Snipers shot at us."

"That's right, Sam. Snipers, not drug dealers."

"Making it all the more reason to leave."

Georgia felt like screaming. It was all she could do to keep some composure. "Something bad is happening here. I'm not going, and I can't believe you are. I need to help Gene and clear Frank's name."

"Frank's dead. Gene probably is too. You can't help them."

"I can help the people here. I'm not leaving." *The only clue to who I am is here. I have to find Alex.* "I can't leave."

"Georgia, please," Sam said. He leaned over to put his hands onto hers, but she withdrew them, crossed her arms, and looked away.

"Goodbye, Sam."

A few moments later, she heard the chair scrape on the floor, followed by Sam's retreating footsteps. He went in the direction of their room, probably to retrieve the memory card. When he came back, he glanced in her direction. With a shake of his head, he left the hotel.

Georgia picked up the phone. Thankfully, the call was active.

"Dave, are you still here?"

"We're here," Dave said.

"Georgia what the hell is going on?" Not Dave.

"Marcus." Dave must have conferenced him into the call.

"Damn it girl, what have you gotten yourself into?"

Under Marcus' persistent questioning, Georgia relayed the details of the last two days.

"At the clinic, was José the primary target, or the cartel leader?" Marcus asked.

"I couldn't tell. I think the shots came from the roof of the building across the street. But at least one of Ramos' guards was shot and probably killed."

"What happened to the information Ramos gave you? Was that on the card they took from you?"

"Yes, but I sent it to Dave first."

"I'm parsing it out as we speak," Dave said.

Marcus was silent. Georgia knew he was thinking.

"Hey, Dave?" she asked.

"Here."

"Could you guys overhear the conversation?"

"Not so much."

"Oh."

"Which is why I recorded it," Dave said, not able to hide the pride in his voice.

"You are the best."

"I know."

"Right before they left, Messina—the head creepy guy—said something to Mears, his minion. Can you tell me what they said?"

"Hang on. I'll see."

※

Several minutes later Dave was back. "I think we have it. Is Marcus still on?"

"No, but he said he'd be back and not to hang up."

"I'm going to play it."

The conversation played out again. She waited until she heard Sam say, "I'll get the card and meet you out front." Then chairs creaked as the two men stood up and left the table. "It doesn't matter. In two days it's done and then we'll deal with her."

"Did you hear that?" Dave asked.

"Yes."

"What does that mean?"

"I have no idea."

"Georgia, where are you?" Marcus was back on the line.

"I'm in Catacamas at the nicest hotel in town."

"I don't suppose I can talk you into coming home."

"Nope."

"That's what I was afraid of. Stay there. I'm on my way."

"What?"

"I pulled in some favors and am heading out in an hour. I'll be there sometime tonight."

"Marcus, you don't—" she began.

"Stop. I don't have time to talk," Marcus said, then hung up.

"Crap. Marcus doesn't have to come down here," Georgia said. "I don't need him to do that."

"He's stubborn, like you. And don't tell him I said that."

"Can you guys keep looking at the data and see what you can find?"

"Our number one priority."

"Thanks. I'll call you back when I can."

"George," Dave said. "Marcus is going because cares about you. And so do we."

The comment caught her off guard.

"You there?" he asked.

"Yeah. Thanks, Dave. For everything."

"Thank me later. For now, be careful. And wait for Marcus."

Georgia did not heed Dave's advice. Instead she consulted the hotelier, whom she now knew to be named Jorge Diaz. The old man had laughed until he cried when he learned they had the same name.

"Jorge?" she asked.

"*Qué?*"

"How many hours of daylight do we have left?"

"About three."

"Do you know the towns of Chilasco, Tucuru, or Morales?"

"Not well. The closest is Morales, and it's a few hours away."

"Is there somewhere I can rent a car around here?"

His amused look told her this was a foreign concept.

"Does someone have a car I can borrow? I can pay."

"My nephew has a motorcycle. He may be able to drive you."

"No, I can drive myself. Can you call him? I need to go now."

While they waited, Jorge showed her the location of Morales on a map and gave directions interspersed with warnings. They were still talking when they heard the roar of a motorcycle.

A teenager with a bright smile got off the bike, a no-nonsense cruiser. He was tall by Honduran standards, taller than Georgia by several inches. He eyed Georgia with a mischievous grin and sparkling eyes. "You want to rent my bike?"

"Yes. Don't worry, I know how to ride."

"She wants to go to Morales."

The smile was gone in a flash. "Now?"

"Yes."

"No."

"I know how to ride," Georgia said.

"It is far and will be dark before you get back. The roads are dangerous."

"Please. I must go."

The teen sucked on his cheek, contemplating. Then he smiled again. "I will take you. I know the roads."

"Thank you. What's your name?"

"Jorge. I was named after him," he said, pointing to the old hotelier.

❧

They drove on paved roads for a few miles before turning onto a rough dirt one-lane. Georgia was glad Jorge was at the wheel. In places the road was nearly washed out, and potholes created a continuous obstacle course. Jorge anticipated each and skillfully navigated the course.

They traversed a series of rolling hills, flanked by rows of coffee plants, and then drove down into a deep gorge, losing the sun to the western ridge. Night came early in the valley.

"We are here."

A barn and several storage sheds, constructed from leftover ply-wood, was the closest thing to a town center. Banana and coconut trees, corn, and other row crops surrounded the structures. A few dozen shanties spread across the valley. Coffee ringed the hillsides.

There was a high level of activity. People were moving contents from the barn into a twenty-foot container on a flatbed. Much of it was farming supplies, in the form of hand tools and bags of fertilizer, but she also saw banana slips and boxes marked with an unmistakable red cross. An old pickup truck was loading up with men who stared openly at her.

Georgia found a squat man standing on the outskirts of the action, leaning on a walking stick and wearing a wide brimmed hat. His heavily tanned face bore the deep wrinkles of many years spent working in the sun.

She addressed him in Spanish. "Good afternoon, sir. You all seem to be very busy today."

He did not seem surprised to see her, which was itself surprising. "You the lady from the government? I thought you were coming in a few days. We are almost ready to leave."

"No sir, I'm not from the government."

Now his brow furrowed in confusion. "Then who are you?"

"I'm a friend of Dr. Young from Doctors With Wings. And of José Rodríguez, with Hondureños Para El Progreso."

"Then you know why we are busy. Of course we are thankful to El Progreso; without them we'd have nothing. And doubling the payment to leave early will allow us to truly start over—to buy more land. But to make us leave more than a month early, with only a few days' notice, that is crazy."

"They are doubling your payment?"

"The lady is supposed to come in two days. We must have everyone here, to account for every person in every family, before they will give us our checks."

"Why do you have to leave early?"

The man squinted at her. "We cannot be here when the land is flooded, now can we?"

❧

By the time Georgia and Jorge returned to the hotel it was dark. She paid Jorge one hundred US dollars, and he gleefully informed her he could take her anywhere she wanted to go at any time.

Back in her room, Georgia checked her phone and found it to be almost eight o'clock. Nine in Atlanta, not too late. She texted Dave to see if he could talk.

He called her immediately. "Trish is here, too."

"Dave said someone tried to kill you," Trish said, her voice full of nervous energy. "Are you okay?"

"Yes. José Rodríguez got shot, but he'll be fine." She gave no details as she did not want to relive the events again.

"Oh my God. And Sam left you there all by yourself? What a jerk."

Georgia bit her lip. She was so very angry with Sam.

Fortunately, Dave changed the subject. "We looked at the data. Do you want the good news or the bad news?"

"Good first."

"We got all the data formatted and loaded and are able to analyze it. It gives the hometowns, names, and birthdates for several thousand people and tells how they are all related."

"Go on."

"The full dataset has been really useful. It turns out that many women experienced infertility a generation ago, but it lasted only a few years. The effect was broader, spreading to other towns, but the sterility was only temporary. This time, sterilization seems to be limited to three towns, where there are no births at all to girls under seventeen. The other towns exhibit a high teen birth rate, about twenty five percent of those girls are pregnant by the time they reach sixteen."

"So that's your baseline."

"We were also able to calculate a window of about five months during which the original exposure must have taken place."

"Great job, guys."

"But you still haven't heard the best part. You want to tell her Trish?"

"Sure," Trish said, triumph in her voice. "These timelines coincide with Hurricane Mitch. Mitch caused tremendous destruction, with massive flooding and landslides."

"I heard."

"Seventy percent of all Hondurans lost access to clean water. Water was terribly polluted for a long time. So it would not be too surprising that very bad things were unleashed into the environment."

"You think it was an accident after all?"

"We're not saying that. We just said it happened at the same time."

"Are we still in the good news?"

"Uh, yeah."

"What's the bad?"

"We know the when, but not the where or the how. We mapped the major water sources and river flows, and this new information just doesn't fit. These three villages are close together on a river, but others are on the same river. Maybe the virus could have come from well water—but again, other nearby towns should have been impacted."

Georgia thought back to her conversation with the old man in Morales. The new timeline, two days. Someone wanted these people to move—fast—and was willing to pay a lot for it. To cover up the evidence? They had to figure this out and quickly.

"Could Mitch have been used as a convenient scapegoat, or as cover?"

"Maybe both. Assuming the evildoers planned to stick around," Trish said.

As Georgia pondered this, images flashed through her mind. The water truck in which she and Sam fled. Pallets of bottled water delivered to victims of Hurricanes in Puerto Rico and Texas. Boxes being loaded into the trailer in Morales, emblazoned with a red cross.

"Trish, you're a genius. Anyone could have come in after Mitch, handing out relief supplies. It's the perfect cover."

✧

Georgia heard a noise and opened her eyes. Another strange room, another moment of confusion, the feelings becoming all too unremarkable. Then everything fell into place. She bounded out of bed and opened the door.

She was met by a tired-looking Marcus in black jeans and a dark t-shirt. He was holding a small leather travel bag.

"Hey, Marcus."

"Hey yourself. Nice look by the way." He pointed to her nightshirt, a duplicate of the one she purchased for Sam, in neon yellow.

"I haven't had a lot of time to shop."

Marcus stepped into the room and wrapped his arms around her. Georgia leaned her head against his powerful chest.

He sighed, "Georgia Steele, you are a handful."

She pushed back and was about to make some lame excuse, but he cut her off.

"Tomorrow. I'm beat. I'm going to my room to get some sleep. We'll talk in the morning."

⤚

Georgia was up early, her mind racing. She ordered a cup of coffee and took it in the hotel lobby. The morning light flooded in through open windows and the only sounds were from singing birds. A small bird with yellow and black stripes landed on a nearby sill. She opened a sugar packet and dribbled some onto the corner of her table, beckoning him.

She felt transformed from the day before. Jorge Sr. had laundered her clothes, and Marcus was there. Yesterday felt a mile away.

Only it wasn't. She needed to talk to José, to ask if he knew about the change in schedule and payment to the locals. Assuming he was well enough to talk after being shot. Then she remembered that Sam had all the information, and she did not even know where José was. Phone in hand, she could not get herself to call Sam. She was so angry at him for leaving.

Alejandra Castilla might know, but a quick search showed her number to be unlisted. It was Sunday and the embassy was closed, so Vice-Consul Evans would be no help. If she were at home, with access to real resources, she could have found the number, she knew. And it was too early to call Dave. *Damn.*

Compromising with herself, she sent Sam a text message, letting him know of the schedule change and asking for José's hospital, cell number, and any other relevant information. Then Georgia turned on a tablet computer, courtesy of Marcus, and started researching Hurricane Mitch and subsequent relief efforts.

Most of what she found was in the context of historical analysis, written years after the storm. The stories were different, but the theme was the same: horrific destruction, lack of access to clean water, food, and medical supplies, estimates of the dead and missing, and heart wrenching photos. But there was little contemporary information. The online version of the Honduran newspapers did not go back that far. If she needed them, she'd have to go to a local library or newspaper archives.

Then she found a report from the International Red Cross with an urgent plea to the global community to continue support for Honduras. The article detailed the impact of the hurricane on a district-by-district basis. It was punctuated by photos and shots of the Red Cross and other humanitarian groups delivering aid.

She read for a while, then scrolled down to the Olancho section. As in other places, the people had no electricity, the water was heavily polluted, and food was scarce. The author noted that the massive land and mudslides were the result of clear-cutting the hillsides to make crop lands.

Georgia zoomed in to study the two color photos included. They both referenced a newly formed group, Hondureños Para El Progreso. The first picture showed a young woman about Georgia's age shaking hands with a local man, as boxes of supplies and water were transferred from a jeep.

The woman was identified as the founder of El Progreso, Alejandra "Alex" Castilla. The boxes were marked with a blue P, in the El Progreso script font. A local man seen in the background was drinking from a water bottle with a simple blue label.

The second photo was that of a one-story concrete structure partially obscured in brown mud, twisted trees, and foliage. The caption explained that El Progreso lost their new building and water filtration facility to a mudslide. A quote from Alex Castilla noted, "We are not going to give up what we've just started. We'll find a way."

"You have got to be kidding me," Georgia whispered.

CHAPTER 43

OLANCHO REGION, HONDURAS

GEORGIA WAS STILL looking at the report when Marcus entered the lobby. She got Jorge's attention, and they ordered more coffee along with breakfast.

"What have you heard about Emiko?"

"Not much. There's still no evidence it was anything but a hit and run, and they haven't been able to find the car." Marcus wrapped both hands around his coffee cup and it nearly disappeared from view. "We can talk about Emiko when we are back in Atlanta. What's the plan?"

Georgia showed him the pictures of El Progreso's headquarters from the report. "I think we need to find this place."

"Why?"

"I'll tell you on the way."

"Do you know where it is?"

"No. But I think I know someone who does."

She waved at Jorge again. "Can we get the check, please? And do you know where we can find little Jorge?"

⤶

They found nephew Jorge in the garage where he worked, repairing an old Ford pickup truck. He lay under the truck, his exposed feet bouncing to the beat of bouncy techno dance music.

"Is that K-pop?" Marcus asked, his expression one of clear distaste. He turned off the music, and Georgia grabbed one of Jorge's boots.

The teen inched out on his back. His dirty face broke into a bright white smile when he saw Georgia.

"Señorita Jorge!"

She showed him the picture on the tablet. "Do you know where this is?"

He nodded, then his eyes widened.

She laughed. "This is my friend, Marcus."

Marcus shook his hand, pulling Jorge up from the floor in the process.

"Jorge, can you give us directions to this place?" Georgia asked.

"No Señorita. Too many turns, and the roads are not marked. I can take you there." He eyed Marcus, who had nearly a foot and at least a hundred pounds on the teen. "Do you have a car?"

Georgia pointed to the Jeep Marcus had rented. "You can drive with us."

"Is okay. I will ride, and you can follow."

"Tell me the short version," Marcus said. He and Georgia were in the Jeep, following Jorge out of town. Georgia drove while Marcus scanned the Red Cross report.

"The researcher who created the virus was named Alex. I assumed it was a he," Georgia said.

Marcus zoomed in and brought the tablet close to his face. "Alejandra Castilla?"

"I don't know how I missed it earlier. Some of the things she said, one about building her next facility on top of a hill. Never mind. Yes, I think it's her."

"Did you know her from before?"

"Not that I recall. She was a researcher for Frank. I think she came here to continue her research."

"If that's the case, we need to let someone know."

"But she's not alone." She told Marcus about how Messina knew Castilla, and that Mears had taken them to see her. "I think they're all working together. Messina is the Regional Security Officer for the embassy. Who knows? Our government could be supporting them. You heard how they made Sam leave."

"That's a big leap."

Georgia slowed to go around, over, and through giant potholes and breaks in the road. She said, "Imagine being able to pretty much eradicate your enemies over the course of a few generations, without violence, and in such a way that they would never know until it was too late. It's ingenious and would be worth a fortune."

Marcus grunted.

"I think they are using this dam to cover it all up," she said. "They pay the villagers to leave, and they naturally disperse across the country."

They rounded a corner and saw Jorge waiting ahead at a fork in the road. The left side was so overgrown as to be barely noticeable. He took it.

Georgia downshifted and followed. Bush scratched the side of the Jeep, screeching like fingernails on a chalkboard. They quickly rolled up their windows to keep the thorny branches at bay.

"I also think they moved up the timeframe because we are here poking into it. They're looking to hide something, and I think this is it." She tapped the tablet's screen. "She had to have somewhere to create her virus."

"The building looks completely destroyed." Marcus squinted at the screen as it jerked in his hands.

"Nonetheless, it may hold some answers."

"Mad scientists, international conspiracy, and government cover-up. You've upped your game on this one, Dr. Steele."

❧

They drove for another hour before coming to a wash out. Jorge stopped and parked his bike. Together they examined the remnants of an old bridge, hanging into the ravine. Below, a river meandered through, eight feet across, but less than a foot deep.

"Hard to imagine this little water could do so much destruction," Marcus said.

"Add in twenty inches of rain over a few hours, accumulating across all of those hills," Georgia said, nodding upstream to the jagged ridge line. "Jorge, where do we go from here?"

The teen pointed to a narrow path leading around the wreckage of the bridge and into the ravine. "I can get the bike across the river and you can take it from here. It is only a few kilometers. There is another way, but it is from the west, near the dam, and would take us many hours to reach."

Marcus shook his head. "We should walk, so no one hears us coming." He was in work mode, and Georgia was glad.

"If you are going to walk, follow the creek. It is closer that way."

❧

Marcus and Georgia left the Jeep with Jorge and set off upstream. The devastation due to hurricane Mitch was still visible but the forest coming back. The few old trees to survive towered overhead, branches spreading in a loose canopy. Immense dead trunks had become living monuments, hosting colorful bromeliads and leafy philodendron. The many new trees were small by jungle standards, and dense bush grew where sunlight reached the forest floor. Overhead, birds sang and tree frogs chirped.

Georgia put a hand on Marcus' arm. "Do you hear that?" she whispered.

He raised his eyebrows. "The birds?"

At the next bend, a fallen tree formed a bridge across the shallow stream. Georgia bounded across it, light as a cat. Marcus swore to himself and shuffled across, arms in the air like a tight rope walker. He jumped from the tree, landing with a thud. Georgia placed a finger to her lips. They picked their way into the forest, stopping frequently to listen.

"Now?" she whispered, asking if he heard. He nodded in reply.

Ten more meters, and the sound proved to be the whir of a generator inside a concrete bunker, half buried and covered in vines.

"We must be getting close," she whispered.

A few more steps and forest opened onto a pair of parallel ruts running around the larger trees. The area around this primitive road had been cleared.

"That must be it," Georgia said.

"Someone might be home. Let's go back to the river and approach from there."

Doubling back, they dropped into the ravine and out of sight. They had not gone far when Georgia heard a voice. She scrambled up the rough bank but could not see the source of the sound.

"That's all we can fit. How much more is left, Señor?" A man's voice. In heavily accented English.

"One more trip should do it." The response came with a British accent. "I'll stay here and box up the rest. Go on. We don't have much time."

An engine came to life. Georgia held her breath as a flash of white glinted through the foliage, the vehicle passing within twenty feet of their hiding spot. She counted to ten, then motioned for Marcus to follow her up the bank. She crawled through a tangle of vines, stickers catching on her hair and clothes. The big man swore as he extracted himself from the dense brush.

Partially demolished but still recognizable, the low-slung concrete building nestled up to a steep hill at the base of a wooded plateau. A gabled roofline extended past the front half of the building, creating a wrap-around porch. Oddly, the back side of the El Progreso headquarters was built into the hill.

The undergrowth had been cleared around the building, offering Georgia and Marcus limited cover. They left the security of the jungle and made their way more cautiously, hiding behind trees and shrubs. Closer now, Georgia saw that the building had not, in fact, been built into the hill, but had fallen victim to a mudslide.

The walls were still standing, and most of the roof remained intact, but vines covered much of the building. A faded "No Trespassing" sign was posted on the front door, which was secured with a heavy metal bar.

Without warning, Marcus took off at a sprint and she hurried after him. They reached the west corner of the building and crept along the front walk, peering in through broken windows, stepping over glass and other debris. Anything not covered by several feet of mud had long ago been stripped from the inside. If Georgia had not just seen the van and heard the conversation, she would have left, convinced this was an abandoned wreck.

Thump. Thump.

She mouthed, "Did you hear that?"

"What?" Marcus mouthed back.

Georgia closed her eyes and focused. A faint beat.

She followed the sound to the eastern side of the headquarters, Marcus close behind. This far side housed a loading dock, though plywood barricaded the garage door. "*No Traspasar*" had been spray painted on the wood. The rutted driveway ended here. Marcus brushed aside some leaves, revealing fresh oil stains on the cracked concrete pad.

In silence, they moved to the back of the building and were faced with the same wall of mud and brush. Here, a back entrance had been excavated out of the earth and a concrete-block retaining wall ensured its survival. A metal door stood slightly ajar, a heavy lock dangling from a clasp on one side. Marcus positioned himself next to the entrance, slipped a hand in and eased it open.

A vestibule, about six by four feet, had been carved from the dirt. One side was an original wall. The others were made of plywood fastened into the floor and secured by a wooden ceiling. It gave new meaning to a mud room.

Thick concrete tiles, probably original, covered the floor. In the center a metal hatch rested open against the original wall. Light from below revealed the top of a spiral staircase, adjacent to a concrete wall. The sounds were now clearly audible. Music.

They retreated outside and back around to the loading dock. "Was that REM coming from the basement?" Marcus whispered.

Georgia recalled Manuel's comment: *You want to keep something safe here, you have to encase it in concrete.*

"There's only one way in or out. If we go in, we could be trapped," Marcus said.

"This may be our only chance to get any evidence."

"You armed?"

She plucked one of the two wooden sticks from her hair. "Just these, how about you?"

"Stopped and got this along the way." Marcus palmed a four-inch knife.

"So?"

"I've had worse." He grinned. "Besides, I'm hoping this guy is the brains, not the brawn."

"We just have to get out of there before the others come back."

"Let's do it."

Marcus went first. At the bottom of the stairs he signaled Georgia to follow. She descended as quietly as she could into the brightly lit room below.

A lone doorway divided the far wall. Empty shelves and cabinets lined the others. Shreds of packing paper, a mangled box, and used coffee cups littered the floor. They tiptoed across the concrete floor, stopping at the entrance. Michael Stipe sang about the end of the world. Georgia smiled, taken with the irony of it all.

The inner room was double the size of the front storage area. Though practically empty, it could have housed a functioning lab. High metal chairs fronted an expansive counter dotted with electrical outlets. A coffee maker and a stack of Styrofoam cups occupied the corner. A conspicuous gun safe occupied the far corner. A dozen taped and half-full boxes lined the floor.

A man with a wild shock of white hair stood with his back to them at the counter, covering a piece of scientific equipment with copious amounts of bubble wrap and tape. He wore a white lab coat, which seemed strange under the circumstances. He turned to place the bulky item in a box. His eyes flew open when he noticed Georgia, Marcus, and the knife. He hugged the bundle protectively against his chest. "Who are you?" he asked. His accent confirmed he was the Brit they had heard outside.

"You first," Marcus said.

"What are you doing here?"

"You first," Marcus repeated. He took a step forward. "Come on, what's your name?"

"Bruce." The man's eyes darted nervously from Marcus to Georgia and back.

"Great. Hi Bruce. I'm Marcus and this is Georgia."

"What are you doing here?" Bruce asked.

Marcus stared down the diminutive man in the white lab coat.

"We're packing up the lab," Bruce said.

"Where's it going?" Georgia asked.

"I'm not sure."

"Well, where are you going?"

"I don't know yet. We were supposed to have another month to pack. This was a sudden decision." His eyes scanned the room.

"Made by?" Georgia said.

"By me, of course." They turned to see Alejandra Castilla,

alone in the doorway, a wry smile on her face and bronze skin glowing against a white linen shirt. "Georgia Steele, what are you doing here?"

Georgia's voice caught in her throat, blocked by conflicting emotions and a hundred questions fighting for the chance to be asked.

"And who is this handsome man?"

"Marcus West. And yourself?"

"My name is Alejandra Castilla."

"We know who you are. Who you really are," Georgia said, her voice cracking. It was all she could manage.

Alex raised one eyebrow, but the smile stayed on her face. "Of course, you do. I'm actually surprised it took you so long."

"Why are you doing this?" Georgia had to pull herself together.

Alex looked shocked. "You have to be joking. I thought you were smarter than that."

Marcus took a step towards her.

"Take it easy." She put her hands up, palms to them. "Bruce, you may want to put that down," she said to the scientist, still clutching the package to his chest.

Alex selected the closest chair and placed it in the center of the lab, her back to the door. She sat and crossed her legs, one elbow resting on the arm of the chair.

"The Guardians of Mankind were formed out of an intellectual curiosity—and a sense of responsibility—to see if humans could be improved at a rate faster than natural selection. This was not just to make people smarter but also to protect against disease. This was the 1850s and the third cholera pandemic was killing hundreds of thousands." Alex's speech seemed rehearsed, but she spoke with passion. "At the same time, Pasteur had discovered vaccination and Darwin evolution. History had shown that diseases like smallpox could wipe out entire populations of people while others had immunity. Unlike the narrow-minded eugenicists who were beginning to emerge, the Guardians believed that devising a superior human required blending the best of the different races across the world."

"I don't see the point," Marcus said.

"Have you ever been sick?" Alex asked Georgia.

"Of course she's been sick," Marcus said.

"Really?" Alex fixed on Georgia.

Georgia avoided the question. Now that she knew the truth about her appendix, she would have had to answer in the negative. "Times have changed since then. Science has eradicated most disease."

"Indeed. Now we are threatened by things of our own design: biological agents, nuclear weapons, and cyber terrorism."

"But the threat of retaliation keeps things in check," Marcus added.

"Tell that to the terrorists," Alex said. "So far we have been lucky, but we have had many close calls of which the public is blissfully unaware. The Guardians have often intervened to keep the human population from killing itself. But these efforts are temporary. The true problem is to ensure the long-term survival of humans and other species."

"Isn't that a little extreme?" Marcus asked.

"Is it? The key casualty of man's time on Earth has been the Earth itself. We've known for decades that human population and consumption is growing at a rate that is not sustainable. We cannot scare the planet into complying with our demands. It cannot produce more water, oxygen, or land. And it is critically dependent upon the living creatures and plants that we are extinguishing at an alarming rate."

"People can adapt. Or change," Marcus said.

"You tested a retrovirus on innocent people. You sterilized children," Georgia said.

"Georgia my dear, can't you see? This is a nonviolent, safe, and effective way to control the human population, which we have to do in order to save the planet. We've reached a tipping point. If we don't act, others will. The result will make the worst pandemic look like a walk in the park."

Marcus swore under his breath.

"You killed my parents."

"That was not my doing," Castilla said, her gaze dropping to the floor.

"They threatened you."

"True." Alex nodded. "But I left the States. They were no danger to me. They were a threat to the organization. And that's a perilous situation to be in."

The words stung, and Georgia fought to stay focused. "And that's when you came here?"

"We set up manufacturing here under the guise of El Progreso. Then Hurricane Mitch hit and that gave us the perfect cover to test our product. We only needed to wait to confirm that the condition would be inherited. Later when the hydroelectric dam project got approved, I pushed for the exact location and selected the impacted villages for the second test stage. Once they flood the river valley, the people will be gone. And we'll be done here."

"And so that's it?" Marcus asked.

"What?"

"Your little experiment is over?"

Alex expelled a choked laugh. She leaned forward in her seat. "No Marcus, this is just the beginning. Now that we finally have our results"—she nodded to Bruce, who in turn looked at the floor—"we can begin to save the world."

"At a massive profit," Georgia said.

"Of course, and why not? You'd be amazed to know what people will pay to eliminate their enemies. Now that we have real proof, we can start a full-scale operation."

"You've already sold this?"

"To a few."

"Unbelievable," Marcus said.

"Georgia, won't you join us? You could make a big impact in the world. And we are cut from the same cloth, as they say."

Georgia crossed her arms, trying to steady herself. "How long have you known?"

"I've always known." Alex left the chair and went to Georgia. She stood inches from her and said in a soft voice, "I know your mother. Your real mother." She emphasized the word real. "Would you like to meet her? You look so much like her. You have her eyes."

"Is she a part of this?" Her voice cracked.

Alex smiled.

"Did you send that phony email from José?" Marcus said.

Heavy steps on the metal staircase. Messina entered the room, followed by Mears. "That was my idea," Messina said.

"You certainly took your time getting here." Alex said, keeping her back to the newcomers.

"Who's he?" Messina said, referencing Marcus.

"Is there anyone else out there?" Marcus said. "I hate repeating myself."

Messina pulled his gun from his hip holster and pointed it at Marcus. "Funny now?"

Marcus raised his hands.

"Tie them up," Messina grunted.

Mears searched them both, taking their cellphones and Marcus' new knife. He then moved two of the high-backed metal chairs into an empty corner, and using zip ties, bound their hands behind them to the back rails of the chairs and their ankles to the front.

With Marcus and Georgia out of the way, the four went to work packing the remaining contents of the lab. The men driving the white van came back, and while surprised to see Georgia and Marcus, said nothing of their presence. They gathered up the rest of the equipment and left with Bruce.

"Are we finished?" Messina asked Alex.

"Just one minute."

Alex unlocked the gun safe and removed a laptop, a set of keys, a few file folders, and other smaller items. These she placed in a backpack. She spoke to Georgia, her face unusually soft and pleading. "What do you say, clever girl? Will you come with us?"

Georgia did not answer. She was afraid she would say yes.

"Pity. A real pity. A great mind, ruined by the influence of ordinary parenting." Alex started to leave but turned back and strode purposefully to Georgia. "Goodbye my dear," she said, her expression solemn. "I am so very sorry we could not come to an agreement." She leaned over and kissed Georgia's cheek. Then she spun around and quickly exited the room.

Messina was completing a detailed search of the space, opening cabinet doors and checking every shelf.

"You know, this is a very bad idea," Georgia said to Messina. "You are going to get caught. Someone will find us and figure it out."

"Can't see how. You'll be under thirty feet of water come tomorrow morning." Mears was standing by the door, waiting to leave. As Messina passed through the doorway he said, "Kill them both." Heavy footsteps echoed as he ascended the staircase.

Danny Mears stood still, but the anxiety roiling within him was palpable. His Adam's apple bobbed up and down as he swallowed.

"You don't have to listen to that thug," Marcus said.

Danny looked from Marcus to Georgia, then closed his eyes and shook his head. His fingers fumbled as he released the gun from his shoulder hostler.

Georgia's voice cracked, "Please, no."

"Forgive me." He raised his gun and fired twice.

CHAPTER 44

OLANCHO REGION, HONDURAS

GEORGIA CLOSED HER eyes. The sound was deafening, the shots echoed throughout the concrete bunker. The expected pain never came. She opened her eyes. Mears was gone. Marcus was grinning at her.

"Looks like our boy Mears has a soft spot for you."

"I think he's just in over his head."

"Speaking of, what did Messina mean about being under thirty feet of water?"

"We're right in the middle of the new reservoir that is going to be created when the temporary dam is dismantled." Georgia explained. Then it hit her like a ton of bricks. "So are the three villages, but the people can't move until they collect their checks, in person. Tomorrow. Alexandra and Messina must have decided to flood the basin early, destroy the evidence, and kill most of the villagers. And of course, they get to keep all the money that would have been paid out."

"We have to get out of here."

Georgia twisted in her seat, but her hands were tightly bound.

Marcus gave the chairs a once over. "I think these are Emeco chairs too, just our luck. I saw them on Navy ships. Solid and built to last a hundred years." Marcus heaved his massive frame, twisting back and forth. His chair scraped a few inches across the floor and nearly toppled over.

Georgia scoured the room for anything they could use to free themselves, while Marcus struggled with his bonds. He swore repeatedly, and Georgia felt herself succumb to cold resignation. The windowless concrete room would make a silent tomb.

"All this time, I was so caught up in finding new relatives. But I already have a family with you and Dave, and even Trish."

"I know, sugar."

"I really love you all."

"I love you too, and I know the geek squad would go to hell and back for you."

Georgia closed her eyes, feeling euphoric. She wondered if this was common before death. She let her mind wander and relaxed her body. Her head felt heavy and she leaned to rest it on the back of the chair. Something sharp poked the back of her neck, wrenching her from the meditative state.

"Ouch," she yelped, eyes flying open. "I have an idea," she said.

"You are a strange but beautiful woman," Marcus said.

"I may be able to pop these ties open with one of my sticks if you can get it out of my hair."

With some doing, they rocked until they fell sideways onto to the floor, landing with a painful thud. Marcus pushed himself close to Georgia using his knees and shoulders. Twisting his body, he freed one of the turquoise-topped sticks from Georgia's hair with his teeth. Many minutes passed before he was able to maneuver the pick into her hand.

"Stay very still," she said, feeling for the zip tie binding his hands. "If I can just get it into the slot, maybe I can depress the clasp."

"Ouch, you skewered me," he squeaked.

"Don't be such a baby. Stay still," she said. "Now, try to pull your hand away from the chair, slowly." A zipping sound followed by a low moan.

"Nice." Marcus used the stick to free his other hand and feet, then released Georgia. "Let's get out of here."

They scrambled up the stairs. Marcus pushed the heavy hatch open and leaned it against one of the walls. They climbed into the small vestibule.

He tried the door. "Figures," he said. "With the hinges on the outside and that bar across the door, there is no way we can get out this way."

They looked at the other three walls. The original was concrete block, but two others were wood. Marcus pounded on them and shook his head.

Georgia pointed to the low ceiling. "It's not bearing any weight. Maybe it's just for weather."

"Hang on, stay here," Marcus said. He went back down the spiral staircase into the lab.

"And where else would I go?"

He came back with one of the Emeco chairs and handed it to Georgia. Maneuvering around her, he replaced the concrete cover and stepped on it, bouncing up and down a few times. Marcus then placed the chair on the cover and climbed up. He banged on the ceiling and it gave a gratifying creak. "Good call. It's just a piece of plywood nailed across the top." He put his hands together and banged them against one corner. The wood creaked but did not move.

"What I need is some leverage."

"Maybe one of the chair legs?"

Marcus jumped off the chair and rammed the two legs against one edge of the ceiling. "We need more force."

Georgia fetched a second chair. She held it against the ceiling, while he used the other as a hammer to drive a chair leg into the joint. They continued the process, methodically moving around the edge of the ceiling until Marcus was able to force the plywood apart. He stood on one of the chairs and punched the ceiling out, then grinned. "Come on."

"You're not kidding about these chairs," Georgia said, climbing on a chair and following Marcus up onto the rafters. "They rock."

The roof directly above their heads was solid and offered no way out. Georgia headed for a patch of daylight visible through a tear in the roof, using the ceiling joists like a balance beam. She smiled as she heard Marcus swearing about her being part cat, but he followed, albeit at a much slower pace.

They crawled across the roof to the rear of the facility where the mud had not yet been cleared. This gave them about a six-foot jump from the roof to soft soil below.

"Think Jorge is waiting?"

"Let's find out."

CHAPTER 45

OLANCHO REGION, HONDURAS

JORGE WAS INDEED waiting for them when they got back to the road. They found the teen sitting in their Jeep, head back and eyes closed. Marcus roused him with a poke to the shoulder.

"Everything okay?" Jorge asked, giving them a once over.

"We're fine," Georgia said. "But the villagers won't be. They are going to blow up the dam. People could be killed."

Jorge's eyes widened. "When?"

"Today. I don't know exactly when. Do you have a cell phone?"

Jorge checked his phone, but it had no reception.

"How far is the old dam from here?" Marcus asked.

"Maybe three hours."

"How can that be?"

"Like I said before. You have to go back," he said, nodding to the road they drove in on. "Then go around the mountains past Chilasco."

"What about straight ahead?" Marcus asked. He pointed past the collapsed bridge.

"Sí. Yes. Less than one hour if you go that way."

"Jorge, we need to borrow your bike," Georgia said. "You take the Jeep and call for help. Try to get word to the people in the villages. But be careful."

❦

Before they left, Jorge told them what little he knew about the original dam. It was built to divide and contain the existing lake to enable mining the bed for gold and other heavy minerals. Incorporating the refuse from the mining process, the dam grew over the years and stopped or diverted much of the river flow. When the rains were heavy, water would spill over into the fields and flood the crops; the causeway not able to handle the increased volume.

They picked their way down the road through the forest, with Marcus driving and Georgia nestled behind. She was the better driver, but Marcus' large frame barely fit on Jorge's motorbike. Their progress was slow; they had to avoid low-hanging branches and potholes in the road, and also keep the sound of the engine down.

Finally, they rounded a bend and the mine pit, and the processing plant came into view. An eight-foot chain link fence, overgrown with grass and bush, ran parallel to the road. The surrounding hills were marred by jagged tears, the ancient layers of sediment crudely exposed and eroding. A rock crusher and a tractor sat abandoned next to a storage shed flanked by piles of gravel, sorted by size.

They saw the dam a quarter mile farther on. Marcus cut the motorcycle engine. While Marcus hid the bike, Georgia located a spot where they could see the dam, but hopefully not be seen. She re-secured her long hair, using the wooden picks to keep it in place.

Marcus joined her. "Christ, it's big."

The dam's low-slung earthen wall was built at the mouth of the river between steep hillsides. It stood thirty feet tall and a football field wide. Below, a narrow river split the empty lakebed, a vast plain otherwise overgrown with tall grasses and scrubby brush. At each end of the dam was a building. Perched on top of the dam, at the far side, was an enclosed plywood observation deck. The building closest to them was a more substantial two-story. The first floor was concrete block. An open deck fronted the second floor, both built with wooden planking. A single lane road angled up from the building's base, crossed the expanse of the dam, and terminated at the top of the dam outside the observation deck, where a dusty black SUV was parked. Armed men clad in gray camouflage patrolled the ridge.

Marcus whispered, "Let's get a look from the other side."

The road afforded no cover, so they took to the dense thorny bush. Both were heavily scratched by the time they found an animal trail several yards off the street. Once above the dam, the lake widened, encompassing the upper valleys.

"It's enormous," Georgia said, taking in the expanse of the lake. "I can't see where it ends."

"Unbelievable. If this thing goes..." Marcus said.

Without another word, they backtracked the trail, then cut through the bush to get a closer view of the main building.

The concrete block first story was built into the dam. It was unclear which had been constructed first. Access was through a set of roughhewn wooden doors. Two more dusty SUVs were parked nearby, blocking a worn pick-up. A pair of guards approached and one of the men stared intently in their direction. Georgia feared they had been seen. The guard finally turned back to his counterpart, and Georgia exhaled. The men lingered outside the building, smoking cigarettes. They dared not move as long as the two stood there.

An upstairs door banged open and a man burst forth, yelling and gesturing. Georgia could not understand—*something about blocks?* The two guards immediately headed down the road away from the dam, taking their cigarettes with them.

"Shall we get a closer look?" Marcus asked.

They dashed to the base of the dam, hiding in its shadow, and ran to the parked vehicles. Marcus continued to the building, pulling one of the wooden doors open wide enough to slip through. Georgia shadowed him into the darkness and waited a few seconds for her vision to catch up. They were in a storage room that housed everything from a Bobcat tractor to walls of hand tools. Marcus headed for the far wall. Turning left, she promptly tripped over a cord and fell onto a workbench.

Screw this. Georgia activated the flashlight on her phone, facing it down. The offending green cord cut across the aisle through the center of the room. She followed it, circling a tiller and a brush mower and stepping over pallets stacked with bags of sand. The cord ran to the far corner, the part of the room farthest beneath the dam.

"Oh crap," Georgia said. She was not an explosives expert by any means but knew this was a lot of firepower.

She looked for Marcus. A dim light gave away his form, bent over and still, too far away to signal. She moved quickly along the back wall. Even with the light, she slipped on something slick and nearly fell. Holding the phone closer to the floor, she saw it was blood. A trail led from her to Marcus, ending with bodies lying in prone position. She forced herself to keep moving.

Four men dressed in jeans, boots, and simple work shirts lay side by side, hands behind their backs, shot multiple times in the head and chest. As Marcus stood, she saw the anger on his face.

Quickly she told him about the explosives. "Can you disable them?"

"I don't know," he said. "How many men do you think they have?"

"If we assume that the truck belonged to the workers, that leaves three cars, so then at most a dozen. Probably less."

"They're all going to be armed," said Marcus. "And I don't think Messina will take kindly to us being here."

"I don't think he's here yet," Georgia said, recalling the shine on his SUV. She pointed to the dead men. "They might have a cell phone or radio."

"Maybe in their truck. Not on them. I checked already."

"Go look at the explosives. I'll check their truck for a radio."

"Be careful, George." Marcus started towards the back corner.

Once outside, Georgia got into the worker's truck and closed the door. In a matter of seconds, she found a radio in the glove compartment and turned it on.

She spoke in Spanish, "Hello, is anyone there?"

"Who's this?" The reply was immediate.

"I am at the old dam near Chilasco. Four of your workers are dead. A group of men are going to blow the dam and flood the villages. You need to warn the people and get some police out here to stop them."

"Are you sure?"

"I've seen the bodies."

"Where are you?"

"I'm here at the dam."

"Where exactly?"

Georgia froze. Something was wrong.

"Get out slowly with your hands where I can see them." The words came from behind her and were spoken in English with a Midwest accent. She turned to see a rifle pointed at her head.

She got out of the truck. Above her, on the deck outside the second story of the building, a man in a wide-brimmed hat waggled a radio. Of course, how stupid. They had one of the dead men's radios and were monitoring it for activity.

"Let's go." The Midwestern guard was bigger than Marcus. He was just a kid, barely legal, with pink cheeks and short blond hair. He pointed the way with the rifle, and she trudged up the steps to the top floor of the building.

The man with the radio was Hispanic, but he spoke to her in English. "How did you get here?" he asked. He was much smaller than the corn-fed American, and several decades older. His right cheek bore a thick scar.

Georgia said, "How can you do this to your own people?"

"Take her inside. Do not take your eyes or gun off her," he told the kid. A pair of the armed sentries jogged over. "There may be more," he told the pair. "Bring them back here if you can. Shoot them if you cannot."

The kid pushed her thought the door into the building, which she now saw was really just a cabin. Georgia sat on a long bench at a rustic table facing the front door and rested her head on folded hands. The kid stood by the window, rifle in hand. Surely Marcus would be okay. She heard nothing from outside. She tried talking to the kid, pleading for him to let her go. He just stared impassively through her.

Then came the shuffling of boots up the stairs. Marcus entered the doorway, eyes blazing and hands clasped behind his head, the barrel of a rifle held against his back. The guard, jaw clenched and eyes glaring, pushed Marcus into the room and told him to sit down in rough English. This guy was not American or Honduran, but sounded Eastern European.

Marcus joined Georgia on the bench. She squeezed his hand.

Both sentries remained, guns trained upon them. They stood on either side of Marcus and Georgia, but not in line with each other. They had training.

Marcus looked around the small cabin. "Figures," he whispered under his breath.

"What?"

He nodded over his shoulder. "On the counter."

Georgia saw a small black object like a cable box, branded Firebox.

"Remote detonator. It wasn't down with the rest of the explosives."

The Russian guard took two full steps towards Marcus and cracked him across the face with the butt of his rifle. "Shut up," he growled.

Marcus groaned and cradled his jaw.

᪥

A wordless hour passed. Georgia was the first to hear the approaching car, but soon all were at attention. The motor shut down, a door slammed, and a familiar voice said, "Is everything on schedule?"

The older Hispanic man answered. "Yes, sir. We had to disable the workers, as you warned. But everything is almost ready."

"You were supposed to be done an hour ago."

"We had an issue. Two Americans, a black and—"

"Let me guess. A pretty little Jap."

"We caught her trying to call out on one of the workers' radios."

"Where are they?"

"Inside."

Loud steps on the deck outside were replaced by a grunt as Messina pushed the Midwestern kid out of the doorway and into the room. The guard accidentally let off a round, and it shot into the wall a few feet over Marcus' head.

"Damn," Marcus exclaimed.

"Mears, get in here," Messina yelled.

Danny Mears entered the room. Upon seeing Georgia and Marcus, he closed his eyes and dropped his head.

"I'm not even going to ask," Messina said. His right hand went to his hip, and he pulled a Glock out of his holster. Messina glared at Georgia and Marcus, then shot Danny Mears twice in the chest.

CHAPTER 46

OLANCHO REGION, HONDURAS

Georgia opened her mouth to scream, but no sound came out. Mears slumped to the floor, his eyes locked on hers.

Messina turned from Mears to Georgia and Marcus, the gun following. "How long?" His comment was directed not to them, but to the scarred man visible through the window, radio against his ear.

"We are ready. We just have to connect the remote starter."

Messina holstered his gun and retrieved the Firebox. He passed it out through the doorway, over Mears' lifeless body. "Do it now. We leave in five." He made his way into the small kitchen and opened the refrigerator, coming out with a bottle of water. Messina regarded them for a few minutes while he drank the cold water. He screwed the cap back on the half empty bottle. "I can't understand why you're here. What's the freaking point?"

"I couldn't just stand by and watch while you kill those innocent people," Georgia said.

"Don't worry, you won't have to." Messina put down the bottle and got his gun. He pointed it at Georgia.

Three shots rang, but the sounds came from afar. The scarred man fell against the door frame and crumpled to the ground.

Marcus scrambled under the table, and Georgia squeezed in next to him. Messina's footfalls echoed across the floor, moving towards the back of the cabin. She heard shouting. "Put down your guns, hands in the air," first in Spanish, next in English.

An eerie moment of silence was quickly followed by a flurry of shots. Georgia covered her ears as deafening gunfire erupted in all directions. Bullets ricocheted off the concrete floor inches away, a chip biting into her arm. Then it was quiet.

Marcus motioned for her to stay and crawled from under the table. An excruciating minute later, a hand beckoned for her to follow. The cabin looked empty.

"Messina?" Georgia asked.

Crouching over Mears, Marcus turned the body in order to extract a gun from the shoulder holster. "I don't know. He's not here." He positioned himself behind the door frame, aiming Mears' gun.

Georgia peered through the window. The kid who had guarded her earlier had been shot in the shoulder and was leaning against the cabin, his eyes wide with fear. A group of men, armed with guns in various shapes and sizes, approached the dam on foot.

"Come out with your hands up." The command came in accented English. "You cannot escape."

Georgia caught Marcus' eye, and she nodded her agreement. They had no choice. He stepped into the open and raised his hands. The revolver hung from one thumb, pointing harmlessly to the floor.

"Don't shoot," a second voice shouted. "They're with us."

Georgia recognized it. She flew out of the house, jumping over the dead man. Sam and Juan Carlos Ramos were among the group of newcomers.

"Sam!" she shouted, rushing across to the deck railing. "I thought you left."

"I almost did," Sam said.

"Messina?"

"My men will find him," Ramos said, his tone calm and confident. Georgia saw three groups of armed men fanning out across the property.

"The dam is rigged to blow," Marcus called out. "Do you see a small black box? It's the detonator." He held up his hands in the shape of a small square.

Both men shook their heads.

"Shit. It could be anywhere. We have to find Messina," Marcus said.

Georgia figured the detonator would be triggered either via Bluetooth or Wi-Fi. "I need a phone," Georgia said. She searched Mears' pockets, apologizing to him as she did, and found her and Marcus' cell phones.

"Georgia, we have to get out of here!"

"Just give me a minute. I think I can disable it." She found no Wi-Fi signal in the area, which meant the firing box had to be Bluetooth enabled. "It has to be Bluetooth. If he's firing it from his phone, he'll probably have to be within fifty feet of the box."

"George," Marcus' said, his voice tense and impatient.

She saw the Firebox Bluetooth signal on her phone. "I found it. I'm going to try and jam it." She tried a program to connect to the box but got no response. "I'm too far away." She went out onto the deck to try and get a better connection.

Sam pointed to the SUV parked near the observation deck. "Messina's behind the car." He took off running up the road to the top of the dam.

Georgia started down the stairs that led from the deck to the base of the dam. "I've got to get closer."

She heard Marcus' heavy steps following. "Shit."

Georgia caught movement on the other side of the SUV. Messina had left his hiding place, and Sam would be an easy target. "Watch out!" she shouted.

Messina leaned over the hood of the car and started shooting at Sam. Marcus pinned Georgia against the side of the dam for protection. She wiggled free and saw Messina entering the observation deck on the far side. Sam shot at him but missed. Messina returned fire as he ducked inside.

Georgia kept an eye on her phone as she tried to pair with the firing box. She crept along the base of the dam. Marcus followed closely behind, keeping watch. Sporadic shouts and gunfire continued from the surrounding area as Ramos and his men engaged with Messina's men. But nothing from the top of the dam.

"I think I got it," Georgia said, when they'd gone about thirty yards. "I'm in range. Now let's see if I can force pair or jam it."

"Hurry."

She ran two programs: one to try to connect directly with the device and another to spoof the signal so that Messina would not be able to control it. A few agonizing minutes later, the latter worked. She had, in effect, blocked anyone from being able to remotely detonate the explosives.

"We did it," she called out and waved her hand. "Sam, I jammed the firing box. It's safe."

Sam gave her a thumbs up from the top of the dam. He reached the SUV just as Messina started shooting again. Bullets pelted the SUV but return fire from elsewhere forced Messina back inside the observation deck.

"We've got him pinned," Sam said, yelling between rounds.

Seconds later, Messina —who must have climbed out a back window—shot from the far side of the deck, where he was protected from both Sam and Ramos' men. Messina lay on his stomach at the top of the wall. One hand continued to fire the gun, another searched across the top of the dam.

"What's he doing?" Marcus asked.

It hit her. "He's trying to light the fuse!" Georgia screamed.

Sam left the safety of the SUV and fired multiple rounds.

Messina cried out, swearing, and his gun clattered down the embankment. He scrambled back into the tower.

Sam mouthed, "Are you okay?"

Georgia nodded. It was over. She closed her eyes and took a deep, calming breath. Opening them, she looked around, expecting to see Messina being led away. Instead, she saw wisps of smoke rising into the air. She ran up the road leading to the top of the dam to get a better look.

"The fuse!" she screamed. The wire was burning fast, the lit ends moving in two opposite directions.

Sam slid down the side of the dam, passing one flaming trail. He grabbed for the wire as his momentum carried him across the earthen wall. He finally stopped on a shallow ledge, halfway to the ground below. He took something from his pocket— amazingly, he still had the wire in his hand—and cut the fuse seconds before the burning end reached him.

Georgia was watching Sam and too late she saw that the other end of the burning fuse had almost reached a bundle of explosives hidden in the grass next to the road. She turned to run and the charge went off, the blast knocking her over. She hit hard, landing heavily on her left ankle and skidding down the dam before catching herself on a narrow wall anchor. Georgia cried out as sharp metal scraped across her arm and bit into her hand. She leaned into the dam to redistribute her weight. She could hear nothing through the ringing in her ears.

Below her, Marcus rushed away from the base of the dam, his arms full of explosives and lengths of wire. He laid them gently at the base of the chain link fence and then looked back at the dam, undoubtedly, to assess the extent of the damage caused by the explosion. He caught Georgia watching him and flashed an okay sign. She peered over her shoulder and saw Sam slowly making his way across the ledge coming in her direction. She waved to him. They had done it.

Sam waved back, his expression changing from happy to one of horror. She saw him scream her name, as he pointed over her head. Darks spots punctuated the dam's wall, slowly spreading in diameter. Water began to trickle down the side of the dam, blackening the earth.

She had to get out of there. But her legs were trembling and the wall was precariously steep. The trickle grew to a rivulet. One agonizingly slow step at a time, Georgia felt her way down the embankment. Water reached the lakebed and began to pool.

With a loud groan, a section of earth around the blast point broke away in slow motion. A mass of dirt, rock, and concrete slid down the dam wall. Water spewed from the deep gash.

Marcus met her partway up the wall. He slid an arm under hers and half carried her away from the rift in the direction of the cabin. Turning back, she saw, to her horror, that Sam was gone.

She shook free of Marcus and climbed up the stairs leading to the deck to get a better view, ignoring the pain in her ankle and Marcus' calls to come back. The tear in the dam grew wider, the earth breaking apart in the torrent. Water engulfed the riverbed. She saw a flash of white being carried away downstream. Sam.

"Sam!" Georgia screamed, then flew back down the stairs. She rushed past Marcus – "I have to get Sam, you find Ramos" – and headed towards the brush where they hid Jorge's motorbike. She jumped on, started the engine, and sped away, taking the dirt road that followed the river.

Georgia made good progress on the well-worn road. Fortunately, the current of the water had slowed, with the force from the dam far behind. She was able to go faster than the flow of the debris and hoped that meant she could get downstream of Sam. She ran some quick calculations in her head. If he was able to grab onto something and stay afloat, she might have a chance.

She sped around a corner and braked hard, almost losing control of the bike. Just ahead, the road disappeared into the flooded riverbank.

"Damn."

Georgia backtracked, stopping in several places, studying the water flow, the currents, and the debris patterns. If she was going to save Sam, she'd have to do it soon. She found a place where the river widened, creating calmer pockets on her side of the bank. Further upriver, she recalled a downed tree hanging over the water. Georgia backtracked to the tree, got off the bike, and tested the log. It felt solid. She would have only a few minutes. Leaving her phone on the bike, she cat-walked as far as she dared down the tree trunk, scanning the horizon. Nothing. The water was getting deeper and faster, with larger pieces of debris now passing by. These would be treacherous.

She had almost given up when she spotted him upstream. She yelled, "Sam!" He had grabbed onto something resembling a log or a post. He appeared to be face down in the water and made no response to her cries.

She concentrated, planning her jump and the moves she would need to make after that to get them to safety. If she jumped too early, she would get struck by the log; too late and he'd slip from her.

She jumped. Submerged brush scratched and clawed at her legs before the swift current caught her. Sam was ahead and she swam as hard as she could to catch up. Grabbing the log, she pulled Sam's head back from the water. He groaned, barely conscious.

They needed to move to the side quickly, to find calmer water. The log jostled and was now facing almost perpendicular to the current. She wrapped her arm around Sam's chest, keeping his face out of the water as best she could.

Using the log as protection, she was able to pull herself and Sam along it towards the shore. When they reached the end, she kicked off as hard as she could, grabbing Sam by the collar. Instantly she was pushed under water but kept kicking and pulling them in the direction of the shore.

Georgia's injured ankle slammed into a rock. She screamed and swallowed water, coughed and swallowed more. She closed her eyes and did not let go of Sam. The flooded river was not deep, but whenever Georgia managed to surface, it threw them back under. Finally, she felt the force of the water lessen.

She surfaced with Sam beside her. They had gone far past her intended point, but here was a deep cove, where the water eddied. She kept their heads up and eventually her leg swept across vegetation. As she pulled them closer to shore, leaves and sticks turned to ground. She dragged Sam to a small embankment, pulling his head and shoulders out of the water. Georgia pulled herself out and collapsed onto the ground, shaking uncontrollably.

Sam was unresponsive. His heart was beating, but he was not breathing. She had to get him out of the water. Crawling, she positioned herself behind his head and reached under his arms. "Come on," Georgia cried out as she pulled. She was unable to move him.

She forced herself back into the water. Georgia lifted one of Sam's legs up and over, rolling him up the bank and onto his stomach. She repeated the process again, rotating him onto his back and onto dry land. For the moment. The water was rising.

She started CPR. Between forced breaths, she called out his name. She turned him on his side and pounded on his back. Nothing.

She repeated the process, breathing and turning him on his side. "Breathe, Dammit!" Sam convulsed and water spewed from his mouth. After more CPR, he began to breathe and cough up water. He opened his eyes, looking around wildly.

"Take it easy," she said. "Just breathe."

He curled into a fetal position, coughing and choking for many minutes.

"How did you…what happened…?" he asked between coughing fits.

"We have to get out of here before this all comes apart. Can you move?"

Sam nodded. Slowly, they crawled up the slope on hands and knees, through rows of coffee plants, which they used for bracing, until finally the ground leveled out. They collapsed, panting and coughing.

Sam croaked, "I can't believe we're alive."

It hit her like a brick. "The villages, the people. They'll be killed."

He reached for her, laying a hand on her arm. "No. We got to them in time. Marcus?"

"He should be okay. He was near the cabin last I saw him."

Sam rolled onto his back and closed his eyes. "How did you save me?"

She was too tired to answer.

⤙

Georgia woke to Sam shaking her. Had she fallen asleep? Passed out?

"We should go," he said.

"Let me look at you first," Georgia said. "Are you hurt?"

Sam felt his side, grimacing as he poked at some ribs. His denim shirt was ripped, the collar almost completely detached. He had a deep abrasion on one shoulder. One cheek was starting to swell.

Georgia had a gash on her arm in addition to the cut on her hand. Sam tore a bandage from his shirt to bind the cut on her arm. Though Georgia's ankle was not broken, it was swollen and sore. They were both covered in mud.

"Let's do it," Georgia said.

They continued up the hillside, looking for a road or a house. Once they left the coffee field, it was slow going, and they were forced to crawl through thickets and climb over several downed trees.

"How did you know we were at the dam?" Georgia asked, during one of their frequent stops.

"Your text message. I got it when I was at the hospital visiting José. My phone had died—I had to borrow a charger—anyway, he knew there were no plans for the villages to be evacuated early, and certainly no extra money. We knew something was very wrong. I tried calling you, but it went straight to voicemail."

"You were supposed to leave."

"And miss all this excitement?"

They scaled a short rock face and soon after found a single-lane dirt road. Each leaned on the other for support as they limped along.

"What about Ramos?" Georgia asked.

"Once we figured out what was going on, José got in touch with Ramos. We convinced him to send people to evacuate the three towns. And of course, Ramos came to the dam to stop Messina. That did not take as much convincing. Messina seems to have many enemies."

"I can't believe you got him to help."

"I played to his sense of country. Ramos is a very dangerous man, but he is not a mass murderer of women and children. Plus this makes him a bit of a hero, and every guy wants to be a hero."

"I hate making a murdering drug dealer a hero," Georgia said.

"Sometimes you don't have a choice. Sometimes it takes bad to fight evil."

"Who are you? And what have you done with Sam Bennett?"

In lieu of a response, he took her face in his hands and kissed her. Georgia heard the approach of a vehicle, then the blast of the horn, and reluctantly pulled away.

Even the strong glare on the Jeep's windshield could not stop Jorge's smile from shining through.

CHAPTER 47

OLANCHO REGION, HONDURAS

Two DAYS LATER Georgia and Sam visited the best private hospital in Honduras. José had been moved from the ICU and a security guard was stationed outside his private room.

"My friends," he exclaimed as they entered.

"José, you look great," Sam said. "Much better than before."

"I wish I could say the same for the both of you."

Georgia wore a conspicuous ankle brace and her arm and hand were bandaged to protect the deep abrasions and stitches. Sam's face was badly bruised and one cheek was still swollen. His broken ribs were wrapped, but at least they were concealed beneath his shirt.

"Happy to be alive, my friend," Sam said. "It was a miracle. Georgia saved my life."

"Looks like you've had a lot of visitors," Georgia said, changing the subject, for what felt like the hundredth time. The room was brimming with flowers and balloons.

"Yes, many people from DWW and El Progreso. We are all devastated."

"I can imagine," Georgia said.

"To think Alejandra fooled us for so long. And she escaped?"

"Yes," Sam answered. "Castilla's house was cleaned out by the time the police got there."

"We couldn't find any trace of her or the contents of the lab," Georgia said, eyeing an arrangement of bright red heliconias.

"I imagine both are out of the country by now," Sam added.

"What will happen?" José asked.

"We are gathering whatever evidence we can," Sam said.

"Sam volunteered to stay and act as a liaison for the US," Georgia said. "He'll work with Martin Evans from the embassy to try to clean up this mess. The people in the villages seem to trust him."

"I want to make sure they are given the settlement that was promised," Sam said.

"Good. I never did like Messina. Or Mears."

"I think Mears was in over his head. He wasn't a bad guy," said Georgia.

"Messina is another story," Sam said. "The other men were mostly guns for hire, brought in to supplement the local State Department resources. Fortunately, they have no problem talking."

"Did they find him? Messina?" José asked.

"No," Sam said, "but he was probably killed when the dam collapsed."

"You sure you want to stay?" José asked Sam.

Sam nodded. "It's going to be a challenge to prove what happened. Without hard evidence, it's going to be very difficult to get anyone, including both of our governments, to admit any of this took place. So far we just have a rogue employee who blew up a dam in order to steal the money promised to the villagers as settlement."

"But we have the villagers' DNA," Georgia countered.

"Yes, we do. But we can't connect that to Messina or Alejandra Castilla."

Georgia had been moving from one bouquet to another, stopping at a lovely mix of red ginger and pink and white caladium leaves. "This is just gorgeous." She read the card aloud. "Real Estate Especial?"

"Gene was trying to find us a place of our own. Where we live—where we used to live—we rented. He wanted to move out of Honduras, but it is my home. We fought about it. Then I found out that Gene had been sneaking out to look at homes for us."

"That's nice."

"He was even going back to look at one house for a second time, one he found through Real Estate Especial. It was only partially constructed and needed a lot of work, but it was on four acres with a barn for my horse and plenty of room for us to have a garden. But he never..." José's voice faltered. He pinched the bridge of his nose, holding back the tears. "The appointment was on Monday, the day we got back from Roatan."

"The day after your trip?" Georgia said, thinking aloud.

"Yes."

"José, can you give me the phone number for Real Estate Especial?"

"Of course."

"Sam, you up for one more trip before I leave?"

"You know it."

They found the house on the hill and the cistern turned hurricane bunker with little problem. The owner, Eduardo, confirmed that he had given Gene Young several bottles from a case of El Progreso post-hurricane relief water, which his deceased father had stored away after Hurricane Mitch. He was more than happy to let them take the rest.

The next day, Sam drove Georgia to the airport. She had all the evidence she needed to prove Frank's innocence and Castilla's guilt. And to bring exposure to the atrocities committed to the people of Olancho and the danger that this decades-long experiment posed to the rest of the world. And unlike Frank or Gene, she was not alone. She had many friends, including Sam. She felt very thankful for that.

"You better get going." Sam squeezed her hand, which he had been holding tightly in his.

Her flight to Miami left in an hour. They had lingered outside the entrance to the airport security screening, neither wanting to say goodbye.

"You're right."

"Does Marcus know you are coming back today?"

"Yes." Marcus had slipped out of Honduras quickly and quietly after the dam explosion, leaving that very night. Georgia surmised he must have entered the country illegally in the dead of night and left in the same fashion.

As if reading her thoughts, Sam said, "I'll make sure we keep him out of this, I think he wanted to stay under the radar."

"You know, you've come a long way, Sam Bennett," Georgia said.

"It was your idea to come."

"You know what I mean." She brushed his cheek, the rough stubble scratching her hand. "I'm proud of you."

He wrapped his arms around her and kissed her. "That means a lot to me, Georgia Steele."

She laughed. "Call me George."

CHAPTER 48

NOVEMBER, ATLANTA, GA

GEORGIA SAT DRINKING coffee on a bench outside the front door of a Sandy Springs office tower. It was a perfect November day in Atlanta—blue sky and sixty-five degrees. She was dressed in a tailored pantsuit and looked like any other white-collar worker, perhaps one waiting for her ride home as it was nearing five o'clock.

Facing the high rise, she was unable to see the man approaching her from behind. But she did hear him.

Just as he reached for her shoulder, she stood and spun around, ready to throw hot coffee at her potential assailant. She gave a cry as pain shot through her still healing ankle.

"Whoa." The would-be attacker gripped her elbow, steadying her.

"Sam," she exclaimed, and felt the smile stretch across her face. She put down her coffee and hugged him. "Nice tan. When did you get back?"

"Just now."

"How long are you going to be here?"

"Only a few days. I had to be here for this."

"How did—" they both started, then laughed.

"How did you find this jerk?" Sam asked.

"It wasn't too hard, once we really started to look. The APD had a description of the car and driver that hit Emiko. We wrote a pattern-matching algorithm and persuaded the APD to run it on camera footage across the city. We found about a half-dozen potentials, and the police took it from there. Easy really, just time consuming."

"The geek squad strikes again."

"Now you sound like Marcus."

"And this guy is just a run-of-the-mill lowlife?" Sam asked.

"Not even that. Just a run-of-the-mill guy, probably drunk driving."

"Shitty."

"Yeah."

Sam took a step back, giving Georgia a chance to check him out. He looked confident and collected in a black suit worn over a linen shirt. When her eyes returned to his face, she saw he was looking intently at her.

"I missed you, George."

"Me, too."

"Can we have dinner tonight?"

"We're having a get together at Dave's house to celebrate this and the Atlantic-Pacific case. Most of the guys plead out and rolled over on the few who didn't."

"So I hear. It's all over the news. Nice work on that."

"You should come over to Dave's tonight."

"I'm sure those guys don't want to see me."

"Just because you lied to them about who you were? And how I almost got killed after you left me in Catacamas?"

Sam looked strickened.

"They're over it. Just bring a bottle of good champagne. It'll be fine."

Sam shifted his weight, still looking uncomfortable. "I guess so."

"Why don't you pick me up around six thirty? We can catch

up before we go over." Georgia winked at Sam and the discomfort on his face vanished, replaced by a toothy grin.

A pair of men crossed the parking lot walking toward them. Both were lean and of medium stature, an older man with very dark skin and man about her age with a lighter complexion. They both sported very short hair, off-the-rack suits, sunglasses, and black dress shoes.

"First we need see this guy to his new home," Georgia said. "And this must be his escort."

The younger man walked past them, while the older stopped and put out his hand, "Dr. Steele?"

"Yes, and you are Detective Adams, or Bell?"

"I'm Adams," he said. "That's Bell."

Bell had positioned himself close to the building entrance.

"This is Sam Bennett, with the FBI."

"Detective," Sam said, shaking hands.

"Bennett," Adams said, nodding. "You're the fed who was tailing Mori the night she was killed."

"Uh, yes," Sam said hesitantly.

Georgia's heart leapt into her throat. "You never told me that."

"I know. I'm sorry."

Before Georgia could question Sam, Detective Bell joined them. She extended her hand and introduced herself.

Bell ignored her hand and stared at Georgia. "Wow, you look just like her. I mean, you could be her older sister."

Georgia folded her arms across her chest. "Something like that." She then repeated the lie she had told many times and would tell many more. "We shared a sperm donor at the in vitro clinic, so we have the same biological father. Emiko found me. She was killed the night we met."

"I knew that. I just wasn't expecting such a resemblance."

"What do we know about the guy?" Sam asked.

Detective Adams took over. "The suspect is Ralph Gardner, age forty-eight, middle manager at an accounting firm here. He's in his office now and usually leaves between five fifteen and five thirty."

They all looked at their watches or phones.

"So anytime now," Sam said. "Any chance of resisting or weapons?"

"Very little. You carrying?"

"Yep."

"Okay. We shouldn't need you, but you can act as backup if you like."

"Sounds good."

"I'll help, too," Georgia said. All three men looked as if they had eaten something sour. "Just kidding. I'll sit on the bench and drink my coffee."

Georgia and Sam sat together while the detectives moved to opposite sides of the entrance.

"Were you ever going to tell me about Emiko?"

Sam fidgeted. "I think that's him."

Adams and Bell closed in on a balding Caucasian man with glasses who had just exited the building through the revolving door. He looked older than his forty-eight years and wore a rumpled white dress shirt, striped tie, and khaki pants. When Bell approached him, he made an about-face and saw Adams.

"Mr. Gardner—police. We'd like to talk to you," Adams said.

Gardner bolted, running straight towards Georgia and Sam.

"Stop," Bell yelled.

Gardner came to a dead stop, a few feet from Georgia. His eyes wide, his mouth open, like a man who has seen a ghost.

Sam grabbed his arms, forcing them behind his back. He did not fight or even move. He just stared at Georgia. In one smooth motion, Adams handcuffed him. It was all over in less than a minute. The detectives took Emiko's killer and left, Mirandizing him as they walked away.

"Am I still invited for dinner?" Sam asked.

"I'm not sure." Georgia looked at him sternly, "That will depend upon how well pre-dinner goes. Six thirty—don't be late and don't forget the champagne."

⤜

"Okay, you can go," Georgia said, still breathing hard.

"What?" Sam panted, elbows supporting him while he ran two fingers through her damp hair.

"You can go to dinner with me at Dave's house."

He dropped onto his back next to her in bed. "I am never going to live any of this down, am I?"

Georgia leaned against a pillow and extracted the bottle of Veuve Cliquot from the ice bucket on the bedside table. She refilled their glasses and handed one to Sam.

"Eventually. But we all have to pay for our sins." She smiled wickedly.

Sam put his glass down on the night table and rolled out of bed. After rifling through the pockets of his jacket, he retrieved a wrapped rectangular box and placed it in front of her.

"I didn't mean it literally. You didn't—" Her words were abruptly cut off as Sam kissed her. When she finally opened the box, she found a pair of silver hair sticks, the ends bejeweled with fossilized amber. "How beautiful!"

"Replacement for the pair you lost saving my life."

"As I recall, you saved my life too," Georgia said, pulling him back into bed. "How can I ever repay you?"

⤜

The welcome reception at Dave's house was decidedly cooler than at Georgia's apartment. The remaining bottle of Cliquot was reluctantly taken by Trish at the door. "We're out back," was all she said. Dave, his hands full of plates and napkins, would not even make eye contact with Sam. They went out to the patio and saw the remaining guests for the evening, Marcus and Diane.

Marcus rose, shook Sam's hand, and grabbed his shoulder. "Good to see you, man."

"You, too."

Diane stayed seated and greeted Sam with a smile, and for a split-second Georgia thought she winked at him. Maybe she had something in her eye.

Trish followed Dave out onto the patio and began passing around champagne. "George, tell us about the arrest? I assume, since we have champagne, that they got the guy?"

Georgia recapped the arrest. She raised her glass. "To Emiko. My... daughter. I'm so glad I got to meet you and put away the bastard who took your life." Her voice cracked, but she managed not to cry.

No one spoke. A car backfire broke the silence, making them all jump.

Georgia raised her glass again. "To Emiko."

"To Emiko," they all echoed. They clinked glasses and drank. And looked uncomfortable.

"Marcus was telling us that most of the criminals in the Atlantic-Pacific scandal have already admitted guilt," Diane said, clearly trying to change the subject. "Does that mean you two can avoid testifying?"

"Unfortunately, I said most of them, not all of them. I doubt those at the very top will roll over," Marcus said.

"My boss, Sean Kelly, says that there will be a trial or two, but with so many admitting to it, there is a good chance of conviction for even the ringleaders," Sam said.

Dave and Trish pointedly ignored him.

Georgia started to say something, but Marcus hushed her. He addressed Dave and Trish. "Listen to me," he said, authority in his voice. "When the government owns you—either in the service, the

FBI, the CIA, or even the IRS—they own you. You do not get to decide what to do or who to tell about it. If you try to go against an order, you risk your career, possibly your life. Even if you know it's the right thing to do. Remember Ed?" This was a reference to Edward Snowden, one of Dave's heroes.

Dave started to protest, but Marcus stopped him. "Sam is the reason why Georgia and I are standing in front of you today. Do you have any idea what kind of risk he took when he disobeyed an order to leave? And not only that, then convinced the head of a drug cartel to drop everything and save the lives of around seven hundred people including George's and mine?" His voice had gotten louder over the course of his monologue. He boomed, "Do you?" He breathed deeply, and said in a normal but firm voice, "He saved our lives. So quit your bitching and thank him right now."

Diane's mouth dropped open. Trish looked at her feet. Dave's face was flushed.

Trish and Dave started to apologize, but Sam dismissed them.

Dave sighed, "It's not your fault. I know that. I'm just not sure I can deal with all of this. We're the good guys here."

"I have a recommendation on how to handle things in the future," Sam said.

"Go on," Trish said.

"The best and only weapon you can use against the government is publicity. The last thing the Feds need is for respected civilians"—he swung a pointed finger across the room—"that worked with local law enforcement and the FBI to break up a sophisticated organized crime ring, to tell the world that they themselves were being spied on by the FBI. That would do incredible damage."

"Are you saying we blackmail the FBI?"

"Oh no, I would never say anything like that," Sam smiled and raised his hands. "I recommend a gentleman's agreement."

"And a lot of counter surveillance for good measure," Marcus added.

"I don't want to quit," Dave said. "I love doing this. It's important work, not just publishing crap no one will ever read. We just have to up our game."

"Go super geek on their asses," Marcus agreed.

"We're gonna get to buy some cool tech shit," Georgia said.

Everyone laughed and the tension melted away.

◅

After the pizza delivery man came and the pizza boxes were inspected for listening devices by Dave—"I saw Inside Man"—they all sat down together to eat.

"Tell us what's going on with you, Sam," Trish said.

Sam described how he had stayed behind in Honduras, working with José to ensure that the displaced villagers received their settlement, now partly funded by the US government.

"Did they ever find Dr. Young?" Dave asked.

Sam shook his head. "No. At this point we have to assume he's dead, and that Castilla and Messina were probably responsible. José's getting better. I think the work keeps him going."

"Speaking of Castilla," Georgia said, trying to move the conversation in a positive direction, "Sam was appointed to a new joint task force with the CIA and Interpol to find Alejandra Castilla, aka Alex Castle."

"Not much new to report, I'm afraid. You all already know that we followed Castilla's trail and lost her, but we did find one of her scientists."

"The British guy we met in the basement lab," Georgia explained.

"Through him, we found that two additional groups were targeted by the virus. This first involves a pair of sheiks in the Middle East and their families; the other warring, religious factions in Africa. Fortunately, both are relatively isolated, but the fallout is going to be intense. We're bringing in the Saudis to help negotiate the first case." He looked to Diane. "Did you tell them yet?"

"No. I was waiting for you," she said, beaming. "Sam's recommendation helped secure my new position with the CDC. Our group was created in conjunction with the World Health Organization. We are working to create a vaccine for the retrovirus. Given the extent of Dr. Anderson's research and the cooperation from Castilla's scientist, it shouldn't be too difficult." Diane's characteristic serious expression returned. "The more complex issue, at least from a technical side, is how to assist those who have already been infected."

"You can't just give them a vaccination?" Marcus asked.

"I'm afraid not. Their genes have been permanently altered. There is gene therapy and CRISPR splicing, but all of this will require significant research and development. For now, there really is no other option but containment."

The group looked at her in horror.

"Sorry. I don't mean physically containing the people. I mean containing the spread of the virus. As bad as it is that for the hundreds—or even thousands—of women and girls who are now sterile, others will spread this to future generations, and there is no plan yet for addressing this situation.

"Currently, my group consists of one lab technician and me, but the CDC is soliciting funds for a world-wide testing and monitoring program, and also for gene therapy research. The proposed short-term plan is that the US, via the CDC, distributes testing kits and vaccines to those who demonstrate need, but keep confidential the composition of the retrovirus.

"What's the timing?" Sam asked.

"We are presenting a plan to Congress right after the holiday break. They've already requested that Georgia testify."

"I plan on being there to scare the bejesus out of Congress so that they act quickly," Georgia said. She addressed Dave, "We'll demonstrate our infection models. Add some cool computer graphics and show them what can happen under some simple scenarios.

We'll use Washington, DC as ground zero. That should put the fear of God into them."

"You both are aptly qualified for that." Diane's expression was unreadable, and Georgia could not tell if she was berating or complimenting them.

"Thanks, I guess," she said.

"Ongoing, my small team will need a partner to predict the spread and watch for new outbreaks. We know the virus can be modified so we are chasing a moving target to some extent. I've drafted a request to use West Intelligence and Analytics for that work."

"Who?" Sam asked.

Now Diane's front collapsed. She smiled sheepishly. "Well, I needed a name, and West Security already has a great reputation, so I thought a new subsidiary would be appropriate."

"Aren't we all full of secrets tonight," Marcus said.

⨯

As the group toasted their new endeavor, Georgia's thoughts kept returning to her own secrets.

Though the feds were actively pursuing Alejandra Castilla, the same could not be said for clearing Frank's name or exposing the Guardians. She was told point blank by Agent Kelly that she should not get dragged into conspiracy theories and that there was no hard evidence this organization ever existed.

Of course, she knew differently. Nevertheless, she promised both Marcus and Sam that she would leave this to the experts. It was not really a lie. She would not involve her friends, but she would not stop looking either. After all, she was an expert, wasn't she?

She would find the Guardians, learn all she could about them, and try to stop them from destroying any more lives. She owed it to Emiko, her parents, and Frank.

And then there was her mother. Her *real* mother. Was she part of the evil or just a good person trapped in their web as her own parents had been? She would find out.

The search for her secret family had only just begun.

Message from the Author

Thank you so much for reading my debut novel "The Crucible of Steele." I would love to hear what you thought of it and would be ever so grateful if you could leave a review on Amazon or Goodreads. Reviews and personal recommendations are the only real ways for a new, self-published author to be successful in this highly competitive market.

Please keep in touch. You can email me at linda@lmwhitaker.com or contact me through my website (lmwhitaker.com). I am hard at work on the next Georgia Steele novel, and will post updates.

Though the science and technology in this book are grounded in fact, I'm sure things are off in places; sometimes this was on purpose for simplification, but there could be times I just got it wrong (apologies in advance to my experts, any mistakes are all on me). Any feedback is welcome and appreciated.

Acknowledgements

Many people helped me along the way to writing this novel. First and foremost, thank you to my sister, Heather Whitaker, for everything. This would never have happened without you. A big thank you to my husband, Steve Silver, for so much love and laughter, and hardly ever asking when I was going to be finished. More thanks to Patrick Coleman, Steve Wechselblatt, and Leissa Shahrak for years of teaching, friendship, and support.

So many other people lent their time and expertise, I am very humbled. Subject matter experts, beta readers and proofreaders: Prof. Sean Conner, Bridget Kromhout, Darryl Bollinger, JoAnne Manse, Maggie Powell, and Paul Goldsman. Kind authors who offered valuable classes, advice and/or encouragement: Ellen Hart, Darryl Bollinger, Michael Grumley, Marcus Sakey, Adair Sanders, and everyone in the Greenville, SC, Sisters in Crime.

Many more encouraged me along the way, from good friends to total strangers. Thank you all.

Made in the USA
Columbia, SC
05 July 2020